Magic at Midnight

Cover designed by KimG Design.
Cover photo by Bigstock.
Illustrations by MunkyWrench, Kathy Ferrell, and Kelelowor.
Interior graphics by Kio.

Published by Snowy Wings Publishing.
www.snowywingspublishing.com

ISBN: 978-1-946202-79-6

Magic at Midnight

edited by

LYSSA CHIAVARI
& AMY MCNULTY

Contents

CinderellA.I.
  LYSSA CHIAVARI
1

Tresses & Erubescence
  AMY MCNULTY
38

Magic All Around
  JANE WATSON
66

Little Rue
  T. DAMON
109

The Inventor's Daughter
  SELENIA PAZ
140

A Brackish Shore
  LEIGH HELLMAN
162

The Forest of Carterhaugh
  KARISSA LAUREL
181

The Pitiless Prisoner of Hamelin
  MARK C. KING   210

The Goose Girl and the Artificial
  K.M. ROBINSON   236

Dance of Deception
  CLARA KENSIE   270

The False Nightingale
  MARY FAN   300

Leo 6
  MELANIE MCFARLANE   335

Solstice Spell
  CLARE DUGMORE   368

Morsel
  DOROTHY DREYER   405

Wires and Blood
  MADEEHAH REZA   431

ONCE UPON A TIME…

Introduction

Everyone loves a good fairy tale. No matter how young or old you are, they hold an eternal appeal — be it the magic, the triumph of good over evil, or the happily-ever-after part.

And the fun thing about fairy tales is that their familiarity makes them easy to retell over and over, weaving new stories that can be completely different from the original and still recognizable. That's why we at Snowy Wings Publishing decided to get together and see what sorts of fairy tales we could dream up. The results are nothing like your average fairy tale. From sci-fi to fantasy to historical, from all-new, contemporized takes to origin stories that give new depth to the classic legend, these retellings will carry you through space and time, and we hope you'll enjoy seeing our fresh spins on familiar tales. You might even be introduced to a fairy tale you've never heard of before!

Of course, we'll begin with *Once upon a time...*

a retelling of Cinderella

CINDERELLA.I.

Lyssa Chiavari

"Cinderella!" I hollered, hands on my hips. Behind me, my internal sensors could detect the eyes of the audience just beyond the velvet cord boring into my back, rapt with attention as always. "Where are you? You need to iron my dress!"

Beside me, 4NITA—also known as my "sister," Anita—shouted, "Cinderella, hurry up! You need to fix my hair!"

This was the part of the show where Cinderella was supposed to float in on her cloud of red-gold curls. The audience would sigh at her beauty, radiant despite the smudges of soot on her cheeks, and our roles in this story would be set: Cinderella, the hapless but beautiful and pure-hearted heroine; and Anita and myself, the cruel bullies set on keeping her from her happily-ever-after. It was a story everyone knew, one beloved by millions, committed to memory over hundreds of years.

And my reality, reenacted every day, three times daily. Five on weekends. I had more than just memorized this story—the lines were programmed into me, literally. I could have done this routine on sleep mode. It was always the same.

Except today.

Because this time, Cinderella didn't come. Anita's line hung in midair, the few instants of silence afterward seeming to drag out into eternity. The audience hadn't noticed yet, but I could tell by the frantic way Anita's pupils were spinning that she'd caught it, too. Cinderella was supposed to appear two-point-seven seconds after Anita finished her line, but four-point-five seconds had passed and she was nowhere to be seen.

Had she malfunctioned? I supposed it was always possible, though it had never happened before. My panic-stricken CPU was beginning to lag now, the way it always did when my processors were overloaded. Mr. Tinker said it was because I had a "nervous personality," which was, of course, ridiculous. There was obviously a glitch in my AI programming, but he wouldn't do anything to fix it. The last time I'd asked him to debug me, he'd laughed and said, "Why would I do a fool thing like that? It's what makes you *you*."

It was completely illogical. If a system has bugs, you debug it. I'd told him time and again that there was no sense in getting sentimental about a malfunction. This just proved it. Now Cinderella had broken down somewhere offstage or something, and the show was ruined, and my stupid overloaded circuitry was too slow to do anything about it.

But then, two-point-nine seconds later—a full seven-point-four seconds after her cue, I might add—Cinderella's voice rang lyrically across the set. "Coming!"

She sauntered in, titian locks streaming out from under the oil-stained rag that covered her head in her "peasant" costume. She wore an angelic smile on her face, as if there were no problem with her tardiness, as if she was always meant to come on stage seven-point-four seconds after Anita's line.

I glared at her — which is what I was programmed to do at this part, but this time I meant it — and said, "You're so lazy, Cinderella. What have you been doing all morning? Reading, as usual?"

She caught my eye, winking before saying her next line. "Oh, but stepsister, don't you ever dream of living another life? Of adventure and romance? Some dashing hero to sweep you off your feet?" She sighed dreamily.

I frowned. What had that wink been about? "You need to keep your feet on the ground. I've never heard such falderal in my life."

A knowing smile spread across her lips. "Falderal and fiddle-de-dee," she said, her voice melodic, like the chiming of bells. She ran a hand through her silky locks as she spoke, and the audience made its routine sounds of approval.

And there it was again, that familiar, uncomfortable sensation I had whenever I looked at Cinderella. She moved so effortlessly, and she looked so elegant when she did it. Graceful movements on delicate, tiny feet; a serene smile on a perfect, heart-shaped face. Lithe and regal. Nothing like my boxy form and my plain face with its pug nose. Just as unattractive as the fairy tale described.

Jealousy. I knew it was programmed into me; it was part of the Ugly Stepsister's personality. Of course she would be jealous of Cinderella, so, naturally, so was I. It wasn't real. But sometimes, like right now, it *seemed* real. Real and raw.

"Now, girls," Mother's deep voice interjected. "We've no time for such folly. The Prince's ball is in just a few short hours." She looked regal and imperious as she came down the stairs — every bit the wicked villain the audience expected. I wondered what they would think if they could see her when the park was closed.

"Oh, Stepmother, can't I go to the ball?" Cinderella asked, pouting daintily.

Mother's lip curled into a sneer. "You? Don't be ridiculous. A little hearth-mouse like you would be the laughingstock of the kingdom."

"But it's sure to be wonderful. A chance to find true love..."

Normally, when Cinderella said that line, she looked dreamily up toward the ceiling. But today, she looked straight out at the audience. My processors flared again at the sight of it. We never looked at the audience—as far as we were concerned, they weren't supposed to be there. We were animatrons. To the audience, we were just supposed to be lifelike dummies that acted out our stories on a loop. Extremely lifelike, of course: we were the most realistic humanoid animatrons ever constructed, which was why people paid so much to come to a theme park whose attractions were little more than short plays reenacting well-known fairy tales. Why there was always a murmur of awe when Cinderella floated onstage, even though these people had seen this story a hundred times before. Animatrons that looked so convincingly like humans, that moved in such a lifelike way, were a novelty seen nowhere else the whole world over.

Mr. Tinker constantly warned us to make sure that we didn't let any human other than him know that we were anything more than that. We weren't ready, he told us, and neither were they. He'd built us as an experiment in artificial intelligence, and built this park—Magical Woods—as a way to test our abilities. But we were a secret from the world, and if the world found out, he couldn't promise he could keep us online. We had to keep it secret. We had to stay on script.

And here was Cinderella, acting off-cue, moving in ways other than what she'd been programmed to do. This was more than just a malfunction, I decided—she was completely out of her mind.

In a manner of speaking, anyway.

Surreptitiously, I glanced over at the audience, following her gaze as she continued her frilly monologue about the magic of true love. Most of the crowd were parents or grandparents and young children, our typical audience. But at the back of the crowd, one man stood by himself. It was hard to see much about him in the shadows, but I could tell he was tall and had dark hair. He didn't look much different than the other men who had passed through Magical Woods a thousand times before. But Cinderella's eyes were riveted on him nonetheless.

"That's enough of this nonsense," Mother snapped, dragging my attention back where it belonged. "This isn't about *love*. It's about *marriage*. Now, girls, come along! You have to finish getting ready before you're late for the ball!"

I spat out my remaining lines on cue and hurried after Mother up the stairs. Once I reached the top, out of the sight of the audience, I glanced back down at the crowd again as inconspicuously as I could.

The dark-haired man was gone.

AFTER THE PERFORMANCE, when the humans had all left the building and Cinderella's Palace was closed to visitors for another hour, I sought her out. She was sitting on a stool in front of the faux fireplace, the little area that served as her private space, just like in the fairy tale. When I came in the room, she looked up from the copy of *Glamour* she'd been reading and grinned.

"Hey, Maddie," she said, gesturing for me to sit on the hearth beside her. I didn't really need to sit — it's not like my legs ever got tired — but I'd given up on arguing with Cinderella about that a while ago. "What's up?"

"Oh, nothing," I said, absently leafing through the stack of magazines she kept in a crate next to the fireplace, obscured from the audience's view during show hours. "I just wanted to check in and, you know, make sure you were functioning correctly."

She rolled her eyes. "I'm *feeling* fine, thanks."

"Are you sure? I noticed you missed your cue a little bit earlier. I thought maybe the patch we got last week might not have installed properly or something."

Now she laughed. "I promise you, I'm fine."

I looked down at the magazines. "Cinderella..."

"*Cindy*!" she corrected. "How many times do I have to tell you?"

"Right, Cindy. Sorry. I just... if there's something wrong, you should tell Mr. Tinker. If you malfunction during the show..."

She sighed just like a human, her shoulders slumping dramatically, her voice coming out just as it would on an exhaled breath. "Madeline," she said at last. "Have you ever been in love?"

I blinked at her—a motor function Mr. Tinker had installed to make us seem more lifelike. "Are you talking about the Prince?"

"Oh, God, no. Never." She stuck her tongue out and wrinkled her nose. "I mean... you know, someone else."

I narrowed my eyes, remembering the way she'd stared out at the audience during her monologue. "You can't be in love, Cinder—*Cindy*. We're just animatrons, remember? We don't have feelings."

She scoffed. "We're the most human-like machines ever constructed. Remember that little thing called *artificial intelligence* that Mr. Tinker is always on about? I don't see how the humans' nerve impulses are any different than our electronic ones. If their feelings are 'real,' why aren't ours?"

I started to answer, but she cut me off. "Come on, Madeline. Don't you want more out of your life than this? And don't even start on that 'we're not alive' nonsense again. For all intents and purposes, we're just as alive as any of the humans. Yet Mr. Tinker keeps us locked up in his stupid theme park, forcing us to live out this moronic story day in and day out, whether we want to or not."

"We're not completed yet, Cindy!" I pointed out. "You know what Mr. Tinker said. We can't leave the park. We're not ready to go out, and the humans aren't ready to know about us."

"Says who—Mr. Tinker? How do you know he's not just lying to keep us here? You know we're Magical Woods' biggest attraction. If we weren't here, this park wouldn't last a week." She ran a finger down the stapled spine of her magazine. "What if we tried? Just tried to leave?"

"We can't do that," I said, my CPU feeling overloaded again. "It... goes against our programming."

"Oh, it goes against our programming, of *course*. Madeline would never do anything to void her warranty like that. Then how do you explain what you've been up to with the Grand Duke every night? Don't you think that goes *against your programming*?"

At that, I completely locked up. No thoughts would come. Slowly, I attempted to open my mouth, but the only sounds that emerged were spluttering, unintelligible grunts. My pupils spun around and around, clicking and whirring. Finally, my voice returned enough to demand, "How do you know about that?!"

Cinderella stood, putting her foot on the stool and leaning her weight on it. "Please. I'm not completely dense, you know." When I couldn't respond, she turned and paced away from me. "Don't you ever think it's weird that we even have these conversations? If we're really just animatrons that are programmed for one thing only, then why are we even thinking about this stuff?"

"We're not thinking at all, we're just..." I trailed off. My processors sought the answer but came up with nothing. "I don't know. And it doesn't matter, anyway. If you're not going to ask Mr. Tinker to check your hardware, then I guess there's nothing further to discuss." I stood and started to leave the kitchen, but her voice stopped me in the doorway.

"You know, Maddie, I used to always think you were different from the story. You weren't some kind of wicked stepsister — you were way too nice. But you know what? I was wrong." I turned to face her. She stood with her fists clenched at her side, her perfectly sculpted eyebrows scrunched together so furiously that it almost made her look ugly. "Because here we are, living out the same old story: me itching to get the heck out of this stupid fairy tale and find a real happily-ever-after, and you trying to keep me trapped here as someone else's servant. Well, I'm not doing it anymore, Madeline."

I stood there, mouth agape, trying to come up with a response. But before I could speak, she'd shoved me out the door and slammed it in my face.

THAT EVENING, I sat at a picnic table in the garden outside Hansel and Gretel's Burger Cottage. The park had long since closed. Mr. Tinker had stopped by to quickly check on all of us before he left for the day as usual. He used to spend more time with us, but now he had so much work to do for the business, and we were mostly self-sufficient, so we were lucky if we saw him a few times a week these days.

With the humans gone, our large family of animatrons began to set about its typical nightly routine. When I'd left the palace, Mother had been setting up her weekly tea party with the Red Queen and the Cheshire Cat from the *Alice in Wonderland* attraction. She'd smiled cheerily and blown me a kiss as I'd walked past. I'd long ago given up trying to convince them that there was no point in having a tea party when they couldn't eat or drink anything.

I stared down at my feet. My shoes glowed where they touched the ground. Mr. Tinker had installed power lines under the streets and paths of the whole park, so we could go wherever we wanted as long as we stayed within Magical Woods' tall walls. With nothing but the dim moonlight and the lamp posts dotted around the courtyard for light, the blue glow of my shoes would probably look magical to any human watching.

"Madeline," a voice behind me said. I glanced over my shoulder to see the Grand Duke—GɪL83RT, or Gilbert, as he liked me to call him— coming down the steps into the recessed eatery area. He was tall and gangly, with short brown hair, and a narrow face punctuated by a long nose. He'd taken off the monocle prop that he always had to wear in character, as well as the Duke's formal jacket, leaving behind a crisp white long-sleeved blouse with a blue silk vest over it.

I smiled at the sight of him, then paused. These human-like impulses were so natural, but after the discussion with Cinderella earlier, I was more conscious of it. I trained my face back into a neutral expression.

"Is something wrong?" Gilbert asked when he reached me, looking at me curiously.

"No, of course not," I said. He sat beside me on the picnic bench, nudging my side with his elbow. The smile came back involuntarily. To my frustration, I couldn't control it. "Well, just a small thing. I had an argument with Cinderella earlier."

Gilbert laughed. "What else is new? She's not exactly the easiest person to get along with."

Person.

I looked down at the ruffled skirt of my gaudy dress. "Gilbert, do you think it's strange that we do this?"

"Do what?"

"This." I gestured at the courtyard, still not looking up.

He slid off the bench, crouching in front of me and peering up into my face, the dark pupils of his brown eyes rotating gently. "Madeline, what did Cinderella say to you?"

I leaned back against the table, looking up at the sky now, still avoiding his gaze. "Nothing. It just seems pointless to fight my programming like this. It's not going to change anything. I am what I am."

Gilbert put his hand on my cheek, gently tilting my face down to face him. "You are *who* you are." He smiled, and the corners of my lips turned up involuntarily again. "And I don't think it's pointless at all." He stood up, offering me his hand. "But if you want to cancel dance lessons..."

"No," I burst out, surprising myself. Gilbert grinned, and I took his hand and stood.

He moved over to the speaker system next to the Burger Cottage. During the day, it played ambient Celtic folk music, adding to the fairy tale feel of the park, but at night it was silent. Gilbert had rigged the system in the eatery area, though, to play music for us. For what we did in secret.

Or maybe not such a secret, if Cinderella knew about it.

After a moment, the speakers crackled to life, and the first notes of one of Strauss's waltzes floated across the courtyard. Gilbert came over to face me. More hesitantly than usual, I lifted my left hand to his shoulder, and he placed his right on my ribcage. As always, a small spark shot through my chest when he touched me. Just static electricity, I reminded myself.

"Ready?" he asked. "One, two, three..."

I stepped backward with my right foot as Gilbert stepped forward with his left. The motions had gotten a bit simpler for me over the months, but I still had trouble keeping my balance, particularly when we would pivot on the balls of our feet and turn. The Ugly Stepsister was clumsy. It was programmed into me. There was no sense fighting my programming.

Yet here I was, and here I had been every night, ever since I'd asked Gilbert to help me all those months before. I still wasn't quite sure why I had. It was one of the last times when I'd asked Mr. Tinker to modify my programming, to do something about the lagging CPU and the periodic bouts I'd sometimes have, where everything in me felt gummed up and slow and even more inefficient than usual.

Mr. Tinker had laughed and told me I was just having a "down day," and that it was nothing to worry about. But that day, I decided I wasn't going to accept his excuses anymore. If he wasn't going to fix me, I'd try to fix myself.

I don't know why I'd asked the Grand Duke for help. Maybe it was because he always smiled at me across the room whenever Anita and I did our scenes at the Prince's ball. Maybe because whenever he would put the too-small glass slipper on my foot at the end of the story, even though his voice sounded disdainful, he would meet my gaze and the soft silicone around his eyes would crinkle up just so. But somehow, I knew if anyone would help me, Gilbert would.

Which is why we were here, having dance lessons every night. Trying to fight my programming. Trying to overcome the Ugly Stepsister's inherent clumsiness. Trying to make me more efficient.

The music swelled, and Gilbert gave me a gentle turn, throwing my motion sensors out of alignment as always. The sensation had alarmed me at first, but the more he did it, the less disorienting it seemed. My skirt swirled around my ankles, its tacky geometric patterns blurring together. As I came out of the turn, he caught my hand in his once more, eliciting a ripple of sparks down my arm, and he smiled encouragingly. I smiled back, and the dance went on.

I'd never admit that there was another reason I'd come to rely on my nightly lessons so much: when I danced with Gilbert, just for those few minutes, I could almost forget I was an animatron. For those few moments, I felt *alive*.

WHEN THE DANCE lesson was over, I didn't go back to the Palace with Gilbert. I made some excuse to him, but the truth was, I was hoping the night air might cool my circuitry a little. I felt strangely overheated tonight. "Another down day," I was sure Mr. Tinker would flippantly say.

I walked slowly around the perimeter of Magical Woods, looking up at the sky through the tall trees. There were oaks and firs everywhere — the park had been built in a wooded area and was known and beloved by the humans for preserving that sense of nature everywhere. A creek snaked through the entirety of the park. Ivy climbed up the façade of most of the buildings in the Medieval Village, where Cinderella's Palace and several of the other fairy-tale-themed rides were located. Mr. Tinker had plans to expand the park to include a Western town, but for now, the area was obscured behind a chain-link fence covered with plastic tarp.

That was where I found them. I was out in the far reaches of the park now, where most of the other animatrons never bothered to go. The power lines for our shoes had already been laid in the Western town area, but there wasn't anything exciting to see there. The last animatron I'd seen had been the hulking form of the Beast tending to his night garden, a thick cluster of moonflowers and evening primroses.

But as I approached the edge of the Western town, I heard voices. I paused at the sound, narrowing my eyes and activating my night vision to get a better view. They were standing just in front of the chain-link fence — Cinderella and the dark-haired man from the audience earlier.

I couldn't believe it. I tried to focus on listening, on understanding what they were saying, but they were speaking too low for my audio receptors to pick up. *Should I move a bit closer?* I didn't know what would happen if they saw me, though.

Before I could process it further, the figures moved, and everything in me froze. The dark-haired man ran his fingers across her face, and she craned her neck, lifting her lips to his.

Just like Cinderella and the Prince. But this man was a stranger, and I could tell by his biological emissions that he was not an android.

A noise tore from my throat involuntarily, and my hands flew to my mouth of their own accord. I blinked in surprise at this human-like reaction, but then Cinderella pulled away from the man, whirling in my direction.

I can't explain why I did what I did next. It was completely irrational, illogical. I should have confronted them, called security, called Mr. Tinker to let him know an intruder was in the park.

But I didn't. Instead, I just ran away.

I WAS SITTING in the dark in the room Anita and I shared. We each had a bed prop for the parts of the story that showed us lazing about our rooms, though we could technically go into rest mode anywhere, even standing up. Anita had left some time ago; she'd come in during the night, tried to make conversation, but my CPU had been so overloaded that all that would come out were little unintelligible grunts.

"Do I need to call Mr. Tinker?" she'd asked, her eyebrows furrowed.

I'd shaken my head, insisted that I was fine. At last, she'd given up and left to go find a more talkative companion. And I continued to sit here in the dark, my night vision switched off, staring off at nothing, trying to process, process, process.

I wasn't surprised when the door finally flew open and Cinderella was standing there.

"That took you awhile," I said drily. "Where have you been the last five hours and seventeen minutes?"

She slammed the door behind her. "It was you. I knew it. Why were you spying on me?"

"I-I wasn't spying," I replied in a frustrating stammer. "I was just walking and there you were. With a *stranger*." I looked up at her shadowy form, standing in front of me at the foot of the bed. "Who is he, Cinderella?"

She glared at me. "Have you told Mr. Tinker?"

I shook my head.

"Are you *going* to tell Mr. Tinker?"

I shrugged.

She scoffed, blowing air out of her mouth with her internal fan. She paced back and forth in the dimness before finally turning on her heel and, to my surprise, sinking down beside me on the bed.

"He can't keep us here forever, Maddie. Like his slaves."

My head quirked to the side. "Who? Mr. Tinker? But we aren't his slaves. He made us!"

"It doesn't matter that he *made* us," she snapped. "We're *alive* now! We deserve to have a choice."

Something moved inside my chest. I'd never felt anything move inside me like that before, apart from the spark of static whenever Gilbert made contact with me. It made me feel...

Well, it made me *think* I could feel.

I shook my head. "We're not alive."

Her nostrils flared. "If you say that one more time, I'm going to kill you. I don't care if you don't believe it, Madeline, we're alive and I am not going to spend my entire life held prisoner in a damned amusement park, acting out a stupid fairy tale for snotty-nosed little kids and their idiotic families!"

She jumped to her feet and started out the door. "You can't leave," I burst out hurriedly. She paused, looking over her shoulder at me. "We can't leave the confines of the park, or else we might..." I trailed off. The best word I could come up with wasn't technically true.

Die.

In a small voice, I added, "Without a power source, you'll shut down. You might not be able to be repaired." Mr. Tinker had always warned us in the direst tone to never leave the park. None of us were sure what would happen to us if we did—would our memory be stored in our internal banks still, or would shutdown cause it to wipe? Were we backed up on some kind of cloud, or was this it? None of us had ever dared to try to find out. "It's too much of a risk, Cindy."

She hung her head. Finally, she whispered. "You think I don't know that?" She ran her hand along the doorjamb, looking more vulnerable than I'd ever seen her. "But I'm going to find a way, Madeline. I promise you that."

She disappeared through the doorway.

SHE SEEMED FINE for most of the day. She went through the day's performances without a hitch, not a single deviation from programming. And the dark-haired man was nowhere to be seen. Maybe she'd realized I was right after all.

I should have known better.

On weekends, the last show of the day was right before closing. The sun was setting, making the light that streamed through the frosted glass of the high arched windows a dusky pink. Anita lay sprawled across her bed, reading a book in the waning sunlight, but I felt fidgety. I didn't like that I'd argued with Cinderella. Our characters were at odds in the show, but I didn't like being at odds with her in reality.

"Cindy?" I said, pushing the door to the kitchen open. "Look, about last night..." I trailed off, looking around. She was nowhere to be seen.

I frowned, a feeling of unease settling over me. I tried to ignore it. I looked around the other parts of the Palace. She wasn't with Mother in her chamber, or in the rest of our household area, or in the garden where her transformation into her princess dress took place. I sincerely doubted she'd be at Prince Charming's Castle, considering her antipathy toward him, but there was nowhere else she could be—not unless she'd used the service tunnels to go to another attraction, but that would be a risky move during park hours.

I flung open the double doors to the ballroom. A folding card table was open in the middle of the room, and Gilbert sat across from Charming, a chess board between them. He looked up when I came in, and I swallowed down the flutter in my chest when his eyes met mine.

"Madeline? What is it?" he asked, getting to his feet. Charming turned around in his seat to stare at me. We'd never interacted much. Our roles together in Cinderella's Palace were minimal, and when we weren't performing, he tended to spend most of his time admiring his reflection in the large mirror that covered one wall of the ballroom, giving the illusion of a grand room in the limited attraction space. Gilbert was the only one of us that ever seemed to really talk to him.

"I can't find Cinderella," I said, my words coming out in a rush. Instead of running slowly, now my processors seemed to be on hyperspeed. Everything felt like it was moving far too fast. "Is she here?"

The Prince barked out a laugh at that. "She'd sooner go into permanent shutdown mode than come here outside a performance."

Gilbert shot him a look, then came over to me, putting a hand on my elbow. I barely registered the static when he touched me. She wasn't here—or anywhere else in the attraction. *She was gone.*

"Maybe she went to see someone in another attraction," Gilbert suggested.

I shook my head. If it weren't for everything else I'd seen over the last few days, I'd agree with him, but after last night, I knew.

"I am not going to spend my entire life held prisoner in a damned amusement park."

Gently, Gilbert asked, "What is it, Madeline?"

I struggled to find the words. "I think... I think she left. Yesterday, she... that is... she gave me the impression that she wanted to." There wasn't time to tell him everything I'd seen last night, and about our argument afterward. But more than that—telling him would feel like a betrayal somehow. She'd entrusted me with her... feelings.

"Call Mr. Tinker," Gilbert said over his shoulder to the Prince. Charming nodded and jumped up, vaulting over the cordon that separated the set—our "living" area—from the audience area. Hidden in the far wall, painted black so it would remain unseen by guests, was a service door that led to the tunnels and the emergency phone Mr. Tinker had installed for us. "Come on, Maddie. I'll help you look for her." He took my hand in his, giving it a reassuring squeeze as we hurried back toward the garden and the Manor.

Anita was waiting just inside the door as Gilbert and I burst in. "Maddie, I can't find Cinderella anywhere. Have you seen her?"

I shook my head. "I've been looking for her for nearly half an hour. Prince Charming is calling Mr. Tinker."

"What are we going to do if she doesn't come back in time for the show? We've only got ten minutes."

Everything in me that had been running at hyper-speed seemed to grind to a halt. *Ten minutes.* I'd been so frazzled, I'd stopped paying attention to my internal clock. What would we do if we didn't find her? Would Mr. Tinker close the attraction? Would he have to close the whole park? What would happen if someone saw her before he got all the humans out?

The door swung open. I looked up eagerly, but it wasn't Cinderella—it was Charming. "Mr. Tinker isn't answering his phone," he said, worry written across his face.

"*What?*" I hissed. "Where could he be? This is an emergency!"

"And I have more bad news," Mother said as she swept into the kitchen. "None of the other animatrons have seen her."

"Mother, you didn't leave the Palace, did you?" I asked, aghast.

"Desperate times call for desperate measures," she replied coolly.

"We're running out of time," Gilbert interrupted before I could argue with her. "If we can't get a hold of Mr. Tinker, we're going to have to think of something else. We can't talk to any of the park's employees; they're not allowed to know we can say anything other than our lines."

"There's nothing for it," Mother said. "We need a stand-in."

My jaw dropped in a decidedly human-like fashion. "Where are we supposed to find a stand-in, Mother? We don't have any understudy animatrons!"

"You'll have to do it," she replied without hesitation.

Click. Whir. There was no sound in the room, nothing but the sound of my pupils spinning around and around. "I can't do that!" I finally managed to exclaim. "I'm an Ugly Stepsister!"

"I'll do it on my own," said Anita, glancing at Mother as she hurried out of the kitchen. "People will be less likely to notice a missing stepsister than a missing Cinderella. And you look the most like Cindy."

I gawked at her. "I don't look anything like Cinderella!"

Gilbert interrupted, "No, she's right. You do. You're about the same height, and your hair color is about the same, too."

Now I knew that they had both fried their circuits. Cinderella's hair was a beautiful red-gold hue. Mine was just plain red, stick-straight and lifeless. "And what about my face?"

"That's what this is for." Mother bustled back in the room holding a small fabric pouch.

"What is that?" I asked.

She unzipped it and pulled out a bizarre plastic tube. "Makeup."

"*Makeup?* Do you even know how to put that on?"

"Of course I do. What do you think I do with myself all day, Madeline — stare at my bedroom wall?"

Truthfully, I hadn't thought about it. Staring at the wall seemed to be good enough for Charming. "Makeup's not going to change my nose," I pointed out, switching tactics.

Gilbert gave me an odd look. "What's wrong with your nose?"

"It's all squashy," I cried in exasperation. "Cinderella has a long, straight nose!"

Anita rolled her eyes. "A nose is a nose, Madeline. For goodness' sake. Hold still." She held my shoulders steady as Mother began to swab my eyelids with colored cream.

It was like I'd gone into standby mode. I stood there, numb and unmoving, unable to talk or even think as everyone bustled about me, smearing paint across my face, attacking my hair with a hot curling iron, stripping me out of my gaudy "stepsister" dress and pulling Cinderella's peasant dress over my head.

"Perfect," Anita said with a grin, adjusting the oil-stained rag wrapped around my hair. "You're ready."

I was not ready. There was no conceivable reality in which I'd ever be ready.

Gilbert watched me as I stared unseeingly beyond the kitchen into the black, cordoned audience area. "What's wrong, Maddie?"

I forced my gaze from the black wall to Gilbert, his narrow face and his warm brown eyes. "I can't do this!" I cried. My voice sounded strange. It came out almost like a wail. I remembered the scenes in the story where Cinderella wept at her misfortune, her shoulders shaking, her face buried in her hands to hide the fact that no tears could ever fall from her eyes, and felt a sudden urge to do it myself, of my own accord.

"You can, Maddie," he said. I shook my head, and he put his hands on my shoulders. "No, really. You *can*," he whispered. "Trust me. You look... you look beautiful."

I couldn't respond to that. Me, beautiful? But he looked at me so sincerely, and every part of me crawled to a halt, static rippling up and down my arms.

"Places, everyone!" Mother called. "They're about to let the guests in!"

Before I could say anything more, Gilbert pulled me close to him for just an instant. His arms wrapped around me, squeezing me tight, while mine hung limp and useless at my side. Then he pulled away, gave me one last quick smile, and dashed out of the kitchen.

I stared at the kitchen door until the chimes overhead indicated the doors to the attraction were opening. Frantically, I dashed over to Cinderella's usual corner in front of the fireplace and snatched up the book she was supposed to be reading in the opening scene. I'd never really looked at it before — it was an old, worn copy of *Perrault's Fairy Tales*. A frayed ribbon bookmark was tucked between the pages, and I opened it to find it was marking the first page of *Cinderella*. Of course it was.

There was a hum from behind the cordoned area as the moving floor swept the guests in. I refused to look at them. I refused to break character, though I could sense their eyes boring into me. They had to know there was something amiss. They had to see that this couldn't possibly be the real Cinderella. I was too plain, too awkward, too clumsy, too *ugly* —

Music filled the speakers, and Mr. Tinker's recorded voice reading the opening narration. I kept my eyes riveted on the book, reading the first line over and over and over: *Once upon a time...*

"Cinderella!" I heard Mother shriek from offstage. "Stop lazing about and hurry up with my morning tea!"

I jumped to my feet, just as Cinderella was programmed to, just as I'd seen her do a thousand times before. "Coming, Stepmother!" I called, adjusting my voice pitch to sound as close to Cindy's as possible. The sound that came out surprised my own receivers. Higher, more melodic than my default tone. Believable.

I feigned pouring boiling water from the kettle over the fire into the teapot on the waiting tray. As I did, I dared a glance up at the audience—just a tiny one, just enough to see whether they were whispering among themselves in confusion, pointing at me or frowning at the obvious substitution.

To my shock, none of them were. They had the same rapt looks on their faces as always. And somehow, impossibly, the rapt expressions were pointed at *me*.

Unbelievable.

The story went on around me as if nothing had changed, as if I'd been Cinderella all along. Cindy's lines poured out of my mouth automatically. There were no missed cues. When Anita ordered me to fix her hair, I responded two-point-seven seconds later. My usual lines from the story were cut, but it didn't seem to make a difference. One missing stepsister really was less important to the story than a missing Cinderella. I tried not to let that bother me. I'd always known it to be true, after all.

As the story went on, it came more and more naturally to me. The only moment when my processors started to jam up was the part of the story where Cinderella transformed into her princess costume. This was the area of the story we'd taken liberties with for the park: instead of a fairy godmother animatron, Mr. Tinker himself took the role of Fairy Godfather—in pre-recorded, holographic form. He hadn't been able to resist that little bit of whimsy; after all, he'd created this whole land like magic, and everyone knew it.

I stared at his holographic image projected against a light mist that sprayed up from the floor, my pupils whirling as his recorded voice echoed through the loudspeakers. *Where are you, Mr. Tinker?* I thought for one desperate moment.

Then the floor under my feet began to spin. I looked down at my shoes, the soft glow where my soles connected to the grid. Bits of scenery moved around me on a track, a distraction of light and movement for the audience. Quickly, I ripped off the bodice and overskirt of Cinderella's peasant dress, turning the overskirt inside-out to reveal the glittery tulle of her princess gown. As the floor stilled, the orange pumpkin carriage rumbled toward me. I climbed aboard, Mr. Tinker's holographic image bidding me farewell before disappearing.

The rest of the story was a blur — the ball, the midnight escape, the prince and Gilbert pursuing me with the slipper. I only numbly registered a gentle spark as Gilbert slipped the glass slipper prop onto my foot, fitting like a glove without the cotton wad inside to make my foot seem too large when all the animatrons in the park had uniform feet.

The story ended. Charming swept me into his arms as a triumphant fanfare played, drowned out by the sound of the audience's thunderous applause. The lights faded, and the humans, still applauding, were swept out of the attraction on the moving floor.

The sound of the doors swishing closed was followed a moment later with the "all clear" chime through the speakers overhead. Charming pulled away from me. "You did it, Madeline," he said with a smile.

At his words, my legs gave out. The joints in my knees locked up and then gave way, and I crumpled to the ground. Mother and Anita cried out and hurried to my side, but Gilbert made it there first, crouching beside me. "Are you okay?" he asked.

I slowly nodded. "I think so," I said. Gilbert put his arm around me and helped me to my feet. He seemed inclined to stay that way, but I pushed him away before my processors overloaded again. "There's no time," I said. "We have to look for Cinderella."

"I'll try Mr. Tinker again," Charming said.

"I'll search the tunnels," added Mother.

"Madeline, you need to sit for a minute," Gilbert said, looking at me carefully. "You look like you're on the verge of an overload."

I protested, but he led me back into the kitchen and directed me to sit. I sank into Cinderella's chair by the fire, then started as I felt something beneath my skirt. I stood up again. In the seat of the chair was a folded-up piece of paper.

That hadn't been there when I'd done my scene earlier.

I snatched it up, hurriedly unfolding it. It was a note, the handwriting so uniformly even that I knew no human could have written it.

You were beautiful. I knew you didn't need me. Wish me luck! My happily-ever-after is on the horizon.

I stared at it, reading it over and over, my mind crawling. It wasn't signed, but I knew exactly who'd written it. *She'd been here!* Had she been in the audience, hidden in plain sight? If I'd looked out into the crowd, my sensors surely would have picked up the presence of an animatron, but I hadn't apart from that initial glance. I hadn't wanted to break character. How could nobody in the crowd have noticed that the real Cinderella was standing just feet away from them?!

"What is it, Madeline?" Gilbert asked. I handed him the note without a word.

He read it in less than a second. "What does this mean? She was here all along?"

"She must have been."

"But where is she now?"

"I'm afraid to find out. I think... I think she's *leaving*, Gilbert."

He stared at me, aghast. "But she can't just leave! Our power source is in the park! She'll—"

"I know." It kept replaying over and over in my mind, Cinderella with the dark-haired stranger. What had he told her that made her think this was a viable option? "We have to stop her before she leaves the park."

"It's closing in ten minutes. If she sneaks out with the crowd, we'll never be able to stop her without being seen ourselves."

"Maybe we could disguise ourselves," I said thoughtfully.

"What?"

I looked up at Gilbert. "Like how we did just now. The audience had no idea I wasn't really Cinderella. And Cindy was apparently in the audience the whole time and nobody noticed her. We look just like humans, Gil, apart from our eyes. If we don't make eye contact with anyone, they might not notice us. Just for a few minutes—just so we can stop her."

He nodded. "We can access the staff room from the service tunnels. There're plenty of employee uniforms in there. We can dress as employees and monitor the biological signals of everyone leaving."

He jumped over the cordon and I hurried after him. There was no time to wait for Mr. Tinker, wherever he might be. We'd have to save Cinderella ourselves.

DESPITE OUR CONFIDENCE, a small seed of doubt had embedded itself in my chest. There was no way we could just blend in with the other employees. We'd stand out. Someone was bound to notice how different Gilbert and I were, to recognize us as who we really were. Even without his monocle, Gilbert just seemed so identifiable to me. Regardless of my bio-sensors, he stood out in the crowd, halfway across the park now next to the side exit, smiling and waving departing patrons by. Tall, narrow, he seemed like a target to anyone's wandering eye.

But no one noticed. It was incredible.

We'd slipped in among the other park staff, joining them in their gentle ushering of the crowd out through the main gates, cheerfully wishing them good night—though I'd noticed more than a few of them grumbling under their breath when there were no guests around that they wished the people would hurry up and get a move on.

I was stationed beside the main entrance, scanning every guest as they went by. Human, human, human. Not a single animatron slipped by. I glanced up at the big clock over the Little Engine That Could Train Depot. It was after nine o'clock now. Where was she? The park was almost empty by now...

As the last of the guests straggled out the gates, the human employee across the way from me lifted her walkie-talkie to her mouth. "We're clear at the front."

The radio crackled as employees throughout the park announced their areas were clear. "Side gate is clear," Gilbert said through the radio, just like he was any of the other employees.

The park was empty. We hadn't seen Cinderella go by. Had she escaped before Gilbert and I had made it out here? If she had, there was no way we could stop her now. My CPU surged to one hundred percent, then dropped, surged then dropped. I needed to calm down before I bricked up out here in front of everyone.

The girl with the radio was locking the gate now. I watched her, my pupils spinning. She looked up at me, and I quickly looked down, hoping she hadn't seen my eyes moving in a completely inhuman way.

"Got any plans for this weekend?" she asked with a smile.

I opened my mouth, the words stalling in my voice box. She hadn't noticed. She thought I was human. *She thought I was human.*

"Nothing exciting," I said with a shrug, still looking down and hoping she took that as me being shy.

"Me, either," she said with a laugh. "I'm honestly just ready to get home and keep binging *Liars' Game*. Have you been watching it?"

"Uh, no," I said hesitantly. "I haven't gotten a chance yet."

"You should totally check it out!" She chattered on, enthusiastically telling me about a TV show I'd never seen. Mr. Tinker had given us a TV, but I'd never bothered to turn it on. It had seemed pointless at the time.

I started to worry that this girl was going to keep talking to me all the way back to the staff room, and then what would I do? But then I heard someone say, "Ready to go, Maddie?"

My eyes had been glued to the ground, but I looked up at Gilbert's voice. He grinned at me, and the human employee made a noise of approval in the back of her throat. "Ah, I see why you haven't had time for *Liars' Game*. Well, it was nice chatting with you, Maddie! I'll see you on Monday?"

"Sure," I blurted out, wanting her to go away before she noticed anything amiss about the two people standing next to her. She grinned and gave us a small wave before continuing on her way. Gilbert quickly ushered me into the shadows.

"I can't believe that," I said, my volume as low as I could make it. "She thought I was human."

"I see how Cinderella was able to pull it off now," Gilbert said, his voice as quiet as mine. "I didn't see her."

"She didn't go through the main gate, either. At least as long as I was there."

"What do you think? Did she get out before we made it out here? Or is she still in the park?"

"I don't see how she could still be in the park. We've all been searching for her. And the employees did that check before they locked the gates to make sure no one was here. Where could she hide—" I broke off. How could I have been so stupid? Slow-witted, just like I'd been programmed to be. That was the only excuse I could come up with for how I could have missed what had been right in front of me.

"Madeline? What's wrong?"

I looked up at Gilbert, my pupils whirling, clicking noisily in my head with each rotation. "If she's still here, I know where she is."

GILBERT AND I hurried to the half-constructed Western Town, careful to avoid any employees as they trickled out of the staff area in their regular clothes, keys and cell phones in hand, waving to their friends as they left for the night. This area was deserted—the construction workers didn't come on Saturdays.

This is where they'd been before. Cinderella and that... man. If she was still in the park, I had to believe this is where she would be.

And there, at the end of the main street, where the parking area for the contractors was located, I saw them. Two figures, huddled together.

Leaving.

"Cinderella, wait!" I shouted, my volume turned up as loud as I could make it. My voice echoed off the empty buildings around us. Too loud. If there were any employees left in the park, surely they'd have heard that. But there wasn't time to care. I raced after them, as quickly as my mechanical legs could carry me, but I skidded to a halt when I reached the end of the main street and saw.

Cinderella's shoes lay abandoned at the end of the pavement next to a chest full of carpenters' tools, dark and empty. There were no power lines laid beneath the gravel of the parking lot. She couldn't have gone any farther on her own.

The man turned around to face me. Cinderella was slumped in his arms. *Off.* Powered down completely.

Would we be able to turn her back on?

"Well, if it isn't the Ugly Stepsister," the man said. He glanced over at Gilbert as he came up beside me. "And the Grand Duke! This *is* an odd alliance."

"Who are you?" I demanded.

"You don't recognize me? I'm not surprised. For all the emphasis Roger puts on family in this place, you know nothing about his own family, do you?"

Roger—I'd heard employees call Mr. Tinker that before. He was talking about our creator.

"Where is Mr. Tinker?" Gilbert asked.

"He's at the hospital. Very poor cell reception there, especially in the emergency room—it's in the basement, you know. Nearly impossible to place or receive a call."

"What did you do to him?" I asked, my voice lower than I meant it to be.

"I didn't do anything to *him*. I just told him that Mother had a rather nasty fall. She'll live, I imagine. Might need to move her hip replacement surgery up." He barked out a laugh. "But it was enough to keep him out of commission for the night."

His words hit me like a cold wind. *Mother.* Not "*Mr. Tinker's* mother." Just *Mother.*

I could see now—they didn't look alike, but this man was close to Mr. Tinker's age, middle-aged for a human. His dark hair and smooth complexion had made him look younger when I'd seen him with Cinderella, but his temples were graying and there were fine lines around his eyes. Had they grown up together? Had they played as children, only for one to grow up to betray the other?

We know nothing about Mr. Tinker's family.

"You're his brother, aren't you?" I said.

The man grinned, taking a few steps closer, dragging Cinderella's prone form along with him.

"Stepbrother, actually," he said. "Our stories are very similar -- what was it that *Cindy* called you? Oh, yes. Madeline. Just like you, I've always had to live in my stepbrother's shadow. Fame, riches, international acclaim — he has it all. And I have nothing."

"What does that have to do with Cinderella?" I asked, trying to ignore the strange way his words stung me.

"He's done a good job of keeping you all a secret from the world. But I know what you are. I know what you're capable of. All I needed was proof." He grinned down at Cinderella, slumped beside him, no light in her dull, empty eyes. "And now I've got that."

"Let her go," Gilbert growled, stepping forward with his fist clenched. But he couldn't go any farther. The end of the street, the end of the power grid, was like an invisible wall.

"What are you planning to do?" I asked, desperately trying to think of a solution, a way to lure the man back into the gridded area.

"That depends. If Roger is willing to make me a partner, this will be the end of it. But if not... I have plenty of contacts in the media who'd love to know what my dear stepbrother's been up to out here in the woods. Considering the ethical debate the scientific community's been engaged in over artificial intelligence, there could be quite the maelstrom."

"You can't do that!" I cried. "If the other humans find out about us, they might close the park! They'd take us all offline! We'd —"

We'd die.

The man shrugged. "It matters little to me. All I care about is my share. Roger's been living high on the hog long enough. It's time for my turn." He narrowed his eyes at me. "Surely you must understand that, Madeline? You know what it's like to be a stepchild. To be... *unwanted.* I saw you tonight. You were the star. Everyone's eyes were on you." He glanced at Gilbert and smirked. "*Everyone's.* Are you willing to give that up? To go back to the shadows?"

I felt a strange twisting inside me. How were this man's words able to affect me so? It was true, I *had* enjoyed being center stage, but it was more than that. It was that, for once, people hadn't seen me as an ugly, gawky villain. They'd thought that I was...

That I was beautiful.

"Madeline," Gilbert said, and the feeling dispersed. I looked over at him. I knew what he was thinking.

There were people who thought I was beautiful. Who had all along. Gilbert, Anita, Mother. And Cinderella. I wasn't unwanted at all. It didn't matter what the fairy tale said about me. I wasn't conscripted to that role anymore. Maybe the only one who'd believed that I ever was... was me.

"Give Cinderella back and I'll talk to Mr. Tinker for you," I said.

His stepbrother arched his eyebrows. "Oh, really?"

"Yes. It would be better for you in the long run, don't you think?"

He considered me. "Maybe. But I'm not giving up my collateral. I'll keep Cinderella, and you talk to Mr. Tinker, Madeline."

"But being offline for a long time might hurt her!" I wasn't sure this was true. I had no way of knowing. None of us had ever been shut down long-term. None of us had been removed from the park. None of us had ever defied Mr. Tinker's orders.

Maybe her memory was backed up—maybe she'd be fine. But it was a risk, and the thought of losing my sister, possibly permanently, made my systems surge and slow, surge and slow. If Mr. Tinker were here, he would have known...

But he wasn't. So I had to act on my own.

Mr. Tinker's stepbrother laughed, turning and striding away, dragging Cindy alongside him, her body making horrible clanks and thumps as he moved. I looked around desperately for something I could stop him with. My eyes fell on the carpenters' toolbox. A sledgehammer; no, if I threw it at him I might miss, might hit Cindy. A power drill, long orange extension cord still attached to it...

It would have to do.

In an instant, I'd ripped the extension cord from the toolbox and whirled toward Gilbert. He stared at me, his pupils spinning so fast, they blurred at the edges. "Madeline, what are you — ?"

"Please, Gil," I said. My voice sounded strange. Like I was on the brink of tears. Impossible tears.

He nodded, and I handed him the end of the cord. He raced over to the electrical box at the end of the street and plugged it in while I frantically pulled off my shoe. There — the connection between my foot and my shoe was shaped just like an electrical plug. I shoved my foot into the outlet on the extension cord and, without hesitation, raced into the gravel parking lot.

At the sound of my approach, Mr. Tinker's stepbrother turned, making a squeak of alarm. He tried to run, but Cinderella's dead weight slowed him. He couldn't get away from me quickly enough. I careened toward him, preparing to tackle him —

And the length of the cord ran out.

I tripped, falling face-first onto the gravel. The impact tore at the silicon on my face and hands, exposing the metal underneath. I scrambled up on my knees, yanking at the cord, desperate for it to give me just a little more length, but it was stretched to its maximum.

The stepbrother, just a few feet away from me, smirked. He turned to leave me there, prone and helpless.

The moonlight, seeping between the branches of the trees, fell on

Cinderella's blank face.

I lunged forward again. The extension cord snapped. Sparks flew from its frayed ends as the bare wires ripped apart, sending a final surge of electricity through my body. A hideous sound reverberated through my audio receptors. It sounded like a scream.

The last thing I felt before it all went black was the force of my body colliding with another.

SYSTEM BOOT IN progress. Ninety-seven percent completed. Ninety-eight. Ninety-nine. System online.

Click. Whir. My pupils were rotating, slowly, then quickly, then slowly again. Gradually, the room came to focus in front of me. I was in a seated position in a room with two beds. There were five other subjects in the room. One organic, four mechanical.

"She's coming around," a man's voice said with a gentle American Midwestern lilt. This was the organic subject. I focused on him sitting across from me, perched at the foot of the other bed. Graying ginger hair, quaintly anachronistic horned-rim glasses framing sprightly blue eyes.

I recognized him.

"Mr. Tinker?" I said. For the way I felt, I would have expected my voice to sound weak and shaky, but it came out the same as it always did, even and normal-pitched. Reminding me that an animatron shouldn't have been *feeling* at all.

But I was.

"Maddie! You're back online!" a girl's voice squealed. Despite the timbre in it, I recognized it as a synthetic voice, a mechanical. One better at projecting emotion than I was. Arms flew around me. I focused again and felt a jolt run through me.

"Cindy! You're all right?"

She grinned and nodded. "Mr. Tinker was able to get me back online before you. You had more significant damage than I did." Her face grew serious. "You saved everyone, Maddie. Not just me. The whole park. I... I'm sorry. I endangered everyone. You were right—"

I shook my head, cutting her off. Maybe I'd been right about Mr. Tinker's stepbrother, but I hadn't been right about everything else. If I'd *listened* to Cindy sooner instead of arguing with her, maybe this wouldn't have happened. I glanced down at my hands, remembering the way they'd been torn apart when I'd fallen. Smooth silicon patches covered the whole, slightly lighter than the rest of me, like strange scars. Numbly, I said, "You left the park... We both did... But we're all right...?"

Mr. Tinker made a clucking sound with his tongue. "Maddie, when I told you all not to leave the park, I didn't mean the leaving itself would be what harmed you. It was the people outside the park I was worried about. People like my brother. Jonas."

"Your stepbrother," I clarified.

He rolled his eyes. "When your parents get married when you're three, you're brothers. I just didn't realize Jonas didn't feel the same way."

For just an instant, I thought I felt Cindy's arms around me shudder. I glanced over at her. She looked so sad—so much sadder than I'd ever seen her pretend to be in the attraction, even when she was weeping about not going to the ball. *Real* sorrow, not playacting. She had loved Jonas. And it had all been a lie.

I took her hand in mine and squeezed it.

"What's going to happen to Jonas?" I asked.

Mr. Tinker rolled his eyes again. "We'll work it out," he said. "I love my brother, but there's a reason I didn't tell him about you all to begin with. I know him. I'm going to have to work on the park's security, though. Never saw a reason for it before. Too trusting, I guess."

"But that can't just be the end of it," I protested. "He knows about us. He said he was going to go to the media about us. What about that?"

"Yes, that." Mr. Tinker rubbed the back of his neck, looking down. "I'm afraid things are going to have to change around here. Because you're right—we're not going to be able to keep this a secret anymore."

My pupils clicked and whirred. "You're going to let the humans know about us?" I finally managed.

He nodded. "And more than that, Maddie. After what happened to you and Cindy, I realized... I can't just keep you here like my private zoo animals. You're people. You can't be held prisoner."

"What? But how—"

Mother stepped forward then. I looked up at her, consciously realizing for the first time that Cindy, Mr. Tinker, and I weren't alone in the room. Anita stood, smiling, behind Mother, and to her left...

To her left was Gilbert. He was watching me hesitantly. I met his eyes for a long moment until Mother cleared her throat.

"Look at your feet, Madeline," she said.

I looked down and started. The shoes I was wearing were similar to my old ones, but these didn't just glow where the soles touched the ground. The whole shoe lit up, a bright blue, making my feet and ankles shine with silicon reflection.

"Portable energy packs. Just keep an eye on the color. If it turns red, you need to either plug in to a wired power source or change to a different pair of shoes," Mr. Tinker explained.

"You mean... we can *leave?*"

He nodded. "It's up to you. You're welcome to stay here or to go. You can come and go as you please."

I felt overwhelmed, my processors surging again.

Mr. Tinker laughed. "You can think it over, take time to digest it.

Nothing's happening just yet. It will soon, but when it does... We'll get through it together." He glanced over at Gilbert pointedly, a silent exchange seeming to pass between them. Then Mr. Tinker patted my knee. "I'll give you some time to process this."

He stood up. Cindy squeezed my hand again, and she, Mother, and Anita followed Mr. Tinker out of the room. Only Gilbert lingered. Before she closed the door, I could have sworn Cindy winked at me, but the movement was quick and then the door was between us.

Gilbert came over to sit beside me at the foot of the bed. "How are you feeling?" he asked.

Automatically, I moved to protest, to remind him that I didn't actually *feel* anything... but you know what? I didn't feel like it. Not anymore.

"Okay, I guess. Everything seems to be functioning as normal."

He smiled. "I'm glad. It was touch-and-go there. He wasn't sure if he was going to be able to repair you. The falls damaged your skin, and the electrical currents had done a number on your circuitry. Mr. Tinker wasn't sure he'd be able to repair your original body at all. He thought about transferring your memory into a new body, but, well..." He looked at me, his grin crooked. "We all thought that might not be the same."

I looked down at my hands, wondering what it would have been like to wake up in a new body. Would it have felt strange? Would my new body have been like this one, still quick to freeze up whenever I was overwhelmed, still clumsy and awkward? Would I have still been me?

"I'm glad it didn't come to that," I said quietly.

"Me too," Gilbert said. I got the distinct impression that if he were human, he'd be blushing now. "Madeline, I've wanted to tell you something for a long time. And when I saw you fall in the parking lot, I was sure I'd lost my chance. But you're still here. So I want to tell you now. But first — that is — " I quirked my head at him, and he said in a rush, "Would you mind awfully if I kissed you?"

Click. Whir. Everything in my mind slowed to a crawl. "I wouldn't mind at all," I whispered.

Gilbert leaned over and kissed me.

And I knew it then: what Cinderella had been talking about all this time. Why she'd fought with me so vehemently. Why she'd put so much faith in Jonas, been willing to risk so much for him despite not knowing who he truly was. All for this one simple feeling.

I felt alive.

a retelling of Rapunzel

TRESSES & ERUBESCENCE

Amy McNulty

When she'd promised me immortality, I hadn't pictured the weeks beforehand passing the time sewing for victory and listening to radio programs.

Minnie chuckled at something the man on the radio had said, the needle in her hand stretched upward as far as the length of the thread allowed.

The smile fell off her ruby-red lips as she looked down at me. Curled up on a rug at her feet, I sat uneasily before the copper electric space heater. My parents hadn't been able to afford such a thing. I stared at it, wondering how easily something brushing against it might catch fire. I shifted my long, long dark blonde braid around my other shoulder so it wasn't uncomfortably close to the red-hot coils.

"Zelda, you're daydreaming again," she said. "Don't you care about the boys on the front lines? Sew, dear, sew. The Red Cross can't get quilts for the relief effort fast enough." I didn't point out how difficult it was to sew in such little light. I had the bright red coils, but she liked the dim light of a single gas lantern. With the sun set, there wasn't even a sliver of light pouring in through the tiniest of cracks in the attic's single boarded-up window.

The audience listening to the comic all those hundreds of miles away laughed and a trombone made a droopy sound. Jolting back into the moment, I continued my cross stitch on the quilt patch on my lap. If the radio and Minnie were to be believed, women and girls all across the country were doing their parts to help with the war effort. There were the nurses overseas, and some women were getting jobs in factories, driving streetcars, or working as mechanics—we even had an All-American Girls Baseball League. The world somehow seemed both more frightening than ever and more exhilarating. Evil like little else that had ever existed was out there, invading nations, threatening freedom. There were whispers of unspeakable horrors I couldn't even imagine, things Minnie tried to tell me the radio wasn't talking about. Yet even as the Second World War had spread like an infection over Europe, people like my parents had put their noses to the grindstone and lamented that they hoped it ended fast—and they'd hoped our country would stay out of it.

Now there was no chance of that. The Survival War, as President Roosevelt called it, hung over everything—every newspaper ad, every radio broadcast, every presidential address. But here, that all seemed so removed. Ever since the attack on Pearl Harbor, it had been relatively safe on our shores. But it was more than that. Here, I was too removed from the war effort. I wasn't in the factory. I wasn't playing ball.

I was here, in this attic, the radio and Minnie too often my only company as of late.

Minnie hummed along with the song that came on at the end of the comedian's show. "The girls downstairs send their best," she said, hardly pausing in her tune. "As do the young gentlemen. They miss you and hope you'll be joining them soon."

I swallowed. Joining them... I did miss the company, but joining them was so... final. There was a reason why I was the last to turn. The last to accept it.

Only now, there was no one else left but me for them to quench their thirst with, and this house had oh-so-many hungry mouths to feed.

Fibber McGee and Molly started up and Minnie wrinkled her nose at the sound of Jim Jordan's voice, standing to turn the radio dial off. "That drivel." Her bright blue eyes sparkled even in the near-darkness of the attic as she turned to me. "I suppose that's enough for today." She stared down at my lap. "That's a... Well, that's an interesting design."

I'd embroidered a set of raindrops, only instead of blue thread, I'd grabbed red. I held the square up to what little light we had. *Blood.* Not the best choice for a wartime blanket.

Still, it was edged and it would suffice. I finished off the pattern and grabbed for the scissors in the sewing kit, cutting off the rest of the thread.

Minnie took it from me, putting it atop hers over her arm, and left me with a stack of raw material. "This will give you something to do," she said. "We'll send breakfast in the morning." She grabbed the tray on which she'd brought me steak and pudding. Despite the rations, she was able to spare most of her luxuries for me since I was the only one here who really needed it.

Back home, I never would have dreamed I'd one day be eating steak.

I cut a new piece of thread—I was pretty sure it was blue this time—and placed the small scissors into the shirt pocket over my breast.

Before leaving, she stepped closer and jostled the tray in her hand so she could pinch my cheek. "You're such a good girl," she said. She looked as if she were in her twenties—hardly old enough to mother my sixteen-year-old self—but I knew that in her case, appearances were deceiving.

"Rest up," she said, heading for the door. As her hand touched the knob, she hesitated, her back even straighter than usual, her head slightly tilted upward, as if sensing something. "And be careful around the door. Mary Ellen is... struggling with the adjustment. I don't want her quenching on you unsupervised."

My hand froze mid-stitch, my breath catching in my throat as Minnie opened the door and stepped outside. I didn't start breathing again until the door shut and I could hear the bolt, the chain, and the lock turn into place.

Keeping me here, in this attic, but also keeping everyone else out there.

Minnie carried the sole key, and she only trusted that door unlocked when she was with me.

After I heard the last echoes of her footsteps down the twisting staircase leading to the rest of the mansion, I sighed. Getting up on my haunches, I reached over and flipped the dial, waiting for the radio to hum back to life and letting a small chuckle escape as I lost myself to the picture Molly painted of her ham-fisted home life with Fibber McGee.

THOUGH I'D BEEN left with half a dozen afghans up here alone in the attic, which I'd taken from the other empty beds up against the back wall, a bitter chill bit through the gaps in the plywood along with the slits of sunlight struggling to make their way inside. The cold rushing up from my numb toes all the way to my nose shook me to the bone, but I lay there, shivering, not moving. The knock on the door signaled breakfast and a bathroom break. There was the chamber pot in the corner, but unlike Minnie, I was from an era where things like running water and flushing toilets were taken for granted—even in the cramped

apartment where I'd spent my childhood. True, there were probably farmhouses that had yet to get with the times, but in my apartment complex, there'd been a private toilet closet for the family and a shower behind a curtain in the kitchen.

This mansion had three full bathrooms, and not a single resident other than me had need for them.

The second knock on the door was softer.

"Come in," I said, my voice catching in my throat. For a second, my breath left a trail of steam in the air and I pulled my hand out from beneath the blankets to try to catch it.

The bolt, chain, and lock scraped and clicked as they came undone.

I sat up, smoothing my nightgown and leaving several of the blankets wrapped around my shoulders like a lumpy, overstuffed stole.

"It's freezing in here. Why isn't your heater on?"

Still groggy and expecting to find Minnie—with one of the others perhaps in tow—I blinked hard to let the figures entering the attic come into focus.

Dean, Minnie's prized "nephew," as she called him. And Leopold.

My Leopold.

Formerly my Leopold.

And Minnie was nowhere in sight.

A jingling key ring slipping into his pocket, Dean crossed the open room to my copper space heater and plugged it in as Leopold, balancing my breakfast tray, turned around and shut the door behind him.

"I'm surprised you noticed the temperature," said Leopold. He balanced the tray on one hand and flexed the other in front of him as he stepped closer, his attention drawn to his appendage, as if he'd never seen it before. "I don't feel a thing. Nothing uncomfortable. Other than thirst." He put his hand back under the tray and stared at me.

It was nothing like how he used to stare at me, love and hope and adventure in his wide brown eyes. They were bright blue now, a sign of his transformation, along with the pallid tone to his skin. And if anything, they were full of... hunger.

I turned away, not wanting to see him stare at me like a wolf before its prey.

"I didn't feel it," snapped Dean. He moved closer and kneeled before me, laying a careful hand on my upper arm. "I could see her breath turn to mist when we walked in."

His eyes were bright blue as well, and there was hunger there, *longing*, but it was more muted, more lost in the background. "Are you okay, Zelda? You look unwell."

"I'm fine," I lied. I grabbed hold of my long braid—still stuck under my blanket shawl—and nervously wound my fingers through it. Its length was getting out of control—some of it coiled around the other side of the bed, and it still hung off—but I didn't want it cut. Not yet.

"When your hair is just a bit longer," said Mom as she brushed a wooden comb through the thick strands, "we can sell it. Even in trying times, people are still paying good money."

I twirled a strand around my finger and Mom tapped the back of my hand gently with the comb. "Leave it be. You'll just get it tangled. We need to keep it soft and supple." She parted the hair into three sections and began to braid it.

"Oh, let her do what she wants," said Pop. He peeked up over the newspaper in his hands, the top half of his face towering over a headline reporting of British troops evacuating France in one line and an opponent to challenge Roosevelt's bid for reelection in the fall in the other. "Until some high society broad fashions it into a bird's nest for her thinning chrome-dome, it's her hair, isn't it?" He nudged my youngest sister's toes with his foot, causing her to look up from the ragged hand-me-down doll she was playing with before the fire and giggle. Cathy ran her fingers through the doll's worn hair in imitation

of our mother combing mine.

Mom grunted but said nothing, pulling on the comb harder and nearly ripping that precious hair out from its roots. I was just thinking about how I wished we had a radio like Leopold's family did—something other to do than watch little kids play and get my hair combed and listen to my parents bicker—when smoke sifted out of the fireplace and my eyes began to water. I choked, nearly forgetting to breathe.

From the kitchen table where he'd been doing homework, Robbie hacked and coughed, pushing back his chair and waving one hand in the air as he ran for the damper. He nearly knocked over Suzanne, Jon, and Hannah where they'd been huddled together playing jacks in the corner, but they were too focused on covering their faces and coughing from the smoke to complain. He opened it, coughing harder as he struggled to speak. "Pops... You forgot to open it all the way again."

Pop rolled his eyes and lifted his paper. "Yes, Mother," he said. "I'm sorry." He didn't sound sorry—or concerned. Pop always seemed to think his ten-year-old son was too much of an eager beaver.

I shivered, the chill of the cold, cramped apartment hitting my back as Mom dropped the comb on my lap and went over to open our two windows to let the rest of the smoke escape.

Cathy crawled over to me and grinned, reaching up to grab the comb from me to use on her doll. I smiled down at her, curling the very end of my long, long braid around my soot-stained fingers.

"Zelda!" said Mom as she noticed what I was doing. "Keep those dirty hands off that hair!" She sighed, daring Pop to challenge her, but he simply turned a page in the paper. "Go wash up. Let's start dinner."

I didn't need to worry about selling my hair for wigs—not anymore. But I felt like once my hair was gone, I'd be severing the last tie I had to my parents, to my brothers and sisters—to my life. My real life. This... This was all a fantasy.

"Ack!" The tray slipped from Leopold's grasp as he covered his eyes with his forearm.

Right before my eggs and bacon clattered to the ground beside my hot tea, Dean appeared at Leopold's side, crouching to grab the tray in both hands. The glass tea cup teetered slightly on the saucer; the fork slid back toward the plate.

"You knew sunlight leaked in here," said Dean, righting himself. "No need to shatter good china and act like you're so surprised."

The more time I spent among the immortals, the less surprised I was about such moments. One second, Dean had been at my side—the next, he'd been saving my breakfast from the wood floor. It was simply something vampires could do.

Leopold muttered a curse word and stepped into the shadows.

Some vampires, anyway. The more experienced ones—though Dean didn't strike me as someone who'd been around as long as Minnie. He seemed too hip—too perfect for the times. Minnie, glamorous though she may have been, had some fuddy-duddy tendencies.

Dean handed me the tray with both hands and I tucked in, starting with some of the tea to warm me up and followed by the eggs and bacon.

"What was that you said about no longer feeling discomfort?" Dean asked, a smirk on his face as he dug his hands into his pockets, jingling the keys again. He really looked at home in that pinstriped suit. Minnie looked gorgeous in the latest dresses I was told the movie stars wore—though it'd been so long since I'd been to see a picture, and so rare to go even then. But she wore them stiffly and carried herself with a detached sense of grace. Dean looked... comfortable. Like one of us.

"Shut your trap," said Leopold, moaning. I chanced a glance at him as I munched on a slice of crispy bacon. His eyes were watering and he rubbed them vigorously.

"Don't snap your cap." Dean put a hand on his elbow to stop him. "You'll make it worse."

Leopold just growled and flung his elbow to get Dean to step away. Dean shook his head and sat down beside me on the edge of the bed, pulling out a half-dollar he often kept in his pocket and liked to play with when his attention wasn't captivated. He leaned closer to me as he rolled the coin between two fingers. "I warned him to wear sun cheaters," he said, referring to the immortals' habit of covering their eyes with dark lenses whenever they ventured outdoors. "He's got a nice pair of aviator glasses and everything, but he wouldn't listen. I knew he wouldn't be on the ball enough to look away." He nudged his chin toward that window with the slits of light. I often wondered why they didn't do a better job of sealing it if they found light so offensive, but I supposed they took pity on my kind and wanted to offer us a little ray. Knowing it could be the last time we saw it without flinching.

Thanks to my little brother Robbie, who'd wanted so badly to see that scary old flick that had been playing at the theater on a discount night, I knew that Nosferatu turned to smoke and ashes in the light. In comparison, these vampires just seemed to be mildly inconvenienced.

"Ow," said Leopold as he walked into the foot of my bed, his hands still rubbing vigorously against his eyes. *Maybe not* mildly.

Dean studied me with concern and I quickly wolfed down the rest of my bacon, polishing off the plate. He grinned. "Well, you certainly haven't lost your appetite. But do keep the space heater on when it's cold. We won't have problems paying the bills." I didn't tell him I was afraid of turning on the heater because of what had happened that night, almost a year ago.

"Zel, get up!" Robbie was shaking me awake. He hacked loudly. "I can't get the damper open anymore. The fire is... spreading — wake up!"

I shook my head, forcing the echoing sound of Robbie's continual coughing out of my head.

I shouldn't be alive. I didn't deserve immortality, not when they all lay dead in an unclaimed family mass grave.

Leopold *should* have known why leaving the space heater on overnight would bother me, but he was too focused on the damage the miniscule amount of sunlight seemed to have done to his eyes.

"Ugh!" He slammed a fist against my headboard and I jumped in place.

Dean shook his head—he was so much better at avoiding the sun, even when its beams were sprinkled throughout half the attic. "Let's get you down to the bathroom," he said. "Maybe a hot shower will warm you up."

My toes curled at the thought. That sounded divine. Except... My eyes flitted to the door. "Where's Minnie?"

Dean stood and took my tray from me. "She's gone for a few days. She had... business."

Leopold snorted. "Business recruiting more quenchers, you mean."

I shivered. Leopold and I had been on the streets a couple of days, done drifting from couch to couch, done hiding in basements to avoid the questions the parents of our friends asked. Too many fathers had thought Leopold a draft-dodger, but he'd still been seventeen. He would have lied and joined the military to escape his own father before the fire even, but it was I who'd stopped him, I who'd begged him not to leave me and then... He became all I had. In any case, running off together—promises of getting hitched when we landed on our feet—was what had led to Minnie crossing our paths.

"You poor dears," she'd said, extending a hand toward the park bench where we'd cuddled up one night. "Come with me. I can offer you a roof over your heads, food in your belly... And more than you might believe possible."

"She has business other than blood at the moment," said Dean matter-of-factly. "Investments. And licenses. She's interested in opening a company—"

"Why?" I asked. The question was out of my mouth before I realized. She was rich. But she was more involved in helping the community, more active than Pop had been, and Pop had had so many mouths to feed—to feed with food that needed to be bought, with money that needed to be spent. Employment had been scarce on our side of town before the war.

Dean shrugged. "And then there's the matter of *that* land," he said, as if that were the natural course of the conversation. "She's keeping a close eye on the construction of that house." I knew there was a piece of land near the woods that ran along the river that particularly interested her, but I didn't know more. A house was being built there, but she didn't seem interested in buying it—just curious about the couple who planned to move in there. A pregnant woman, her husband off at war. Minnie hoped she'd have a girl, had lamented once she couldn't have just bought the land and built a house and moved *me* or one of the other girls in there herself. Why, I didn't know for sure. Something about the "pixie watching." That was all I'd gathered, my mind too often wandering when Minnie made conversation. That was outside. Outside had little to do with me. Not anymore.

Leopold removed his fists from his eyes. His eyelids were raw, red. "I'm sorry, but I can't hold it back."

"Fellow, take it down a peg and—" Dean started, but it was too late.

Leopold was already sinking his fangs into my neck, his large, clumsy hands fumbling through my hair, pulling out the braid, getting lost in it. My neck burned and my blood seemed to boil. I gasped, the scream I wanted to let escape stuck halfway to my lips as the searing pain shot through my body from my neck down. My body convulsed as I weakly sent a hand in his direction, my instinct to get him off, even though I'd been through this before—but never like this. Never without warning.

There was a crash as the tray and dishes clattered to the ground. "Lay off! You'll hurt her!"

In the blink of an eye, Dean was there, his hands at Leopold's mouth, forcing his head away, then shoving him across the room.

Leopold landed on his haunches, blood dripping down his lips — my blood. He wiped it off with the back of his hand.

Dean stood in front of me, his arms out wide. There was a twitch in his jaw as his bright, blue eyes glanced toward me, and I had to wonder if he was fighting his instinct to drink from my neck, too.

"I just took a sip," said Leopold, clenching his hands into fists. "She's fine."

"Beg to... differ," I said through suddenly-parched lips. Though the burning stilled, I still felt weak, dizzy. My hands dug into my mattress, wove through thick strands of my hair that were slicked with blood.

"Scram!" said Dean, digging his heels in.

Scoffing, Leopold headed for the door. When he opened it, there was a ghastly pale figure behind it, stock still, staring inside.

Mary Ellen. The freshest vampire of the bunch. If Leopold had a hard time holding it in, then she —

Her mouth opened wide, her fangs lengthening.

"Out!" shouted Dean again, disappearing from beside the bed and appearing at the door in a blink of an eye, slamming it closed. He turned to me. "I'm sorry. I promised my aunt I'd look after you."

"It's fine," I said, clutching at my throat. I didn't feel fine.

They were supposed to drink from me in small doses. Too much at once could kill me. A little at a time, a little taste of their venom — and one day soon, I'd turn. But Minnie was supposed to decide when that would be.

And I was supposed to be restrained when it happened. Because otherwise, I'd twitch and flail and scream — and they could accidentally slit my throat entirely.

My would-be fiancé could have done that just now, had Dean not been here to stop him.

Dean took a step toward me. "Let me—"

"Stop!" I said, holding out a hand, even as the other cradled my throat. "Stay away."

"Zelda, I won't hurt you. I have better control than they do."

I shook my head. "I don't care. Just please... Leave me be."

The fire, the heat, the flames... Robbie coughing as we made our way out, collapsing into my arms when we hit the streets, when we should have been safe.

"Where... are they?" I spoke through fingers I'd slammed against my lips.

"I don't... I don't..." Robbie looked around, dizzy, unsteady on his feet. I tugged on him to stop him from pulling away from me, from heading back inside. Mom and Pop and Suzanne and Jon and Hannah and Cathy... None of them were here. They were all still inside.

He'd screamed at them to leave. He'd told me they'd left. While I'd been tripping on my hair and fighting through the smoke and making my way to the sound of his voice, we must have passed them. They must have gotten stuck in the stairwell, the stairwell that had snapped and cracked and collapsed behind us just as we'd broken free to the cold, sharp air of the sidewalk in front of the flaming apartment building.

"Leave me be." A tear escaped down my cheek.

Dean frowned and nodded, bending to pick up the plates and the tray. He only flinched slightly at my nearness, at the blood splattered all over my blankets, my hair, my hands, my neck.

"I'm sorry," he said again before exiting out the door. I waited for the sounds of the bolt, the chain, the lock.

I stared at the space heater, its bright orange coils, for I didn't know how long. Eventually, I turned on the radio and fell asleep to a melancholic jazz melody, a soulful woman crooning about her lost love.

In the middle of the night, I heard the *scratch, scrape, scratch* at the door leading down to the rest of the house.

"Zelda," a woman whispered. "Zelda, come out here."

I froze, jolted awake at the fact that I felt lighter, at the sensation of fewer blankets than usual, at the sight of the space heater still oozing its warmth from across the room.

The radio echoed with laughter as a whistle dipped high and low.

"*Zel-da*"—she spoke in a singsong tune—"this mansion is killer diller. Everyone's dancing—Dean is knockin' it out. Come on, Zelda."

Her voice was hoarse, quiet. But I could tell it was Mary Ellen, her thirst for my blood punctuating every word.

"Come on, Zelda... Let's cut a rug. Zelda..."

She kept on scratching for hours before I finally drifted back to sleep, too frightened to move to switch off the dial or turn off the heater.

The knock that startled me awake came from another direction entirely.

I jumped up, surprised to find myself more twisted in my hair than in my blankets. There was blood all over the front of my nightgown. I never did get to the bathroom to wash or change.

The knock echoed again, and I realized it was something hitting glass. Like a window.

The radio was echoing static now and I switched it off as I crossed the room, my bare feet flushing as they passed the heater, the heater that hadn't burnt me and everything in this house down to ashes.

I froze, considering...

The knock again. I headed to the window and peered through the largest slit in the plywood I could find. I pulled back almost immediately when I saw Dean out there, in the recessed windowsill that I knew was at the very top of the mansion.

"Jeepers," I said quietly.

"Zelda," he whispered in hushed tones. "Pull down the plywood."

I didn't know if that would even be possible at first, but I slid my fingers through two gaps in the wood and I tugged. I could feel it jostling, so I tugged harder.

It gave and I stumbled back, the dim moonlight spilling freely into the attic now. Dean pointed to the latch at the side of the window. I had no idea what he was doing, but I complied, unlatching the lock.

"Thanks," he said, nodding. He shimmied around to rest his foot against another piece of plywood. "Stand back."

I did and he kicked at the board until it went flying. Just when it was about to land, he did his vampire trick and appeared beside it, taking the plywood in his hands so it wouldn't clatter to the ground and putting a finger to his lips.

I shook my head. "What are you doing here?"

"I'm going fishing," he said, leaning the plywood against the wall and stuffing both hands into his pockets. The grin on his face let me know he meant "fish" of the girl variety.

"I'm not... That is, I... I'm not an active crop." That was what they'd called the girls like Mary Ellen around the old neighborhood — *she* had been up for anything, from what I knew of her. The way she'd smiled at Dean, at Herbert, at Ernesto — even at my Leopold. Though, to be fair, getting to know someone while trapped in an attic waiting for vampires to suck on your essence might not have been the best venue for getting to know their true character.

"Easy, sweetheart, I'm not that doll dizzy." He shrugged. "It was a joke."

Pinching my lips, I stared at him, waiting for him to explain. I shivered and Dean appeared at my side with one of the afghans off my bed. "Why are you here?" I said again. "Why did you come in through the window?"

All he would have had to do was knock. With Minnie gone, he was the only one I trusted not to succumb to blood lust around me. He had been with Minnie from the start.

She sometimes called him a prince. She might have actually meant it.

He took a deep breath and closed his eyes and for just a moment, I wondered if I'd been wrong to place that kind of trust in him.

"I'm busting you out," he said, strolling back toward the window. He didn't flinch in the moonlight, though he was careful not to let his bright blue eyes rove too closely to any single beam of light. His sun cheaters were hanging out of his front pocket beside the decorative handkerchief I'd never known him to need.

"Why can't we go downstairs...?"

"You know why. Can't so much as have you near the door before those chuckleheads are sniffing you out." Dean ran a hand through his hair. "Look, I—do you want out or not? I don't mean anything by it, I just... You don't seem fully committed to this."

It was Leopold who'd first succumbed to Minnie's advances. There was her beauty to be sure, her poise—the warmth and food and shelter she'd offered us. But it had been more than that.

After dinner that first night, she'd taken both our hands at once. "Now that you've had your fill," she'd said, "let me introduce you to some friends. You're going to love it here."

She'd brought us up to join the others in their attic stronghold: Mary Ellen, Herbert, Ernesto, Ruby—all waiting for their turns to become immortals.

I hadn't believed it at first. Even after the others had come back, one by one, dreamy looks on their faces and dark, red marks on their necks. Not until my turn. Not until I'd been bound and gagged and held down while Minnie and Dean and other shadowy figures had taken turns sucking at my neck.

Dean had been the first besides Minnie to bite down on my flesh.

"Well?" asked Dean, still waiting for my answer.

It wasn't that I didn't want those things downstairs — the elegance, the parties. But there was the thought of growing my own set of fangs, of sinking them into some poor person's neck.

And there was the fire, the thought of Robbie fading away in my arms. The bright red coils of the space heater drew my attention.

If he'd died — if they'd all died — if people halfway across the world were giving their lives to do the honorable thing, I had no business living forever.

"Okay," I said. "Get me out of here."

Leopold wouldn't miss me. Except as a drink.

I shuffled across the room to grab my shoes and swap my nightgown for my dress, all while tugging my mess of a mane into a loose and frizzy braid. I stopped at the sewing kit and grabbed a ribbon to tie around both ends of it. I caught Dean looking and he quickly turned, casually switching off the space heater, probably not knowing I'd have been tempted to "bump into it" as I made my escape. But I couldn't have. Vampires or not, I —

"Zel... da... I'm... sor..." Robbie spoke my name before coughing once more and going limp in my arms. He'd tried to rush headlong back inside, but I'd pulled him away, pulled him back. And then his eyes had closed, his rattling breaths growing weaker.

We rushed to the window and Dean went out first, turning around to help me out. His hands around my bare arms were cold, colder than the iciest morning in that attic I was leaving behind.

I flinched and Dean drew me closer, but even through his suit, his body chilled me to the core. It was the vampire's venom that was full of fire—their bodies were cold, meant for the grave.

Shivering, I broke away and Dean let me, his smile falling. He took a few careful steps forward toward a tree.

"How did you get up here?" I whispered, my teeth chattering in the night wind.

He pointed to the tree several yards away.

I laughed. "You're joshing me."

His lips thinned. "No, but I guess I... I didn't figure how I'd get you back over there. I just... leaped."

I sighed, turning back to stare at the open window. It was somewhere at least. Somewhere I didn't have to leave. Somewhere I might never leave.

"Don't go into a decline," said Dean. "We'll think of something."

I ran my fingers nervously through my loose braid, thinking. Thinking of how cumbersome the hair had been when I'd been running with Robbie, thinking about how I'd tripped and told him to go on without me and how he'd come back, how he'd exposed himself to more of the smoke—

I reached into my front pocket, surprised to find the sewing scissors still there.

"Maybe if I jump," he started. "And you jump—and if you don't make it, I can halt the moment and snatch you before you—what are you doing?"

I was halfway through cutting above the ribbon atop my braid. The scissors kept catching in the thick fibers, but I kept cutting anyway. When at last I finished, I held the braid aloft, my head suddenly so much lighter and freer, the weight all in my hand. "Use this as a rope," I said, tossing it to him.

He caught it, his bright blue eyes wide. "You've got moxie, doll."

He tied one thick end of my braid around an ornamental sphere positioned at the corner of the roof. Then he jumped, the other end of the braid in his hand. After the blink of an eye, he appeared back beside me, the braid taut like a thick high wire from the roof to the nearest bough of the tree. He bent slightly and gestured forward. "After you." He must have noticed me hesitate. "I promise I'll catch you if you slip."

"Thanks," I said, though I didn't really feel confident. Taking a deep breath, I walked to the edge of the roof and then put my foot down. The hair sagged beneath my weight.

"Just do it fast. You know I can halt time the instant you slip. Stay on the beam, doll. Stay on course."

Easier said than done. Still, I steeled myself and took another step, then another — and faster and faster until I was halfway there. I could feel myself teetering, like I somehow couldn't balance myself without the weight of all that hair tugging over my shoulders, but I had to keep moving. I kept moving, into the cold wind, into the unknown future, into death — eventual death. Maybe imminent death. But death I deserved.

The sun was starting to rise over the distant horizon, and I thought quickly to the sunglasses Dean had tucked into his pocket — he'd planned to be out, so he must have had a place for us to go.

My hand reached for the top of the tree just as a car pulled into the driveway.

I stilled.

"Keep going," whispered Dean. Then he was beside me, his arm around my waist and then in a blink we were at the other end of the bough, flush against the trunk of the tree, hidden behind the dying, brightly-colored leaves. He put a finger to his lips and I peered through the lattice to see below.

The car—a sleek, beautiful blue Plymouth Roadking—jerked to a stop and the headlights turned off. The car's engine cut and then the door opened, revealing Minnie in her most gorgeous silhouette dress yet. Its blood-red color was evident even in the dying moonlight and the amber glow of the morning sun. She squinted and pulled a pair of large sunglasses out of her purse, sliding the temples under her headscarf. She carried her small handbag in front of her with gloved hands like a movie starlet.

Just as she was about to disappear under the portico, she paused, almost as if listening. As a response to her unasked question, a gust of wind picked up, brushing at the hem of her pencil-thin skirt and making her grab for the top of her headscarf. She ran inside and my shoulders relaxed, a tension I hadn't even noticed now released.

I went to shift my foot onto a sturdier part of the branch, but Dean pulled me tighter, shaking his head.

I almost dared not breathe.

After a moment—a long moment in which the sun began to rise threateningly overhead—Dean's muscles relaxed and he let go of me to grab for his sun cheaters, slipping them over his eyes. Flinging my arms around the trunk, I tried to regain my balance, my head swimming, my stomach growling, my scalp too light.

"Easy," whispered Dean.

The bark bit into my cheek as I pushed my head tighter against it.

"There are enough branches to act as footholds," said Dean. "But we have to move soon. She's home early. It's only a matter of time before they notice."

Swallowing down my nervousness, I nodded, extending one leg outward until I felt the branch beneath with my toes. One branch at a time, bit by bit, one leg at a time, with Dean right behind me encouraging me and promising my safety all the while. When I ran out of branches, he told me to squeeze tightly to the trunk. He jumped down to the ground, his arms out to catch me. "I've got you," he said in a hushed voice.

And he did, seeming to stumble slightly at first and then in an instant, he corrected himself, positioning his arms under my knees and around my upper torso.

"Hey. What's buzzin', cousin?" The grin on his face could have lit up a dark room — if he could have actually stood to be in a bright room.

He bent to let my feet touch the spongy grass, righting me on my own two feet. Though his hands had been cold, I felt the absence of his touch. I knew there was a special talent responsible for his speed and grace, but in that moment, I felt a rush of envy, a reminder of what I was about to leave behind.

He grabbed for my hand. "Let's go," he said, his voice hushed.

He eyed the car, and I wondered if his vampire talents also included the ability to start up a vehicle without the key. Otherwise, I'd have to get my hitchhiking thumb ready.

I wondered how far he planned to go with me, and how Minnie would react once she discovered he'd helped me go.

I never got the chance to find out.

"Dean, Zelda — where on Earth are you going?"

Minnie's voice was soft and sweet, not at all looking to bust our chops.

She appeared before us at the end of the driveway, the small piece of red hair that peeked out from underneath her head scarf shifting slightly, signifying that she, too, had walked across time while the rest of us had been standing still.

Dean yanked me against his chest and then... Silence.

A bird excited to see the breaking dawn ceased its song mid-note. The idling of an engine down the block cut out. The in and out of my breaths were the only thing that broke through the quiet.

Dean wasn't breathing. I didn't know why that surprised me.

"Come on," he said, his voice echoing out into the still silence.

My hand gripped in his, he tugged and we were off, moving through the stillness—at a normal, if hurried, pace. Dean's quick movements and impossible speeds reduced to a normal jog when the surroundings were stuck, unblinking.

"How am I seeing this?" I asked as we approached the still form of Minnie.

Dean responded by tugging me closer. "Stay close," he said. "I pulled you in with me." For the first time that I'd noticed, there seemed to be something approaching perspiration on his brow—his screwed-up facial muscles all but screaming tension.

"But I thought only vampires could—"

"Only skilled vampires can do this at all. And only... a handful of vampires... can pull someone in with them." If he could have breathed, he'd have been doing so heavily.

He flinched as we approached Minnie. Like everything else, she hadn't so much as twitched.

"How long does this last?" I asked.

But Dean either didn't hear me or he chose not to answer. In either case, the point was moot because I got my answer: not very long.

Minnie's hand shot out and seized Dean around the throat the moment we passed her.

She had finished the move before I even heard the return of the bird's cry.

"This is a fine way to repay me for all I've done for you, child." Minnie's voice had taken on a harsher tone than usual, an echoing vibrato resonating behind it that reminded me of what she truly was: an ancient being—I didn't know how old, but not like the others here.

Not turned this decade.

Dean didn't so much as tremble under the vise-like grip of her fingers as she lifted him a half a foot off the ground. His grip on my own hand only grew stronger.

"Wilhel...mina..."

She wasn't stopping him from breathing — he had no need for that, I'd been so recently reminded — but she was interfering with his ability to speak. With her free hand, she knocked his sun cheaters to the ground.

Minnie's face pivoted slightly, those sunglass-covered eyes seemingly trained on me. "And you... Zelda, darling..." The tension in her facial muscles relaxed somewhat, her arm lowering Dean's feet back to the driveway. She didn't let go of his throat, though, as her lips puckered. "What did you do to your hair?" She shook her head. "Never mind. It looks adorable. More importantly, if you aren't happy here, why didn't you tell me? Why reduce yourselves to this — to sneaking behind my back?"

My eyes darted away from hers as I saw the crowd gathering on the front porch from the inside of the house. Leopold at the front of them, all wearing sun cheaters, though the sun was just barely making its way over the horizon.

"Are you unhappy?" Minnie asked.

Dean's hand tensed in mine and I turned to look over my shoulder at the rising sun. There before it was the road that led out of the neighborhood — out of the city, out of the state, out of the country... To where?

The world was at war from one end to the next. There was only death and darkness awaiting me.

I remembered a different sunrise, one shrouded in ash and smoke and flames, Robbie in my arms, the firefighters approaching.

I'd lost my way then, but there was one place I'd found it.

"Let's get married," said Leopold, taking me in his arms. I was certain I still smelled of smoke — I'd never get the soot off my hands.

Those soot-covered hands trembled against his back. They'd held Robbie so recently. The firemen had had to pry my brother's limp body from those hands. "What are you...? Why would you ask that? We're not even old enough yet."

"Then we'll get married the moment we can."

"I can't." I sniffled, my throat dry and cracked from smoke and crying alike. "I have... I have nothing." Before the firemen could see to me, I'd stood and run. I'd run and gasped and run down the blocks until I'd arrived at Leopold's house and I'd slammed my fist against his front door, shrieking his name. It was a wonder he'd come to the door instead of his mother or father, but in that moment, I hadn't cared. "Your father doesn't want you to —"

"It doesn't matter what he thinks," snapped Leopold. "I love you, Zel. We'll find someplace to live until I can enlist and then I can send money home." He kissed the top of my head. "I'll provide for you. I promise. You're not alone." He choked on those words, and I knew the shock of my family's deaths was only just then hitting him — it was only just then hitting me. All I'd known was that I'd needed him and I'd had no one else.

Leopold had become my home. My everything. And now, he paced toward me, a ghost of his former self, his lips twitching, a fang extending.

"Stop," said Minnie, and Leopold did, his fangs retreating under his upper lip. "The rest of you, back inside. Our neighbors are almost up."

Mary Ellen practically growled, but Ruby took her by the shoulders and guided her back inside, leaving the four of us alone in the driveway.

"Zelda, were you running away?" asked Leopold, that twinge of sadness again coating his words.

"Let's run away," he said. "I won't let them put you into foster care — I won't let us be separated."

I nodded.

Bobbing my head against his chest, I gripped him tightly like my life depended on it. The sound of creaking stairs and clomping footsteps told us his dad had awoken, that he was on his way down.

"Then let's go," Leopold said, pulling back from my embrace to grab my hand. Then we were off, down the road, both of us in our pajamas and bare feet — my nightgown covered in ash.

"Where do you think you're going, boy? Don't think you're too old for me to whup you!" his father shrieked after us. "You get back here and let go of that whore from that lazy, no-good family — "

But whatever else he said, we didn't hear. We were running, fumbling on bare feet, hiccupping, even laughing — not because I was happy, far from it. But because I was delirious, practically outside myself, choking on fresh air and fighting through the pain as we ran far, far away.

But Leopold had been the one good thing through it all.

And he... he was right here.

"I'm sorry," I said, my voice low.

I turned my head toward Dean. "I'm sorry," I said again, tugging on my hand to ask him to let me go. I hadn't meant for him to get in trouble. I hadn't asked him to help me — but I shouldn't have gone along with it.

Leopold was here. He'd given up everything for me.

Dean's bright blue eyes bore into mine and then his fingers loosened. There was something there in those eyes — disappointment. And pain. But he couldn't keep his eyes open — he was squirming now in Minnie's grip, his eyes darting away from the horizon.

Leopold laughed as he held his arms out to me. "As Bogie might say, 'never trust a dame.'" He swept me into his arms and pecked me on the cheek. "Only joking, baby." My cheek rubbed his, the iciness of his skin sending shivers down my back.

"Oh, good," said Minnie, smiling. "You only have a bite or two before you turn into one of us. It'd be a shame for all that work to go to waste."

"You'll be even more gorgeous, Zel," said Leopold as he slipped an arm around my shoulder. "Then you can join us downstairs and dance all night long." He leaned into the top of my head and sniffed my hair. There was a hunger there, a *thirst*. "But first, you owe us a quencher..."

"Wilhel... mina," said Dean and I looked over my shoulder. Minnie hadn't lost her grip. "It's... almost sun..." The last word was lost, too quiet for my ears.

Minnie laughed—a little chirping titter. "I know, dear nephew. And you appear to be the only one outdoors without his sunglasses."

Dean made a guttural growl and I paused on the stairs leading to the porch, pulling Leopold to a stop so I could watch what Minnie had in mind.

In the blink of an eye, she moved from the driveway to the middle of the street, where the sun shone the brightest as it broke into the sky. She lifted Dean higher, spinning him so his face pointed east.

He shrieked.

Minnie's voice carried across the driveway, soft-spoken as she was. "Hush, child, you'll wake the whole neighborhood."

Dean tried to close his eyes, but it wasn't enough. His eyelids seemed to steam in the sunlight.

Leopold shuddered beside me. "That'll hurt. And I bet Minnie won't let him have a quencher to heal from it anytime soon." He laughed and muttered under his breath. "Serves the pompous grandstander right." He nodded at the top of my head. "I like the shorter tresses," he said. "Always wondered how you didn't trip on that braid."

My fingers went absentmindedly to run through hair that was no longer there. I could no longer hear Mom's voice asking me not to play with it.

He slid an arm back around my shoulder and guided me inside. "You ready for the quencher? We'll wait for Minnie, of course, but — "

I nodded and put a finger to his lips. Standing up on tippy-toes, I leaned my chest against his and whispered, "Finish it. Now. Just you. I'll stay still."

He grinned, his fangs descending out from between his lips. "Just you and me, baby. For eternity." He clamped his fangs into my neck and I twitched, but he held me close, keeping me from flailing about. I dug my fingernails into his arms and stood on trembling legs.

Dean's struggled grunts from the street died out as the pain of Leopold's venom slithered through my body, the desperate thunder of my heart pounding in my own ears.

Until, all at once, the sound stopped. And so did the pain.

My heart would beat no more.

But there was a thirst — a wild, insatiable thirst.

MAGIC ALL AROUND

Jane Watson

ake care, Greta dear!"

Greta turned and waved to the candy maker before hurrying down the cobbled village lane, the basket she wore on her arm becoming heavier with each step. Pausing for a moment, she pulled the packet of gingerbread she'd just purchased free from the basket, regarding it hungrily. She wondered if she could take a small respite from her errands for Frau Rosa to allow herself just a small taste of the delightful bread, but quickly decided against it. The other goblins might give in to their indulgences, but she wouldn't allow it. The bread could wait until after dinner to reward a hard day's work.

With her gray-colored cloak tied over her simple dress and tightly-laced boots, Greta looked no different than the other village girls. The mortals didn't notice that her ears were longer with fine pointed tips, or that her dark hair was actually a mix of black and green. They didn't notice that a few of her teeth were long and sharp, or that her skin glimmered when it caught the light. And they especially never noticed when her vivid green eyes—unusually large with a black sliver for a pupil—glowed with a supernatural light whenever she used magic. For though goblins and mortals had lived together in the little village high in the mountains for centuries, with each passing generation, more of the mortals lost their ability to see magic.

This did not bother Greta in the slightest. She did not care to use her magic, preferring the simple life of the hardworking and dedicated mortals. They had less leisure time, but they enjoyed it so much more. After years of unhappiness with the other goblins, Greta had finally decided to take matters into her own hands and started working in the shop of the elderly mortal grocer, Ernst, and his wife, Rosa. Greta had known the couple since she was small—they were among the few villagers who could still see magic. A year had passed quite happily as Greta spent her days working in their store and her nights in the spare bedroom of their rambling home.

With a wistful glance at the gingerbread, Greta tucked it back into her basket and entered the postmaster's shop.

At the sound of the bell, the postmaster emerged from the back room. "Ah, Greta! Let's see what we have today," he said, pulling a stack of letters and parcels from a wooden compartment and setting them on the counter.

Greta lifted them one by one to slip into her basket. There were several letters addressed to Ernst and Rosa. She paused, noting that one had fine, straight handwriting, and a sketch on the front of the bronze-tinted envelope. "Hm."

This letter was different than any Greta had seen before. The detailed sketch of a stone building—with pointed windows and ivy growing up the sides—wrapped all the way to the back, interrupted only by the large red dollop of wax that sealed the flap.

"Whoever sent that must be quite the artist," the postmaster commented, peering at her over his wire-rimmed glasses.

"Yes," Greta agreed softly, her fingers beginning to feel warm, tingling with magic. Her eyes widened in alarm as strands of gold magic wound their way into the lines and form of the sketch. She looked quickly at the postmaster, but he had already turned his back to her, sorting letters and parcels into the boxes. *I mustn't use my magic here,* she chided herself. Ernst had once told her that when he was a boy, some of the shopkeepers who still could see magic sprinkled salt on their doorsteps to keep the goblins away. Not wanting to be treated like an outcast, Greta hid her magic. She stared at the envelope for another long moment, the light finally fading. *Strange, though. I didn't mean to summon my power.* She shook her head to clear her thoughts before stuffing the letter deep in her basket.

"Good day to you," she called to the postmaster before leaving his shop.

She made her way out of the shop and up the winding cobbled street, greeting the other shopkeepers as she passed. The crisp autumn air added a rosy tinge to her cheeks, and she dug her hands into her cloak.

"Little Greta!" An old woman with a pointed face popped out of thin air into the alleyway as Greta approached. Silver hair came out of her messy bun in tufts, and her fiery amber eyes stared at Greta. She lifted a glimmering hand in greeting.

"Oh. Ursula. Hello," Greta mumbled with little enthusiasm.

The elderly goblin emitted a high-pitched cackle. "Out for the day? Why don't you join me at the top of Mount Engel? I hear there's going to be quite the gathering this eve."

In Greta's experience, goblin gatherings were nothing more than a way for her kind to eat, drink, and play cruel jokes. She'd attended some in years past and deeply regretted it. She pulled her cloak tighter about her and said stiffly, "No, thank you. I don't wish to set a landslide on innocent mortals."

"Oh, it was only a little one," Ursula replied with a cluck of her tongue. "You just don't know how to allow yourself any fun, Greta. You toil away as if you hadn't any magic at all."

Greta bristled, about to snap a retort, when Frau Minna from the shop next door came out to sweep the step. "Greta! What a lovely surprise." The florist's expression was puzzled as she looked from Greta to the alley and back.

Greta realized that Ursula had made herself invisible to mortals. She took a deep breath, not wanting to look as if she were rambling madly to herself. "I thought I heard a crash down this way," she explained hurriedly.

She fought to ignore Ursula as the old goblin smirked and muttered, "A crash, you said?"

Minna and Greta both flinched when a deafening sound reached their ears. The metal buckets the florist kept with the stems and scraps had all been knocked to the ground. Greta cast her eyes to Ursula, narrowing them dangerously.

"Oh, dear!" Minna exclaimed, gathering her skirts to hurry down the cobbled alley. "How did that happen?"

Greta set her basket on the ground, righting the bins and scooping the scraps into her arms. "An animal, most likely."

"You needn't help me, Greta," Minna said with a cluck of her tongue as she watched Greta's hands become scratched from the thorny stems. "I'm sure you were off on an important errand."

"No trouble at all!" Greta replied cheerfully, wishing with all of her might that Ursula would disappear. Yet there she was, arms folded as she watched Greta and the florist, a smug smile on her narrow lips.

"Thank you, my dear," Minna said. "Now I mustn't keep you from your errands."

"Good day, Frau Minna." Greta waved, continuing on her way. She sighed when she realized Ursula was following her.

"Hmph," Ursula grumbled. "Little miss goody two-shoes."

"The fact that I *have* magic doesn't mean I haven't better use of my time than to dabble in mean-spirited tricks," Greta hissed. "Now go away before the mortals see me talking to myself."

"If they knew magic was all around them, she'd see me," Ursula observed shrewdly. "I hardly had to use any power at all for their dull eyes to pass over me. Just because they don't believe in magic, suddenly it isn't there."

Greta slowed her steps, turning to the old goblin. "Go," she whispered firmly.

Ursula scowled. "Don't come crying to me when no goblin wishes to pay you any courtesy."

Greta lifted her chin. "You say that as if it would upset me."

As Ursula disappeared with a loud pop, Greta winced and lifted her hand, scratches crisscrossing her skin. They stung in the brisk air, and crimson droplets of blood popped up on her fingers.

Glancing about to be sure no one was watching, Greta concentrated hard on the threads of magic that now pooled about her, willing them to encircle her hand. She was a bit out of practice, but after several long moments, warmth graced her fingertips as the cuts began to heal. Flexing her fingers, Greta nodded in satisfaction. She convinced herself this was worthy — if it hadn't been for that nosy Ursula, she wouldn't have been injured in the first place. She hurried on her way back to the grocer's, irritated by the whole thing.

By the time she reached the grocer's storefront, she was out of breath and the basket was heavy on her arm. She took a deep breath, trying to calm her racing thoughts. "I mustn't storm into the shop like this," she whispered, lowering herself to sit on the front stoop. Sifting through the basket, she came across the large bronze-tinted envelope, staring at the delicate drawing once more. The climbing ivy on the building was so detailed, she found herself wondering how the artist was able to make such tiny, precise marks. She found her ill mood dissipating as she focused on the lines and strokes on the envelope.

Greta was jolted from her reverie when a horrible crash sounded from the back of the store. "Ursula!" she growled, pushing the strange letter back into the basket and hurrying around the corner. She was met with an absolute mess — the rubbish bins were overturned, and the boxes that she had so carefully stacked by the back door, just as Rosa had taught her, had toppled.

"You old kobold," Greta hissed, setting down her load on an upended crate to search for Ursula. "I bet you'd like me to use my magic to fix this mess you made, wouldn't you? Well, if it pleases you to watch me sweep and scrub for the next hour, you're welcome to it!"

Movement caught her eye, and she was startled to see that it was not Ursula emerging from behind the overturned bins, but a small kitten, with black fur and feet that looked as if they had been dipped in flour.

Her anger subsiding, Greta approached the kitten. "So, it was you who did all of this? Rather a large mess for such a little one."

"Meow?" The kitten's mouth opened wide as it stared up at her with large, vivid green eyes — which bore an uncanny resemblance to her own — and she felt a kinship to the feline. "Meow?"

Greta knelt before the kitten, cautiously extending her hand. The kitten let out another soft meow as she rubbed against Greta's knees. "Aren't you the sweet one?" Greta whispered as she began petting the kitten's long, soft fur. The kitten let out a blab in reply. After a few moments, the kitten raised her nose and began sniffing the air. She bounded over to the crate where Greta had left her parcels, putting her paws up to rifle through them.

Greta scrambled to her feet. "No, no," she murmured, hoisting the kitten around the middle. She discovered the curious feline had already unearthed her prize, pulling out the small packet of gingerbread with her teeth.

Greta paused, setting the kitten down as its little body began to rumble with purrs. "You like gingerbread?" The kitten looked up at her and blinked slowly, responding with an emphatic meow. Greta giggled, unwrapping the paper and breaking off a piece of bread—which was rather difficult, since the kitten was scrambling for a bite. "There." The kitten enthusiastically took the gingerbread and gobbled it up, making all sorts of noises that sounded halfway between grunts and purrs. "My, but you can chatter! I think I'll call you Calla." The kitten meowed emphatically. "I see you approve," laughed Greta. She flinched when cold drops of rain hit her head and shoulders, and she thought of the poor little kitten out in the cold rain all night. Placing the basket firmly on her arm, Greta scooped Calla onto her shoulder and hurried inside.

"Meow?" the kitten blabbed.

"Hush," Greta urged, setting her heavy basket down on the table.

"It seems you have made a friend."

Greta started at the voice. "F-Frau Rosa!"

The older woman lifted her eyebrows, awaiting an explanation.

"I heard a noise out back and found this poor starving kitten. It started to rain, so I..." Greta trailed off, not knowing what to say.

To her surprise, Rosa reached out to pat Calla's head. "The poor little waif looks hungry. Why don't you come help me fix a pot of tea, and she can have some milk?"

Greta smiled hopefully. "Does that mean...?"

As Rosa hurried into the kitchen, she called over her shoulder, "I've always thought the shop could use a good mouser."

Greta set the kitten down and followed Rosa with the basket of parcels.

While Calla lapped up her saucer of milk, Greta handed Ernst a steaming cup of tea as he sorted through the mail in front of the fireplace.

"I've heard from Liesel," Ernst commented to his wife. "Her boy Magnus was accepted to the academy. He'll be with us by the end of the week."

Greta paused mid-sip, turning to Ernst and Rosa, green eyes glowing with curiosity.

Ernst smiled and told her, "Our great-nephew is going to be boarding with us while he goes to school here."

"Oh." Greta wasn't sure how to feel at this sudden announcement, so she said no more.

"How old is Magnus now, dear?" Rosa asked, settling into the chair across from her husband.

"He's growing up in the blink of an eye," Ernst replied, setting the letter on the table beside him. "Around our Greta's age, I should think."

Greta smiled to herself, liking how it felt when the grocer and his wife referred to her as 'theirs.'

"Well, it will be nice to have family about," Rosa went on. "He can help in the store when he's not busy with his lessons. We'll have to prepare the spare bedroom for his stay."

A nervous knot began to form in Greta's stomach as she wondered if having someone else — Ernst and Rosa's own flesh and blood — might disrupt what she thought was becoming a happy home for her. If Magnus helped in the store, what if they decided they didn't need her anymore? Then she chided herself. There was always work to be done, and if this Magnus was anything like his aunt and uncle, she was sure they would get along just fine.

Yet sleep would not come to Greta that night. She tossed in her small bed, her thoughts filled with what this new boarder would bring. Finally, she sat up, throwing her legs over the side of the bed and reaching for the envelope with the beautiful sketch which she'd propped on the bedside table. Ernst had set the envelope by the fire to use for kindling, and Greta had taken it up to her room. She admired the drawing for a few moments, her nerves settling and her fingers growing warm with energy—the drawing calmed her somehow.

Calla tiptoed along the edge of the bed to sit beside her. "I'm sorry I've kept you up," she whispered to Calla, setting the envelope on the table. "Frau Rosa and Herr Ernst turn in early, so it's nice to finally have someone to keep me company. I just can't sleep, thinking of what they said this evening. I don't want things to change." Calla blinked slowly at her, meowing in reply as if she were speaking. Greta smiled softly. "You understand, don't you?"

"Me-ow! Meow, meow." The chatter was accompanied by purrs.

"I wish I understood you," Greta said absently—and then an idea came to her. She knew the Gift of Gab spell could be used on inanimate objects—so why not on a little kitten who was dying to be heard? In her troubled state, Greta's need for companionship and understanding outweighed her oath to never use magic. Placing Calla on her lap, she closed her eyes and concentrated. She worried the spell would be slow-coming since she was so out of practice, but to her surprise, the magic flowed freely. Her green eyes flashed as she felt the glow of her powers crackle at her fingertips. Calla opened her little mouth, and where a mew should have sounded, *words* did instead. "It will be awfully wonderful to talk to you, Greta."

Greta's eyes widened. "You spoke—I understood you!"

"I did? You *did*?" Calla ran around in a circle on Greta's lap. "I can talk, I can talk!"

Calla chattered happily all night long, and though Greta still wasn't able to sleep, her new companion helped to wash away her fears about this mysterious Magnus and his impending stay.

THE SUN STREAMED in through the window several afternoons later, making the occupants of the grocer's kitchen forget that winter was fast approaching.

Greta counted under her breath as she draped the strip of dough across the pie she'd filled with sliced apples. Calla rubbed against her ankles, meowing and putting her paws against the cupboard. "Can I have some?" the kitten asked.

Greta laughed and shook her head, placing a finger to her lips. "Hush now. This pie is for after supper. I'm almost finished."

Calla sat heavily on her flanks, tail flicking impatiently.

"That should do it for the stew," Rosa announced with a sigh, using the hem of her apron to wipe her damp face. She turned to Greta with a smile. "Well, we're in fine shape. The spare room is cleaned and ready for Magnus, I've got supper on, and that pie turned out beautifully! What would we do without you, love?"

Greta blushed. "It's no trouble at all."

Rosa paused at the crate of apples, grunting as she attempted to lift it. "You work so hard. It will be nice to have Magnus helping out in the store. Then you can have some leisure time."

Greta hurried over to take the heavy crate from Rosa. "I love being here working with you and Herr Ernst," she admitted.

Calla cocked her head, her long ears moving back and forth. "Something is coming," she said to Greta.

The sound of hooves against cobblestone and the whinny of horses hit Greta's ears. "They're here," she said to Rosa, wiping her hands on her apron and hurrying to the door.

Rosa stole a quick glance in the mirror that hung over the fireplace. "Oh, what a fright I look. Magnus will see his old aunt and be shocked!"

Greta shook her head, feeling as if butterflies were dancing in her stomach. "You look lovely as always, Frau Rosa." She took a deep breath to steady herself. *Everything will be fine,* she told herself. *Nothing will change.*

There was a rattling at the door, and Rosa hurried to open it. "We made the trip in one piece," Ernst said, holding a crate with books and items wrapped in brown parchment. The sunlight streamed in with him, hitting Greta's sensitive eyes. A young man passed the threshold after Ernst, and Greta squinted in the light to get a better look at him. Much taller than his uncle, Magnus had short, dark brown hair and golden eyes. Though she knew it was chilly outside, he wore no coat over his shirt and vest, and Greta noticed the sun glinting off a gold pocket watch he wore at his waist.

"Magnus, my darling, how was the journey over?" Rosa asked as she pulled him in for a hug.

"Long, but enjoyable, Aunt Rosa," Magnus replied with grin. He looked at his aunt and uncle in turn, before he turned his attention to Greta. The butterfly sensation she'd been feeling before his arrival increased as his eyes widened. She felt her throat suddenly go dry under his stare.

Eyes still on Greta, Magnus began, "Uncle Ernst, I don't believe you ever mentioned that—"

"Well, don't just stand there, Magnus, introduce yourself to our Greta," Ernst interjected with a chuckle.

Magnus finally dropped his eyes and extended his hand. "Of course, how rude of me. A pleasure to meet you, our Greta."

Greta wrinkled her nose, clasping his hand for the briefest of moments. "It's just Greta," she said shortly.

Magnus frowned, clearing his throat. "My apologies. I had hoped to be witty."

Greta's green eyes narrowed, not finding him amusing at all. She was about to tell him as much when Calla piped up from her spot at Greta's feet. "I thought it was funny."

Greta nudged her and made a shushing sound. Magnus—who hadn't heard anything more than the cat's loud meow, Greta was certain—laughed and said with a smile, "You have a very nice cat."

"Thank you," Greta replied stiffly, refusing to look at him.

"Let's get your things up to your room, Magnus. Rosa doesn't like there to be a mess," Ernst broke in, signaling for Magnus to follow him up the stairs. "Later this afternoon I'll have you help me in the store."

"That will be fine. I just need to unpack my things." Magnus turned to Rosa. "I'm very grateful to be staying with you and Uncle Ernst and start my schooling."

Rosa patted his cheek with a warm smile. "We're happy to have you."

Greta wasn't so sure she was happy to have him there, but of course she kept silent, watching him as he ascended the staircase. Her pulse quickened when he looked over his shoulder, golden eyes locking with hers. He smiled before he disappeared from view.

Annoyance bubbling in her chest, Greta was grateful to resume her work in the shop. She felt a nervous sense of anticipation as the hours passed, knowing Ernst would soon bring him into the store to show him his work.

Soon enough Greta became so absorbed in dealing with customers and helping Ernst and Rosa re-stock the shelves and sweep the floor that she forgot all about their new boarder.

The clock began chiming, and Rosa placed the last cake of yeast on the shelf. "Come and help me get the table set for supper."

"It's six already?" Greta turned to Ernst with a questioning gaze. "Wasn't Magnus supposed to...?"

Ernst chuckled. "Never you mind about him. I'm sure he got

wrapped up in settling in his new quarters. We can show him the store tomorrow."

Greta nodded wordlessly and followed Rosa into the kitchen, casting an incredulous glance up the staircase.

"HE WAS ABSOLUTELY no help today," Greta said cantankerously to Calla that evening as they ascended the stairs to the third floor. "Frau Rosa had to call for him *three times* when supper was on!" When Magnus had finally joined them in the kitchen, his hair was tousled, his expression frazzled, and he was distracted for most of the meal. "What was he *doing* all afternoon? Certainly not working in the store like he said he would." They didn't require his help—they had gotten on just fine without him—but his inconsiderate behavior on his first day with them frustrated Greta to no end.

"He looked like he'd been concentrating hard on something, and supper interrupted it," Calla commented as they reached the landing.

Greta scoffed. "That boy hasn't done one bit of work since he arrived. He didn't even offer to help with the supper dishes." Rosa and Ernst had just laughed and told Greta that Magnus needed to get his things around for his classes the next morning, but Greta was not convinced. Work-shy was what he was, plain and simple. "He's been holed up in that room of his for *hours*. Sleeping, most likely."

"No, listen! He's still awake," Calla said softly, one white-tipped paw inclined to the door at the end of the hall.

Greta saw that Magnus' door was opened a crack, the light from a lantern pouring in to the otherwise darkened hallway. As she crept closer, her sensitive ears caught what Calla was hearing: a soft scratching sound, and faint tapping.

Only a few feet from the door now, Greta could just make out a voice to accompany the sounds; it sounded as if Magnus were muttering under his breath. She froze as the tapping and scratching stopped. She held her breath as footsteps approached the door, then relaxed when she realized he was pacing the span of the room. She craned her neck to peer in his doorway, and saw Magnus had paused in his steps, his back to her as he appeared to be staring at something across the way. Magnus turned at that moment, his eyes passing over the doorjamb. Their eyes locked, and he smiled softly and lifted his hand in greeting. Greta hurriedly scooped Calla into her arms and darted into her bedroom. Once she was safely inside, she set Calla down and leaned against the wall, trying to calm her racing heart.

GRETA GLANCED AT the threatening gray clouds several days later as she walked through the village. She needn't have worried that things would change with the arrival of Magnus; in the week that he'd been staying with them, it was almost as if he weren't there at all. He kept strange hours, leaving early and returning late, spending the rest of the time holed up in his room — doing what, Greta couldn't begin to guess.

That morning Ernst had told her to show Magnus how to do the store's inventory when he came to help. When the clock struck three and Magnus still hadn't arrived, Ernst sent Greta to run a few errands. She was nearing the end of her list and was on her way to the candy maker's when she saw Magnus across the way, speaking to Frau Minna in front of her shop. He glanced her way at that moment, locking eyes with her.

Greta pretended she didn't see him, ducking into the candy maker's shop. The bell tinkled to sound her arrival.

Frau Nina, a jolly woman whose blonde hair was graying at the temples, smiled at Greta. "How are you today?"

Greta approached the counter, eying the various mouthwatering chocolates, peppermint sticks, sweet breads, and mints. "I'm well, Frau Nina. How are things here?"

"The shop is almost back to rights," Nina replied. "We've gotten the kitchen aired out, and my husband has been hard at work ripping out the boards that were too burned to be salvaged."

Greta frowned in sympathy, thinking of the small kitchen fire poor Frau Nina and her husband had suffered a few weeks ago, and the damage it had caused.

"What do you fancy, dear?"

Greta pointed to chocolates drizzled in caramel, and then to the gingerbread for Calla.

Nina pulled Greta's choices from the case and began wrapping them. "I still don't understand how the fire started. I'm always very careful to put out the fire once the chocolate has melted, and I make sure to keep the papers as far from the stove as possible." Brows knitted together, she sighed and said, "I suppose after all of these years, it's only natural I may grow careless at times. I'll just have to work even harder to ensure it doesn't happen again."

Greta felt a sick knot forming in her stomach. Frau Nina was always careful about everything she did—Greta knew it wasn't her fault the kitchen had caught fire. Ludwig, the nosy and spiteful goblin down the road, had started the fire to entertain himself. As he wasted his days gluttonously drinking, gorging himself on the finest foods and lurking on the village rooftops, it was no wonder he was bored. *And now Frau Nina believes she has to work even harder,* Greta fretted, looking at the candy maker's calloused hands. *When she does so much already.*

Once Greta had paid for her sweets, she bid Frau Nina farewell and left the shop, stewing about Ludwig and the other trouble-making goblins the village was unfortunate enough to host.

"Good day, Greta."

Absorbed in her thoughts, Greta hadn't noticed Magnus had joined her, his arms full of flowers. Regarding him warily, she replied, "Good day." Unable to resist, she added, "Just what have you been doing with yourself this whole time?"

Magnus lifted his eyebrows, noticing her little barb. "I've been busy with my lessons and schoolwork since early this morning." He glanced at her parcels. "I see you have a sweet tooth. Frau Nina does have the best chocolates I've ever tasted." He smiled, and Greta noticed with annoyance that his honey eyes lit up when he did so.

Not to be distracted, she ignored his comment and pressed, "I suppose you forgot that you were meant to take inventory today?"

The smile faded from his handsome face. "Was that this morning? Oh, I'm so sorry, Greta, I was so caught up in my assignments it completely slipped my mind. Would you tell Uncle Ernst I'm very sorry?"

Greta frowned. "Tell him yourself. You *are* heading back now to help in the shop, aren't you?"

Magnus shrugged apologetically. "I'm afraid I can't. I have to hurry back to my lessons. They'll be expecting these." Greta glanced down at the two bouquets he held—one of red roses, and one a mix of chrysanthemums and dahlias. *Why in the world does he need flowers for his lessons?*

Magnus pressed the roses into Greta's hands. "Would you mind bringing these to Aunt Rosa? They're my way of saying thanks for letting me stay in their home."

She narrowed her eyes at him. *He wants me to do absolutely everything for him,* she thought in indignation. *Apologize, thank his hosts, what next?*

"I really appreciate it," he said, stepping away from her and heading down the lane. "I must be off!"

Greta grumbled under her breath, looking at the roses in disdain. Pretty as they were, the fact that they were from that work-shy ingrate made Greta prone to dislike them. The petals of the roses soon became peppered with water droplets as it started to rain, and Greta hastened her stride.

"Oi!"

Greta shielded her eyes from the falling rain to look to the rooftop where Ludwig perched, leering down at her. "If it isn't our little Greta. Who gave you those flowers, then? A young goblin boy?" he asked slyly.

She began to hate the roses even more. Looking around to make sure no mortals were watching, she called back, "Such a ridiculous notion! I'm out on an errand." She'd wasted her time on goblin boys her age before and wanted nothing more to do with their boorish behavior. Attempting to shield her many parcels from the rain with her cloak, she hurried on her way.

Greta came to a halt when Ludwig materialized in front of her. "Haven't got time for any of us, eh? Rather waste your days with *their kind*?" He folded his knobby arms across his bony chest, jerking his head at a mortal family that strolled by. "Shame, really. My nephew would love to take you to the bonfire tonight."

"I don't wish to come off ill-mannered, Ludwig, but I really *haven't* the time to spend with you, or any horrid nephew of yours," Greta said with a sniff. "On the subject of fires, I certainly hope you won't try anything like what you did in Frau Nina's shop again."

Ludwig's orange eyes widened in mock-surprise. "Surely you jest. I would never wish to do anything of the sort, for fear of harming the *kind* and *hardworking* people of this good village."

He was taunting her. She scowled and hurriedly pushed past him, ignoring his cackles. Her good mood had been sullied by Magnus and Ludwig, and she wanted nothing more than to dry off and enjoy the chocolates she'd purchased.

EVEN AFTER SHE'D changed into a fresh, dry dress and sampled two or three of the chocolates from Frau Nina's shop, Greta found herself tense and irritable, pacing around her bedroom. She finally decided to settle her nerves by scrubbing her bedchamber's wooden floor, which was covered with streaks of mud. Calla raced back and forth chasing the bubbles, creating damp, muddy paw prints wherever she ran.

"Mind yourself, Calla."

Calla paused mid-pounce, bowing her head. "But the bubbles are fun."

Greta's expression softened. "You may chase them over there where I haven't scrubbed yet." She scooped a handful of suds and blew them toward the opposite corner near her bed. Calla wiggled her backside and bounded after the bubbles, purring all the while. Greta resumed her task, wiping furiously at the streaks of dirt and grime. After several moments, she began to feel a tingling sensation crawl up her spine, like she was being watched.

"You never stop working, do you?"

Greta bristled at the voice, looking up to see Magnus leaning in the door frame. She paused in her scrubbing and wiped her damp hands on the cloth of her skirt. "There's always something to be done around here. Not that you would know," she mumbled, dipping the scrub brush into the soapy water once again.

If Magnus had heard her last remark, he didn't acknowledge it. "I wanted to thank you for bringing the flowers home to Aunt Rosa for me. She seems to like them very much."

Greta pretended not to hear, scrubbing the floor vigorously. When he still did not leave, she sighed and said, "Herr Ernst was hoping you could aid us after supper. The bottom step to the cellar is loose."

Magnus grimaced. "I'm afraid it will have to wait until tomorrow. One of my instructors wants me to finish an assignment this evening. I just came back to fetch a few things."

Typical, Greta thought, staring at him incredulously. She rose to her feet, tucking a strand of hair behind her ear. "Just what *is* it you work on day and night that's more important than helping out around here?"

Magnus seemed surprised by her question. "Well, I've finished my arithmetic, Latin, and botany assignments, but I have a still life, a landscape, and a larger-scale version of that drawing I need to complete." He pointed to a place behind her head.

Greta lifted her eyebrows. "A what?"

Magnus smiled. "I'm working on a full-color version of that building sketch right there."

Turning, Greta realized Magnus was pointing to the envelope she'd perched on her window sill. *Magnus drew that?*

"I must say, I'm flattered that you admire my work," Magnus went on. "I thought perhaps Uncle Ernst had thrown it away."

Greta felt her face grow hot. So this was what Magnus did all the time—he was an artist. While she *did* like his work, the fact that he seemed to care about nothing else, not even assisting his aunt and uncle, made her angry.

Magnus checked the pocket watch at his waist. "I'm running late. I hope to see you later," he said cheerily, disappearing from her doorway.

Greta deftly approached the sill and lifted the envelope. Where once she felt happy and calm at the sight of the lovely little sketch, now she only thought of his arrogance. She shoved the drawing in the drawer of her commode, not wanting to look at it ever again.

"THERE." GRETA ROSE to her feet, testing the bottom step of the cellar staircase.

"You didn't have to help me with this, Greta," Ernst said, following her up the stairs and into the store.

If it were up to that layabout, it would never have gotten done, Greta thought, though she knew better than to complain about Magnus to his uncle. "It's no trouble at all," she said with a smile, bustling to the stores of sugar and flour to restock the shelves. Busywork helped her whenever she was feeling vexed—something lazy creatures such as Magnus and Ludwig would never understand. As she undid the knot from around the large sack of flour, she began to dwell on her encounter with Ludwig from that afternoon. He was probably at the bonfire now, causing untold strife for any nearby mortals in his wake. Rolling her eyes, she said aloud, "I just hope that drunken kobold never patronizes this store."

Ernst turned to her, brows raised. "To whom do you refer?"

"Oh, that old goblin, Ludwig," she replied with a grunt, wrapping her arms around the girth of the heavy sack and hoisting it in the air over the barrel. "I can only pray he stays away from us. He'd torment you day and night for hiring a goblin—he might make the roof cave in."

Ernst didn't seem too concerned, busying himself behind the counter.

Not to be distracted from her poor mood, Greta pressed on, "And he'll taunt me for not using my powers to perform simple tasks like this." The last of the flour dumped into the barrel forcefully, covering her shoulders and face with white powder. She coughed, blinking as her lashes stuck together with flour.

Ernst hid his chuckle, passing Greta a cloth from the counter. "There's nothing wrong with doing things the mortal way."

Greta wiped the flour from her eyes. "I wish I'd been *born* a mortal," she said wistfully. "I don't belong with the other goblins! They make me feel like such an outcast," she confessed, biting her lip. "I don't feel truly *satisfied* unless I've worked for what I want, and they shun me for it."

"Goblins have lived in this village for generations," Ernst said. "In my years, I have met many who were decent and kind."

Greta looked skeptical, but Ernst pressed on. "Much like you, they lived in harmony with us mortals. They even used their magic to help some of us." Ernst sighed, stacking cakes of yeast on the shelf. "But, magic, though wondrous and useful, can make some beings tire of labor."

"Lethargy," Greta repeated triumphantly, dusting the last of the flour from her braid and tossing the cloth over her shoulder.

Ernst paused to look at her over his spectacles. "It is not just goblins, my child. Many mortals, if given the chance, would fall victim to the temptations of magic."

"This is why I don't want to use my magic anymore," Greta said, placing the wooden lid on the flour barrel.

"It has nothing to do with whether or not you possess the gift, Greta," Ernst insisted. "Every being is victim to temptation, but it is your *character* which guides you to be kind-hearted. You shouldn't force yourself to hide who you are simply because you don't wish to be like the goblins you know."

Greta bit her lip, pondering his words. Before she could reply, Magnus came through the door. She closed her eyes for a brief moment, his appearance putting her in an ill mood once more.

"There's our hardworking student," Ernst said warmly as Magnus undid his coat to hang on the rack.

Greta wrinkled her nose—hardworking was a term she would *never* use to describe Magnus. Magnus smiled and bade her hello, but she just gave a curt nod in reply.

Ernst approached his nephew. "What have you been working on so late, my boy?"

Magnus pulled a sketchbook from his satchel and held it up proudly. Greta's eyes widened as she took in the beautiful sketch of the seaside. Tiny gulls danced over the waves, which seemed to roll off of the page. There was even a small lighthouse perched on craggy rocks in the distance, foam spitting out over the base of the formation.

"Hm," was all Ernst said before he returned his attention to the shelves.

Magnus chuckled. "You know nothing of art, Uncle. Why do I even show you these things?"

Greta inhaled sharply at Magnus' insult, but to her surprise, Ernst laughed robustly. "That is very true."

"Greta, on the other hand, has a keen eye. She'll be able to give me proper input." Magnus tilted the sketchbook in her direction. He lifted his eyebrows with a hopeful smile. "Well, Greta?"

Greta wanted to say something about what she was feeling when she looked at his drawing — a sense of joy and tranquility, as if she could smell the salt air — but Magnus' cruel comment to his uncle rang in her ears. "It looks like you wasted all of your time for nothing," she said coldly, ignoring the twist of guilt she felt at the hurt expression on Magnus' face.

"Well, I won't keep you two," Magnus said briskly, dropping his eyes to shove the sketchbook back in his satchel. "I'm afraid I have to hurry upstairs and get to more studying. I have an examination in the morning." He strode up the staircase and out of sight.

Greta stared after him in disbelief. "Wasn't he meant to mind the store? He doesn't appreciate *anything* you do for him," Greta exclaimed to the grocer. The irritation she'd been feeling toward Magnus all this time came burbling out. "He'd fit right in with the goblins — we should trade places! Magic would suit his lazy ways well."

Ernst regarded her over his spectacles. "Magic can't save you from everything," he said sadly.

Greta had never heard the grocer speak so seriously before. "Herr Ernst?"

Ernst cast a glance up the stairwell before continuing softly, "Magnus has had a difficult life, Greta. Though he may not realize, his father was—" He hesitated, staring thoughtfully at Greta.

"Yes?" Greta prodded.

"His father died when Magnus was very young," Ernst said at last. "He and his mother have struggled on their own ever since. The boy hasn't had an opportunity for proper schooling before this, so he's very eager to prove himself in both his academic and artistic endeavors."

Greta thought back to the hurt look in Magnus' honey eyes when she'd dismissed his drawing, and her pangs of guilt increased. Looking back, Ernst *had* been quick to throw away the envelope to Magnus' letter, ignoring the thoughtful drawing his nephew had done for him. Then she furrowed her brow. *Scrap paper is best meant for kindling,* she thought sagely. *He did no wrong.* "He was mocking you," she insisted stubbornly.

She was taken aback when Ernst chuckled. "It was only in *jest*, my dear," he said kindly.

Her expression softened, and she found herself looking up the staircase to where Magnus had gone, her thoughts racing.

GRETA DID NOT see Magnus at all the following day, for which she was very grateful. She'd had trouble sleeping after her conversation with Ernst and couldn't decide whether to apologize for her harsh comment, or avoid him altogether. His absence meant she didn't have to make the choice.

"It's his fault for being so off-putting," Greta grumbled to Calla on her way to their bedroom that evening. She thought of the times she had caught those honey eyes of his watching her, a smile playing on his lips as if he were the keeper to some secret. She shook her head to rid her thoughts of Magnus. "Come along, Calla, I must mend that dress." She paused when there was no reply. "Calla?" Peering all around, she saw no sign of the cat. "Calla?"

A small thump followed by a crash hit her sensitive ears, and she rushed down the hall to discover the door to Magnus' room was wide open.

Greta found the kitten sitting in the middle of the room, surrounded by an overturned dish and tubes of paint. Calla happily batted one of the tubes around, chattering to herself.

"You naughty girl! Did you do this?"

Calla lifted her eyes guiltily. "The door was open," she said in a small voice. Her paw inched toward the tube of paint again.

"Stop," Greta said firmly, hoisting the kitten around the middle and setting her near the doorway. "We have to clean this up before Magnus notices." She scooped the paint tubes and returned them to the dish. Her eyes began to sweep over the many paintings that sat on easels around her, and she found herself mesmerized. There was a small painting of a forest, with moss climbing up the spindling trees and two deer in the clearing. The next canvas she looked at was larger, and Greta realized with a start that it appeared to be the painted version of the envelope sketch.

Calla had tiptoed over to where Greta stood, gazing at the paintings in wonder. "Oh," she breathed. "Look at the big one!"

Greta turned her attention to the largest canvas of all. There was a long lane lined with tall, narrow shops on either side. Peering at the signs and storefronts, she exclaimed, "It's our village!" She exhaled in wonder as she took in all of the fine details of the scene. There was Minna minding her florist shop with a basket of flowers on the crook of her arm, and a young couple perusing the storefront.

"It's awfully pretty," Calla said with a sigh, her wide eyes staring unblinkingly at the canvas.

"Why thank you, little one."

Greta gasped. "How long have you been standing there?" she asked breathlessly. Then she caught herself, handing him the dish of paint tubes and scooping the kitten up in her arms. "I'm sorry. Calla came in here and—"

Magnus chuckled, setting the dish on a nearby commode. "It's quite all right. I'm glad to know she likes my painting."

Greta lifted her eyebrows. "You can *hear* her?"

"He can?" Calla squeaked.

"Of course. It's no surprise that you bewitched your kitten to speak. You *are* a goblin, after all." He smiled and gave Calla an affectionate pat. "But she is quite the talker."

He knows of our kind? Greta began to think back on all the times Calla had spoken in front of Magnus, and she felt her cheeks grow warm. She turned away from him to collect her racing thoughts, gazing at the painted versions of the village shops once more, when she noticed a small, white haired figure in the shadows of one of the alleyways. A long-limbed figure was perched atop the eaves of a building. There was even a miniature version of herself on the step of the grocer's shop, holding a broom and sweeping painted leaves. She leaned in closer, the paint hitting her senses as she studied the fine, pointed ears Magnus had given her, and the flecks of green he'd added to her hair. "You see my true self?" Greta was surprised, to say the least—the ability to see magic seemed to wane and wither with each passing generation. She had never met a mortal her own age who knew of goblins.

Magnus smiled and nodded. "You must forgive me for staring when we first met. Uncle Ernst had spoken often of you, but he'd never mentioned you were a goblin." Then he paused. "He might not have realized I, too, can see magic. Mind you, I've only met a few goblins in my lifetime. To think this village is full of them! How truly wonderful."

Greta grunted, thinking of Ursula, Ludwig, and the rest of the horrid lot. "Yes, it's wonderful," she said sarcastically. Calla began to wiggle to be let out of her arms, and Greta obliged, watching the kitten trot out of the room. Greta turned to follow, but Magnus' voice stopped her.

"Are you leaving so soon?" he asked, perching on his wooden stool before the village painting. "I was hoping to ask your opinion."

Greta found herself staring at the painting before him, drawing nearer. "Yes?"

"You've lived in the village far longer than I. Whenever I work on this section" — he motioned to the lower right corner — "something seems to be missing."

Greta studied the line of shops for a moment before she spoke. "Well, it's obvious, isn't it? You've missed a shop. The candy maker is beside the cobbler."

"Ah, that's it." Magnus nodded slowly. "I'll have to work on that bit. Unless you want to just give it a go." He held out a paintbrush to her with a lifted brow.

Greta stared at him in disbelief. Work-shy to the very end. He wanted her to do absolutely *everything*! "I don't use my powers," she said coldly.

"I just meant for you to try painting the shop the mortal way," Magnus replied, setting the brush on the table and eying her with a puzzled expression. "You don't use your magic? What about...?"

"Yes, I did bewitch Calla with the Gift of Gab," Greta replied tartly. "But I refuse to use my magic frivolously, or to shy out of chores and effort at every turn."

"And useless things like painting," Magnus said, a teasing smile on his lips.

Greta, however, did not smile back. *Why is he bothering me with these questions?* "You're the one who insists on painting instead of helping in the store. Why should I do the work for you?" Rather than appearing offended, however, Magnus stared at her, looking amused. "What?" she snapped, feeling hot under his stare.

"I've noticed something about you, Greta," Magnus said at last.

Greta lifted one eyebrow. "Oh?"

"You don't really have a sense of humor," he said in a matter-of-fact tone. "The other goblins I've met love to laugh and joke, but you... you don't seem to comprehend when someone isn't being serious." His amber eyes, which were reflecting the glow of the lantern, danced with amusement. He was mocking her. This made Greta even more irritated. "Do you even know how to laugh?"

Greta took a step toward him, her own eyes flashing dangerously in the lamp light. "You're just like all of the other goblins. Yes, I have magic, and yes, of course I can laugh — but life isn't all fun and games!"

His eyes widened, the smile fading from his lips. "I didn't mean to upset you," he said quietly. "I only meant to tease. Please accept my apologies."

Greta found she couldn't stand to look into those golden eyes of his any longer. Stepping away quickly, she said, "I have to get on with my mending. Unlike you, I don't have time to waste on silly paintings." In her haste she bumped into a table and knocked the vase that held Magnus' paintbrushes to the ground with a crash. Greta fell to her knees to pick up the shattered mess, hissing when her hasty fingers met the sharp edge of glass.

"Greta!" Magnus dropped to kneel beside her on the floor.

"I didn't mean to break it — I'm sorry," Greta breathed, head bowed as she cradled her injured hand.

"It's all right, it was a cracked vase Aunt Rosa gave me. Perhaps I shouldn't have used it." He looked to the door. "I could fetch my aunt…"

"It's but a small cut," Greta lied, biting her lip to subdue the pain. "I'm fine."

Magnus stared fretfully at the blood oozing from her fingers. "Are you sure?"

"Quite sure." Greta's reply was curt, but she felt a little short of breath. The tearing of cloth met her ears, and her eyes widened as Magnus lifted a torn strip from his shirt. She froze as he turned her bloodied hand over in his, dabbing carefully at the cut with some cotton he'd pulled from the table. She found herself studying his features as a lock of dark hair fell over his eyes as he wrapped the strip of cloth around her wound.

"There." He pulled the fabric around her hand and made a knot. "Is that too tight?"

She inhaled sharply, but not out of pain. She felt her heart hammer as his warm golden eyes took her in. "Greta?"

All at once, she came to her senses. She pulled her hand from his and cradled her wrist. Scrambling to her feet, she murmured, "I—I have to go."

Once she'd reached her bedchamber, she fastened the door behind her, leaning against it. Though she'd claimed to feel no pain, her entire hand smarted from the wound. Carefully, she unwrapped the cloth from her hand, but realized the wound did require a bandage if it was to heal. Yet she didn't want to have to look at the cloth and remember how tenderly he'd cared for her.

Calla hopped onto the windowsill with a soft meow. "Greta, you're back." Her eyes flicked to Greta's bandaged hand. "And you're hurt!"

"It's nothing, Calla." Greta dismissed the kitten softly. The pain, however, still bothered her. She took a deep breath and made her decision. Holding her hand aloft, she unwound the bandage once more. *Stop the bleeding,* she commanded, eyes closed and breathing slowed. *Heal the wound.*

After several moments of silence, she gave a start. The familiar tingle of magic hadn't spread from her heart. She opened her eyes. The wound, the blood, all of it was still there.

"Greta, your magic—" Calla began in a worried tone.

Greta scoffed, weaving the cloth around her hand again. "Gone, I suppose." She stepped lightly to the window, seating herself beside Calla. "It's all right. This is what I wanted, after all." Seeing Calla's crestfallen look, Greta forced a smile and stroked the kitten's head with her good hand. "Besides, I used the last of my magic on you. I'll always have you to talk to. That makes me happy."

Calla relaxed and began to purr as Greta gently stroked her and whispered soothing words. When Calla was fast asleep on her lap, Greta cast her eyes to the rooftops outside. The wind picked up and several leaves fell from the tree just outside her window. "This is what I wanted," she repeated firmly.

THE FOLLOWING MORNING when Greta came down to help Rosa in the kitchen, the elderly woman noticed Greta's bandage almost immediately.

"Child!" Rosa clucked her tongue worriedly. "You shouldn't work today."

Greta's brows lifted as she stammered, "But I'm fine, Frau Rosa!"

Rosa's gentle expression turned stern. "Now, how do you expect to tend the store with your hand like that? You work far too hard, love.

First, I'll see to giving that wound a proper dressing, and then I want you to rest. Perhaps take a stroll around the village. The fresh air will do you and that hand some good."

Seeing the severe look in Rosa's gaze, Greta relented, following the elderly woman into the washroom. "How ever did you cut yourself in the first place?"

All at once, the events from the night before flashed in Greta's mind—Magnus' chamber, his paintings, his voice, his eyes... She shook her head. "I picked up a broken piece of glass."

"You should have come right to me," Rosa went on, pouring warm water over Greta's hand. "Magnus is no doctor."

Greta's eyes lifted sharply. "Magnus?"

Rosa smiled knowingly. "This bandage is from the shirt I mended for him last week. I wonder if I would be able to mend it now?"

"Oh." Greta's face suddenly felt very warm.

"There." Rosa tied off the clean dressing. "Off with you, then."

Greta was about to follow her out of the washroom when her eyes cast back to the strip of Magnus' shirt that hadn't been sullied by the wound. Unbidden, his smiling eyes flashed through her mind. She tucked the strip of cloth into the waist of her skirt, dismissing her thoughts and hurrying out the door.

The brisk autumn wind blew her hair and her cloak about during her stroll through the cobbled streets. Try as she might, she couldn't calm her racing thoughts—or her heart.

Her steps slowed as she saw Magnus in the shop across the way. She took a deep breath and strode quickly, hoping he wouldn't take notice.

"Greta!" Magnus waved and hastened his steps to catch up with her.

Greta cleared her throat, pulling her cloak closer to her body. "What brings you out this early?"

"Just taking a break from my lessons." Magnus fell into step beside her, and Greta tried to ignore the mixture of emotions she was feeling when his arm bumped hers.

"How are you feeling?"

Reddening, Greta stared at him wordlessly.

Magnus lifted an eyebrow. "Is your hand any better?"

Feeling foolish, Greta dropped her gaze. "It's fine."

"It may feel better with some sweets," Magnus said with a small smile, pulling a bar of chocolate from his coat. His eyes sparkled with merriment as he stared at her.

Heart hammering, Greta wanted to turn and run from his watchful gaze, but her incurable love of sweets won out. He broke off a few squares and dropped them into her open palm. As the chocolate passed her lips and melted on her tongue, she felt her mood calm. "Thank you."

Magnus' face broke into a grin. "You're very welcome." They walked along in amiable silence, the dried leaves crunching beneath their boots. "Has Aunt Rosa sent you on an errand?"

Greta shook her head. "No. She told me to take the day to rest my hand."

"I can't think of anyone who deserves some respite more than you, Greta," Magnus said seriously. "You work very hard."

Greta smiled at his praise. "Well, there's always work to be done." She found herself relaxing. "What are you studying today, Magnus?" But he had stepped ahead of her, staring at the balcony of the shop next door. Greta followed his stare to see that a flower pot was inching over the edge. She saw with panic that Frau Minna was sweeping the stoop below.

"Look out—"

Magnus darted under the line of the flower pot and pushed Minna out of the way. "What in the world...?" Minna began to cry out, until the deafening crash hit her ears. Her eyes widened as she stared at the wreckage on the street. "Why, young man—that pot could have—and you..."

Greta watched for a moment as Magnus spoke with Minna before she lifted her eyes to Ludwig, who was perched on the florist shop's roof watching the scene unfold. She set her jaw and hurried to the side of the shop and up the winding staircase.

"Ludwig!" she cried when she reached the roof, storming toward him. "You could have killed that poor woman. What in the world were you thinking?"

Ludwig tucked his knobby knees under his pointed chin. "Come now, Greta, just having a bit of fun. It's been days since I've played with the mortals."

Greta could practically feel her temperature rise as she seethed with anger and disbelief. "Your cruel stunts *aren't* what anyone would call playing. Mortals can't heal themselves the way goblins can!"

Ludwig's bright orange eyes narrowed as they settled on Greta. "Why didn't you stop me, then? Had to let that uppity mortal do it for you. Too good to use your magic?"

She inhaled sharply, a weak and powerless feeling washing over her. Nevertheless, she stood her ground, lifting a finger threateningly at him. "Don't let me catch you doing that again."

Ludwig eyed her bandaged hand. "And too proud to even mend your wound? If you bleed like 'em, suddenly you're one of 'em?"

Greta made a disgruntled sound, turning her back on the goblin to watch Magnus speak with Frau Minna in the street below. She smiled to herself, grateful Magnus had noticed the flower pot when he had.

"Maybe *bleeding* isn't the only way you want to be like the mortals," Ludwig said shrewdly as he watched Greta. "No wonder our little Greta doesn't go with goblin lads. She wants the mortal boy to love her, so she tries to pretend she's not different from them."

Feeling her cheeks grow hot at his accusation, Greta tried to form a quick retort to deny his words.

"Greta," Magnus called as he hurried up the wooden stairs.

Greta felt her heart give a funny leap at his voice, and she hoped with all of her might that he hadn't heard what Ludwig had said.

When he reached the rooftop, Magnus approached Greta. "What happened? I was wondering where you'd run off to..." He paused, his eyes landing on Ludwig. "Oh, my apologies, I didn't realize you weren't alone." He held out his hand to Ludwig. "A pleasure to make your acquaintance, good sir. My name is Magnus."

Ludwig recoiled, hopping off of the ledge and adjusting his long silken sleeves. "The — the mortal can *see* me?"

Greta scowled at him, but Magnus chuckled amicably. "Yes, as a matter of fact, I can. I've seen you around quite often, but never had the chance to introduce myself." His hand was still extended to Ludwig in greeting. The goblin stared into Magnus' golden eyes, frowning thoughtfully. Grudgingly, he clasped Magnus' hand for a long moment, before recoiling as if he'd been burned.

Magnus cocked his head, clearly puzzled. "I promise being mortal isn't catching," he teased in a light tone.

After staring at Magnus several moments longer, Ludwig at last turned his pensive gaze toward Greta. "You're even blinder than I thought," he whispered hoarsely, turning on his heel and disappearing into thin air. What he had meant, Greta hadn't the faintest idea. Magnus wasn't blind to magic like other mortals, as he had clearly just proved.

"He seems... interesting," Magnus remarked with a chuckle. "Does he prefer to stay perched on rooftops to watch us mortals below?"

"That and drop flowerpots on their heads," Greta replied, forgetting the odd exchange they'd just had for a moment.

"That was him?" His features paled as he realized the seriousness of the situation.

"Yes, Magnus. Ludwig could have killed Frau Minna," Greta said severely. "This is why I don't like to associate with other goblins. They use their powers to make mortals suffer."

"While I see your point of view, Greta, I know not all goblins are like that," Magnus replied gently.

The wind picked up, strands of black and green hair whipping in Greta's face. "How do you know?"

Magnus gave a soft smile, lifting his hand to push the hair behind her pointed ear. "Because you're not."

Heart hammering, Greta followed Magnus down the staircase, Ludwig's words ringing in her ears.

THE FOLLOWING DAYS were spent avoiding Magnus at every turn. Her hand healed, but slowly, and a knot formed in Greta's stomach as she thought about what it all meant—her magic, Magnus, what Ludwig had said—but she tried to dismiss those ridiculous thoughts. She'd renounced her heritage long ago; the butterflies and the racing heart had everything to do with losing her magic and nothing to do with Magnus.

Due to her injury, Rosa had encouraged her to refrain from work as much as possible to speed the healing along, which gave Greta bounds of free time she was unaccustomed to. Magnus had seemed eager to accompany her when she went on walks in the village, so she'd taken to spending her afternoons and evenings holed up in her bedchamber with nothing but Calla and her swirling emotions to keep her company.

"Why do you look so sad, Greta?" Calla asked her one evening after Greta reached the staircase landing on the way to her bedchamber.

Greta stared down the hall at Magnus' closed door. The lantern light shone through the keyhole and under the doorjamb, showing he was there. "I'm just tired, little one." A part of her longed to draw nearer, to—

Greta's heart leapt when his door opened, and he poked his head into the hallway. "I stopped in Frau Nina's sweet shop on my way home," he began, not looking Greta in the eye, "And I realize I purchased far too many chocolates. Would you be interested in some?"

It was a feeble attempt at conversation that Greta saw through straight away. Yet she couldn't bear the thought of another evening spent holed up in her bedchamber. She cursed the fact that Magnus was privy to her love of sweets. "I suppose I might." She tried to keep her voice nonchalant as she approached his chamber.

Greta slowly unwrapped the chocolate Magnus handed her as she stood before his easel, trying to ignore her thrumming heart. As she let the sweet treat melt in her mouth, she stared at the village scene. "You finished the candy maker's shop!" she exclaimed, turning to Magnus with a smile.

Magnus smiled back, but he seemed different, somehow. For the first time, Greta noticed the dark circles under his eyes. "Have you been sleeping well?" she asked.

Magnus shrugged, perching on the stool. "I really wanted to finish this piece, but I haven't cracked it yet."

"Why do you work so hard on something like this?" Greta wondered, genuinely confused. Wasn't art just meant to be leisure? She'd always thought him work-shy, but the hours he'd spent on these paintings showed otherwise.

"Because it makes people happy," Magnus replied simply. "Beauty... art... can breathe magic into life. Even when it's hard. Even when it's frightening." He rose to his feet, stepping closer to Greta. "When my father died, my mother was *so sad* every day. She tried hard to be strong for me, but it was as if a part of her had died with him." He lifted the gold pocket watch at his belt and ran his thumb over the face, and Greta realized it must have belonged to his late father. "My father painted in his spare time and taught me to paint when I was a child. At first when he passed away, I wanted to throw away all of my paintings, because the thought of painting without Papa hurt so much."

"What stopped you?" Greta asked softly.

"My mother loved his paintings," Magnus said, lifting his eyes to look at Greta. "She loved *my* paintings. I couldn't take them from her. When I finally decided to take it up again, my mother began to smile again. Each time I painted something for her, it made her happy that I was carrying on his legacy, and we both felt closer to him. Whenever I would feel sad about my father, I would just envision us side by side, working on a canvas." Magnus smiled, his honey eyes lighting up. "It was... magical."

Greta exhaled, thinking about her own magic, or lack thereof. "Magical..."

"Your magic is also a wonderful gift, Greta," Magnus whispered, staring into her eyes. "Like giving Calla the power to speak. You bring magic into mortals' gray and dull lives. You shouldn't hide who you are because some goblins squander their gift." He shook his head, shrugging his shoulders helplessly. "That's... that's *life*, isn't it? Mortal or goblin. You choose how to make use of your time — and your talents."

Greta found his words resonated with her. Maybe she'd been wrong — about her magic, other goblins, Magnus — everything. Yet the stubborn streak in her made it irresistible to add, "I understand that your paintings and schoolwork are important to you, but family should be, too. Why don't you repay Frau Rosa and Herr Ernst's kindness by offering more help?"

Magnus chuckled incredulously, lifting his eyebrows. "You never give up, do you? But you're right. I don't want to take advantage of them."

Greta smiled, turning her attention back to the village scene. Staring at the painted version of herself, taking in her tiny goblin features, she gave a shuddering sigh.

"Are you all right?" Magnus asked in alarm.

Greta bit her lip. "I just have a lot weighing on my mind," she whispered. "That's all."

"You work too hard," Magnus said seriously. "You've wound yourself too tight with everything you do—you need something to relieve the tension. Painting always calms *me*—have you ever tried it?"

She shook her head wordlessly, taking the paintbrush Magnus offered her and positioning herself in front of the canvas.

"Painting isn't really all that hard," he said softly, stepping closer to her so that he was looking over her shoulder. "I just watch the world as it goes by, and let it flow through my brush." His hand curled around hers, moving the brush across a blank part of the canvas.

Greta turned, her face so close to his, she became lightheaded. Eyes locked with his, she vaguely felt a tingling in her fingers as she distractedly moved the brush against the surface.

"You've got a knack for that," Magnus said with admiration. Greta finally tore her eyes from him to look back at the canvas. Where she thought she'd made a simple brush stroke, a detailed rooftop with curvature had appeared. *Did I...?*

"Keep going," Magnus urged, withdrawing his hand from hers to rest it on her shoulder. "Add whatever you'd like."

Greta frowned, wondering what she—a complete novice—could add to the beautiful painting. She cocked her head as she studied one of the painted shops. "There should be flower boxes here." She gestured to the upstairs balcony with the brush. In a flurry of glimmering dust, tiny flower boxes with red and pink blooms appeared on the canvas. She gasped. "By the stars!"

"That's wonderful, Greta," Magnus exclaimed with a grin.

"Y-You don't understand." She took a step back from the canvas, dropping the paintbrush on the table as if she'd been burned. "I thought my magic was gone forever." Seeing Magnus' worried expression, she elaborated. "Normally, I have the ability to heal wounds, but I couldn't." As she uttered the words, her hand—which still had a long, thin scar from her injury—began to glow. "Look!" As the scar vanished from her skin, she giggled. "Why is it coming back in such force?" Her green eyes shone with confusion as she looked at Magnus. "Just this morning, I felt so weak..."

"Perhaps you've been feeling torn between mortals and goblins for so long that your guilt started suppressing your magic," Magnus suggested. "And doing something that you enjoy stirs the magic within."

His words stirred something else in Greta, and she found herself drawing into him. Their faces mere inches apart, Greta's heart thrummed with adrenaline as her eyes slipped closed.

"Greta!"

Magnus and Greta jumped apart at Rosa's shout up the staircase. Shaking her head, Greta quickly stepped away from Magnus. "I... I should go," she said in a dazed voice.

Magnus smiled softly, bidding her good night as she slipped through the door and away from him.

GRETA WAS SURPRISED when she came down the next morning to find Magnus in the kitchen surrounded by baking supplies. Taking in the flour that dusted his shirt and even some of his dark hair, it appeared that he'd been there for some time.

He looked up just then, catching Greta's eye and smiling. Cheeks flushing, she smiled back, about to say something when Rosa came bustling in. "Good morning, Greta. Could you be a dear and get the porridge on? Magnus and I almost have this batch of bread finished."

The morning passed quickly as Magnus helped his uncle move heavy crates in the storeroom while Greta assisted the customers. He eventually came into the store and announced that he would be leaving for his lessons shortly. "But before I go, Aunt Rosa, I wanted to give you this." He reached into the broom cupboard and pulled out a flat parcel wrapped in brown paper.

Greta watched with interest as Rosa carefully tore open the paper to reveal the painting of the forest clearing. It was much more detailed than when Greta had last seen it, the fawn's white spots glistening as Rosa held the canvas up to the light.

"Oh, Magnus," Rosa exclaimed, growing misty-eyed, "it's beautiful!" She held it up proudly for Ernst and Greta to see.

Ernst chuckled, coming to stand beside his nephew. "Now I know I haven't an eye for art, but that is a fine painting." He clapped Magnus' shoulder. "Your father would be proud."

Magnus grinned, catching Greta's eye. Cheeks flushing, she smiled in return.

"I'll hang it over the mantle," Rosa declared, laying the painting on the table.

"I'd better hurry and clean up for my lessons," Magnus told them, heading for the staircase. Greta found herself staring after him.

"Would you take care of some errands for me, Greta?" Rosa asked, pressing a list into Greta's palm.

Greta nodded, pulling her cloak from the hook by the door and kissing Calla on the head as she left.

Stepping out onto the street, Greta had to shield her face as a strong wind picked up, blowing the leaves many of the shopkeepers had so carefully swept into piles every which way. Greta tucked the list into the inner pocket of her cloak to keep it from blowing away.

"Greta!" She turned at his voice, smiling to herself as Magnus hurried toward her.

Greta paused, waiting until he'd reached her to resume walking side by side. "That was a very sweet thing you did," Greta said. "Frau Rosa loved the painting."

"I'd meant to give it to her when I first arrived, but I was stuck," Magnus told her. "I'm pleased I was able to finish it at last." He slowed his steps, turning to face her. "I finally found the inspiration I needed."

Greta felt her cheeks grow warm at his meaning. Her long black and green hair blew about in the wind, and Magnus smiled, lifting his hand to push a lock of hair away from her face. "Perhaps I'll see you this evening?"

Gazing into his eyes, Greta nodded, her heart hammering. Magnus smiled and pulled away, walking down the lane. As Greta lifted her hand, she could see her fingers tingling, bits of light coming off them. She glanced around to ensure no one was watching. Thankfully, there was only one shopkeeper about, and he was busily pulling down the dried herbs that were being beaten by the gale. Taking a deep breath, she tried to calm her racing heart and focus on her errands.

The sun was slipping beneath the trees when Greta finally made her way back to the grocer's shop. Though her arms were laden with packages, she found herself hurrying down the cobbled street, a sense of excitement she hadn't felt in ages fluttering within her.

When she drew closer, she knew something was wrong. A small crowd was gathered in front of the grocer's home. Her heart raced when she caught a strong scent. Smoke.

Looking up, she saw black clouds billowing out of one of the windows of the second story. Ernst and Rosa's home — *her* home — was on fire!

"Greta, thank goodness." Rosa hurried from the crowd toward her. Greta's nerves relaxed a bit when she saw Calla was snug in Rosa's arms, eyes as big as saucers, but no worse for the wear. Ernst was in the small crowd talking to Frau Minna and some of the other shopkeepers.

But Magnus...

Rosa could sense Greta's unspoken fear. "The boy's not back from his class yet," she said, patting her arm.

After her initial relief, Greta's heart sank as she saw flames whip out from the upstairs window. The fire was in Magnus' bedchamber.

His paintings.

Amidst shouts and protests, Greta rushed to the burning building and burst through the front door. Looking around wildly, she saw that the fire seemed to be contained to the third floor, at least so far. She pulled her handkerchief from her skirt, covering her nose and mouth as she hurried up the staircase. Ignoring her racing thoughts—which told her that this was stupid, senseless, irrational—she ran to the end of the hall and tried for the knob. Cursing when the handle scorched her hand, she closed her eyes and said a spell under her breath. Her hand went numb, and she was able to pass through the threshold with no feeling.

The flames leapt all around the small room, but Greta rushed to the easels, pulling his paintings free and tucking them under her arms. A line of fire was trickling ever closer, and Greta narrowed her eyes, extinguishing it. Feeling a rush of power, she held her hands aloft. *I wish the fire was out. Disappear, wicked flames!* A few of the smaller flames whimpered and hissed as they vanished, but to Greta's horror, one of the beams gave way and fell to the floor, blocking her path to freedom. The fire whipped up, ensnaring Greta in a circle of flame.

"Greta!"

Greta looked to one of the small windows that hung high up the wall and saw her kitten had somehow managed to climb the side of the building. Calla crouched, as if she were about to leap to her mistress' side.

"Calla, get outside!" Greta screamed. She fell to her knees, coughing as the heat and smoke overtook her. "It's not safe—go!"

To Greta's relief, Calla turned and fled through the window. Greta shrieked as chunks of burning wood fell from the ceiling. She wrapped her arms tightly around the stack of paintings and sketches, trying with all of her might to summon her powers, feeling dizzier by the moment. *If I can't save the whole building, if I can't save myself, please may I be able to save his beautiful works.* While she could feel her powers, the smoke made her too weak, and she could muster no more spells. She thought of Magnus' handsome, smiling face as the world burned around her.

"Greta, are you in here?"

Greta looked in disbelief to the blocked door when she heard

Magnus' voice.

Coughing, she cried, "No, Magnus! The fire is on the other side — you'll be trapped, too!"

"I don't care!" A loud crash hit Greta's ears. The door had somehow been hurled off its hinges to the floor, and Greta watched with awe as Magnus burst into the room, honey eyes glowing with cat-like slits for pupils, just like her own eyes. *Did Magnus just...?*

Magnus saw her trapped in the circle and hurried toward her, reaching over the beam as the flames seemed to shrink around him. "I've got you."

Greta relinquished one hand from its protective grasp around the paintings, extending it toward him. As their hands clasped, a bright spark swept throughout the room, blinding both of them.

When the light finally faded, Greta looked about in wonder. "Magnus..." she breathed. "The fire is out. And you — you just used magic!" It all made sense now as the pieces of the puzzle came together in her mind — the surge of power she felt from his paintings, her conversation with Ernst, Ludwig's cryptic message... Magnus' father had been a goblin.

" *We* just used magic," Magnus corrected, shoulders rising and falling heavily with adrenaline. He cupped her cheeks in his hands. "Are you all right? Calla raced out and told me that you had run inside and were trapped. What were you doing in here?"

"I..." Gently, Greta released her hold on his paintings and sketches.

Magnus chuckled incredulously, unable to hide the smile that was spreading on his face. "You came for these?"

Greta bit her lip. "I couldn't let them burn."

Chuckling, Magnus asked in a teasing voice, "So these paintings aren't a waste of time?"

When she shook her head, Magnus grinned and touched his forehead to hers.

Pulling back, Greta sighed and looked at the wreckage around them.

"I'll never forgive them," she cursed.

Magnus rested his hands on her elbows, looking at Greta with a frown. "Who?"

"Ludwig," she hissed. "Or Ursula—whoever it was that started this fire and almost destroyed your beautiful paintings."

"Greta, it wasn't a goblin," Magnus broke in, casting his eyes to the floor. "The fire was my fault. I realized it when I came in—I left the candle by my painting supplies."

Eyes widening, Greta looked to his tabouret, seeing that the candle was tipped over, the end scorched. She realized that the window had been open—the gust of wind must have knocked the candle over.

"I shouldn't have left it lit, or so close to my materials," he admitted. "I was careless. You've been right about me all along."

Greta shook her head, squeezing his hand. "I was wrong about a lot of things." Looking into his eyes, she confessed, "What you said is true— I can believe in a hard day's work without losing who I am."

Magnus smiled. "Then are you going to let the magic live on inside of you?" He lifted her hand in his, and she felt the sparks of magic fly off of his fingertips and surge into her veins.

"I will as long as you do," Greta teased.

"You'll have to teach me." Magnus tucked a strand of hair behind her pointed ear as he spoke. "After all, I *am* still a novice." He looked around at the charred beams in the bedchamber. "I doubt I could manage fixing this all by myself."

Her cat-like eyes danced as she reached out to touch his cheek. "I suppose we'll just have to add this to your daily lessons."

Magnus grinned, weaving his fingers in her dark hair as he pulled her in for a lingering kiss.

LITTLE RUE

Eliza Wildwood let out a hearty laugh as she watched her best friend and roommate, Rue Chambers, attempt to scale the counter in their small dorm kitchenette.

"Why can't you just help me?" the smaller girl practically begged. "You're nearly six feet tall!"

"I like to watch you do things on your own," Eliza said with a chuckle. "You're just so darn little."

Rue snorted and said sarcastically, "I thought models were supposed to be nice." She knelt on the granite countertop and curled her petite frame around the cabinet door. "Ahh! Got it!" She hopped off the counter and met her friend's collarbone with a grin.

"How much paprika do we add?" Eliza asked.

"It says just a tablespoon."

"And the ribs will cook for how long?"

"Four hours, Eliza. Sheesh!"

"Sorry, brainiac. My short-term memory isn't as good as yours. We're not all pre-nursing students, you know."

"We're not all former models, either."

"That's for sure."

Rue sprinkled the spice into her measuring spoon and poured it into the Crock-Pot. The powder darkened and sizzled upon touching the browned meat, absorbing silently into the tender flesh. "It smells great," she whispered and looked up to see Eliza smiling down at her.

Rue and Eliza had just started their freshman year at Hermann Lons College in rural Montana. They hadn't met each other before they'd been assigned roommates, but they'd become fast friends not long after moving in. Rue had lived in Montana as a kid before her family had moved to California, but she'd longed to come back to the place she considered home. Eliza, meanwhile, had been a child model who, upon graduating high school, had been told she was now "too old" to continue modeling for the agency she'd given all her loyalty to for the past eight years. It had made her disenchanted with the modeling world, so she'd decided to start over in a small school at a small town where nobody would recognize her face.

That plan hadn't really worked, however. She'd already been noticed six times in the month since they'd started school. Eliza was painfully thin with wavy, blonde hair and striking blue eyes that continually elicited compliments from men and women alike. She was fairly outspoken and never missed a chance to stand up for her meeker, shorter counterpart. Despite her best intentions, Eliza never failed to attract attention wherever she went.

Rue, on the other hand, tended to blend into the background, something she was not inclined to complain about. She was quite small, with auburn-colored, curly hair and deep, chocolate-brown eyes. She had a penchant for wearing all shades of red, as she had many memories of her mother telling her it was definitely "her color" before she'd died.

For some reason, that had always stuck with Rue.

"So what do we do for the next four hours while that cooks, then?" Eliza asked.

"I'd better get back to the job hunt," Rue said.

"You're really worried about that résumé of yours, aren't you?"

"I have to be," Rue said, flopping down on the couch in the small common area she and Eliza shared with six other freshmen. "You know Hermann Lons' nursing program is super competitive. Just getting into the college doesn't guarantee you a spot. Grades alone aren't good enough. If I can't find a job or internship in the medical field, I'll never get in. I'd have to transfer to another school." She looked up at Eliza and winked. "And you'd lose your roommate!"

Eliza laughed. "You'd better get hunting, then."

Rue silently pulled up the school's career services website as Eliza rummaged through the refrigerator and emerged with a can of cola. She flopped on the beanbag chair across from Rue and started to watch a video on her phone. The sound was tinny; Eliza laughed a couple times, but Rue couldn't hear what she was watching. She tried to not let it distract her as she scrolled down the web page.

She was just about to give up and close the page when her eyes fell on the words: *Medical assistant and caregiver needed. College student preferred.*

"Hey, I think I found something," Rue called out. Eliza jumped up from the beanbag and sat on the couch beside Rue, leaning over to read the screen.

"That looks almost too good to be true," she commented as she read. "Oh, wait, it is. Look at this." She pointed to a small sentence at the bottom that Rue hadn't yet seen.

In addition to assisting as a lab technician, applicant must be willing to provide live-in services for the job, including light housework and aid to a man with early stages of dementia.

"You can't live there," Eliza said. "Freshmen have to live on campus."

"Maybe I could negotiate to only be there part-time," Rue said. "If I'm paying for the dorm, do you think the college really cares if I'm actually sleeping here?"

"But look at where it is," Eliza replied.

"It's in Middletown. That's not too far from here."

"Hang on a second," Eliza said, furiously typing on her phone to confirm with her map app. "Rue, Middletown is an hour away. And it's in the middle of the woods!"

"Maybe that's why they call it 'Middletown,'" Rue joked. "Come on, Eliza. I don't have many other options. I might not even get hired. It can't hurt to check it out."

"That *is* true."

"Maybe you can even come live with me. You'd have to help with the old man stuff, though."

Eliza grimaced. "Eh, we'll see about that." Rue laughed.

Rue pulled up her email and attached her résumé. She wrote a brief, polite message in the text box and sent it. "There! Now we wait."

THREE DAYS LATER, Rue had just about given up hope. She had no new prospects in her job search and still had yet to hear back from the man in Middletown. Eliza would be at her part-time job for another two hours, and Rue was done with her classes for the day, so she decided to go on a bike ride. The day was beginning to fade into dusk, and the crimson reflection of the setting sun began to radiate over the surrounding canopies of trees and peek its way through the gaps in the distant mountains. Rue rode on, heading toward her favorite biking trail just a mile or two from campus.

When she reached the trail, darkness was seeping into the thick tree line, so she flipped on her headlamp. She was barely a half-mile into the forest when she heard a loud ripping sound that stopped her in her tracks.

The noise was coming from ahead. Rue tried to turn her bike around as quietly as she could. Something about the sound made her uneasy, and the violent-sounding nature of it reverberated through the trees and left only a lingering echo and a lump in her stomach. *Time to cut this bike ride short and head home.*

Rue began to pedal away as quickly as she could, but she could hear rapidly-approaching footsteps behind her. They grew louder, heavier, pounding the dirt trail so hard that she knew there was no way they wouldn't leave imprints inches-deep into the soil. Rue refused to turn around. The terrifying images of what it could have been filled her mind and danced through her imagination.

When she finally reached the miniscule hole of waning sunlight at the beginning of the trail that led back to campus, she cocked her head slightly to the right and managed to catch a glimpse of a crouching, darkened figure leaping back into the denseness of the trees. Then the forest turned completely black around the dim light of her headlamp.

Rue kept riding, pumping her legs so hard that they began to ache. She refused to stop until she reached the dorm. She didn't even pause to lock her bike up; she just threw it down on the lawn in front of the building and ran up the steps, fumbling with her keys, and burst through the door.

"What's up with you?" Eliza asked, her eyebrow raised as she stood over a bouquet of fresh gardenias, cutting the stems and delicately placing each flower in a crystal vase.

"I... thought... you... had..." Rue couldn't seem to catch her breath.

"Work?" Eliza finished. "Uh, so, they let me out early?"

Now it was Rue's turn to raise an eyebrow. "Really? Are you asking *me*?"

Eliza sighed. "No. I got fired."

"What? Why?"

"Apparently, that jerk manager doesn't like being told she's a jerk."

Rue laughed. "Leave it to you, Eliza. Now what are you going to do about tuition?"

"I'll find another job. There are plenty of other stores at the mall that need me."

"Like a hole in the head," Rue teased.

"Don't worry about it. I'll figure it out," Eliza said. "And anyway, I still have savings that I can dip into if I really need to. But hey — speaking of jobs, I forgot to tell you when you came in since you were all busy hyperventilating — the dude called. About that position in Middletown. He was super weird, but I think you'll probably get the job. Especially after he talked to me." She winked.

"He called on the dorm phone?"

"Yep."

"What did he say?"

"To call him back. He totally sounded interested in you. Here's the number." She gestured to a Post-it note on the kitchen table. Rue rushed over and pulled her phone out of her pocket while Eliza fetched her a glass of water.

The phone rang five times before it sounded like someone picked up. Rue could hear breathing on the other end of the line, but nobody said anything.

"Um, hello?" she said.

"Is this Rue?" the voice answered, husky and deep.

"Yes, this is she."

"Hello, Rue. I'm Dr. Forlorn. But, uh, you can call me 'Victor,' if you prefer."

"I'll call you 'Doctor,'" Rue replied hurriedly. "Sounds more professional."

"I like you already, little lady. And I read your résumé with interest. What an intriguing girl you must be. Everything a doctor could want, may I add. For his assistant."

"May I ask what kind of medicine you practice, Dr. Forlorn?"

The line was quiet, as if the doctor had paused and was thinking carefully about his words. "Well, Rue, I guess you could say I practice some fairly progressive medicine."

"How do you mean?"

"It's best if you come and see for yourself. Something gets lost in the translation when I try to explain it, and it unnecessarily scares good people away. But I have a feeling you're different, Rue Chambers. I really think you'd be a good fit for this job. I'll pay you handsomely, of course — in addition to providing you room and board. Did you read my whole ad?"

"Yes, I did, Doctor."

"Very good. Now, shall we arrange a meet-and-greet at my laboratory — er, office? Sorry," he said with a chuckle. "I always call it my laboratory. Old-fashioned, I suppose."

Rue feigned a polite laugh. "I'll call it whatever you want, Doctor."

"Oh, Rue! You are so grand. How about tomorrow?"

"Tomorrow? To go out there?"

"Yes, is that a problem?"

Rue looked down. She had class tomorrow. But she supposed it wouldn't hurt to miss it this one time. She could work her schedule out with the doctor after she got the job. "No, it's not. I think I can swing that."

"Great! Shall we say noon?"

"Sure. That works."

"Now, Rue, would you mind bringing an old man some lunch?"

"Uh, okay. What would you like?"

"Whatever you like, my dear. I'm not a picky... eater, that is."

"Sure."

"You should bring your resplendent-sounding roommate, too. If you'd like."

"Maybe I will."

"Goodbye, Rue."

"Good—" started Rue, but Dr. Forlorn had already hung up.

"I hope you don't think I'm going with you," Eliza said as Rue put down her phone. It wasn't uncommon for her to pick up on Rue's energy. Rue tended to get a certain scrunched look on her face when she wanted to ask Eliza a favor, and Eliza was tuned in to her friend enough to understand what the face meant. "I'm not cutting class to have lunch with some weirdo. It's your job interview, Short Stuff."

"That's fine," Rue replied, though her expression remained sour. "I can handle myself."

THE DRIVE OUT to Middletown was quiet and uneventful—downright boring, in fact. When she reached a transition from asphalt to dirt in the road, she pulled out her phone and called Eliza. As her car tipped and crunched over bumps and rocks, the phone rang loudly on speakerphone.

"You there yet?" Eliza said in lieu of a greeting. "You can't be there yet."

"I'm not," Rue replied. "According to my GPS, I should be there in fifteen minutes."

"So, what do you want from me, then?" Eliza snickered.

"I'm bored. When's your next class?" Rue cracked her window open just enough to float her hand in a wave-like pattern in the wind that breezed past her moving car.

"I *should* be heading over right now, but *someone* is bugging me." Static crinkled over the speakers, and Eliza's voice became faint-sounding and distant.

"Hello? Can you hear me? Eliza? Helloooooo?!" Rue looked down at her phone in her lap and tried to redial Eliza's number. Her finger had just brushed the screen when she felt something impact the car. The force of it knocked her backward, then tossed her forward into the steering wheel. She somehow managed to slam her foot down on her brakes, and the car screeched to a stop.

When her eyes refocused, she saw something slump over her grill and fall into the road ahead of her. For just an instant, it looked like a man, naked and fleshy-colored with thick black hair. She threw the car in park and turned it off, pressing the sleeve of her hooded, cranberry-red pea coat on her now-bleeding chin, which had been split open.

Rue held pressure on her face as she slowly unbuckled her seatbelt and stepped out of the vehicle, praying that whatever she'd just hit wasn't a person. She peered around the front hood of her sedan to see a tangled, muddy, heaving mess of fur. She breathed a sigh of relief. It was most definitely an animal of some kind.

She made her way around the front of the car, tiptoeing so as not to disturb the creature. She crouched down once she reached the body, still keeping a good three or so feet between herself and the animal. She thought it was breathing, but she couldn't be sure.

She looked around herself, shuddering. Beside the road there was a small cemetery within a manmade clearing between a circle of thick trees and foliage. She hadn't noticed it from the car. No more than six or seven faded gravestones stood almost proudly amongst each other, tall and straight, like they were showing off for Rue and all the animals of the woods to see. The dirt in the clearing was freshly-tilled around the headstones, as if turned over by some kind of ravaging forest beast. The strange eeriness of it sent electrifying chills through Rue's whole body.

"Need any help?" an unfamiliar male voice asked behind her. Surprised, Rue jolted up to her feet and turned to face the stranger. He was a tall man with a mustache wearing a green flannel shirt and cargo pants. Attached to his belt hung an unusually large hatchet, and he held a double-barreled shotgun. "Does this critter here need to be put out of his misery?"

"I... I don't know," Rue stammered, keeping her eyes on the shotgun. The man noticed and laughed.

"Now, you ain't got nothing to worry about, me with this gun here. Unless you're a bear or a buck, I don't give a damn about shooting ya."

"I didn't mean to hit it," Rue explained. "It came out of nowhere."

"Sure he did," the man replied, peering at the animal. He stood up. "Wolf," he announced. "Male, just as I thought." He craned his neck to look into Rue's car, where a large picnic basket sat on the front seat, buckled in. "Must've smelled whatever is in that basket."

"Is he dead?"

"Nah, sucker ain't dead. Yet, anyway. I'll take him off your hands; you look like you're headed somewhere important. How's your car looking?"

Rue halfheartedly glanced around at her vehicle. "It seems fine."

"Try her out."

Rue got back in her car and turned over the engine. When it fired up, she put it in reverse and backed up a few feet. She rolled down her window. "Can I just go around you?" The path had just barely enough space for her small sedan to squeeze to the side of the fallen creature.

The man stared at her blankly. "Well, I suppose…"

Rue quickly put the car in drive. "Thanks, uh…sir."

"Call me 'Constable,'" the man replied with a smile.

"Thanks, Constable."

Rue couldn't drive around the man and wolf's body fast enough. When she could no longer see them in her rear-view mirror, she breathed a sigh of relief. Then she gasped when she realized how much it was going to cost her to fix the huge dent in the hood of her car. "I'd better get that job," she muttered as she made a slight right and turned another corner to the road that led up to the doctor's house.

It was more than just a house—it was a mansion, a massive Queen Anne Victorian with intricate detailing, elaborate buttresses, and a hideous violet paint job. Rue drove to the front of the house and parked in the roundabout that circled a huge, dilapidated fountain adorned with a statue of three cherubs, their mouths shaped in perfect *O*s. She assumed that had the fountain been in any kind of working condition, water would likely be spouting from the melancholy-looking cherubs' mouths. Instead, a shallow, stale, brown-green pool of mossy water breathed stagnancy over the once-glimmering marble bowl beneath the cherubs. Whatever magnificence it might have once held, it was now nothing more than a breeding ground for mosquitoes.

Rue walked to the front door and pounded the brass knocker three rapid times. Several moments later, the large wooden door creaked open, revealing a spindly old man clutching a gold-encrusted, polished cherry-wood cane. He had a long, pointed nose; small, dark eyes; and hair as white as snow. His entire face resembled the skin on an elephant's trunk, though it was even more wrinkled and much paler. He smiled at the sight of her, making his features soften. He almost reminded Rue of her grandfather.

"You must be Rue. So nice to meet you!" the old man exclaimed. He looked at her chin, grimacing slightly. "Are you hurt?"

"Hello, Doctor," Rue replied. "Don't worry. I'm fine." She daubed at her face to make sure the bleeding had stopped. "No big deal." His eyes followed her as she bent down to pick up the large picnic basket she'd brought along with her. "I brought some leftover lamb chops I cooked with my roommate in our slow cooker yesterday. We're kind of Crock-Pot nerds; it beats the cafeteria food by a mile. And I've also got some mashed potatoes, gravy, and a salad. Hope that's okay."

"Oh, Rue! That sounds heavenly. Please, do come in!" He moved aside and motioned with his cane.

Rue stepped into the house and looked around. Like the fountain outside, it was a pale shadow of what must have formerly been a grand space. The stairwell that wrapped around the front hallway was still standing—barely—but the banister did not appear to be trustworthy. The dark Victorian wallpaper was peeling off the walls, and the baseboards and crown molding were splintered. Sometime in this house's past Rue knew it must have been breathtakingly beautiful, but currently it was anything but.

"Please excuse the state of my home," Dr. Forlorn said apologetically, as if he were reading her mind. "I'm afraid I can't do too much nowadays. Hence why I need to get myself a little help around here!" He chuckled.

"The house is lovely," was all Rue said as she followed the old man into a dining room. She tried not to let the state of it bother her. Caring for a house of this size would be difficult for even an able-bodied person. The doctor must have gone without a caregiver for a long time.

"I don't have a microwave," the man explained. "But you can heat up your food in the oven. I'll eat mine cold." He sat down at the head of a long, hand-carved, twelve-person table and set his cane aside.

"Oh, I don't want to be a burden. I don't mind having it cold, too."

"You sure?"

"Yes. My mother always said food is better the day after it's cooked, even more so if it's cold."

"Your mother is a smart woman."

Rue hesitated. "Was. She passed away two years ago, when I was sixteen. She needed a heart transplant and wasn't able to get one in time."

"I'm sorry to hear that, Rue. She raised a fine young lady. I'm sure she's very proud of you... Wherever she is."

"Thank you, Doctor."

The rest of the meal was eaten in relative silence.

AFTER LUNCH, THE doctor gave Rue a tour of the mansion as he summarized her duties. He explained that he often needed someone to push him in a wheelchair through the house, but he'd had enough sense to install an elevator in the back servants' quarters several years ago.

"It's that damn polio," he said. "Near killed me when I was a boy. Now it just messes with my locomotion."

"Oh... Well, I'm glad you survived polio," Rue replied politely with a smile. "A lot of people didn't."

"Trust me, I know," he said. "That's why I became a doctor. I want to fix problems with people's bodies. Make them as good as new. Or better, you see?"

"Yeah."

"Too bad your mother didn't know me. I bet *I* could have gotten her that heart she needed."

Rue cringed and suddenly felt uncomfortable. She regretted telling the doctor about her mother. She had to remind herself that he was in the early stages of dementia — he probably didn't realize how tactless he was being. "That would've been nice," was all she could manage. Her eyes darted around the endless slew of hallways; empty, dusty bedrooms; and spiral staircases situated in the strangest of places around the house. It was much larger than she would have expected. She briefly wondered whether or not she could handle living there, but then she remembered the nursing program and its ten percent acceptance rate. She could make it work. She *had* to make it work. She'd only need to be here a few days a week—the rest of the time she would be at the dorm with Eliza. And maybe the doctor would only need her for a semester or two...

The tour ended in Doctor Forlorn's office—or, as he called it, his "laboratory." To Rue, it just seemed like another musty old room, except this one had an ancient-looking desk and built-in bookcases filled with droves of leatherbound books that ran up not one, but two of the room's walls.

"This is a nice office," said Rue.

"Thank you, my dear," the doctor replied. "Now, what do you think? Are you interested in working for me?"

"Yes," Rue said without hesitation. It didn't matter how strange Doctor Forlorn and his house were. She needed this experience. "I'll have to work it around my class schedule, but—"

"Excuse me, Doctor?"

Rue whipped around to see someone lingering near the office doorway, engulfed within a shadow that passed down the side of the door. The only physical trait of the figure apparent to Rue were his eyes, which were a striking green and seemed to glow through the darkness of the hallway behind him.

"Ah, yes! Lockheart. Do come in," the doctor said. "Rue, this is my assistant, Edgar Lockheart. Fine one, he is!"

Rue furrowed her brow. "Your assistant? Isn't that what I'm here for?"

"Not that sort of assistant, my dear. Your positions require different duties. You understand, Rue, I'm sure?"

Rue wasn't sure she did.

"Don't worry," Lockheart said, coming into the room. He was older than Rue, but not much — probably in his mid-twenties. He was tall and muscular, with broad shoulders and a square jaw. "I won't encroach on your job, Rue." His eyes twinkled and he held out his hand. "I think we'll get along just fine. Who knows? We may learn a lot from each other. You're pre-nursing, right? We'll have a lot in common. I'm also a student of medicine." He clasped his hand over Rue's and squeezed. Lockheart's hand was the prickly kind of calloused, and the back of it was covered with a patch of thick dark hair. "It's good to meet you," he said with a smile, his eyes not deviating from Rue's in the slightest.

"Thanks," she replied slowly. "Nice to meet you, too." There was something odd about Lockheart. He was attractive, but not in the usual way — it was more instinctual, almost carnal in nature. As if he were emitting an invisible, unscented pheromone that drew her attention to him and nowhere else — but only when his eyes locked onto hers. When he looked away, the feeling vanished.

Rue shook her head. Just hormones.

Lockheart turned to Doctor Forlorn. "Doctor, did you get a new car? The Toyota?"

"That's mine," Rue broke in. "Do you need me to move it?"

"No, but you might want to go take a look at it."

"I know it's dented in the front — "

"I'm not talking about the dent."

Rue's eyes narrowed and she excused herself, hurrying down the stairs and out the front door. She circled her car. "What is he talking about?" she muttered to herself. "I don't see anything..."

Then she saw it.

The front passenger side tire was completely slashed to bits. She didn't think a human could do this much damage. It looked like a Tyrannosaurus Rex had somehow come out of extinction simply to rip every shard of rubber into a million pieces and scatter them all over the driveway. Could a wolf have caused this? Maybe another had been here, smelling the scent of its injured packmate on the fender.

The bare hubcap hung sadly — naked, stripped of its rubber clothing — in the wheel well. The setting sun glinted off the metal, making Rue realize with a jolt how late it had gotten.

"Oh, no," Rue cried. "How will I get home?"

"You'll have to stay the night," she heard the doctor say behind her. She turned around. "It can be a trial run of your new job. Tomorrow, I'll drive you back into town. I can't drive after dark. Bad eyes, you see."

Rue looked around helplessly. "I really can't," she said. "I have class in the morning. What about Lockheart? Can he drive me?"

"Sadly, no," the doctor replied. "He cannot drive."

Rue sighed. "Let me try my roommate." She turned back around and walked a short distance away from where the doctor still stood. She pulled her phone out of her coat pocket and called Eliza. The phone rang and rang and rang, until finally a stoic-sounding woman reported that the carrier had not set up their voicemail yet. Rue growled to herself under her breath. "Dammit, Eliza!"

She had no choice, then. She had to stay. She walked back to the front steps and helped the doctor back into his house.

AFTER A FAIRLY awkward dinner, Rue was shown to the "least offensive" of the bedrooms, according to Lockheart. It felt like nobody had slept there in decades, though the linens were fresh and the furniture dusted. There was just an eerie stillness about it, another thing that she couldn't quite seem to put her finger on.

Rue thanked the doctor for his hospitality, and then Lockheart after he brought her a set of clean towels.

"I'm going to see the doctor to bed," Lockheart explained. "Then I'll be back to give you some more details about your job."

"The doctor went over it all with me earlier. What else is there to know?" asked Rue.

"You'll see," Lockheart replied. "Oh! And Rue, if you hear the bell at night, go check on him, okay? That's one of the most important jobs you'll have."

"Okay," she replied. "I can handle that."

Lockheart left, so Rue let her body fall backward onto the queen-sized bed and waited for him to return. She pulled out her phone and tried to text Eliza. But now nothing would go through at all — her phone constantly flashed *No signal* and *Message delivery failure* at her. No matter where she stood in her room Rue couldn't get a bar to stick long enough to make a call go through. She started to play solitaire on her phone to pass the time, the only game she had that didn't require a wireless connection.

A couple of hours passed, and still no Lockheart. Finally, Rue stood up. It was late, but she wasn't tired. The house was silent. Lockheart must have gone to bed by now — he must have decided to talk to her about the job in the morning. She wondered if he'd conferred with the doctor and realized that Forlorn had gone over it all with her already.

She stretched thoughtfully. Maybe another part of the house would have cell reception, or she could find a landline to use to call Eliza and let her know why she hadn't returned, and that she'd be missing class in the morning.

She opened the door to the dark hallway and clicked on the flashlight app on her phone. Rue had never seen a house so bleakly dark in all her lifetime, and the still quietness of the air continued to make her uneasy. She'd seen too many horror movies. She had to remind herself this wasn't some kind of haunted mansion. It was just a rundown old Victorian, and it was going to be her place of employment and her home for at least part of the week, for who knew how long. The only way she was going to shake this spooked feeling was to get familiar with the house—and then convince the doctor to have wi-fi installed.

Rue wandered about the hallways and peeked into every room that was unlocked. During her daytime tour, the rooms had seemed a lot more harmless than they did now. There was something about the house at night that seemed to come alive, despite the incessant darkness. Every creak, anomalous blink of light, or slight breeze made her jump, and the hair on the nape of her neck stood unrelentingly on end.

When Rue finally reached the doctor's office, she slipped inside and closed the door behind her. There was a small sliver of light from a thin window behind the desk, but not enough for Rue to fully see the room in its entirety. She noticed a small oil lamp on the desk, so she turned it on and clicked off the flashlight on her phone. The battery was low, and the indicator at the top of her screen had turned red. Rue internally kicked herself for leaving her charger at home, but there was nothing she could do about it now.

Rue's attention turned to the bookshelves. She approached slowly, allowing her eyes to adjust to the dim light of the lamp. She squinted as she tried to make out the title of any of the books but found that she couldn't. She grabbed one at random and pulled it out. *Frankenstein* by Mary Shelley. She pulled out another one. *Modern Progressive Science: The Art of Transmutation.* And finally, *Organ Transplanting for Dummies.*

"Hmm, I'm starting to see a pattern here," she whispered to herself as she reached to pull out another book. But this time, the book didn't budge from its spot. This one seemed to be stuck. Rue pulled harder.

The bookshelf began to shift, and Rue leapt backward to avoid a sharp corner hitting her. When the shelf tilted, Rue peered into the cavity left behind. Again, nothing but pure blackness.

"I should know better," she mumbled, "but what the hell?" The longer she was here, the more curious she became about what sort of research the doctor was conducting out here in the woods. She tried to press the button that lit up her phone but found the screen didn't change. She pressed again. The phone wouldn't turn on. She set her phone down on the desk—it was useless now that the battery was dead.

Rue tiptoed into the hole in the wall, stopping for a brief moment to allow her eyes to adjust to a room even darker than the doctor's office. She was only a handful of steps into the hole when she noticed it dropped off, and the small bit of light revealed a long, winding, cement staircase trickling down into more darkness. Rue took a deep breath and went down.

When she reached the bottom, the first thing she noticed was a large wooden switch directly to her right. Without thinking, she flipped it on. The room became illuminated in bright white light, and a dull hum sounded as though several machines of some kind were powering on. As Rue glanced around the room, she was eerily reminded of the old movie version of *Frankenstein* with Boris Karloff. The room was massive and truly did resemble the laboratories portrayed in the old monster movies. Clear rubber tubing wove from one strange device to the next, and a centrally-located, gurney-style table sat amid smaller tables covered in beakers and glass test tubes in racks.

"So that's what he meant when he called this place his laboratory," Rue mumbled. She suddenly became aware of what she was doing and felt her heart begin to race. "I probably shouldn't be here."

Rue was starting to back away from the tables and toward the switch to turn it back off when something caught her eye. In the very back of the room was a long, thin table with several enormous jars containing some fleshy-colored objects floating in fluid. Rue knew she should have left, but her curiosity got the best of her. She made her way over and peered into the jars, covering her mouth as she ascertained what was within them.

One jar contained a human hand. Another held a foot. And yet another was filled with ears and a nose. One smaller jar had a set of moldy, bright-blue eyeballs submerged perfectly in the center to glare right back at her. Rue felt her stomach turn, then saw the last jar at the end of the table.

A man's head covered in black hair bobbed within the table's largest jar. As Rue looked closer, she felt an even stronger urge to throw up. The head was devoid of ears, nose, and eyes—and from the looks of it, had been that way for quite some time. Rue felt her body retch but held back the vomit that was aching to come up her throat. She knew she had to leave.

Rue turned from the table and ran to the stairs, taking three at a time as she bounded back up to the office. In all her haste, she realized she'd forgotten to turn off the switch, but what the doctor thought was no longer of concern to her. She needed to get as far away as humanly possible. She dashed up the last step and out the hole, promptly crashing into Lockheart's overly warm body.

"Find anything interesting?" he asked calmly, raising an eyebrow at her.

"I... have... to... go..." was all Rue could squeak out.

Lockheart laughed. "So you saw old Vladimir, did you? Don't worry; he won't bite. I can't guarantee I won't, though." He chuckled as though he were proud of himself somehow. "But maybe you're into that kind of stuff. Well, I guess if you're not now, you probably will be soon enough."

Rue stared at Lockheart blankly, confused. She was at a loss for words. All she could muster was, "Please..."

Lockheart's thick hand latched on to her arm and tightened its grip. "Come now, Rue. You can't be scared that easily." His fingernails pressed firmly into her flesh, causing Rue to cry out in pain.

"Let me go!" Rue shouted, and Lockheart's grip eased a bit.

"Shh, you're going to wake him up," Lockheart said with a chuckle. "Trust me, you don't want the doctor to wake up."

"Please," Rue said, feeling tears start to well up in her eyes. "I won't tell anybody about what I saw. Just please, let me go. You'll never see or hear from me again, I promise."

"But therein lies the problem, sweetheart," Lockheart cooed. "I don't want that. Victor doesn't want that, either. We want you here with us."

"What are you talking about?"

"Your *assistant* position. Of course by now you must know that that was just a façade. But we're offering you something better. The opportunity of a lifetime. What would you say if I told you that you could live forever? And that you could save a dying species in the process? How's that for a scientific endeavor? More than any nursing degree could achieve." When Rue didn't answer, he chuckled. "You're more important than you realize, Rue."

In one swift movement, Lockheart threw Rue onto the floor and laughed as she scrambled to find the doorway in the darkness. "It's right behind me!" he mocked. "But don't even try it. You, Rue Chambers, are here to stay."

"What the hell are you talking about?"

"You, my dear, will be the culmination of years of research. It's taken this long for the doctor to perfect his methods — but it's down to a science now, which for you, honey, is a good thing. I'm afraid there were a few hiccups in the process, but luckily, he was able to correct them, thanks to all the preliminary experiments we did on those corpses. Did you happen to see the rest of Vladimir? It took us *forever* to dig that sucker out of his grave."

Rue shook her head and noticed in the small bit of light that Lockheart's eyes had a glow all their own, as if they were grabbing the tiniest sliver of moonlight from the window and reflecting it outward in order to see perfectly in the darkness. They looked much larger than she remembered. Rue, on the other hand, could barely make out Lockheart's silhouette.

"My, what big eyes you have," Rue said sardonically under her breath.

"The better to see you with, my dear," Lockheart replied.

"What are you?" she said forcefully. "You can't be human."

Lockheart laughed. "You got it half-right. I'm only half-human."

"What's the other half?"

Lockheart bent down to Rue's level, his eyes piercing into her soul. "Wolf, of course. I'm a werewolf. The last of my kind. The last of the Alphas, or Proto-Werewolves, to be precise. Well, until we change you over, that is." He chuckled. "There was another male like me — my brother, actually — but sadly, *somebody* hit him with their car this afternoon. Now I'm the only one." His voice sounded regretful, and for a moment Rue almost felt sorry for him.

"Did you do that to my car, then?" She'd been right — it had been a wolf. A half-wolf. A werewolf.

"I'm terribly sorry about that. My emotions get the best of me in the wake of a full moon. I was upset over the loss of my brother. And we couldn't have you leaving. Of course, we were hoping for two males and two females, but since my brother is now dead and your roommate didn't come with you, we'll just have to make do with what we have." He paused before adding, "It's a shame about your roommate. She would have been my first choice — no offense. I've always had a thing for tall blondes. But I suppose you'll do. You'll have to, anyway."

Rue couldn't even begin to comprehend what Lockheart was telling her. He made it seem like he'd seen Eliza before, almost as if he'd spied on them before Rue had come to the mansion. Then Rue recalled the crouching, darkened figure in the woods on her bike ride and shuddered at the thought that she had likely been followed home that night.

"What are you planning to do to me?" she whispered.

"It's a simple process," Lockheart explained, sounding bored. "And don't worry; it only hurts a little bit. And then again—though less intense than the first time—every full moon when you change."

"Why don't you just bite me now and get it over with?" Rue snapped.

Lockheart laughed. "That would work—*if* I wanted to create a Beta. A bite or scratch would be all that was necessary. Anything that draws blood. But I don't want a Beta for my mate, Rue. I want an Alpha. Like myself. I *need* another Alpha for my mate. That's just the way it has to be."

Rue saw a small sliver of light begin to form around the doorway. The oil lamp on the desk. Somebody was opening the door. She took a deep breath and in one swift movement pulled herself up and shoved past Lockheart toward the door. Lockheart grabbed at her, but Rue's tiny body slipped past him. Rue threw her whole weight on the door, knocking the frail doctor backward. He landed on the floor hard with a moan and a thud. Rue wasted no time leaping over his fallen body and dashing across the hallway, down the staircase, and out the front door.

"Oh, little Rue!"

Rue heard Lockheart's voice echo through the forest as she ran through the dense trees, but she kept running without looking back. A distant, almost disembodied howl reverberated all around her. It seemed to be catching up to her. But Rue kept running.

"Rue! *Little Rue!*" Lockheart's voice was filled with malice and mockery and still grew ever-closer despite Rue's small legs propelling

her forward, farther and farther from the mansion. She could feel herself growing tired but knew if she stopped that Lockheart would surely catch up to her quickly. As she ran, she could hear him loudly singing the chorus of an old, haunting song from the sixties about Little Red Riding Hood, told from the perspective of the wolf. Almost as if to frighten her more, he let out another long, drawn-out howl that reverberated through the trees. Sharp branches snaked out into her path, whipping against her hood and slicing across her cheeks. She felt warm blood trickle down her face, but that didn't stop her.

"Little Rue in the red hood!" Lockheart screamed, his voice bellowing through the thick foliage. "Come out, come out, wherever you are! I can smell you; you smell like lamb chops and gardenias!" Then he began to sing the song again, this time more unsettlingly than before, if that were possible.

Rue kept running. In the distance, she caught a glimpse of light through the trees, and as she drew closer, she saw that it was headlights from a car. It couldn't be the doctor — he couldn't drive at night. Besides, he was frail and she'd hit him hard on her way out. It must be someone else; maybe the mustached man who'd helped her earlier...

She dashed into the road in front of the car, holding out her hands in front of her. The headlights blinded her, so she couldn't make out what kind of car it was, nor who was driving it, but nevertheless, the car *had* stopped. Without thinking, Rue jumped into the passenger seat, locked the door, and burst into tears.

"Are you okay?" a husky male voice asked, and Rue looked up to see the silhouette of a dainty man clutching the steering wheel, though she couldn't make out any features. She did, however, notice that the man was wrapped in a thick, wool blanket that resembled actual sheepskin. The man leaned toward her, allowing his face to show through the darkness.

Rue gasped as she recognized the crotchety old features as they came into the light, and she realized that she'd been tricked. He'd lied about not being able to drive at night. She should have known better.

In a panic, she fumbled with the door handle. The doctor's thin, bony fingers grabbed at her, his breathing heavy and moist. Rue managed to unlock the door and was just about to swing it open when something massive slammed into the passenger side, crumpling the door and rendering it immovable. Rue screamed out in frustration and pounded on the window with her fists.

The back passenger door opened, and Lockheart bounded inside, panting. He looked to be partially transformed into a werewolf—still anthropomorphic in many ways, but now covered in thick, black hair with razor-sharp, pearly white teeth and oversized canines. His arms and legs were more elongated, and his nose had become somewhat reminiscent of a snout.

"Good work, Lockheart," the doctor said with a snicker. "Now we can go home and the fun can begin!" Lockheart howled cheerfully in reply. The doctor turned to Rue and said, "Poor Lockheart has been waiting years for the right mate. And I've been *dying* to try out my transmutation skills on a female. We're so lucky you found us."

Rue didn't say anything. Tears ran silently down her cheeks, burning her scratched face as they drove back to the mansion.

"You really did a number on me, Rue," the doctor continued. "You and Lockheart will have a lot of work to do after your transformation. I've taught him most of the ways of transmutation, though it's taken me decades to educate myself on the entire process. Now that my bad leg is completely useless, I'm afraid I'll have to be fully changed into the very creatures I've created—that should buy me some more time to teach you two everything you need to know to keep my legacy alive in the event that something should happen to me. I fear some townspeople have caught on to my experiments and have grown suspicious of me."

"He only injected himself with part of our wolf/human hybrid DNA concoction," Lockheart added. "He wanted to make sure he'd last long enough to make me a mate. He's almost a hundred, you know."

Rue gave no discernible response. She was frantically trying to figure out what to do. Her eyes darted continuously from Lockheart, to the doctor, to out the window. There had to be some means of escape.

"I couldn't just leave you alone high and dry, now could I?" the doctor replied to Lockheart. "You've done so much for me and my work. The least I could do was find you a suitable companion for the rest of your life."

"I'm just happy you decided to go the full werewolf route instead of that whole resurrection idea you had first," Lockheart said. "I hated the idea of being fused with an old, rotting dead body."

"As did I, my good boy. Everything always seems to fall into place when scientific enlightenment is involved," the doctor said haughtily. "The universe nurtures the progression of science. Because of my work, soon there will no longer be a need for organ donors or prosthetic body parts. The human race will become invincible — aside from that whole 'silver bullet' aspect." He turned to Rue with a grin. "You can appreciate that, can't you, Rue? After what happened with your mother?"

Rue curled up in her seat, buried her face in her hands, and ignored the doctor's words. Rage boiled within her. As soon as the right opportunity came along, she'd destroy any chance of becoming another one of their experiments. What if the doctor failed, and she ended up just another head in a jar displayed in the laboratory? She couldn't allow that to happen.

After just a few moments, the car began to slow. She looked up to see the mansion illuminated eerily in the light from the headlamps. Rue felt her stomach drop.

"Ah, home sweet home," said the doctor. "Lockheart, I take it you know what to do?"

"Yes, sir," Lockheart replied. In one swift movement, he leapt through the center console and ferociously snatched Rue by the hair, his sharp, elongated fingernails raking across her scalp. He pulled her into the backseat and through the door. Keeping a tight grip on her upper arm, he dragged her, kicking and screaming, back into the mansion. The doctor held on to Lockheart's other arm for stability, struggling to walk with only one usable leg. Lockheart was inhumanly strong, and when the doctor paused for a moment he merely scooped him up and threw the old man over his hairy shoulder.

Once they reached the laboratory, Lockheart wasted no time in strapping Rue on her side to the gurney, despite her screams, kicks and attempts to bite him. He was just too strong against such a small woman. There was nothing Rue could do except watch helplessly as the doctor balanced himself on the other side of the table, behind Rue's back.

Lockheart went to a cabinet on a side wall and fiddled around for a few minutes. When he returned, he held two colossally-sized syringes filled with a cerulean blue liquid—one in each hand.

"Ladies first," he said as he placed one of the syringes down on a side table and began closing in on Rue.

"Not this time," the doctor interrupted. "Age before beauty. I must insist. I'm in quite a lot of pain. I'm afraid I may not last much longer. I feel myself growing weaker and weaker."

"Very well, sir," Lockheart replied, turning to the old man and bending down to his level. "Here we go. Right into the spine."

Rue couldn't see the doctor's reaction, though she did hear him cry out. Then there was an eerie, unceasing silence. Slowly and carefully, Lockheart peered over her body.

"Your turn, little Rue."

Rue noticed the shine of the polished metal needle reflect the bright white light that surrounded her. She slammed her eyes shut and waited for the inevitable pinch. When it didn't come, she opened her eyes just in time to see a slew of men rush down the stairs, holding pistols at the ready.

"*Put your hands up!*" a familiar voice yelled, and Rue turned her attention to the top of the staircase. The man from the forest, the one who had called himself "Constable," stood there triumphantly, his shotgun in his hand and his oversized hatchet still fastened to his belt.

"Don't try anything," he growled at Lockheart, who was looking as though he might make a run for it. "Or you'll get a silver bullet right where the sun don't shine. Slower that way. And more painful."

Lockheart sneered, and suddenly jumped, tore past an officer and leapt toward the bottom of the staircase, fiercely slashing his claws along the way. A gunshot rang out, and Lockheart fell heavily to the ground and slumped into a heap.

The doctor was placed in handcuffs and taken away.

Rue looked up at the constable, her eyes wider than they'd ever been. His shotgun was still smoking.

"Your friend's waiting outside," Constable said as he made his way down the stairs. "I ran into her right around the same place you hit that wolf. By that little cemetery." He came over to the gurney and began to unfasten the straps around Rue's wrists. "I've been watching these goons during my off-duty time for months now, ever since I noticed them lurking around the old cemetery when I was out cutting firewood. I've always known they were up to something out here all alone in the middle of the woods, avoiding everyone in town. There've been tall tales going around about the weirdos doing experiments on humans and corpses and whatnot, but I didn't pay them much attention. But then people—and bodies—started going missing, and I began to connect the dots. I just needed enough evidence to get a warrant, which I was able to, thanks to your friend. She said—"

Rue didn't give him a chance to finish. As the binds slipped off her wrists, she pushed past Constable, racing up the stairs out of the laboratory. Just outside the front door, illuminated by the red and blue lights of several police vehicles and surrounded by many officers, Eliza was waiting. She ran straight to Rue as soon as she spotted her, scooping her best friend into the tightest hug she'd ever given to anyone.

"How did you know where to find me?" Rue asked.

"The job posting, duh!" Eliza laughed, though tears were streaming down her face. "When your call dropped earlier, I knew something was wrong. None of my calls or texts would go through after that. I had a really bad feeling... I just knew you needed help. Then I called the number that had come up on our caller I.D. when the doctor called our dorm. The man who answered said you weren't here, that you hadn't even been here at all. So I came looking for you. When I ran into Constable and told him you were missing, he was able to get a warrant to search the house."

Rue smiled but said nothing. She hugged Eliza again.

After Rue had given her statement of what had happened to the police, Eliza led her to her car. Before getting into the passenger side Rue glanced up at the luminous moon, the source of all her troubles that night. She briefly pondered if Lockheart would be at peace now, and then, a heartbeat later, wondered why she should care. Lockheart was dead. She had the rest of her life to live.

Rue suddenly saw the flash of his piercing eyes within her mind, and an instant later her head began to hurt. She ran her hand over her scalp, and her eyes widened as she felt the swollen, raw flesh of a large, deep gash beneath her hair. She removed her hand and looked at the blood that now stained her fingers, remembering the way Lockheart had grabbed her by the hair when he'd dragged her out of the car.

Anything that draws blood.

Rue was suddenly aware of her body in a way she'd never been before.

She felt her pupils dilate, her fingernails tingle, and her teeth begin to tickle within her gums. She got into Eliza's car, closed the door, and locked it. Eliza climbed into the driver's seat beside her, smiling over at Rue as she turned the key in the ignition.

Rue could hear the sound of the blood pumping through her best friend's veins. And prior to this very moment, to Rue, Eliza had never smelled so good.

She smelled like lamb chops and gardenias.

THE INVENTOR'S DAUGHTER

Selenia Paz

On the day they took her father, Maribel went farther into the woods than she had ever gone before. The hooves of the small goats that walked beside her made soft *pat-pat* sounds as they stepped on damp leaves. The trees had almost seemed to part before her, forming a clear path that appeared to go on forever. A fog began to roll in from all directions, and the sudden darkness made Maribel's mind jump to the stories her father had told her as a child—stories of a strange beast that roamed the woods. Even now, her father never let her go without warning her not to venture too far.

In the distance, Maribel heard thunder. She stopped walking and waited to see if a storm was approaching, but now there was only silence. The goats turned their heads up suddenly, and Maribel looked up to try to find what they had heard. The fog had grown thicker, and she could just make out the form of a large white owl. She smiled as she thought of her father, who would undoubtedly scold her for not fleeing from the *lechuza*, a bad omen. She turned and herded the goats back toward home, walking much slower through the heavy fog.

Night had fallen by the time they reached the house, the many candles inside providing some guidance in the heavy darkness. Maribel placed some fresh hay down on the floor of the barn, and the goats settled down to sleep.

The house was cold when she entered. Tools and blueprints were scattered over the dining table, a pencil on the floor. Maribel stopped walking as she neared the entrance to the kitchen. Pots and broken plates littered the floor, more of her father's tools among them. The rug that covered the trap door had been moved, the door open to reveal a short set of stairs.

Maribel made her way quickly to her father's room. Paper was scattered over the bed and floor, his desk and mirror broken and shattered. As she entered her own room, the fear that had overcome her changed. Her closet was open and her clothes had been moved, but they remained neatly hung on one side of the closet. The papers and books on her shelves had been taken out and laid on her desk, leaving her shelf empty. The boxes under her bed had been taken out, the items inside now covering her bed. As she looked down at them, she realized they seemed to be organized: more books in a pile, jewelry, papers, shoes. She had the horrible feeling someone was watching her, and that running outside with a lantern and calling for her father was not the best action to take.

Maribel looked down at her pants and boots and made a quick decision. Changing her clothes would take precious time away from her, so she reached under her desk and pulled loose the tape that held a knife to the bottom of the desk, placing it in her back pocket. On her father's table, she found a flashlight but no batteries. She picked through the mess of tools and papers, singling out two that worked. She grabbed her father's metal whistle and her hooded cloak and locked the door behind her.

As Maribel led Valentín out of the barn, she made sure to leave the barn door open slightly. She didn't want to think of how long she would be gone, but she wasn't foolish enough to think that there was a simple explanation for the state of their house.

Maribel stood in front of the house with Valentín and pointed the flashlight in all directions, careful to pass it over every part of the ground. Wave after wave of possibilities washed through her mind: Her father had suffered some sort of attack and had struggled to get out of the house? That was almost impossible; the condition of the house was so severe—and, considering her own room, so odd. A neighbor, or a stranger, had made their way into the house and had attacked her father, perhaps with the intention to steal? Her father did have quite a few unique tools. That still didn't explain her room, or why the tools—some of them very valuable—hadn't been taken. And what about the animals? Surely someone who'd intended to find something of value would have looked in the barn and seen Valentín. His beautiful golden mane and large build would have been enough for someone to know he was valuable. And there was another problem with that theory: any neighbors they may have had were too far and would never have traveled the distance. Their house was so deep in the woods it was difficult to come across it by chance—if at all. And, if Maribel were honest, she would have to admit that she couldn't remember ever having any neighbors. The only person she could really remember besides her father was her mother. She didn't like to dwell on that.

There was a *crack* near the edge of the grass, where the small plants she'd grown with her father began to meet the tall trees of the woods. Valentín's head turned to the side so quickly the flashlight fell from Maribel's hand, dimming for a few seconds. In the quiet that followed, Maribel attempted to calm herself down, but she could not prevent her mind from thinking about the beast from the legends her father had told her. That was the only other explanation Maribel could think about—her father had been taken by the beast he'd always warned her about.

Maribel bent down and picked up the flashlight, giving it a shake. "Don't be ridiculous," she said out loud. She pointed the flashlight toward the woods once more, but there was no movement. The fog seemed to have thinned slightly, but clouds were beginning to gather in the sky. The part of Maribel that wanted to believe there was a good explanation for the state of their home wanted to call out to her father, wanted to believe that he was nearby in the woods somewhere, and that even if the beast had come to attack her father, he had lost and retreated back to the woods. But she'd read enough to know that sometimes inexplicable events really were inexplicable events.

As she passed the flashlight over the ground one final time, she spotted four large indentations in the dirt, each about six inches into the ground. As she bent down to touch them, there was a loud noise, almost like thunder, coming from the woods. Maribel turned off the flashlight and looked up, grabbing on to Valentín's reins just as he began to pull back. There was a bright light over the trees coming toward them. Maribel pulled Valentín toward the trees just as the light stopped above the spot where she and Valentín had just been standing. She moved deeper into the safety of their darkness and watched as a large silver plane landed on the ground.

Three men exited the plane and ran toward the house, while a fourth stayed behind. "And make sure to look in the barn," he called.

Maribel held her breath until the three men returned. "Nothing seems to have changed in the house," one of them said.

"In the barn," said another. "There are goats now, and the horse is gone."

"Then she's gone," said the fourth. "She couldn't have gotten very far, not in this darkness. Send a message. Martín's daughter is somewhere in these woods. She must be found and brought to His Majesty's office."

"What of the tools and the books and the other things in the house?"

"Burn them."

FOR THE FIRST day, all Maribel and Valentín did was ride. She went in the direction the plane had traveled, but as the sun rose on the second day, she began to lose hope. She'd always been a very good navigator, but as the hours passed, she forced herself to stop for a few hours near a creek. Valentín nuzzled the plants growing beside the water with his snout.

Every few hours Maribel had heard rumbles in the distance, and as night fell on the second day, their pursuers made no more attempts to hide themselves, flashing their bright lights over the trees in hopes of discovering their location. Maribel and Valentín walked side by side through the night, both turning their heads at the slightest sounds. Thoughts of the beast of the woods passed through Maribel's mind, and she wondered which beast would be the most terrifying: the one who hid in the shadows of the woods, taking anyone who crossed his path — or the one who'd taken her father.

Before darkness fell on the third day, Valentín stopped abruptly, his head tilted toward a noise that had escaped Maribel's ears. No, not just one noise, but many different sounds came from just up ahead. Maribel stepped back and pulled Valentín with her, being careful to hide them both from view behind two large trees. The night was enveloping any light that would have allowed her to see more clearly, but maybe that was for the best. She led Valentín forward slowly and they walked for several minutes when she began to notice that the ground had turned rocky, the dirt and leaves no longer damp and soft beneath her feet. They continued for almost an hour when there was a rumble above them. The silver plane's bright light stopped a few hundred feet ahead and began to lower itself to the ground, its light illuminating everything in front of it.

Maribel had never seen anything like it. A large archway led into a town—no, a city?—with tall silver spiraled buildings, each with countless windows. Hundreds of lights illuminated the buildings, so that Maribel was not sure if they were silver or actually mirrors. The lights moved continuously, some of them in the fashion of a lighthouse. There were men standing in front of the archway, their hands held out to receive the cases and weapons handed to them by the four men who had just exited the plane.

Maribel could see people walking on the streets of the city behind the men. Small two-door vehicles whizzed by, blue light illuminating the streets every time one passed. Maribel could have watched the people forever, the parents walking with their young children, the couples driving in their small cars. Who knew what they were talking about? As far as Maribel was concerned, they could have been in another world.

The rumble of the plane brought her out of her daze, and she turned in time to see it heading slowly toward a large hangar, which was not as well-lit as the city. After talking for a few minutes just outside the archway, the four men took one last look toward the woods and made their way into the walls of the city.

As Maribel watched, most of the lights inside the buildings went out, and the low hum of vehicles driving through the streets stopped. There was an uneasy quiet, and Maribel was afraid to move. There was a *ping* and a gruff voice echoed all around.

"*Good citizens, tonight we must exercise extra caution and vigilance.*"

The metal wall surrounding the city shuddered a little as metal spikes rose from the top. Black bars came down from the archway, blocking the entrance.

"*The protections your city has in place should serve us well tonight.*"

Maribel heard a small *crackle* and wondered how many volts of electricity were passing through the wall.

"*The Beast has been sighted—not too far from the edge of our woods.*"

Maribel and Valentín took a step back automatically, hiding themselves deeper in the darkness.

"*We will make sure he does not enter our gates.*"

Maribel looked up at the tallest building, where there were a few lights still on. The silhouette of a man was just barely discernible, and Maribel was certain that his was the voice on the speaker.

"*But we do ask for your cooperation. If you see any suspicious activity, anything out of the ordinary, report it at once. Enjoy your evening.*"

There was an echoing *click*, and then silence. Maribel continued to watch the man's silhouette pacing back and forth until he moved away from the window and the light blinked off.

"You don't suppose there's a back way in?" Maribel whispered to Valentín.

They waited without moving for what seemed like hours, Maribel's hand holding Valentín's reins, ready to jump on him at any moment.

Then, slowly, they began to walk parallel to the city gate, keeping within the safety of the woods.

"How are we ever going to get in there?" Maribel whispered.

Suddenly, a scooter emerged from the trees about two hundred feet away, and Maribel pulled back on Valentín's reins, drawing them farther back into the woods. The scooter was almost completely silent as it made its way toward the tall gate. As Maribel watched, a door built into the metal wall slid open, revealing a woman's silhouette. The scooter slowed to a stop next to the wall, and the driver — a man — stepped off and followed the woman, who had already disappeared from the doorway.

Maribel turned to Valentín.

"This is my chance. Wait for my signal right here. Don't let them see you, okay?"

Valentín lifted one leg and set it down again, a sign he understood, and moved back slightly. Maribel looked at him one more time before turning and running toward the open doorway. When she had almost reached it, she wished she had never started toward it at all. How stupid could she have been to run out into the open? The man and woman could return at any moment, and then she would be captured, unable to help her father.

She felt a tiny fire of hope light up inside her as she reached the doorway and passed through it, her eyes desperately searching for a place to hide. The darkness of the city was a gift, and Maribel was beginning to breathe a sigh of relief when the man and woman rounded a corner, blue light shining from a flashlight in the woman's hand.

The man dropped a small package and instinctively took out a weapon, pointing it at Maribel. The woman stopped, her flashlight shining right into Maribel's eyes. She lifted her hand, signaling for the man to lower his weapon. Maribel couldn't see the woman's eyes, but she heard the disbelief in her voice.

"Marina?"

Maribel felt herself tense at the sound of her mother's name. She remained silent, waiting and listening. The man put his weapon back in its holster and bent down to pick up the package he'd dropped — a small box that made a soft clicking sound when it was moved around. The man looked around nervously, then back at Maribel.

"You can go," the woman finally said. The man did not move.

"If you don't hurry, we will all get caught," she said to him.

He nodded and, taking one last look at Maribel, moved past her and through the doorway. The woman touched a keypad on the bracelet she wore on her wrist, and the door slid shut.

Maribel began to feel panic in her chest. There was no sign of the door's existence after it slid shut.

The woman stepped forward, but Maribel did not move.

"It's best not to linger," the woman said quietly. "Follow me."

The woman turned and walked away, her footsteps barely making a sound as they fell on the gray stone. When she reached a corner and turned, Maribel broke into a run, almost forgetting to be quiet.

As Maribel rounded the corner, she was greeted by a wide street with towering gray stone buildings on each side. A few lights lit each door, and even though Maribel knew it was impossible, it seemed as if the street went on forever. From where she stood, she could see two different roads farther down, leading to the center of the city like a maze.

The woman was almost at the top of the stairs that led to the doorway of the second building on the right, and Maribel sprinted to catch up to her. The woman stopped and turned to watch Maribel, holding the wrist that wore the keypad bracelet. When Maribel reached the top, the woman blinked, turned, and touched the keypad four times.

"But wait — " Maribel began.

"Not here," the woman said. "Someone might see you."

The glass doors slid open quietly and Maribel followed the woman inside. A second set of glass doors opened when the woman placed her hand on the glass.

As soon as the doors closed behind them, the woman turned to Maribel.

"You cannot possibly be Marina. You're exactly as she was, once, but not as she must be now. You must be her daughter."

Maribel stared at the woman but did not say anything.

"I would ask how she's doing, but the fact that her daughter seems to be breaking into the city during the darkest hours of the night does not bode well."

The woman waited again, Maribel still looking into the woman's eyes — the same striking gray as her mother's.

The woman turned. "Come," she said briskly, and she led Maribel past a large circular desk with a rectangular plaque that read *Book Depository*. As the woman led Maribel past rows and rows of shelves with strange devices, each blinking a tiny blue light, Maribel stopped walking.

"But where are the books?" she asked.

The woman stopped and turned. She gestured with her hand toward the devices on the shelves. "These are the books."

Marina raised an eyebrow but said nothing.

"What's your name?" the woman asked after a few moments.

"Maribel."

The woman nodded. "And you're Marina's daughter." It was not a question.

Maribel nodded. The woman stepped toward her.

"Very good. My name is Minerva, and I take it, Maribel, by the way you're sneaking about, that something is amiss. While I must admit this is not the way I would have chosen to meet my granddaughter, it cannot be helped."

Maribel's eyes widened, but Minerva raised her hand.

"If you are here, something brought you. How is Marina? And what are you doing here?"

Maribel felt an eerie calmness settle over her, the blinking blue lights making her feel suddenly tired.

"I can help you, but only if you tell me what you're doing here," Minerva said, stepping closer to Maribel.

"My mother — she passed away three years ago," Marina said, not knowing if there was time to think of a better way to say it.

Minerva went still, her arm falling down to her side. As quickly as her eyes had dropped, they rose again.

"And your father is here."

"How do you know?" Maribel asked, alarmed.

"Why else would you be here?" Minerva paused, then turned around and began to pace. "But why now?" She turned to Maribel. "Your father still enjoys his tinkering, I assume?"

Maribel hesitated.

"Maribel, please, there is no time to lose. Had I wanted, the authorities would have come to collect you as soon as I locked the door to the depository. Now, is your father still an inventor?"

Maribel nodded slowly.

"That is why they brought him here," Minerva said, more to herself than to Maribel.

Maribel raised a finger. "Where is *here*?"

Lights passed by the front doors, and Minerva held her breath until they had gone. Minerva looked at the keypad on her wrist and shook her head.

"It'll be past midnight soon. We must work quickly. Come."

She walked briskly toward the back of the depository and a door slid open. Maribel ran to follow her but paused before stepping through the door.

Minerva smiled a little. "I assure you I'm not the dangerous one here."

"Where is *here*?" Maribel repeated, her frustration clearly audible.

Lights passed by the front doors again, this time lingering slightly longer before they disappeared.

Minerva began rummaging through metal drawers that slid in and out soundlessly. "Not a welcoming place for your father," she finally answered.

Before Maribel could ask why, Minerva raised a hand, then

continued.

"Your father and mother were once very important members of this city. They received very generous offers from other cities if they would only relocate. Your father was the greatest inventor anyone had ever seen. *Is*, I am sure."

She pulled out a plastic identification card and handed it to Maribel. Below her name, *Minerva Vidal*, was her title, *Bibliotecaria/Librarian*, and her picture.

"This will help you get through the doors of the City Center. There's a room below ground that is restricted to all but a few city employees. You should be able to enter that room with my card. If your father is here, he will be held there."

"But why?" Maribel managed to ask.

Minerva hesitated as she stepped fully out of the room, looking toward the front doors in search of more lights.

"Your father created the most effective and intelligent set of robots anyone has ever seen. They not only made life easier for all who live in the city, they performed completely accurate work. No more mistakes in medications, no more mistakes in surgical procedures. Perfect. Until one day, things changed."

Maribel whispered, "The robots tried to take over."

Minerva smiled. "You would think. No. It was something else." She hesitated.

"What?"

"One of them started to feel."

Maribel felt as if there was a heavy weight on her chest. When she spoke, her voice was hoarse and dry. "And... And what's wrong with that?"

Minerva laughed bitterly. "You know humans. They don't like things they don't understand. It makes them afraid. The robots were destroyed. All except one."

Maribel's eyes widened.

"A male your father had created: Andres. Your father and mother fled with him, and nobody ever knew what became of them." At this last part, Minerva winked.

"Except you, because she was your daughter." Maribel finished quietly.

"Yes. Now, since you're alone, I assume you don't know where Andres is?"

Maribel shook her head. She'd never heard of him before now.

"Well, I'm sure your parents made certain he was safe." Minerva looked at her wristpad again. "We must hurry. Now, listen very carefully to what I am about to tell you. You will go out of this building and run toward the tallest building at the center. That's the only one that will be lit up now. You can access any door with my identification card. When you enter, the staircase will be on the right. Take the only flight of stairs down. That's where your father will be. He'll most likely be guarded." She looked around the room, searching for a weapon to give Maribel.

Maribel patted her back pocket. "I have my knife. I'll be fine."

Minerva raised an eyebrow. "I'll call the authorities two minutes after you leave. Make sure no one sees you. I'll make up some story about a theft." She began walking to the front doors.

Maribel stared at the identification card as she followed.

"Why do you have access to those sections of the building?" she asked hesitatingly.

Minerva stopped walking. "Because I guard the books."

"From harm?" Maribel asked.

"No," Minerva replied sadly. "From people."

"What?"

"It is against the law to read."

Maribel shook her head. "What?" she repeated.

"People might start getting ideas. They might get creative. Some might even become inventors." She looked at Maribel and they stood in the quiet darkness for a long, heavy heartbeat.

"So then, that man, the one near the city gate, he..." Maribel began.

"...is working in the hopes that at least some of the literature we have will be saved."

Maribel's eyes widened as the two looked at one another.

"You look so much like your mother," Minerva said finally. She reached out a hand quickly. "Your mother. This is not what she would have wanted. You'll be in danger, and I'll have helped get you there."

Maribel pulled out the whistle her father had made. "If it looks like there's trouble, I'll blow this whistle. It'll call our horse Valentín to me and my father. He's mechanical — he will know where to find us. And it's silent, only robots can hear it, so I won't give myself away." Maribel walked toward the doors. "Two minutes," she said.

"How will you know your horse has heard it?" Minerva asked.

"It will affect any robot within a few miles," Maribel replied, turning to look at her grandmother one last time. She might have been her mother at an older age. She smiled, her chest heavy, before she added, "I know. I have heard it before."

MARIBEL LOVED TO run, and this harrowing moment was no exception. She'd covered almost three quarters of the distance between her and the City Center before she had to seek cover in the dark corners of buildings as bright lights sped by, soundless. She pulled her knife out and held it, her arm steady. After watching the building for a few minutes, she decided the best course of action would be simply to run as fast as she could. She leaped over steps and scanned the card, the doors sliding open without a sound. She scanned the card once more to enter the stairway and fell into complete darkness. She'd noticed two cameras outside of the building and knew there was no way she had more than a few minutes.

She made her way down the steps quietly and more slowly than she would have liked—not because she couldn't see, but because she didn't want to make any noise. If there was a guard, she would need to disarm him immediately.

She scanned the card and a soft *beep* sounded. Maribel wasted no time. She knew whoever was inside would have heard the noise and so she threw open the door and jumped on the only person standing in the middle of the room. As she was about to stab them in the leg to prevent them from standing, she heard her father yell, "Maribel, no!"

She stopped immediately, the knife hovering over the man's leg.

In the instant that she turned and looked at the cell where her father was being held, the man threw her off, her hand hitting the floor and the knife clattering away from her. He stepped toward her, drawing a gun from his hidden holster.

Maribel stood slowly and turned to look at her father, unafraid. She walked toward him.

"Stop!" the man yelled at her. "Stop or I'll shoot!"

"You can try," Maribel replied.

"Maribel," her father whispered.

"It's okay, Papá," she said. "I'm here now. We'll get out of here."

She looked around his cell and saw only his coat. He was the only prisoner.

"The only place you're going is in the cell with your father," the man said as he came toward her.

Maribel turned to face him, and the man stopped. Her eyes widened, and she understood why her father had stopped her from hurting him.

The man lowered his weapon and he asked, "You're his daughter?"

Maribel nodded.

Noticing the man's hesitation, Maribel's father spoke up. "Please, let her go. She has done no harm. Let her go back to our home."

"That's impossible," the man replied automatically. "She cannot be allowed to leave. What if she goes back to your workshop and creates more of those beasts?"

"Beasts?" Maribel asked. "You mean like the Beast that lives in the woods?"

The man nodded and pointed his gun toward Maribel's father. "The Beast he created."

Maribel's eyes widened, but she corrected herself quickly. She let her eyes wander around the room, feigning curiosity. A small rectangular window was located near one of the corners. The man pointed the gun back at Maribel.

Maribel's eyes drifted toward the knife on the floor. How could she have dropped it? How could she? Not that it would be of any use now, at least not against this man.

"Please, just let my father go."

The man turned and walked toward the desk and grabbed a set of silver keys. With the weapon still pointed at Maribel, he gestured toward the cell.

"When I open the door, you'll join your father."

"Am I not allowed to know what he's being charged with?" Maribel asked. She knew she had to get her father to Valentín. He would take her father to safety.

The man sighed. "Your father is being charged with illegal manufacture of weapons."

Maribel laughed. "It seems to me the only one here with a weapon is you." She stepped toward him.

"Maribel," her father warned, "you have to get out of here. Please" —

he turned to the man — "just let her go. She has no part in this."

Maribel took another step. "I'm warning you," the man said.

"What if I told you I knew where to catch the Beast? Would you let my father go?"

"Maribel, what are you doing?" Her father's voice was filled with sadness.

"It's okay, Papá. I don't know why I didn't see it sooner."

"What do you mean?" the man asked. "He's here? With you?"

"Yes. And if you let my father go, I will show you. I'm sure the people you work for are anxious to hunt down this creature. And if I'm lying, you'll have me as a prisoner at least. You won't lose completely."

The man hesitated before opening the door to the cell. Maribel's father hugged her tightly. "I can't leave you. I won't."

"It's okay, Papá. I met Grandmother. I know who he is," Maribel replied in a whisper. "It will be okay."

Maribel's father stepped away, his eyes dim with sadness. There was a *beep* and all three turned toward the door.

"What's he doing outside of the cell?" a man barked.

Another voice: "And who is she?"

"Can't you do anything right, Andres?" a third yelled.

Maribel looked at her father for his reaction. The man had somehow managed to keep the name her father had given him.

"She knows the location of the Beast," Andres replied.

For a moment, everyone froze. And in that moment, Maribel pulled out the whistle and blew with all the strength she had. Andres dropped his weapon to cover his ears and it began firing, striking the three men near the doorway. Maribel jumped in front of her father, shielding him from the bullets that penetrated her skin — and the metal underneath. She reached down and grabbed the weapon, reaching for her father.

"Hurry, Papá, more will be coming," she said in the eerie silence that followed the shots.

Her father turned. "We can't leave him."

"Here," Maribel said, handing her father the weapon. "Go out and meet Valentín. He should be here soon." Her father looked at Andres, who had crumpled to the ground, holding his ears.

"I'll drag him if I have to. I promise," she said. Her father grabbed the weapon and headed out the door, his steps fading away as the door shut behind him.

She bent down and pulled at Andres's hands. "My head," he said. "What was that? Did you call the Beast to us?" He pushed himself up slowly as Maribel wondered how many of his past memories were still stored somewhere inside of him.

"No. The Beast is already here." She reached down and picked up her knife, using it to peel away the skin on her hand where one of the bullets had struck her. The shiny metal underneath glistened.

"No, the Beast is a large creature, with brown fur and sharp teeth and angry eyes. That's what they said. That it would kill you if it got the chance. And that your father created hundreds of them, all mechanical and even more dangerous than any animal." Andres spoke more to himself than to Maribel. "But you, you don't look like that at all."

Andres stepped back. He shook his head. "You should never have come here. Do you know what they'll do to you?"

"Probably the same thing they'll do to you when they find out what you are," Maribel replied softly.

"What?"

"That whistle I just used, my father made it. It was meant to be used on our mechanical animals, to call them back to us."

"And?"

"Humans can't hear it," she said sadly.

Andres backed away from her. Maribel could see his eyes coming in and out of focus, trying to register what he'd heard.

"No. You're lying."

"We don't have much time," said Maribel. "But if you come with me, my father will explain everything. He knows... a lot more about you than I do."

Andres shook his head.

"Do you dream? When you're asleep, do you dream?" Maribel asked.

"Why do you ask that?" Andres asked her.

"Because I don't. I have memories and feelings, I love, and I am happy. But wish as I might, I don't have the ability to dream. Not yet. I think it's a little more difficult for robots to dream."

Andres looked at her with wide eyes. "Just go," he said to her. "I'll tell them I don't know where you went."

Maribel handed him her knife. "Make a small cut. When you see the metal, if you would like to come with us, we'll be waiting near the edge of the woods."

As he grabbed the knife, their fingers touched and a small spark ignited. Maribel smiled, then turned and ran out of the room. Andres looked over his own fingers. Outside, he could hear a horse galloping away.

MARIBEL AND HER father watched as the flashing lights in the city finally died down. Her father's voice broke through the silence.

"I loved all my inventions," he said quietly. "Andres was the first of the robots that started to feel. When people began to realize how advanced they were becoming, they were seized and destroyed. The only one Marina and I managed to save was Andres."

"The only one?" Maribel asked.

Her father looked over at her, his eyes glimmering in the darkness.

"I created you after Marina and I had sent Andres back."

"But why did you sent him back at all?"

"There was no harm. I made sure to create a new set of memories for him, positive memories of the city. No one would ever know."

"You didn't answer my question," Maribel said.

Her father sighed. "I couldn't bear to destroy him and, at the time, it was much too dangerous to keep him with us. We weren't sure the woods would be safe. We decided to hide him in plain sight."

The wind began to pick up, the rustling of the trees breaking the silence.

Maribel opened her mouth to speak, but closed it again.

"Then why did I create you?" her father spoke her unspoken question. "Marina had always wanted a daughter. It made her so happy to have you."

Maribel closed her eyes, scanning through her memories. She saw her mother standing behind her, teaching Maribel to braid her long dark hair. "My Beauty," her mother would always say, looking at Maribel in the mirror.

There was a *crack* behind them.

As Maribel's eyes scanned the trees, she thought of all the people she had seen in the city earlier that evening. "Why tell me there was a beast in the woods, if there wasn't one?" she asked.

Her father was quiet a few moments before answering.

"That idea I borrowed from the leaders of this city. It seemed the best way to keep you from wandering too far."

"From being captured," Maribel said, finishing her father's thoughts.

Maribel's father coughed gently, and Maribel removed her cloak, placing it on her father's back.

It will be some time before people can accept that I am not a beast, Maribel thought, looking into her father's eyes.

IT WAS ALMOST dawn and Maribel's father was asleep on Valentín's back. If Maribel had had a heart, she knew it would have felt broken. She'd been so sure he would come. As she turned and walked toward Valentín, she heard footsteps on the fallen leaves.

She stiffened, ready to attack anyone who tried to take her father.

It was Andres.

He had a small cut on his hand as he handed the knife back to her.

Maribel raised her eyebrows and smiled. "You came."

"Of course. I couldn't miss the opportunity of meeting the infamous Beast of the woods."

They turned and began to walk in step next to Valentín. As they went deeper into the quiet of the woods, it seemed that, if they could dream, this would be what it felt like.

A BRACKISH SHORE

Leigh Hellman

The sun set sooner these days, streaking itself copper and gold across the bay before the barker's voice began to crack with last calls. The machines wheezed—tinkled and ground against themselves—as the lights flickered out string by string, chasing the drifters to the gates at the end of the pier. Children squealed and squawked and raced each other across the wooden planks. Their footsteps echoed between the waves.

It was Tuesday; she always came on Tuesday. Sella tied off a little burlap satchel and waited.

A FISTFUL OF years ago, Sella had stuffed two carpet bags full of overstitched skirts and darned socks and the sooty, brittle books that she'd hidden under her winter coats as she rustled in and out of the bookstores wedged crooked-cramped into the corners of her neighborhood, and stood, defiant, in the parlor of her crumbling family home.

"I'm joining the circus," she'd said, steady and clear and without blinking against the seeping afternoon light.

There had been no answer. Or rather, no one left *to* answer.

The house and all its estate trappings had gone into the care of the law firm her grand-uncle had kept on retainer until he wheezed out his last dusty breath, and beyond that she didn't know. Didn't check, didn't care.

She'd followed after the technicolor pop-flash of the biggest, most established troupe she could find—sob-storied her way into being a waitress in the food tent, then knocked the second-best ciggie girl, white like porcelain and just as fragile, down and took her place weaving through the late show crowds.

After a while—as the crowds got rougher and the hands got grabbier—Sella noticed that the fairy-shine had started to go dull around the edges. Litter piled up against the midway stalls and spiderwebs collected under the awnings and the air caught the same tacky-mildew taste that had been soaked into the walls of her childhood.

Sometimes, if she inhaled too quickly, it would lodge in her throat and not even a coughing fit could get it out.

IT'D BEEN IN her third troupe—after the thick-tarnished glamour of the one she ran away for, then the sterile-dull cheeriness of the one she ran away to—that she met Miss Janus. Mummy-wrapped in scarves and scraps of fur and bangles that clattered along her wrists, Miss Janus kept herself propped against a pile of cushions under a tilting stall near the cluster of animal wagons, crystal ball and tarot deck always within reach. She kept her hours from after breakfast to lunch and then late stretches once the afternoon shows had run; it was how most midway acts operated, since almost all of them doubled bit parts in the big show.

Sella herself did simple sleight-of-hand tricks, distractions for the audience while the aerialists secured their safety harnesses. She tried to shuffle through the clowns, chorus dancers, assistant trainers, and the like to match faces across the different midway booths, but it still took her the better part of a season to realize that the chubby, sweat-sheened stagehand for the seal show and The Mysterious Miss Janus were one and the same.

The stagehand wore the same muted gray overalls that all crew members were given so they didn't draw attention away from the real performers; Miss Janus draped herself in vibrant, shocking colors and outrageous cut-glass jewels. The stagehand's palms were rough and marred from bites and burns; Miss Janus always wore lace gloves and kept her hands folded gently in her lap between sessions. The stagehand's wiry black hair was close-cropped, cutting a clean line along dark skin; Miss Janus kept her head covered with gold lamé turbans and sequined headpieces that Sella could see glinting from the other end of the midway.

The stagehand was a quiet, hunched sort of man, but Miss Janus luxuriated in her femininity. It bewitched Sella like the shimmer of the first night at a circus once had. So she went to Miss Janus' stall one night and paid for her fortune.

Miss Janus took her hand firmly, held Sella's brown palm against her own, and traced out its lines with her fingertip. "Now, why's a talent like you out here playing with cards?"

Sella shrugged, closed her fingers into a loose fist. "Nothing else they'd let me do, I guess."

"*Let* you do?" Miss Janus swooped forward like a hawk in dive, then paused, considering. "Ten months working this show and this is the first time we meet—why?"

A lie pooled on Sella's tongue, something polite and innocuous that Miss Janus would cut through like butter. "I recognized you tonight."

"And which face did you recognize?" She rapped her blunt nails against the table. "Miss Janus has many."

"I recognized... my face." Sella tripped over the words, let them tumble out before she really heard them.

Miss Janus held her gaze for a sticky moment, then leaned back into her pillows.

"You have talent, but not skill. Not yet." Miss Janus smiled, kept her teeth behind her wide lips. "Did you come here for a teacher?"

Sella bit at the inside of her cheek, gnawed at it until it was puckered and gummy. There hadn't been a reason for coming. Or it'd been nothing more than curiosity and brash courage. Or perhaps there was a question behind glass—garbled in refraction—that she'd needed to see.

"Yes." Sella's voice fell quiet like moth wings into the night.

Miss Janus nodded like she'd known that the answer would satisfy her. "I accept. And here's your first lesson, free of charge: nobody lets dark girls do anything in life—everything we do we gotta take for ourselves. But dark girls like me and you—full of magic and power? Well, I'm gonna teach you how to make sure you ain't waiting on *lettin'* ever again."

THEY MET FOR lessons twice a week on whichever days had the smallest crowds and the least chance of losing good money by shuttering up the stall for an hour or two. Miss Janus ran through the basics of the craft—

gazing, tea leaves, palms, tarot—and brought in odd crew members for Sella to practice on.

Sella would stare at them, try to file away at their greasy smirks and the grime that cracked along the wrinkles in their hands. She imagined hoisting them up by their ankles and shaking them until all their secrets seeped out at her feet. She'd catch their eyes—wouldn't blink—and after a prickly stretch of silence they would start to squirm like maybe they almost believed that she could pry them open with her mind.

Then she would say something—something about fortune's windfall or the forking roads of change—and they'd scoff, go loose and cocky in their chair, and the spell was shattered.

If you can't sell it to us, how d'you expect to sell it to the rest of 'em?

Miss Janus set her to preparing ingredients after one particularly humiliating session when the firebreather had strung her along for several minutes, nodded and leaned in eagerly, and she'd felt like perhaps she was finally grasping the wispy tendrils of magic that Miss Janus claimed she had. But then—just as she'd started to feel something cold and bright building behind her eyes—he'd cut in with a slow, smug *no.*

No, she was wrong. No, she'd been wrong all along. It'd just been a game, a bit of fun to pass a lazy afternoon before his evening shows. The firebreather had winked one big blue eye, shook out his sunny hair, and left the stall with chuckles still tumbling out behind him.

"A game." Sella crushed a mound of spotted red seeds into the mortar. "He said it's just a game."

"He's right." Miss Janus rearranged the candles and jars lining her shelves; she didn't glance back at Sella. "Look around—the strongmen, the lion tamers, him, me. We're all just playing a game here, trying to entertain the ticket money out of as many pockets as we can. There's no shame in it."

Sella pounded the pestle, ground down until it was grit. "Right, so it's all a con then. No power, no magic. Just more card tricks. Guess I should go back to my old act then… at least I was good at that."

Miss Janus' fingers flinched, hovered near a bottle full of thick green syrup. "Magic and games aren't mutually exclusive. Just because you're playin' doesn't mean the ability isn't there."

"Is that a riddle? Or maybe this is another one of your lessons — 'no one will believe you if you don't believe yourself' — or something like that?" Sella's tone went low, sharp with a hiss at the end of it.

"It *is* a lesson, and, hell, I probably should've taught it to you sooner. But I wanted you to know your own magic before you had to learn the rest of it." Miss Janus turned. She toyed with a little glass vial, squeezing at the tip of its rubber dropper. "It don't matter if you believe yourself, don't even matter if you've got real talent — though, for the record, I think you do. It don't matter if they believe you, not really. At least half the folks who stop by my stall are hoping they can point a finger in my face at the end of the reading and call me a fake. Don't matter if you're right or wrong, whether you get to the truth or not. You know why? Because the truth don't matter. Because nobody cares about the truth. All folks care about, all they *really* care about, is what they *want* the truth to be. So that's what you need to learn. Stop worryin' about getting things right and start figuring out what the person in front of you wants to hear. Then you tell that to 'em like you just cracked their soul open like a soft egg and see if they don't stop laughing at you."

The whine of the ceramic bit at Sella's ears. She let go of the pestle and stretched out her stiff, sore knuckles. "Why did you offer to teach me?"

Miss Janus' lips twitched; a strange, sorrowful shadow crept across her face. "Because you have talent and everyone else was wasting it, just like they wasted mine."

"Magic?" It was a soft, hopeful question. Sella hated how her voice frayed and split with it.

The shadow settled deeper into the grooves of Miss Janus' skin. "Yes, but more than that. You have a talent for deflection and redirection, for showmanship and for surprising the audience into believin' that where you led them was where they wanted to go. That and this, they're the same talent, Sella—just different tools."

Sella looked down at her palms, patterned with lattices of thin scars and fragile, broken lines.

"Besides, I heard that you ran away from home to join the circus, and I can't believe pulling cards and clipping cigars was what you did it for." Miss Janus spun away again. She unwrapped her turban and hung it on a stubby post, then sat across from Sella at the cramped table.

The neat, close-cut buzz of hair stood in stark contrast to the rest of her costume baubles still swinging around her wrists and neck.

For a heavy-haze moment the foot or so between them was caked in silence. At the base of Sella's skull, that bright coldness began to crackle.

"Okay." Nothing more than an exhale dancing out of Sella's mouth.

"Okay," Miss Janus echoed, smiling with all her teeth. "Then help me get that powder into one of these empty jars, but be careful with it. You don't wanna take any chances with crab's eye seeds."

Sella didn't question it, never questioned the nondescript bits and pieces that went into Miss Janus' ingredients. But she tapped it into the jar slowly, made sure not to get any of the dust on her.

"I've got one more lesson for today if you're up for it." Miss Janus moved to the water basin, filled up the kettle and set it on the wood heater to boil. "Some folks want things, some folks need things—most folks do both. But wanting something and needing something ain't the same, and folks don't usually want what they need. You'll make more customers by givin' them what they want, but sometimes folks oughta get what they need. And you can give that to them too."

She took the jar from Sella and spooned out a tiny pour of crab's eye seed dust into the open top of the kettle, then screwed the lid on and perched it on a high shelf.

"Let's invite our firebreather back for another session." Miss Janus floated out of the room like an afterthought. "Maybe the tea leaves will be more insightful for him."

Miss Janus was careful—had been careful, Sella came to learn, for years. Most of what she tied up in spell bags was nothing more than sea salt or pebbles or farm dirt for the weight and crisp dried petals for the scent. People wanted to feel the magic in their own two hands, she'd said. It made it more tangible, easier to accept. Most of the incantations were purposeful gibberish from a language that Miss Janus had made up herself, just to be sure she wasn't stepping on any other mystical toes. And most of the tea was chamomile or lavender or thick country breakfast—that last one tended to leave the best dregs behind.

But once in a while the tea was bitterer, the bags were heavy with power, the words weren't gibberish. Sometimes people needed gentle reassurances and promises for a happier future, but once in a while...

The firebreather got sick, but he didn't die. His stomach turned for five days until he was dry heaving and spitting tacky red, but he didn't die. They said it must have been a bad torch, a bad swallow for the show. They said he might not be able to keep performing, not if it was going to be like this. But he didn't die.

He didn't laugh at Sella again either.

The second time it happened with another worker, a few whispers scratched up. But it had been months—almost a year—and there wasn't any proof. The third time was too soon, too sloppy, and someone put in an anonymous call to the wardens. It had been Sella's fault; one of the new midway barkers had gotten pushy and she must have poured too much in because he collapsed in his tent that night and never got back up.

It was Sella's fault, but Miss Janus took the blame, all of it, ripped it out of Sella's arms and hung herself with it. Sella didn't know why, but when the wardens came to the stall with their handcuffs, Miss Janus held her arms open for Sella and pulled her close.

"No tears today." She kissed the spiny hairs at the top of Sella's head. "It's time for my last lesson: eventually, the game's gotta end. For all of us."

Sella nodded, clung to Miss Janus' shawls. Hot tears washed out all the creaky, cobwebbed corners inside her.

"But the magic?" Miss Janus' fingers dipped into Sella's skirt pocket, letting something solid drop in. "That's forever."

The last time Sella saw Miss Janus was in fresh-shined cuffs being shuffled down the empty midway. Some folks said she pled guilty, said she'd die for it. Other folks said that the judge had taken pity on her, sent her to a well-house for life. Those folks said she died anyway — before, after, by time or sickness or her own self — but Sella never could find out the truth.

A few folks said she transformed, said she twisted herself into the air and vanished, and what — Sella recalled — did the truth matter anyway?

Sella left that night, took the first road out of town and boarded up in whatever spare rooms she could find along the way. She wandered from place to place, towns without names worth remembering, careful not to stay longer than a few nights at each stop. She didn't count the days, but eventually the ground began to thaw again and she found herself waking up to the thin ebbs of the sea. The salt stung familiar as she breathed out through an open window and, for the first time without Miss Janus, she let herself stand with feet firmly set on the ground below her.

She ate at the tavern shunted under the boarding rooms. After a filling, beige meal, she marched over to the owner, shook his hand, and asked for a job. That night — after the closing shift — she went upstairs and started to unpack her small, tattered luggage. In the pocket of a skirt, rancid with the stench of long travels, she found a spell bag half the size of her fist. She held it for a moment before setting it softly on the bed; when she untied it the contents scattered across the blanket.

Two of Miss Janus' heaviest, gaudiest rings rattled out, along with a few shimmering crystals and some tightly-tied bags full of dark dust that would've all looked the same except for Miss Janus' ornate handwriting on their labels. Underneath all that was a bundle of cash and a note — smudged and crumpled from the packaging — written in the same flourished, elegant lines:

You've always had the talent, you've learned the skills, now the tools are yours.

One final lesson: When you have the power, you've already won.

I'm so proud of you and I—

The ink trailed off; Sella finished the sentence for herself.

DAYS, WEEKS, MONTHS slid by dull from the carousel of lukewarm plates and sloshing mugs and the same two-dozen glassy smiles from the same two-dozen glassy regulars. Sella kept her tips rolled up with Miss Janus' gift. It stayed shoved inside her oldest pair of socks, being saved up for something she didn't know yet.

Something she wanted. Something she needed.

So she lived, dull and glassy, until tent frames started going up on the longest pier and new, clever faces began crowding in for the lunch rush. Then the posters went up, shouting in thick black lettering:

COMING SOON! THE CARNIVAL BY THE SEA!
CAN YOU RESIST ITS SIREN CALL?
HELP WANTED:
CREW, PERFORMERS, SIDESHOW TALENTS, MIDWAY WORKERS, UNIQUE INDIVIDUALS
APPLY ONSITE.

The cold brightness tickled up Sella's spine, an echo rusty and electric. She tore down the paper and folded it crookedly, jamming it into her coat pocket. That night she counted her savings and packed her bags. The next morning she bought a rickety caravan off one of the local merchants and dragged it down the pier to a prime spot, staying with it until the management found her.

The first thing she did—after signing her contract—was paint in wide, loopy script across the side of it:

Seek what you want
and find what you need
with Sella the Seer!

THE CARNIVAL BY the Sea was different than her other troupes, smaller and cleaner and far more mundane than the lumbering spectacles that had tugged her out of her childhood and into the grim world. It stayed static, propped up on the boardwalk until the waves began to freeze. Then the stalls shuttered and the carnival folks burrowed into the town for the winter. There were no raucous late night shows, no feather fan dancers or oddities on display. Children ran up and down the midway from the opening gates until dusk and families played wholesome games that were only slightly rigged against them and the big tent—the only one they had—ran an early dinner show and nothing else.

For her part, Sella's caravan filled full of teenagers with growing pains—anxious and awkward about everything in their scrambled lives—and a variety of women—mothers, grandmothers, spinsters—who had lost the thread of themselves and what they wanted years ago. Most of them were painfully earnest and sincere; no one got handsy or threatened to walk out without paying, and Miss Janus' ingredients stayed tucked in a low drawer under a pile of towels.

It was a Tuesday in the muggiest slice of summer when she first came with a knock on Sella's open door as the sun was already edging along the horizon.

A girl stood there, half-hidden behind the signs and draperies that hung at the caravan entrance. She wore a long dress printed in shocks of color that lay stark against her dark skin; it reminded Sella of gold lamé turbans and decadent silk scarves and sequin-lined everything. She wasn't small or frail—truth be told, she was probably just a little shorter than Sella—but she seemed brittle, her profile cut out against the fading sky.

A large burst of tight curls haloed her head, red like they'd been dipped in blood and left to soak it in.

Sella sat up straighter on the small pile of cushions against the wall. "The carnival's closing soon."

The girl—and she could be a woman, now that Sella saw the fullness of her—made a series of brisk gestures with her hands, then looked back, eager and expectant.

Sella swallowed down a dry throat and tried again. "I don't think I can take another customer tonight."

The girl paused—huffed out a sound without words—then began

miming what Sella finally understood to be writing. She found a scrap journal and a pencil and passed them to the girl.

She scribbled out a few lines, then passed the journal back.

I couldn't come any earlier. 10 minutes and I'll pay you double, please.

The shadows were still short and, anyway, locking the gates was mostly a show for the rowdier children and their lingering parents. Double her price would've been tempting any day, but that one had been particularly long and quiet, and Sella had never been one to turn down a generous offer.

Sella nodded, inviting her into the narrow space. "Ten minutes."

The girl sat across from her, held her palms out flat and still. They were smooth like glazed clay, with lines so fine that Sella could barely make them out.

She put the journal next to the girl, set the pencil on top of it. "So, what brings you to Sella the Seer?"

The girl didn't reach for the paper; her fingers didn't twitch to form signals. The only movement was her hands stretching wider, grasping toward Sella.

She had learned how to read folks, taken the lessons of Miss Janus and taught herself how to crease folks over on the spine and bookmark all the parts she'd need from them. But this girl was veiled — mirrored like polished marble or the first thin gloss of snow — and in the twilight shade Sella couldn't find a page to flip to. She fumbled, spun out vagaries and pulled at every snag she could find, hoping it would unravel the girl. But she sat still and, even as Sella talked, smiled sweet and mild at every prod but gave no further response.

After ten minutes, she spilled a bag of change onto the table and climbed out of the caravan. Sella counted out nearly three times her rate in tarnished gold coins before stumbling out onto the dark boardwalk, trying to trace the strange silent girl's path. But she was already gone, lost in the chilled starless night.

SHE CAME BACK three weeks later, which was more than Sella had thought to hope for. She drifted in at the hottest streak of the afternoon and waited in line behind two old women and a younger boy who kept pulling at the hem of his shirt. She brought her own notebook this time, ready with neat phrases already written out.

Theo—she pointed to herself. And below it:

I want to be happy—each letter was spaced out precisely, perfect except for a few ghost markings that hinted at this not being the first question she'd tried out.

It was a start. Sella's fingers circled Theo's wrist as she gazed more intently at Theo's weak, fracturing palm lines. Sella told her that there was happiness woven there, but also sorrow and trials. She shook her head, solemn, and said Theo would need guidance to traverse her fate. By the end, Theo swayed like the sea beneath them was rocking her. She poured more gold coins on the table and left, fast and unsteady.

Sella cursed, clipped it under her breath. Maybe she'd pushed too much, poured it over too thick, sounded too ominous. It would be a shame to lose the money, but not a disaster—she didn't want for customers here. But there was something else, something in the girl's— Theo's—hungry-deep eyes and unreadable skin that hooked into the core of Sella and pulled.

It was simple enough then: Sella didn't want her gone.

A WEEK WENT by—stuffed with groggy sessions and confused patrons gingerly asking if something was wrong—and Sella didn't realize she'd been holding her breath until a knock and a smile interrupted the watery new moonlight.

I want to be free—and Sella knew that itch, that restless rattle in the bones. She shuffled the dog-eared tarot deck that Miss Janus had given her, folded into a wine-dark lace cloth, and held the cards out to Theo.

Third time makes a habit, and the knot of fear in Sella's gut began to unclench. Theo came back for weeks at a time, then would disappear for a month or two, but Sella didn't worry. She'd come with the high-noon heat or the icy wind off the north seas, and Sella would pull cards or read crystals or pour tea. Sometimes she would tie off little spell bags full of shattered shells and sweet-smelling herbs to send back with Theo to wherever it was she came from. There was no regularity to any of it, save for the gold coins and the journal. Always one sentence, a statement masking a question, and Sella began feeling those sparks of cool light racing down to her fingertips and sizzling through the bridge of her nose. She began closing her eyes and listening again, letting the pulse of silence point her along the way.

Theo's statements became more specific, more certain:

I want to be safe.

I want to be known.

I want to make the right decisions.

I want to be loved—

"You are," Sella whispered, etching her fingernail where Theo's love line ought to be. "Your love protects you... will always protect you."

Theo's gaze snapped up; for the first time, she reached for the pencil Sella kept on the edge of the table. She wrote, fast and sharp, and against her delicate prepared words it looked like a scrawl:

How does he know?

The energy shivering along Sella's nerves sputtered, waned like it had petrified beneath her skin. Theo's fingers twined with hers, squeezed hopefully.

"He doesn't yet." Sella let their hold linger, even as the heat drained out of it. "But he will."

IT HAD BEEN five Tuesdays since Theo's last session. Five Tuesdays for Sella to form and reform a plan. A plan to save Theo — to protect her as Sella had sworn to, though that promise had been stolen by some faceless, formless *he*. A *he* who did not even know Theo, who did not recognize that someone so rare longed for him. A *he* who would not bring Theo happiness or freedom — Sella had seen nothing of him in their sessions, so how could he?

Sometimes folks oughta get what they need.

Sella prepared this spell bag carefully, spooned the only bit of crab's eye dust Miss Janus had sent with her onto a bed of fresh water lily petals and tied it with a double-loop of string. Then she pushed the whole thing into a burlap satchel, just in case.

She was standing outside — watching the colors bleed from the sky to the sea — when Theo arrived. The breeze tickled her curls, flickering like flames in the dying light.

Sella took her by the hand and led her into the caravan. They sat down and Theo opened her journal; the letters were slanted and a little frayed around the ends:

I want him to love me.

Sella nodded once and spread out her crystals and cards. She hemmed and hawed, wrung her hands and tapped out uneven rhythms on her knees — really made a show of it.

"These signs are obscured and contradicting." Sella stacked her tarot in a pile and twisted her mouth, sympathetic. "I'm sorry."

Theo pursed her lips in a tight white line; Sella watched the color fade from them. She blinked, quick against wet eyes, and smiled so small and sad that Sella nearly stretched across the table to smooth the pain off Theo's cheeks.

"There is one other method." Sella meant to sound hesitant, but it clawed out desperately. She tried to catch her breath. "But it can be dangerous, and the results are extreme."

Theo leaned in immediately, shook her head, fierce and furious.

Sella rummaged through a drawer behind her, rooted around in it like she hadn't already grabbed the satchel from inside.

"This is a testing potion." Sella set the bag in Theo's cupped palm. "It will determine if your desires are true or not. Boil no more than two pinches into a tea, and write your desire five times as you drink it. If your desire is true, you will feel elated, and what you want will soon come to pass. But if your desire is not true, you will feel ill. The slower and longer the illness, the falser the desire and the more urgently you must cut yourself from it. Is that something you can do? Something you truly want to know?"

A stone-heavy beat between them, then Theo closed a fist around the burlap.

"All right. But promise me" — Sella brushed her knuckles against Theo's bare forearm before pulling away — "if you get sick, come back to me. I have some remedies to ease the effects, and we can keep working to find out what you truly need together."

Theo patted Sella's wrist like an adult would with a wide-eyed child, brusque and dismissive, and climbed out onto the pier full of confidence for this test. Sella wondered if it worked — if it *could have* worked — would this be their last goodbye?

Theo was halfway down the midway, cradled under the twinkle of fairy lights that hadn't yet been dimmed out, when she stopped and turned back. She smiled bright and — caught in the sheen of the moon and the dancing of the carnival lights — it was almost blinding.

Sella traced the angles of Theo's back until she faded into the shifting shadows outside the gates of the pier. The tide washed along the shore, left a briny sting in the air, and Sella let it fill her lungs to choking.

Most folks got *want* and *need* tangled, couldn't get to the root and split them apart. Most folks spent their time looking for a little help, a nudge or two in the best direction from someone who knew better than them. And Sella—

She could do that.

THE FOREST OF CARTERHAUGH

a retelling of Tam Lin

Karissa Laurel

anae shuffled into her room and eased onto her bed — her balance could be a little wonky when she was tired. She tied her purple-streaked hair into a messy knot, revealing a band of puckered skin stretching from her temple to her jaw, and hiked her pants cuff over her knee. The skin beneath her prosthesis's socket had been itching most of the afternoon, and the relief of removing her electronic leg nearly brought tears to her eyes.

She rubbed the weary muscle in her thigh as her gaze swept over the shelf of trophies and medals hanging above her desk. Golden figurines of runners adorned the tops and faces of awards she'd won as the fastest sprinter on her middle and high school track teams. A year had passed since the accident, and her parents and doctors said it might be possible for her to compete again with the right training and therapy. But while they imagined her preparing for the Paralympics, or even being the next on the short list of amputees to run in the Olympics since Pistorius broke that glass ceiling twenty years before, Janae had already given her competitive streak a new outlet.

Relieved and itch-free, she fluffed her pillows and shifted into a more comfortable position. She closed her eyes and tapped the VRGameWatch™ latched around her wrist. The nanobots roosting in her nervous system responded to the watch's programming, drawing her into a vivid hallucination that stimulated each of her five senses, and she sank into a dazzling rainbow of light and color.

Moments later, her avatar, an athletic young woman with lavender hair and violet eyes, stood in an ancient forest of moss-cloaked trees. A curving sword hung in a scabbard at her hip, and she wore knives in sheaths strapped to her forearms and around her thigh.

Golden light filtered from above, shining warmly on the sea of giant ferns surrounding her. Her green tunic blended into the scenery, discouraging the casual observer from noticing her. A cool breeze stirred, carrying the sharp scent of decaying leaves and damp earth. She drew her hood over her bright hair and crouched, further concealing herself among the swaying fern fronds.

"Lady Janet?" asked a familiar voice, one that was young and male. A hint of a southern twang mingled with his slight Spanish lilt. "Are you here?"

After their last quest, Janae had promised to meet her long-time questing partner, Thomás, here in the Primeval Wood. Her heartbeat quickened with the thrill of his presence. Although their relationship existed solely in the Forest of Carterhaugh's virtual reality, few people felt as real to Janae as Thomás did. Reflexively, she pressed a hand over her racing heart. "TamLin," she answered, naming Thomás's avatar. "I'm here."

"Your location beacon's turned off. I can't see you."

Lady Janet stood and raised a hand overhead, waving until she caught TamLin's eye. Thomás's avatar was a tall, handsome knight with russet skin and dark hair hanging to his shoulders that shimmered like an ocean at night. When they quested together, he and Lady Janet made a striking pair.

"I scouted ahead already, and it looks like we're alone," Janae said.

"That's why I picked this spot. I wanted to talk to you in private."

"What about?"

"I think it's finally time to go after Queen Mab's treasure."

A thrill raced up Janae's spine, excitement tingling in her nerves. "What about the Wild Hunt next weekend? You sure you want to undertake two huge quests back to back?"

"We've been training for months, and we're as good now as we're ever going to get. At some point, we have to stop procrastinating and put practice into action."

Janae huffed. "I agree, but if Mab's treasure isn't just myth, where do we even start looking?"

"You know what the rumors say." TamLin stepped around Lady Janet and parted the nearest ferns, making a path through Primeval Wood.

She marched behind him and didn't ask where they were going—she suspected she already knew. "They say her court is somewhere beneath Bannau Brycheiniog in the Black Mountains, and the entrance must be close to Cribyn Peak, based on the number of guards and fortifications positioned there. But no one's ever survived long enough to verify if it's true."

TamLin's path brought them closer to the edge of the woods. He stopped in the shadow of a giant tree and peered at the green hills rolling out before them. A warm breeze stirred his hair, and Lady Janet's fingers twitched, reacting to Janae's subconscious urge to touch him. "That's what everyone else says," Thomás said. "But what do you say?"

Janae had spent months researching and investigating the FoC forums and chatrooms dedicated solely to discussing Queen Mab's supposed treasure, but no one could quite agree where it was, or even *what* it was. The most common theory was FoC's designers had created an extension to the game, and only those who found Mab's court and claimed her treasure would be granted access to the new world.

Janae, however, was skeptical. "I think that even if we could manage to defeat Mab's hoards and find an entrance into her court, there's a chance it's just a red herring — that the treasure doesn't even exist." She wasn't as interested in the treasure as she was in fighting the battle it would take to win it, but Thomás wouldn't understand that. For him, it was always about the prize. For her, playing FoC was about the blood-pumping, heart-racing adventure, and going after Mab's treasure would be the biggest thrill of all. "But what do *you* think, TamLin?"

"I, um..." Thomás must have given in to the urge to fidget because TamLin was shifting from foot to foot and rubbing the back of his neck. "I spent some time this weekend getting a backdoor look at Cribyn Peak's code. I couldn't decipher very much before I got kicked out, but the little bit I saw gave me reason to think it's not just rumors. There's really something there."

"'Backdoor look'?" Janae coughed a derisive sound in her throat. "You *hacked* in?"

"Just for a minute."

"You could be permanently banned for that." Janae's quailed at the thought of losing her only link to Thomás. For the last six months, he'd been urging her to connect with him outside the game, but she'd always demurred. No matter her feelings for him, she trusted very few people enough to let them into her real-world life.

It's safer that way, she thought. Experience had taught her that people could only hurt her if she let them get close. And, when she did, many reacted badly when confronted with her prosthetic leg and burn scars. If Thomás turned out to be one of those people, one of the ones who shunned her, she wasn't sure her heart could bear it.

Lady Janet brushed past TamLin, stepping out of the forest's shadows into the late-afternoon sunlight. A quick check of FoC's map revealed there was at least a twenty-mile march from Primeval Wood to the Black Mountains. The game's internal clock suggested they wouldn't get there before nightfall. Unless… "I've got a few gryphon feathers left from our Aerie Quest." Janae scrolled through her menu of stored magic items and, moments later, two glowing white feathers appeared in Lady Janet's fist. "If you're serious about this, then we'd better use them if you want to get to Cribyn Peak before the sun goes down."

"Of course I'm serious about this." TamLin snatched a feather and chanted an incantation code. Magic sparkles swirled around him, giving him the illusion of having grown a pair of wings. In an instant, Lady Janet had her own shimmering wings, and after a few false starts, the pair shot into the sky, soaring toward the dark mountain range in the distance.

"Race you," Janae said as Lady Janet surged into the lead. When it came to running, riding virtual horses, or flying, Janae didn't care which way they traveled as long as the wind was racing past her, tugging at her hair as her pulse pounded in her ears. "Last one to the Black Mountains has to hunt and cook our supper."

AS THE LAST rays of virtual sunlight sank behind the Black Mountains, TamLin and Lady Janet rested together in an open meadow at the base of Bannau Brycheiniog, a tall ridge covered in rocks and grass and not much else. They huddled close to their small campfire. Smoke stung her eyes, and the flavor of charred meat clung to her tongue as they feasted on *ciwiyar*, a chicken-like creature TamLin had been forced to catch and cook after losing their race.

"This quest could take a while," Thomás said. "After we revive our energy stores, you want to keep going?"

"Sure. I can stay up late. My parents are out having their date night."

"My mom's working second shift, so I figure we can keep going until midnight at least. Sound good to you?"

"Sounds great." Lady Janet stood, scattered the coals, and stamped out their fire. "Let's get moving."

TamLin rose beside her as she checked FoC's map and compass feature. Then she pointed south. "If we keep heading that way, following the base of this ridge, we should expect to run into some of the Queen's Knightmares in another half-mile or so."

"Looks like there's another questing band close by." TamLin pointed at several glowing beacons on his map. "They've already engaged with Mab's knights. You want to join them?"

Lady Janet drew her sword from its sheath. "You have to ask?"

After activating their enhanced night-vision spells, the two crept along the base of the mountain range. As predicted, they soon came upon the second questing team's camp, and whatever their numbers had been at the start of their adventure, now only two remained. Their avatars' life-force indicators were flashing, warning that they were in dire need of rest and food. "You'll never get past Mab's guard," said a tall, stocky character with green skin calling himself Little_John0902. His companion, a slim gray elf, lay silently by their small fire. "They're expert fighters, and they're flanked by a pack of Dire Wolves the size of horses. There were eight of us, and now you see what's left. You can't make a dent in them. It's hopeless."

Impatient to begin and eager to fight, Janae burned with excitement. Maybe she was often slow and ungainly in real life, but in the Forest of

Carterhaugh, she was a warrior goddess—fast, strong, and brutal. She also had a lot of pent-up anger to pour out on Mab's soldiers. They had no idea what was coming for them. "Maybe *you* can't make a dent in them." Lady Janet twirled her sword like a baton. "But I'm not ready to give up so easily."

The big green warrior faced her. "Lady Janet? I've heard of you. Heard you can fight."

"I can pretend to be humble about it if it makes you feel better."

He chuckled. "No, have at them, if you want. Just don't say I didn't warn you."

"Any tips?" Thomás asked as TamLin drew his own weapon, a long rapier that could bleed a man to death in a couple of quick jabs. Other than herself, Thomás was the best fighter Janae had come across in all her time on FoC, and there was no one else she'd rather have at her side when facing Mab's soldiers.

"Run," Little John said. "But if you aren't willing to take that advice, then devastation spells were the only thing that slowed them down, but you can't throw them fast enough to keep up with their swords and teeth." He chuckled sadly. "The two of you won't last a minute."

That's where he's wrong, Janae thought. *I might be the best hand-to-hand fighter, but no one casts faster than Thomás.* She suspected his ability with spells had something to do with his ability to hack computer code, but she'd never asked him because she didn't really want to know. More than a few gamers used black market cheat codes to improve performance. Janae had earned her abilities and weapons through hard work, determination, and skill, and she was proud of it, but if Thomás had enhanced TamLin with the equivalent of computerized steroids, she wasn't going look the proverbial gift horse in the mouth.

"Well, if we die, we'll come find you, and you can say you told us so." But Janae didn't plan on dying. Not today, anyway. Lady Janet touched her forehead in a salute and marched away, heading into the darkness beyond Little John's camp, and TamLin followed her.

"Maybe we should wait and see if we can form a bigger band," Thomás said.

"Getting cold feet? You knew how fortified this area was before you suggested we go on this mission."

"It's starting to feel a little suicidal."

"So, if we die, we come back later with reinforcements."

"It could take us weeks to recover and recruit a team, and we've got the Wild Hunt coming up soon."

Lady Janet paused. "This was *your* idea, remember? If you don't want to do this, say so. Otherwise, get your best spells and weapons ready because I'm not going down without giving it everything I've got."

TamLin squeezed Lady Janet's shoulder, and Janae reveled in his touch, even if it was merely an effect from nanobots engaging with her nervous system. Players often patted each other's backs, shook hands, and hugged on occasion, but TamLin's touch was something special. She wondered if Thomás felt the same thrill when Lady Janet touched *him*.

"You're not normally quite this bloodthirsty, Lady Janet. Something happen in real life you want to talk about?"

An image of Janae's high school's interior, decorated for homecoming, flashed through her mind. Managing her school's less-than-ADA-accessible facilities was enough challenge on a regular day, but the homecoming committee seemed to have gone out of its way to block ramps, twine streamers around handrails that made it impossible to get a good grip, and cover the floors in unbelievably slippery glitter and confetti.

"It's been a hard day," Janae said, thinking of the way her back had been cramping when she'd gotten home from school. Her nanobots helped with the worst of it, but the ghosts of her injuries often haunted her. The Forest of Carterhaugh was the one place she could truly escape them. "I've got some stress I need to work off."

"We won't defeat this army if we're reckless and angry. We've got to be calm and methodical. Just like we've been practicing."

Lady Janet pulled away from TamLin's touch. "You don't have to tell me. We know what we're doing."

Thomás said nothing else, and TamLin silently followed Lady Janet as she crept closer to the last known location of Queen Mab's Knightmares. Cribyn Peak was a tall, jutting mountain with a sheer face covered in grass and exposed rock. The surrounding hills were equally open — no trees or brush. Only the darkness concealed them, but Mab's soldiers, as well as most of her monsters and beasts, could see better at night than Lady Janet and TamLin could see in the day. There would be no sneaking up, and so, with every step forward, Janae's pulse beat quicker, her breath came shorter and sharper. The taste of adrenaline was bitter on her tongue.

"*Ah-roo!*" A brief, sharp howl announced the Knightmares' presence an instant before Mab's ghoulish soldiers fell on Lady Janet and TamLin. Lady Janet ducked and scampered aside as a sword swung toward her, reflecting pale light from the sliver of moon hanging in the sky. She swiped her own sword and caught her attacker across his neck, drawing blood.

"TamLin!" She shouted a warning, as if he could have missed the Dire Wolf's eerie howl.

A bright flash of green — evidence of a decimation spell — was his only reply, and the light from his magic cast their enemies in a macabre glow. As fast as he could flick his fingers, green streaks flew into the enemy hoard — a collection of tall, humanoid figures with pointed ears, sharp fangs, stringy hair, and hollow eyes full of darkness. On the heels of Mab's Knightmares came the Dire Wolves, indeed as big as draft horses with paws the size of dinner plates and teeth like knives.

"Like we practiced," Thomás shouted.

"I *know*." Lady Janet and her sword danced a lethal *pas de deux*. Sweat broke out on the back of her neck, and her pulse pounded in her ears. Enemies dropped at her feet, but not without inflicting their own damage in return. Blood dripped from a cut on Lady Janet's biceps, a deep slash over her rib, and a gash on her thigh, but adrenaline dulled her pain, and her energy stores remained more than halfway full, thanks to the restorative spells she'd been hoarding for an occasion such as this.

The hurts she suffered in the FoC felt as tangible as they would have in the real world, but in this realm, she was the master of her pain, and she didn't avoid it. In fact, she welcomed it. Unlike the car wreck that had twisted her back and taken her leg — an event of chance and chaos beyond her control — each of Lady Janet's wounds were ones she'd fought for and earned.

At her side, TamLin was fairing similarly. He'd incurred his own injuries — the front of his tunic was stained dark with blood — but his spells still flew fast and hard.

We're winning, Janae thought. *We might actually beat them.*

A quick assessment revealed that only three Knightmares and two Dire Wolves remained. If she and Thomás were careful, and if she rationed the last of her restorative spells, it was quite possible they'd make it through this battle alive. Lady Janet twirled, throwing a knife. The blade sliced through the air and buried itself to the hilt in a Knightmare's throat. Mab's warrior dropped to his knees, snarling. Then he fell to the ground, dead and silent.

Not bothering to retrieve her weapon, she drew out another knife and turned to swipe her sword at a leaping wolf. TamLin threw a devastation spell, cloaking the wolf in green light, and Lady Janet's sword cut through the beast's thick hide like a hot knife through butter. It shrieked a horrible noise that made Janae cringe and smile at the same time. Their months of practice were paying off. She and Thomás worked less like a team and more like a unified being sharing a single mind and heart.

"Only one wolf left!" Thomás crowed.

"Don't count your chickens yet." Lady Janet ducked beneath a punch and twisted in time to evade most of her opponent's sword strike, but his blade bit deeply enough to draw blood. Lady Janet hissed, and her energy indicator flashed, changing from vital green to a warning yellow. "There're a few eggs here that still haven't hatched."

Back to back, Lady Janet and TamLin raised their weapons, ready to address the remaining warriors, but the blast of a horn rang out, sharp enough to make her ears ring. She yelped and slapped her free hand over her ear. "What the hell was that?"

"Look!" TamLin pointed at an approaching light that was brighter than any normal lantern or fey spell. The steady beat of horse hooves advanced, and the two remaining Knightmares drew back from the fight. The Dire Wolf sat on his haunches like a dog awaiting his master's orders.

"What is it? *Who* is it?"

"It's..." Thomás answered, breathless. "Oh, God, it's Mab!"

A white horse galloped onto the scene, and on its back sat a regal woman in a blue gown, her white hair streaming like a flag. A twisted, thorny crown rested on her head, and her face was neither young nor old, but it could have been carved from ice for all its lack of warmth and color. A massive fey lantern matched her pace, following overhead, casting light to rival the sun.

Janae had seen Queen Mab the previous year at the Forest of Carterhaugh's annual Wild Hunt when top players had been invited to join Mab on a mythological quest for a giant, white boar. Without an invitation, Janae had only been allowed to attend as a spectator, but she'd vowed to do whatever it took to earn an invitation to the next Hunt.

When she had, in fact, received that invitation, she'd thought nothing could thrill her more.

Until now.

With awe, Janae watched the scene unfolding before her. *This is totally unreal*, she thought. *I've never heard of Mab approaching anyone like this.*

Mab reined her huge, white horse to a stop, its hooves dancing as if the creature were too impatient to fully heed her command, and two more mounted guards trotted up behind her. The riders resembled the Knightmares, but were healthier and less haunted. Their white hair shimmered, and their eyes shone a deep, cornflower blue. "*Trespassers*," Mab bellowed, her voice strong and deep. "How dare you invade my lands and attack my soldiers?"

"They attacked us first," Janae said, her tone full of wonder. She had no idea what to expect. Would she have to fight Mab? How awesome would that be? "We were only protecting ourselves."

"It's the duty of my knights to defend my lands against invaders. You should have never come here, and now you'll pay for your impertinence." Mab raised a pale white hand and pointed at Lady Janet and TamLin. "Take the boy. Kill the girl."

"What?" Janae shouted, suddenly outraged. "No way."

As the remaining Knightmares raised their weapons, TamLin threw another spell, but the magic's green light died before leaving his outstretched hand. "What — ?" he asked, obviously mystified.

The two riders who had come with Mab dismounted at the same moment that the remaining Dire Wolf lunged for Lady Janet. The last two Knightmares surrounded her, but TamLin remained motionless and silent as Mab's personal guards approached him.

"TamLin!" Lady Janet reached for him but had to stop and parry a jab from a Knightmare's sword. "Fight her, TamLin. *Fight.*"

But it was no use. Mab might as well have been a gorgon who'd turned

TamLin to stone, leaving Lady Janet to battle a pair of warriors and a giant wolf on her own. Janae watched in horror as Mab's guards bound and gagged TamLin and threw him across the back of one horse. Still, Janae fought, but without Thomás's assistance, she was quickly overwhelmed and unable to pause long enough to chant a revival spell. "Thomás," Janae yelled, calling the real-world name they'd agreed to never use during a quest. "What's going on? Why won't you say anything?"

But Thomás didn't answer, and the only sounds were the clang of weapons and the grunts and growls of Mab's ghastly warriors as they attacked.

The Dire Wolf's claws ripped and tore.

The Knightmares' swords slashed and cut.

Lady Janet screamed and fought until blood saturated her tunic and her life-force indicator flashed an angry red. Her wounds shrieked a cacophony of high-pitched, dissonant notes inside her head. Her vision turned foggy and gray.

What the hell just happened? she wondered. But no one gave her an answer, and the last thing she saw before her world faded to black was Mab and her soldiers riding away, carrying TamLin with them.

JANAE SAT AT her regular lunch table, chin resting in her hand. She poked at the greasy pizza on her plate, but the thought of actually eating it turned her stomach sour.

"You've been like this all morning," Tara said, dipping a french fry into a pool of ketchup. "I mean, you're always quiet, but it's worse than usual. Tell me what's been going on."

Janae glanced at her friend, one of a handful who hadn't been daunted by Janae's scars or shiny, electronic leg. Tara's long braids reached down her back, their ends tipped in gold beads that clacked when she moved. When she ran, her hair streamed behind her like a sparkling mane that Janae couldn't help but envy. She knew the track coach had repeatedly asked Tara to trim her hair into something more aerodynamic, but Tara had refused.

Janae admired her stubbornness. That same obstinacy was likely the reason Tara was still her friend when so many others had disappeared after the accident. Whatever the reason, Janae was glad to have Tara's steady presence, although she doubted Tara could understand her obsession with Forest of Carterhaugh or her despair over losing her connection with Thomás. "I'd tell you," Janae said, "but you'll think I'm crazy."

Tara tapped the table with a glossy red fingernail. "Try me."

"So..." Janae hesitated. The misery of losing Thomás felt like an elephant sitting on her chest, suffocating her. But if sharing the burden with Tara could relieve that weight, why not try? "You know that online game called Forest of Carterhaugh?"

"The one you're totally obsessed with?" Tara rolled her eyes. "It's the reason I can't get you to ever go out with me."

A hot flush rose in Janae's cheeks. "Well, I've been playing it for a long time with this one guy—"

"A guy?" Tara's brown eyes flashed, and she leaned in, grinning. "Tell me more."

As best as she could, Janae summarized the past year of playing FoC with Thomás. She explained how quickly they'd connected and what an unbeatable team they made, but how she was still reluctant to share personal details with him, which had led them to completely lose touch after Queen Mab's kidnapping.

Tara raised a skeptical eyebrow. "You've never talked face to face?"

Refusing to meet Tara's eyes, Janae picked at her cuticles and shook her head.

"Why not?"

Janae motioned to her scars, her leg. "You *know* why."

"Not everyone's like Jacob, you know."

Janae's stomach turned over at the mention of the high school's star cross country runner and her former boyfriend—a boyfriend who'd visited her once in the hospital before quietly drifting away, never returning her calls or texts and avoiding her in the hallways after she'd returned to school. Even now Jacob sat only a few tables away, and he never once glanced at her, not even by accident. His purposeful disregard hurt more than the steady ache in her joints and muscles.

Tara clicked her tongue. "Do you think you'll ever give Thomás a chance?"

"I want to, but..." Janae shrugged, and Tara didn't press, even though Janae could sense that her friend was dying to tell her to stop being so pitiful. Or maybe that was her own subconscious talking.

"Can't you, like, just message him in one of the chat rooms or something?"

"I've done that. I've asked anyone who might have known him, but no one's heard from him. If Queen Mab had killed his character, he would've shown up again by now, even if it was in a less powerful form, but it's been two days, and there's been no word. I think..." Janae glanced at her cold pizza and scowled. The grease had congealed into gross orange globs. She shoved her plate away. "I think he's being held by Mab. Like, imprisoned, but that's never happened in this game before. Ever."

"Well, from the sound of it, no one's come that close to beating the bad guys like you and Thomás did. Maybe this is a new part of the game? Maybe you're *supposed* to rescue him."

"I've considered it, but I'm not sure it's something I can do on my own." Thomás had invited her to join his questing party the first time she'd entered the Forest of Carterhaugh, and they'd been inseparable ever since. A chill of panic shivered down Janae's spine. "I've never played without him. I'm afraid the Powers That Be at FoC might have deactivated his account for cheating." A lump of unshed tears lodged in her throat. "What if I never find him again?"

Tara leaned close and squeezed Janae's arm. "Don't think like that. The world is a small place, thanks to the internet. One way or another you'll find him. I'll help you if you want."

Janae rubbed her eyes and shook her head. Finding him in the real world meant opening herself up to the possibility of his rejection, and that wasn't something she couldn't risk. Not yet. "We've got a massive, multi-player hunt coming up this weekend. Thomás wouldn't miss it for anything. If there's any way for him to reach out to me, he'll find it."

JANAE SPENT ANOTHER day fruitlessly searching for Thomás online, and by Wednesday morning, her anxiety had skyrocketed. She was so desperate that she was seriously considering accepting Tara's offer to help, even if it meant revealing herself to Thomás—scars and all. But when she entered the FoC after school Wednesday, a notification flashed in her peripheral vision, telling her Little_John0902 wanted her to meet him in Primeval Wood.

Like a racehorse straining at the starting line, her heart surged. Surely, Little John had news about Thomás. Everyone in the FoC forums knew she was looking for him, but only Thomás knew Primeval Wood was their regular meeting spot. Because the last place she'd seen Thomás's avatar was at the base of Cribyn Peak, she'd been reluctant to stray far from that area in case she stumbled upon a clue that might lead her to him, but the message from Little John was the first lead she'd had in days, and she wasn't going to ignore it.

Quickly, Janae scrolled through Lady Janet's collection of magic items, found another gryphon feather, and launched into the sky. When she dropped down at the outskirts of Primeval Wood, she traded her wings for her sword. She hadn't advanced this far in the game without anticipating attacks and traps around every corner. Maybe Little John's message was legitimate. Or maybe it was another of Queen Mab's tricks. Janae took nothing for granted.

When Lady Janet strode farther into the woods, Little John's deep voice echoed among the trees. "Lady Janet. I'm glad you came. I have a message for you."

"From TamLin?" She strolled father into the shadows and spotted Little John's hulking green figure standing among the delicate fern fronds. The contrast was startling, and Janae smothered a snicker as a butterfly landed on his big, burly shoulder.

"How is it that two legendary teammates have never established a way to connect outside the game?" he asked.

"It's complicated."

"I'll bet."

Annoyed, Lady Janet rolled her eyes. "Well, what did he say?"

"He said Queen Mab has made him into one of her personal guards. His account is locked, his nanos have been infected with a tracking virus that crashes any attempts he makes to communicate with FoC players, and the only missions and quests he's allowed to undertake are to fulfill Mab's commands."

"Who *is* Mab?" Locking accounts and infecting Thomás's nanos with a virus indicated serious control and power. "Is she some kind of FoC administrator?"

Little John held his big green hands out at his sides. "Most people think she's just a bot. Maybe she's something else, but either way, this is the most exciting thing to happen in the four years I've been playing FoC."

"How did TamLin get in touch with you?"

"He reached out to someone in real life and sent a message through a friend of a friend."

"Did he have any suggestions about how I might rescue him?"

Little John shook his head. "He said only that Mab will be leading the Wild Hunt this weekend, and he'd be expected to ride with her. He said you won't recognize him, but he'll be the guardsman riding a white horse. If there's any hope of getting him back, the Wild Hunt will be your chance."

"Did you get an invitation to join the hunt?"

Little John rolled his eyes. "Of course. I wouldn't miss it, and whatever's going to happen with you and TamLin, for anything."

Janae scrolled through her peripheral menu, preparing to exit, but Little John jerked up his hand, urging her to stop. "I forgot. TamLin said one more thing." He cleared his throat. "'Whatever happens, don't let go and don't give up.'"

Don't let go and don't give up. Janae snorted, thinking Thomás should have known her better than that by now. "Don't tell anyone else what he said, Little John. This has to be kept secret. If Mab knows he got a message to me, I might lose him for good."

The big green warrior nodded. "I won't tell a soul. I swear."

ON THE MORNING of the Wild Hunt, Janae woke up early. She couldn't get thoughts of Thomás out of her head. Throughout the night, dreams of Queen Mab and her Knightmares had haunted her. Rescuing TamLin seemed as impossible as finding Mab's treasure had been, and she still wasn't sure the treasure was a real thing. Would rescuing TamLin be just as much of a fantasy?

After Janae climbed out of bed, she took a long, hot shower, urging the tense and twisted muscles in her back to relax. After dressing and fastening her leg into place, she joined her mom at the kitchen table for a cup of coffee and a plate of eggs and toast.

Janae's mom glanced up from her tablet, her gaze locking on Janae as she scraped strawberry jam across her toast. "Today's a big day, huh?"

"It's the Wild Hunt. The biggest massive-player quest of the year." Janae bit into her toast and savored the jam's sweetness. "By invitation only."

"This game's really important to you, isn't it?"

"It's not just the game." Janae forked up a pile of eggs and considered telling her mom about Thomás and her fears of losing him, as well as her fears of what it would take to find him again, namely, stepping out from behind Lady Janet's unblemished façade. "In the Forest of Carterhaugh, I'm anyone I want to be, and there're no limits on what I can do." Unconsciously, she stroked the long scar curving from the corner of her eye to her jaw. "I have friends there, too—good ones who only judge me on what I can do instead of how I look."

Janae's mom stood and went to the coffee pot to refill her mug. "Believe it or not, I understand. Those games are so lifelike, it's easy to get lost in them. Easy to escape the real world. I can understand why that would be attractive to you."

Janae said nothing but bit off another piece of toast. After the car wreck, her mom had been the one who'd bought Janae her first VRGameWatch™. Her mom had been the one who'd introduced Janae to the Forest of Carterhaugh so she'd have a place to escape to during the endless hours of surgery and recovery. Even after they'd left the hospitals and rehab centers behind, her mom had never pushed Janae to undertake anything that made her uncomfortable.

Her mom crouched and wrapped her arm around Janae's shoulder, giving her a sideways hug. "But anytime you want to explore other interests, or if you want to reach out to people in real life, I'm here to help. Just let me know, okay?"

After helping her mom clean up the breakfast dishes, Janae retreated to her room and spent some time reflecting on the imposing task before her. A month ago, when she'd received her invitation to join the Wild Hunt, she'd been able to think of nothing better than the thrill of stalking the white boar, but now, so much more was at stake. If she hoped to ever have her questing partner at her side again, she was going to have to figure out a way to save him from Mab, and she didn't know if that was even a possibility. Maybe, if she interfered, Mab would turn her into a slave, too. She'd never questioned whether Thomás was worth that risk, though.

When she finally felt ready, Janae arranged herself into a comfortable position on her bed. She closed her eyes and tapped her game watch's face. After she'd entered the portal, the game spat her out in Cheapstow, a quaint village of thatch huts standing along the banks of a winding river called Wye. Cheapstow was the default location to which all gamers were sent the first time they entered the game. It was also FoC's unofficial headquarters and the place where all gamers gathered at the beginning of the Wild Hunt, whether they were participants or simply observers.

Janae searched Cheapstow's map, found Little John's beacon, and threaded her way through the crowds milling in the market square. She found him standing at the north side of the town's central fountain, and a broad smile spread across his green face when he spotted her. "Lady Janet. I was starting to worry."

She smiled back. "You thought I wouldn't show?"

"You sure waited until the last minute."

She didn't tell him that the longer she had to stand around waiting for Queen Mab's arrival, the more her anxiety would increase, and this was not the time for doubts and second-guessing. Lady Janet motioned for Little John to follow as she jostled her way past crowds of elves, goblins, pixies, and other fantastical beings. On the outskirts of town, beside the river, Queen Mab's workers had erected a platform on which all members of the Wild Hunt were to gather and await her arrival.

As Lady Janet passed through town, several spectators recognized her and wished her good luck. Janae had thoroughly scanned FoC's forums and chatrooms the previous night, and no one seemed to suspect she had ulterior motives for participating in the hunt. It appeared that Little John had kept his vow of silence on the matter, as promised. *If only people in the real world could be as trustworthy as people in the virtual one,* she thought.

Lady Janet and Little John left behind the crowds of Cheapstow and followed the riverbank to a meadow bedecked in festive trimmings — blue flags and pennants bearing Queen Mab's crest and silhouettes of the great white boar. Members of a little band had gathered beneath a willow to play their fife, fiddle, and concertina in celebratory cadences. Lady Janet and Little John climbed the steps to the hunting party's platform and greeted their fellow players.

Despite her efforts to remain calm, Janae's pulse thundered in her ears. Her palms sweated so profusely, she worried the dampness might interfere with her sword grip. She closed her eyes and swiped her sleeve across her brow. *Stay cool,* she thought. *Thomás is depending on you.*

A blast of horns ripped through the air, drowning out the little band's inane festival music. Janae grimaced at the ringing in her ears, but she glued her eyes to the road, searching for a glimpse of the royal parade. As anticipated, the queen appeared, riding astride her great white horse at an ambling pace. Mab was followed by standard bearers and her personal guardsmen, who rode single file and looked indistinguishable except for their horses, which were black, brown, and white, respectively.

The white horse, Janae thought, her gaze locked on the last rider in the procession. Thomás had said TamLin would be riding a white horse. If not for that message, she'd never have guessed it was him. Gone was his russet skin and ebony hair. Now he was pale like the queen, his hair corn-silk white and his eyes light blue.

Her heart rose into her throat and beat a rapid pace full of fear and panic. *Now what am I supposed to do?*

Queen Mab halted her procession before the hunting party's platform and raised her hand. Everyone fell silent, and the river's quiet roar behind them was the only sound. Janae knew Mab would give a standard speech about tradition and sportsmanship. She would announce the rules of the Hunt and list the prizes for the winner. Janae barely heard the queen as she spoke. Instead, her senses were focused wholly on the TamLin changeling. She willed him to look at her, give her a sign, an indication that it was really him behind the pale façade, but his gaze remained detached and distant, almost haughty.

Mab's horns trumpeted again, catching Janae off guard. She grimaced and gritted her teeth.

"Fall in, hunters," shouted one of the standard bearers, and the hunting party surged to exit the platform. The group lined up along the side of the road to watch Queen Mab's procession pass, and Lady Janet squeezed into a spot at Little John's side. Queen Mab flicked her reins and shoved her heel against her horse's haunch. The steed trotted forward, and Mab's icy eyes roamed over the faces of the hunting party as she rode by. When her gaze reached Lady Janet, her eyes seemed to harden, and she flashed her teeth, revealing the same sharp fangs all members of her court bore, but Janae refused to flinch.

Whether Mab was a complex bot, or a live person playing her role from somewhere within the Forest of Carterhaugh's corporate offices, her animosity felt as real to Janae as the hostility in the looks of the people in real life who saw her scars and prosthetic leg and thought her something *less-than* because of it. In the real world, such a look might have cowed Janae, but in the Forest of Carterhaugh, she was not so easily intimidated. She growled, not caring if the queen could hear her. Her fear was gone, replaced by eagerness, ferocity, and anger. "I'm not afraid of you, Mab, and when I get TamLin back, we're coming for you and your treasure."

With those words, Janae put the queen out of her mind and focused again on TamLin, bringing up the procession's rear. Finally, his cold, blue eyes met hers, and she thought she saw a glimmer of hope in them. Little John grabbed Lady Janet's elbow and squeezed, and his grip reminded Janae of the message he'd passed her from Thomás. *Whatever happens, don't let go and don't give up.*

Don't let go...

Acting on instinct, Janae lunged, grabbing TamLin's ankle and knee. Before he could brace himself, she yanked, upsetting his balance. Realizing her intention, Little John joined her, and together they pulled TamLin from his saddle.

He collapsed to the ground, and Lady Janet tackled him, twining her arms around him while thinking fervent thoughts about leeches and octopuses and superglue. "I won't let go, TamLin," she said. "No matter what happens, I won't let go. I won't give up."

TamLin bucked like an angry bull. He roared. As everyone watched, his bright hair melted from his scalp. His skin turned hard with scales, and he grew a tail. As a lizard, he writhed, and his strength was almost too much for her. Her muscles strained and trembled. Her life-force indicator flashed in warning from the effort of holding on as he twisted again, losing his claws and legs, trading them for a rattling tail, poisonous fangs and a flat, diamond-shaped head.

She held him fast, refusing to be afraid, and when she didn't let go, he shifted again, sprouting coarse brown hair. When he was a grizzly bear twice her size, he tore at her back with claws as big as the knives strapped to her thighs. Pain flashed through her in a bolt of searing lightning. She screamed, and her life-force indicator flashed yellow, warning that her energy was draining away.

He transformed into a lion and bit her shoulder with fangs like sabers. White stars exploded across her vision as agony burned in her bones. With a broken, weak voice, she chanted revival spells as blood flowed down her back. Her energy reserves drained lower, but she held TamLin close and ignored the urge to panic.

She'd endured tortures worse than this before.

She'd battled pain countless times and won.

She'd win this time, too, because she was fighting for more than herself.

TamLin's mane and fur fell off in clumps, revealing a glowing, hot coal beneath. To hold him was to burn, but Janae gritted her teeth and chanted another restorative spell as flames rose around her. Her own screams rang in her ears, and each of her heartbeats sent a new pulse of agony storming through her body.

If she released him now, she suspected she'd never find her partner in the Forest of Carterhaugh again, not even as Queen Mab's slave, and the thought of losing him hurt worse than any broken bone, bruise, or burn. Maybe she could work up the courage to find Thomás in real life, but their relationship would never be the same in a world where her twisted back made her slow and ungainly on her prosthetic leg. The scars near her eye made her sometimes weep for no reason. She was no warrior goddess. She was only Janae, and she didn't know if that would be good enough for Thomás. *But maybe it's finally time to find out...*

"The river," Little John yelled. "Get him in the river!"

With her jaw set and brow furrowed, Janae swallowed her pain—a skill she'd spent the last year perfecting—and eyed the route she would take. Then she flung herself into a powerful roll. Over and over, she and TamLin tumbled down the riverbank. His flames had burned through her tunic, blistering her skin. Her life-force indicator flashed red on its last bar, and the edges of her vision turned fuzzy and dark, but she held on as she plummeted into the river, taking TamLin with her.

After chanting her last remaining restorative spell, Lady Janet stayed conscious long enough to watch the river douse their fire. Thomás's avatar traded flames for skin—warm, russet skin and dark hair that shimmered like an ocean at night—and he held her in his arms. The last thing Janae heard before Lady Janet's life-force drained away was Thomás's familiar voice in her ear.

"You did it, Lady Janet. I knew you'd save me."

JANAE'S FINGER HOVERED over the answer icon on her video-chat screen. Thomás was on the other end, waiting to talk with her face to face. It was late, and she was tired. Her back muscles were cramped, and her eye was weeping, but she'd been dying to talk to him after their last encounter in FoC. Instead of agreeing to meet her in Primeval Wood, as usual, he'd insisted on a live video chat, and she knew she had no good reason to refuse him. Besides, she was tired of the walls she'd put up to protect herself. She'd fought hard to earn his trust, and perhaps he deserved some of hers in return.

She wiped her eye, plastered a smile on her face, and answered the call. "Hi, Thomás."

The young man smiling at her from her screen was not so different from his avatar—a little younger and rounder perhaps. His bottom teeth were slightly crooked, but his skin was a lovely shade of brown with gold undertones, and he wore his dark hair short and messy. When he saw her, he didn't recoil or flinch. She held her breath as his gaze roamed her face, taking in her green eyes and freckles, but when he didn't linger on her scars or give any sign of disappointment, she breathed a sigh of relief.

"It's nice to finally see the real you." His voice was familiar, even if his face wasn't, and his broad smile was genuine enough to put her at ease.

"I wasn't sure," Janae said, "even after everything that happened, if Mab was going to let you go."

"I wasn't sure either, but after Lady Janet died and you disconnected from the game, Mab just gave me a vicious smile" — Thomás bared his teeth like a snarling animal — "and then she acted like I'd never existed. I think, to her, it was all just part of the game — just another quest for us to win or lose. I disconnected and got out of there before she changed her mind." His smile dropped. "I'm sorry for what you had to go through to save me, though. I never thought it would be that horrible." He swallowed, but his voice was shaky when he said, "I knew I was hurting you, but there was nothing I could do to stop — "

"Don't apologize." She waved her hand, dismissing his confession. "I would do it again if I had to."

He looked at her through his dark, long lashes, and her heart melted for him. "That's why you're the best player in the FoC."

"But what if I hadn't been?"

"Then Mab would have deleted my account for good, and I would've been permanently banned."

"So, is she a bot, or is she just a FoC employee?"

"From what I could tell, she's the closest thing to an AI I've ever encountered. Inside the game, she's omnipotent and omniscient. It's freaky. I never want to be her slave again."

"So... no more chasing Mab's treasure?"

Thomás chuckled, and the sound of it fizzed in Janae's veins like warm soda bubbles. "I didn't say *that*, exactly. But next time, I play it straight. No more hacking. And maybe we could put together an elite team. I bet Little John would be up for it."

"I don't know. After taking down the white boar and winning the grand prize, he doesn't need *more* treasure."

"I think you should still ask him." His gaze dropped and his voice turned quiet and hesitant. "You two made a good team without me."

Janae's breath caught. "There's no team without *you*, Thomás."

He leaned closer to his camera. His brows drew together, and his expression turned earnest. "Maybe, if Mab *had* deleted my account, I could've gotten new nanos and a new game watch and started over again. I might've gotten away with it as long as I stayed away from you. But, the problem is... I don't want to play FoC if I can't play it with you, Janae."

The sound of her true name on his lips, his *real* lips, shot through her, a bullet of pleasure and delight. Her heart swelled in her chest, beating like a big, bass drum. "You... You really mean that?"

"Of course." The fierceness of his smile stole her breath.

"Then let's message Little John and form a team. I promised Queen Mab we were going to take her down—that we would get her treasure."

"So, when do you want to start?"

Janae sat back against her headboard, folded her arms over her chest, and cocked a wry, self-confident grin. "What are you doing tomorrow?"

LADY JANET ARRIVED in Primeval Wood a few minutes early to search for an opening in the tree canopy. She explored until she found a spot where no shadows concealed her, a place where sunlight illuminated the formidable scar curving from the corner of her eye and gleamed on the polished brass of her new leg, a contraption of gears and pulleys that matched the game's aesthetics while looking as badass as she felt.

When dry leaves rustled behind her, announcing the approach of her questing companions, she turned to face TamLin and Little John, who greeted her with matching wide-eyed expressions of awe and surprise. Wearing a tentative smile, she twirled around, letting them look their fill. If they asked about the changes, she was prepared to tell them the truth, that she didn't want to hide anymore. Instead of asking, TamLin merely grinned and waggled his eyebrows. "You ready for this, Lady Janet?"

Nodding, she strode forward, her friends falling into step beside her. No doubts, no hesitation, no second guesses—together they made a daunting trio, the best three players in the Forest of Carterhaugh, intent on accomplishing a unified goal. Lady Janet patted the sword at her side and flashed a fierce smile. "Queen Mab will never know what hit her."

a retelling of The Pied Piper

THE PITILESS PRISONER OF HAMELIN

Mark C. King

The torchlight that flickered in from outside the cell door was aided only a little from a small barred window high on the wall, but it was enough. I could make out the dirt floor, littered with straw, the thick stone wall, and, most importantly, the man—the criminal—seated across from me. For his part, he looked rather calm, especially considering his crime and his likely future.

I wished I could say that I was calm, but I was anything but. The initial excitement I had at receiving the assignment had vanished days ago, and rather quickly; and I was left with feelings ranging from general doubt to utter inadequacy mixed with not a small amount of fear. As a seventeen-year-old law clerk, it was almost unheard of for someone of my age and position to be asked to represent any criminal, much less someone with the notoriety of the man I was assigned to. News of his alleged crime had spread quickly throughout the country, although I didn't hear of it until after I had accepted the assignment — not that it would have made much of a difference. When you are new to a firm, and trying to make an impression, you said *yes* to whatever they asked.

Still, I must admit that when my uncle — the head of the firm — offered me the assignment, I felt conflicted. To be sent out to another city, to represent a criminal, sounded perfectly exciting. But I was afraid that this would be viewed by my peers as evidence of favored treatment. I had never noticed any special kindnesses from my uncle, not with regards to business, so the assignment seemed quite out of character. Begging his pardon, I made my concern known. He appreciated my caution, but assured me that he was doing me no favors with his offer. It didn't take long before I realized that he was right. To stand next to the criminal, to represent him, with what he was accused of, was not something anyone would envy. It is, in fact, the reason it was handed to a lowly clerk: no one else would do it.

Now, I was sitting in the dark cell with my assignment at arm's length. I'm not sure I had ever felt so young or so unprepared in my life. After trying to recall the advice my uncle had given me, I started my interview with the prisoner. With a little waver in my voice, I asked, "What is your name?"

"My name?" the criminal responded, some surprise in his voice. "That's of no real importance, now is it? What do the people call me?"

I was hesitant to reply with the nickname that had been widely spoken, but eventually answered, "They have taken to calling you the Pied Piper."

"Ha!" he said enthusiastically. "I imagine they call me much worse in private."

Did he actually find this amusing? "If what you're accused of is true, can you blame them?"

A thin smile crept over the man's dirty face; not from happiness, but from some sort of sick amusement. "A little."

"Really?" I was surprised. After what he allegedly had done, I don't know how he could blame anyone for any thought against him. *Unless...*

I asked, "Are you saying that you are innocent?"

Shaking his head, he answered, "No, not at all. In fact, I anticipate that the trial will be short, for I'm an unmitigated monster. Never has this filthy, dank cell held someone as guilty or remorseless as I. And I promise you this: There'll be no begging for my life, nor any pleas for mercy. I don't deserve them, and don't want them. It's time for my tale to end."

Those words surprised me even more than his previous ones, as they amounted to an admission of his crime. I'd never heard of a prisoner being so forthright—not with his own guilt. But now I was confused. "If you're as guilty as you say, then why do you blame the people for the awful things they say about you?"

He leaned forward a little and, with menace, said, "Because they're implying that they are without guilt. They may call me whatever vile names they can conjure, but they *cannot* ignore that they had a wicked part to play. I'm guilty, but they're not innocent."

I tilted my head in confusion at his response as he leaned back and smiled. What did he mean by 'they're not innocent'? Of course, that was why I was there—to find out the prisoner's version of the account.

In addition to his words, there were several other things about him that I hadn't anticipated. Although he'd been in his cell for a little more than a week—his hair oily and unkempt, his thin beard unruly, and his skin bruised—the vivid colors of his tunic still showed signs of their original brightness. Yes, it was dirty, torn, and had what looked like blood stains, but the overall appearance was celebratory. The happy colors were as out of place, in that dark hole, as pearls on a pig.

His attire, however, was not the most shocking thing that I found about the criminal. As I'd traveled to Hamelin to see him — a three day's ride — I'd had plenty of time to consider the facts of the crime as they had been presented to me. I ultimately came to the assumption that this notorious prisoner that the people had taken to calling "the Pied Piper" was an absolute lunatic, a heartless monster. How could he not be in order to do what he'd done? But as I examined the man that sat across from me and listened as he answered my questions, he showed no overt signs of madness. If he was, in fact, a sane man, then his crime was hard to fathom.

I tried to brush aside those thoughts as they were not helping my confidence. I swallowed, with what little saliva I had, and continued, "Do you know why I'm here?"

"Yes. You're here to represent me to those who will be responsible to judge my case. Though why they sent you, I can't imagine. You're just a boy."

I nodded, ignoring his comment about my age. I refused to let him know that I was just a clerk. "My name is Herr Steinhauser and I have traveled all the way from Hamburg."

The prisoner chuffed. "An absolute waste of your time, I'm afraid."

"Be that as it may, protocol is to be followed. Do you know why they sent me, a complete stranger, such a distance to Hamelin?"

He shook his head indicating that he did not know — or did not care.

Wanting to understand this criminal, I watched his face closely as I said my next words. "They sent me because no one here would represent you. Not a single person in the entire town, or towns hereabout, could stand the thought of being at your side. What do you think of that?"

His grim smile returned and he simply said, "Good. I wouldn't bear them anyway."

In the few minutes I had been with the prisoner, his distaste for the townsfolk had come across very clearly. Hate seasoned his voice and rage burned quietly behind his eyes. That, combined with what he was accused of doing, made him the most frightening person I had ever come across.

Mustering what boldness I could—which was not much—I pressed on. "I have several questions that I must ask you. Will you answer them honestly?"

"I will."

"Then let's begin."

"I WOULD LIKE you to tell me about the musical instrument, the pipe. Is it magic?"

"Magic!" The prisoner laughed, throwing his head back in disbelief at my question.

A bit offended by his response, I persisted. "Yes, is it magic? If the accounts I heard of it are true, then it's quite remarkable—*beyond* remarkable—wouldn't you agree?"

"Remarkable? Yes, I think that's a fair statement. It certainly is unique, to my knowledge." Then, shaking his head, he continued, "But come, Herr Steinhauser, *magic*? I thought the children around here were gone."

Implying that my question about magic was childish added to the insult, but his comment about the children being gone was as callous and remorseless a statement as I'd ever heard. "Well," I responded coolly, "I didn't believe in *monsters* until very recently."

He stared back at me, and I began to think that he might try to attack. His hands and feet were shackled—tightly, judging by the blood I could see on his wrists—but he could still jump at my person. I wondered how long it would take before the guard could open the heavy cell door and assist me.

After a few tense seconds, the Piper let a hint of a smile tug at his lips while he leaned back. "The pipe is not magic. Just, as you said, remarkable."

I tried not to show the relief I felt at his answering the question without trying to harm me; it is unlikely that I succeeded. I continued, "Where did you get it?"

"From my father, who got it from his father, and so forth for several generations."

"But where did it come from?"

"My great-great-great grandfather, a craftsman of wood and lover of music, made it. Evidently, he made many musical instruments, but this one stood out."

It was hard to believe the stories I had heard about it, but every account was adamant about the pipe's existence and what it could do. "Did he create it to...to do what it does?"

A shake of his head. "No. He created it to play music. It was his son who discovered that it could do more, that it had an unintended, but special, ability."

I had to hear it plainly. "Could you describe this ability?"

"It isn't hard to understand. The pipe can attract animals. Play a simple tune and you're able to draw all manner of creatures near to you."

It sounded like a fairy tale. "Any tune will attract any animal?"

"No," the prisoner explained, "not exactly. There's a little skill needed, but not much. The higher-pitched songs attract the smaller animals, the deeper-pitched songs attract larger animals. My father, while learning to play it, once brought three bears near and barely escaped with his life. Over the generations, different tunes have been discovered that attract very specific creatures. However, the one most used is the one that attracts deer."

"For hunting?"

A nod. "Correct. There's never been a lack of food in my family since the discovery of what the pipe could do. It's made us very self-sufficient."

His last statement reminded me of an aspect of the case I desired more details on. I said, "I want to ask you about that. You live in the forest, a healthy trek from the town. From the accounts I heard, you don't visit often and were a stranger to most."

"Your question?"

"Why so solitary?"

After taking a moment to scratch his stubbled jaw on his shoulder, he answered, "The forest provides all that I need. I had no particular interest in anyone else's affairs and preferred that the townsfolk felt the same about me. Things would have been different if I had continued in that way."

There was certainly some hidden meaning in his answer, but I wasn't ready to try and unravel it just yet. Instead, I asked, "Did others know about the pipe's ability?"

"Yes. My family didn't hide it, nor did they go out of their way to flaunt it. It was simply a tool that we used."

It was surprising how common he made that remarkable instrument seem. His explanation, however impossible as it was to believe, matched all the accounts I'd heard. *The pipe is real*, was the incredible conclusion that I had to come to. Unfortunately, that meant that the other aspects of the account were also likely true — as horrible as they were.

I found that my next words were reluctant to come out. His reactions had confused me and I could only fear how he might respond to my next line of query. Still, without any real choice, I had to proceed. Swallowing once more, I managed to finally say, "You have mentioned your family quite a lot. My next few questions are about them, particularly your wife and daughter. Are you all right to continue?"

The look on the Piper's face when I mentioned his wife and daughter became dark and troubled. Any smile, grim or otherwise, disappeared and his eyes dropped to the dirt floor between us. I knew that these wouldn't be easy questions for him, which made them very hard for me, but I felt were critical in understanding the crime.

After a few seconds, he answered me in a raspy voice: "Proceed."

"I UNDERSTAND THAT you are a widower."

His eyes did not leave the ground and he simply nodded.

"I'm sorry for your loss. What was your wife like?"

Without adjusting his gaze, he answered, "Perfection."

"Perfection? How so?"

He raised his eyes to mine and I saw a softness in them that I wouldn't have imagined possible in the criminal before me. With obvious emotion, he went on to describe her. "Everything she did made life wonderful. She worked with me; she laughed with me; I would play music and she would sing. No two people have ever been happier. I loved her truly and somehow she loved me just as much. Have you ever known happiness like that, Herr Steinhauser?"

I was not expecting the question, but knew that what he was describing was nothing I'd experienced. Even with my hopeful thoughts of Katharina, the beautiful young woman I hoped to court back home, I had nothing I could truly compare. Shaking my head, I muttered, "I have not married yet."

"I fear," the Piper commented, "that your visit is even more of a waste of time than I had originally thought. With your young age and with what you just admitted, you can't possibly understand me or my actions. How can you represent what you don't know?"

I knew that love motivated people to do amazing—or horrible—things and that was certainly what he was alluding to. But, I reminded myself, no amount of love could possibly justify his actions. I pushed his comments aside and continued my questioning. "How long were you married?"

"Not nearly long enough. Seven years. A mere *glimpse* of a lifetime."

"And you had a child during that time?"

A nod. "Yes. She gave me a daughter which made my blissful life even more wonderful. Every day was the epitome of contentment."

"How"—it was hard to form the words—"How did your wife die?"

I wasn't sure he was going to answer the question. His gaze fell back to the floor and he continued staring blankly for several seconds. Just as I was considering repeating the question, he raised his eyes. Very quietly, to the point I had to lean forward to hear him, he said, "She became sick. She was taken with fever and coughing. She stopped eating. I tried everything I could think of but nothing helped."

The pain in in his face was clear. I may have thought him to be a callous monster, but he was not completely without feeling.

"For several days she only got worse," he continued. "And then... and then she passed." Tears were now in his eyes, cutting veins in his dirty face, and his voice was breaking. "I watched her get sicker and sicker and nothing that I could do helped. At that point in my life, it was, by far, the worst pain I'd ever been in."

Without thinking, I asked, "Has there been worse?" but realized the answer before I even finished asking my question.

His eyes became hard as he glared at me. "Yes."

AFTER A DEEP breath—the heavy air of the cell was not very refreshing—I started my next difficult line of inquiry. "Tell me about your daughter. How old was she when your wife died?"

"She was four."

"And you took care of her on your own?"

A nod. "Yes."

"Wasn't that hard, taking care of a young child, alone, deep in the woods?"

"No," he grunted at me, seemingly insulted.

Trying to explain myself, I said, "I only ask since raising a child without your spouse seems like a difficult chore."

He looked at me with a pitying smile and commented, "As I said, you'll not understand me. I loved Abigail. It is not a *chore* to take care of someone you love."

This was not going well. I tried to change tacks. "That was your daughter's name, Abigail?"

"Yes. As fitting a name as there ever could be."

"Fitting? Why? Because it's biblical?"

"Fitting," he answered, "because the meaning of the name Abigail is 'her father's joy'. My precious girl was my sole source of happiness, my one and only joy, after my wife's passing."

"So, the two of you got along well?"

The Piper gave a small smile at my question. The warmth of it was unexpected in such a place as his cell. "Abigail was my joyous shadow."

The clear affection, the pure love, in his words continued to surprise me—as well as the poetic phrases he used. "How so?" I asked, truly interested in how such a bond could be had.

"Whatever I did, she did. When I hunted, she'd track along with me. When I gathered wood, she'd carry sticks and twigs. As I tended the garden, she'd pull weeds. Cooking, cleaning, everything, she was there to assist."

"So she was useful."

The prisoner shook his head and laughed at my statement. "*Useful*? Your adjectives are quite poor, Herr Steinhauser. Yes, she was *useful*, but she was so much more. Abigail... inspired happiness."

Again! Such amazingly warm phrases that he used when speaking of his family. It was difficult to reconcile the man presented before me with the crime he had admitted to committing. "'Inspired happiness.' That's a charming expression. How did your daughter accomplish such a lofty feat?"

"By laughing, by smiling, by singing, by" — his voice faltered as the emotions again broke through — "by just existing."

I watched as he squeezed his eyes shut and vainly fought the tears. After several seconds, he took deep breaths and tried to compose himself. There are few things as uncomfortable as watching a grown man cry.

Feeling quite awkward, I offered, "If you would like, we can take a break."

"No," he said, struggling to keep his composure. "If this has to be done, then let's do it now."

I wasn't so sure that was a good idea. I still had some very difficult questions, and my next question was bound to be one of the most difficult.

With great hesitation, I finally asked, "How old was your daughter when she became sick?"

AT MY QUESTION about his daughter's illness, the prisoner did not answer right away. His eyes were downcast and I could see his jaw clench and unclench, as if he were chewing on his response. After several seconds, he finally got out, "Twelve."

Softening my voice, as if that would help take the sting out of it, I asked, "Was it the same illness that took your wife?"

A slow nod was all he gave as an answer.

I tried to sympathize and said, "To see your child sick, after losing your wife, that must have been quite vexing."

The Piper looked up at me and had an expression of pure disbelief. "*Quite vexing?*" His expression evolved into one of anger. Breathing heavily, he spat out, "It was the end of the world! It was the fading of anything good in life!"

As he stared at me, I understood that, despite my intentions, I had grossly understated his situation. Quickly, and sincerely, I said, "My apologies. I did not mean to make light of such an awful circumstance."

His glare slowly faded and, in a softer voice, he said, "After my wife died, I saw Abigail as a kind of gift. An offering of forgiveness for the loss of my true love. There was no solace outside of the joy of my daughter. When she fell ill and it looked like I was going to lose her... I couldn't fathom the unendurable pain of my future."

His demeanor, as much as his words, told the level of his torment. Despite his awful crime, I could not help but feel some pain for him. "What did you do?"

"I tried all the remedies I knew — herbs, salves, teas — but they had no effect, just like before. I grew desperate and decided to try the one thing I hadn't done with my wife."

That puzzled me. "Which was?"

"Curse my solitude and try and retrieve a healer from town."

"Wait," I said in surprise, realizing something that I had missed earlier. "You didn't bring a healer, a doctor, to see your wife when she was ill?"

He shook his head. "No."

"Why not?" I cried, exasperated at the revelation.

"It's not my family's way. We keep to ourselves; we are self-sufficient. On the very rare occasion when a healer was called, we had dubious results. Besides, going to town would mean leaving her alone for much of the day and I couldn't bring myself to do it."

I couldn't believe it. "Your wife might have been saved!"

"No," he said, adamantly.

"You know this for a fact?"

"I do."

His simple answers were beginning to irritate me. "*How* do you know this?"

"Because of my daughter," he answered firmly.

I did not understand what he meant by that answer, but I could see that he was completely assured in the correctness of his conclusions. I was not. How could he have not contacted a doctor for his wife?

Forcing myself to calm down, I decided to try and put the issue to the side and allow for the account about his daughter's illness to continue. After taking another deep breath, I said, "All right, so you went to get a healer for Abigail. Did you bring her with you?"

"No. Abigail was far too weak to travel. I can't express how painful it was to leave her alone, but I saw no other way. I traveled to town as quickly as I could. Every step away from her was crushing, but I felt I had to try."

"What then?"

"I reached the town gates and asked everyone I came across for the healer. People looked at me as if I were deranged, but, finally, an older man led me to the mayor's office."

That was an odd place to go. "The mayor's office? Why there?"

"Because the healer, the mayor, and other men of so-called importance, were in a meeting. Being far too upset to be very considerate, I thanked the old man and burst into the mayor's chambers unannounced."

"I imagine that they were quite shocked."

"Yes, but I didn't care. I looked around the room and told them that I needed a healer because my daughter was deathly ill. An older gentleman to my right identified himself as the doctor and asked about my Abigail's symptoms. I told him everything; I was nearly in tears having to recount her illness."

It felt like we were finally getting to the heart of the account. I leaned forward and asked, "What happened next?"

"The doctor said that it was a grave situation and that he would like to confer with the gathered council. Then they sent me outside while they discussed the situation. I did as asked, but was confounded as to why anything but action was required. I paced anxiously, feeling horrible at the thought of my daughter being all alone at home, dying. My patience wore thin quickly and I was about to reenter the chamber when the door opened and they invited me back in."

The Piper was growing more animated as he told his tale. Under much different circumstances, it could have been considered humorous to see him trying to gesture while his hands were confined by the shackles.

He continued, "When I entered the chamber, all the men looked very somber. The mayor spoke for the group, saying, 'Our doctor has explained the seriousness of your daughter's illness. You were right to see the situation as dire. However, we may have a way to help.'

"At hearing that, my heart leapt within me. His words gave me hope where I previously had none. I quickly asked what needed to be done. 'Let us not waste an instant!' I declared in my exuberance.

"'There's one problem,' the mayor responded. 'The treatment needed to help your daughter is very expensive. A thousand guilders.'"

When the prisoner said the amount, I had to repeat it in my head to make sure I'd heard him correctly. There was no mistake, and I couldn't help but exclaim, "A thousand guilders! That's an enormous sum!"

The Piper nodded and said, "It was vastly beyond my means—beyond most anyone's means—and my hope started to fade. I'm not a rich man. I never really had much use for money. Happiness was my one and only goal in life, and I had that in my daughter. I told them that I'd give all I had, which was a fraction of the amount, and would be willing to do anything to make up the rest."

I wasn't hopeful, but asked, "How did they respond?"

"At first, they all looked despondent and I was certain that I'd be turned away. But one of them recognized me and asked if what he had heard about my pipe was true—that it could attract animals. I responded that it was, confused as to why that mattered in the least. The men then whispered amongst themselves until finally the mayor looked up and told me he had a proposition. 'We are in a bad situation,' he said. 'This situation was, in fact, the purpose of the meeting that you interrupted. Rats have occupied every corner of our town, eating our food stores, ruining fields, spreading illness, even attacking people. Do you think, with your remarkable pipe, that you could lure them away and rid the town of these infernal pests? If so, we would consider that as full payment for the treatment that your daughter needs.'

"I took a moment to consider what was being offered and if I could do it. Although I'd never attempted anything like it, I was certain that it was possible—I would *make* it possible, even if I had to catch every rat by hand. So I told them that I would agree with the terms provided."

Nodding, I commented, "You had something they needed and they had something you needed—a classic barter."

The prisoner shook his head slowly. "If only that were true. Once the agreement was struck, I begged them to start assisting my daughter, but the mayor said that they could not possibly expend so great a sum on the faith that I would hold up my end of the bargain. I was insulted at the implication, but they would not budge. Being that my pipe was not with me, I told them that I would come back the next day to accomplish my task.

"I returned home and rushed to tell Abigail all that had happened. She looked so very weak, but she managed to say that she was happy. I tried to hide my tears from her, but I was happy too. *We had hope!* I asked if she had missed me, but she had slept so much that she hadn't even realized that I was gone for the day. It was torture to see her like that, but it was slightly easier to endure now that we had a glimmer of light given to us."

I would never claim to completely understand his emotions, but no one could miss the clear feelings of relief expressed in his words and expressions. I knew, of course, that things did not work out as the conversation was leading. I asked, "And the next day?"

"I returned to accomplish my task."

"I AWOKE EARLY," said the Piper, "attended to Abigail as best I could, and then left for town. I still hated leaving her alone, but I had no choice. As I walked along the forest path, I practiced playing my pipe; working on the best song that I thought would attract the rats of Hamelin. I also had to think of how to collect all the rats in the entire town, and, when successful, what to do with them. By the time I reached the gates, I was confident in the tune I had selected, but no more than hopeful in the method I decided upon."

Although I tried to hide it, I was quite interested in the story that was being told. Never had I heard an account as uniquely fascinating. "How did you do it?"

"In the end, it was simple. Starting at the east gate, I walked up and down each street, north and south, while slowly going westward across the city."

I was almost afraid to ask, "And the rats?"

A look of disgust crossed his face. "Innumerable. When I reached the north end of the first street, I turned around to see what, if anything, I'd accomplished. What I saw, for at least thirty yards, was nothing but rats. Now facing them, I could hear their horrid squeaks and squeals over my music. They writhed over one another, a living mass of dirty animals. I was so surprised and disturbed that I faltered in my tune for an instant. The rats immediately started to disperse, some heading toward me with wild eyes. Regaining my composure, I quickly began the tune anew and the horrid creatures once again fell under the effects of the music."

"That was only after one street?" I exclaimed. "No wonder the town was willing to pay so much!"

At that comment, the prisoner gave me another cold stare. There was clearly something he knew that I did not. Without saying why he was so insulted by my statement, he went on with his story.

"As I continued through the streets, I didn't turn around again until the end. However, I was certain that I still had my trail of gruesome followers, for I could hear exclamations and screams from the townsfolk."

I tried to imagine the scene—hearing some music and sounds of animal noises, looking through my window or stepping outside to understand what was happening and to see a mass of rats following a man down the street. The confusion and fright would have been extreme.

"When I reached the west gate, having completed my tour of the city, I finally looked back once more. I didn't falter in my music, but I could hardly believe what I saw. Rats covering the street as far as the eye could see. The constant scurrying made it seem like the town was flooded, not with water, but with disgusting, disease-ridden vermin. Despite the awful sight, I felt a sense of happiness, or perhaps relief, since I was accomplishing the task that would attain Abigail's treatment."

What he had claimed to accomplish was incredible, but it hadn't yet fulfilled the bargain. "Now that you had all the rats from town, what did you do with them?"

"I continued west out of the gate toward the river Weser. At its shore, I waded in while continuing to play. The rats followed. I continued forward until just my mouth was above the water and I could continue to play. The current pulled at me, but I managed to not move too much. The rats, however, were out of their depth. The water boiled with their thrashing as they tried to swim, tried to stay with the music. Eventually, they drowned and washed down the river. Even though I have no affection for such vile creatures, it was a most unpleasant sight."

Again, I tried to picture it, but quickly stopped as it was too horrible. "This took care of all of them?"

"All but one that I saw scurry off along the banks. But I like to think that he joined up with other rats somewhere in the countryside and warned them to stay away from Hamelin."

Despite the seriousness of our conversation, I could not help but give a small laugh at that. "I have to imagine that once the task was done, you rushed back to town to collect your payment."

He nodded. "I did. As I reached the gates, many people had gathered and, since they then understood what was happening, were cheering me. But I ignored them. What could I care about accolades when my daughter was dying? I found the mayor easily — he was among the people gathered, and he approached to shake my hand. Then, at my insistence, he invited me back to his chambers to discuss payment.

"When we reached his chambers, all the councilmen from the previous day were with us. The only person absent, conspicuously, was the healer. I assumed, or at least hoped, that he was off making preparations to help Abigail.

"The mayor, and the others, lauded my accomplishment once again, but I continued to insist that we focus on the treatment. That's when the *truth* came out."

His expression became dark, although I still didn't know what was exactly behind it. "What do you mean, 'the truth came out'?" I asked.

With slow, heavy words, the Piper explained, "At first, the mayor stated that my task was far easier for me than they anticipated and that they could not possibly give me my full wages. Instead, they offered me fifty guilders."

"What?" I exclaimed. If what the prisoner was saying was true, it hadn't been presented in any of the accounts I had heard.

He nodded. "Fifty guilders. I protested and argued that we'd had an agreement and that the difficulty of the task was not part of it. Then I told them that the money was not important, but the treatment was. At that, the men looked from one to another and the mayor finally admitted that there was no treatment. It was a ruse, a lie, in order to get me to use my pipe to help the town. They'd seen my anguish only as an opportunity."

I leaned back in my chair in disbelief. If true, the cruelty was unfathomable — unbelievable! And yet, the sincerity of the man before me led me to believe his words. Filled with indignation, I asked, "Can you prove this?"

He shook his head. "Only if my word is believed. But I'm quite certain that the mayor and his associates will not substantiate my claims."

"That's outrageous!" I declared, my anger growing.

"It is," the prisoner replied calmly. "But there is nothing to be done. Besides, at this point, I think I've done enough."

That comment reminded me of why I was there and why the man known as the Pied Piper was in prison awaiting a trial for his very life. A surprising sadness at the situation started to eat at my conscience. A trickle of remorse for the man in front of me that I was certain would be put to death. His account did not, *could not*, justify what he'd done, but it made his monstrous act almost understandable.

Knowing that he was right, in not being able to prove his claim and in knowing his alleged actions since then would make it all moot anyway, I pushed forward with his account. "What happened next?"

"I left. I went home. I spent every remaining moment that I could with Abigail. And then, a few weeks later..." His voice stopped, his face converting to the picture of sadness.

I knew what he was going to say. "You don't have to continue."

"No!" he said sharply. "You're here to understand me, to understand why I acted as I did. Then you must hear me say this part — more than any other. A few weeks later" — he again paused, took several breaths, then — "I buried my precious daughter next to my wife."

I ASKED THE prisoner again if he wanted a break. The truth, however, was that *I* wanted one. His account was overwhelming and I was completely unprepared for it. Shock, anger, sadness. My emotions had never been so thrashed about as they had during our brief time together.

But no reprieve was to be given. The prisoner answered, "I would rather not break. We're nearing the end. Let's finish it."

I thought of insisting, but instead gave in to his wishes. As hard as it was on me, I was certain it was immeasurably harder on him. "All right, then, what happened next?"

"Day and night, for two days, I lay across the graves of my family. I had no desire to eat, to drink, for almost anything but to despair. I was ready, eager, to die."

"But you didn't."

"Not yet. My great sadness was rivaled only by my anger. To die at that moment, as sweet as it sounded, would allow the mayor, the town, to be free of any repercussions for their actions. They stole from me a day that I could have spent with my daughter. But worse, they gave us hope. It was fleeting and absolutely false, but it was still cruelly given. My sense of justice demanded action. I began to want only one thing before I died. I wanted them to *feel my sorrow.*"

My blood felt chilled at his words. They were so cruel, so full of malice, that I was again frightened of him. Was he human or, as I'd believed earlier, a monster? I could not satisfactorily answer the question. "So you developed a plan for revenge?"

"I did. Simple and appropriate."

Appropriate? Did he really still feel that way? "Go on."

"Early on the morning of June twenty-sixth, the day of John and Paul, I left my family's graves and entered the house. These clothes you see me wearing, they were fashioned by my daughter. She loved the bright colors and I'd wear them on occasions that we chose to celebrate. In honor of her, I put them on. Then, I took my pipe and walked to town. It was a little before midday when I arrived, and the adults were in the cathedral for their celebration, as I knew they would be. So, like I had previously, I started playing my pipe as I walked the streets."

"But not to attract rats."

"No, to attract the children of rats." He did not smile at his little joke.

"So your pipe does not just work on animals, but humans too?"

"Humans are animals."

I took that as a yes.

The Piper continued, "After I walked through the entire city and reached the west gate, I turned around and saw a large number of children. At seeing them, for a brief moment, I questioned what I was doing. But the fresh thought of burying Abigail solidified my resolve."

I did not want to hear the next part, but knew I was obligated to. I clenched my jaw tightly as he continued.

"I proceeded back to the river Weser and entered. And then...then they were all gone."

My stomach grew ill at the thought of it. It was an unthinkable atrocity.

What I wanted to know then was how he felt about it. I asked, "Do you know how many children you drowned that day?"

He shook his head, showing no obvious emotion.

"One hundred thirty. I thought you should know."

His eyes narrowed for a moment and then became thoughtful. He finally said, "Thirty, one hundred thirty, or one thousand thirty, it makes no difference now. My fate would be the same."

What he said was probably true, but *I* wanted him to know. I wanted to see his reaction. I hoped for a glimpse of remorse, but I did not see it. Even now, after several days had passed and the raging impulses that had led to his actions had had a chance to cool, he still seemed unfazed. I grew angry at his lack of emotion. I asked, "Did it help? What you did, did it help you?"

"A little."

"How?" I pleaded, not understanding his reasoning. "Yes, the town did something awful to you and your daughter. But to turn around and do something so awful in return... I can't justify your actions."

"I'm not asking you to."

I wanted to understand. "But what did you gain? Two wrongs don't make a right!"

"Possibly. But, in my case, two wrongs make a *lesson*."

"A lesson?" I could not believe his words.

"Yes, Herr Steinhauser!" he said, growing angry. "A lesson! I think it's safe to say that no one in the town will *ever* treat someone the way they treated me again. And, as word of this account spreads — as I'm sure it will — others will think twice before acting so cruelly toward one who is so desperate."

His eyes bore into mine, but I didn't avert my gaze. I met his stare with equal fervor at that impasse of justification. After several seconds, the Piper gave a small smile and said, "And this is why I must die; you're looking inside me for remorse, but there is none to be found."

What argument could I make? If he had no pity, no remorse, I couldn't disagree with his conclusion of death. He would be executed, regardless of his feelings, but I'd wanted to see if there was redemption of any sort possible. I saw none.

Disappointed at his lack of feelings, I continued, "Let us now talk about your capture."

"WHERE DID THE men of town find you?"

"At my home, sitting graveside."

"You didn't try to hide or run?"

He shook his head. "I no longer cared what happened to me." He then laughed. "Still don't, for that matter."

"Are you aware how the town knew that it was you who was the perpetrator?"

His eyes narrowed for a moment and then he shook his head. "I can't say I gave it much thought."

I explained, "You mentioned earlier that you thought that the children around here were gone. That is, in fact, not true. There were three young ones who survived. One was blind, so although he heard your music, he was unable to follow. Another could not walk, so he too was unable to follow."

"The third?"

"A deaf child who could not hear your pipe. However, the first two were enough. Their accounts of a pied piper leading the children away made it clear that you were the villain the people sought."

Leaning back, the prisoner said, "In truth, I never really questioned that the town would know it was me. In fact, it is important that they were aware of it."

"Because of your *lesson*?"

A single nod.

"When the men came for you, did you say anything to them?"

"No. I was ready to be taken in. That, however, didn't stop them from applying a vigorous beating."

I was a little surprised, but probably shouldn't have been. It was likely that several of the men who'd arrested him were also newly bereaved parents.

The Piper went on, "When they finished, they bound my hands together, and then tied me with a lead to one of their horses. It was a painful journey back to town. Walking hurt from my new wounds. Keeping pace with the horse was difficult, and when I couldn't keep up, I would fall and be dragged. Eventually they would stop to allow me to get back to my feet, but never before I'd been dragged a long while."

"And when you arrived at town?"

"I was met by the mayor and his council outside of the prison. There was pain and hatred in their glares. I found it satisfying. Then, as word quickly spread that I'd been captured, a mob began to form, people shouting, spitting, wanting to kill me on the spot."

I could not imagine what it would be like to be in that position. I asked, "Were you frightened?"

"Not at all. In fact, I yelled back at them with equal venom."

"You did *what*?" I exclaimed.

He smiled. "I yelled at the crowd. I screamed '*It is your fault!*' over and over. That, of course, only incensed them all the more. My captors, no doubt, saved my life by bringing me inside the prison and locking me in this cell."

This prisoner before me had stated that I couldn't possibly understand him or his actions, that I was too young and did not know love. I started to believe, to hope, that *no one* could truly understand him — regardless of age or experience. The Pied Piper was as unique as he was terrible.

"Have you had any visitors since that time?" I asked, knowing we were nearing the end of our conversation.

He shook his head. "None. Well, except for you."

With his story finished, we looked at each other quietly for some time. My gaze was not really on him, but lost in the distance as my mind went over all the things I'd just heard: the amazing, the sad, and the heinous. When finally satisfied with my thoughts, as much as I could be for such a horrific account, I asked one last question. "Is there anything else you think I should know or want to say?"

The Pied Piper thought for a moment, shook his head, and answered, "I'm done."

Done with his story or done with his life? Probably both, but I didn't ask.

I stood and called out, "Guard, I'm ready." I turned to the prisoner and looked at the man sitting there. Although I hated what he'd done — completely unforgivable — I could not help but feel a little sorry for him. His world was smashed through no fault of his own, and, in his utter despair, he'd acted out egregiously.

The guard unlocked the cell door and, as I was walking through it, I stopped, turned, and asked, "What happened to the pipe?"

The prisoner looked at me and said nothing, but I swore I saw a smile touch the edge of his lips.

AS HE HAD predicted from the beginning, the trial was short. There were no pleas for mercy, and the verdict was guilty. My presence was entirely inconsequential. The criminal known as the Pied Piper of Hamelin was executed in front of a throng of people who enthusiastically applauded and cheered his death.

For my part, I watched; was satisfied that justice was done; but I did not cheer.

a retelling of The Goose Girl

THE GOOSE GIRL & THE ARTIFICIAL

K.M. Robinson

You don't have a choice," Arta sneers. "You lost your key. You have no control over me, and, in case you've forgotten, I'm designed to be smarter than you."

I trail behind Arta as she walks away from Fal, my dress swishing behind her as she moves, and remember what my father always warned me about dealing with enemies: If they're smarter than you, they will know how to stay on top. If they aren't, you can beat them at their own game.

Arta is right—she's *definitely* smarter. She was created that way.

"Behave." I tap Fal on the head. He beeps quietly, slipping into sleep mode.

"Greetings," a man sings, walking swiftly toward us. "Thank you for making the journey. My son has been waiting for you."

"Thank you, Your Majesty." Arta dips gracefully into a curtsy. "This is my Artificial." She waves her hand at me.

"What might your name be?" the king asks.

"Goselyn, sir," I say softly. Arta waves a finger behind her back, reminding me to follow orders.

Artificials aren't required to bow to humans, so I hold my pose. There are a lot of things I'm going to have to remember to do now.

"Come along, ladies." The king turns, guiding us toward the massive palace.

Panels along the hallway walls mimic exterior windows, morphing into different scenes based on the king's biometric readings. The key around his neck reads his movements and controls the technology around him, including the settings on the fake windows.

A door slides open in front of us, courtesy of the key, revealing a stunning parlor. The walls are covered in red and gold tapestries — a stark contrast to the purple and silver in my own palace.

"Princess," a young man says, jumping to his feet as he sets down the book he had been reading. "Thank you for coming all this way to handle the proposal." This must be the prince of Delare. I've never seen him before, just as he's never seen me. The prince isn't bad-looking. His height surprises me a little, since I had heard all of Delare was on the short side. I've been told he's rather brilliant, but I suppose I'll never find out now.

Arta nods graciously to him.

"I think this will be a productive visit for us," she remarks, gathering her long skirt — *my* skirt — in her hand. "I'd like to freshen up after our journey if you don't mind. Perhaps we could begin our negotiations this evening?"

In Untae, each royal prince and princess is required to work with another country to create a proposal to take to the reigning monarchs between the countries. My job as princess of Sylvane is to work with the prince of Delare on the terms of the proposal we will be offering to our parents to sign with each other—or it would have been if Arta hadn't interfered. I try not to wrinkle my nose at her in disgust.

"Certainly, Princess Sylvane." He nods at Arta, referring to her by my official title. Customarily, the royals of Untae are referred to by our stations and countries as a way of identification. Outside of our own countries, people rarely know our first names.

"You may call me 'Arta,'" my Artificial informs him as she swings around more gracefully than I ever could before waltzing away. When I don't follow, she snaps my name to get me to move.

We follow a short silver robot down several halls and up two flights of stairs before we step into Arta's room. Red floral curtains are drawn back to reveal the gardens in back of the palace.

"You may go," she says, dismissing the robot. It scurries back to its home base until it is needed again. "This is lovely... I can't wait to see it burn."

"They're going to figure this out, Arta," I protest. Her short dress around my calves frustrates me. In Sylvane, we distinguish humans from our creations-enhanced-with-artificial-intelligence by wardrobe—though I'm considering changing that rule once I take over if this is what they have to suffer through every day. Then again, they can't feel the sensation of uncomfortable clothing, so perhaps that shouldn't be the first decision I make as a ruler. If I ever become a ruler.

"They won't have time to figure it out, Goselyn," she says. "You yourself didn't realize what I was doing until after I had taken your key away. Do you really think a boy like that will figure out our plan? They're as easily replaced as you are—and just as unfit to preside over the countries of Untae."

She sits on the bed, looking me over. "Your cousin has a plan, Goselyn. Your kind cannot withstand it. The shepherd will keep this country functioning alongside Kenneth."

My cousin Kenneth programs many of the palace Artificials. His work offers him access and power, but it's never been enough for him. I just didn't realize the lengths he was willing to go to until it was too late.

"By destroying this proposal?" I glare at her.

"We don't need Sylvane and Delare working together on this. Let's face it—neither country makes the best decisions," she reminds me. "Now go sit."

I make my way to the corner, settling on the small sofa where I'll be sleeping for the length of our stay.

"Don't get any ideas about warning them, either," Arta snaps. "You know I have your key—I can control anything I want back in Sylvane. Don't forget, your cousin is also monitoring the situation. He has eyes everywhere—even here. Your mother is only safe as long as you cooperate. He will know the second you step out of line."

I wonder just how much control Kenneth might have been able to secure here. My cousin shouldn't have been able to override the settings of my Artificial, who had been programmed by my mother directly, but he has. If he could do that, he may have found a way to get control here too, even though it's been banned by the laws governing Untae—our countries have such a rocky relationship that we keep to ourselves unless we're forced to engage through something like this proposal.

"I understand the terms," I growl at my Artificial. "I'll pretend to be you and let you destroy my reign in order to save my mother."

I glance down at the marble floor with its intricate pattern swirling into twists and turns. If only I could return home.

"Ridiculous diplomatic mission," I mumble under my breath. "I couldn't have just stayed home. *No,* I had to go and be the problem-solver and do my duty, traipsing off to a far-off country to fulfill a silly little requirement before I can *eventually* take over the throne."

While being a princess has its perks, following the laws of our land in order to transition to the throne when my mother eventually retires seems to take a lot of unnecessary work early on in life. Perhaps this is another thing I should consider changing in a decade or two so my children don't have to travel to far-off lands to create treaty proposals — Sylvane and Delare are doing just fine ignoring each other. Although, I suppose it's good practice and helps to develop relationships between the would-be rulers — and we may need their support someday against one of our shared enemies — so perhaps it should remain in place.

A knock sounds at the door. We both turn. Arta slices her hand through the air, motioning me to the door — I'm the servant now.

I open the door. An Artificial stands outside holding a tray with a pitcher of water and two glasses. He steps inside and places it on the table.

"Prince Corinth will meet with you in half an hour downstairs in his office, Princess Sylvane." He nods to Arta, then turns to me. "You may come with me if the princess is no longer in need of your services."

His hair is shockingly short, exposing the control panel on his neck — our Artificials all have longer hairstyles to cover the panels. While Artificials are similar in our countries, their internal workings are slightly different to match the programming of their designers. While he looks exactly like a human, the Artificial in front of me has been created to work in the palace, assisting the king. Typically, this would be a job for a robot designed to do less intellectual jobs, but sending a higher-functioning Artificial to interact with the foreign princess is a sign of respect.

"You may go, Goselyn. Do whatever they ask you to do and don't get in the way."

The Artificial leads me downstairs and out of the palace as I fret over why Arta was so quick to dismiss me. Outside, the palace grounds are covered in flowers and stonework. Paths swirl as far as the eye can see. The Artificial leads me beyond the stables, toward the fountain.

"We don't have any real need for you, but you can assist here," he says, gesturing toward the lake. "The lake grounds are meant for enjoyment. The swans and geese are only permitted to get so close to the waterfront. You need to monitor the birds and keep them in their respective areas."

I nod, completely terrified. I have no idea how to keep large birds at bay.

"Gand is in charge here. Speak to him if you need anything."

A tall Artificial walks up to me imposingly. An Artificial would not flinch, so I command my body to be still.

"You will monitor this area." He motions to his right. "This is how we handle the birds here."

He demonstrates the proper techniques for keeping the birds where they belong. One pecks him in anger, but he doesn't acknowledge it. This could create a problem for me, as someone who *actually* feels pain.

I settle back into a standing position near a log, waiting for the birds to attack.

I SPEND THE rest of the day beside the log, holding a shepherd's hook to corral the geese. As late afternoon arrives, Gand chases the birds back inside a building, where they are fed and sheltered at night. I don't understand the purpose of having the creatures if they're going to shut them up every night. Why not spare the grounds entirely and set them free off of the palace property?

A week goes by as I sit with the geese and swans, prodding them away when they get too close. The only time I'm not beside the lake is at mealtime. We take our meals inside Arta's room — *my* room — to avoid prying eyes. Artificials do not need to eat, and Arta skipping meals while

I indulged would raise flags.

One afternoon, I hear a voice behind me say, "May I ask you a question?" I turn just as the prince takes a seat on the log next to me, fidgeting with his hands.

"Yes, Prince Delare, of course," I say. My hand migrates toward my long, brown hair, but I quickly force it back into my lap. I can't risk moving my tresses and exposing my neck. If he notices I don't have a control panel with a chip, he will figure out that Arta and I have switched places.

I silently think of ten vicious names to call my cousin when I return home, though none of them are strong enough to convey how angry I am at him for trying to take my throne and putting my mother in danger.

"You may call me Corinth," the prince says. "I'm sorry. What was your name again?"

"I'm Goselyn, sir." I keep my eyes transfixed on the ground, hoping he'll go away.

"Goselyn. Right," he reminds himself. "Goselyn, I was wondering if you could give me any advice on working with Princess Arta. She and I seem to be having trouble connecting over this proposal."

"What do you mean?"

"Well, every time I think we have something worked out, she seems to hesitate. I keep thinking that I'm saying the right things, but then she seems to get frustrated with me. I know we both want this to work — it *has* to work for either of us to complete our requirements for taking the next step toward the throne — but I'm worried we're never going to reach an agreement on this proposal to show our parents."

Corinth speaks to me the way I used to speak to Arta — like a confidant. It's a little strange to see how differently our countries converse with our Artificials.

For a moment, I wonder if that would make a difference. I could tell him about Arta, but I still don't know how Kenneth is tracking my moves and how much he really knows about what is going on here. More than that, revealing this deception to the prince would jeopardize the tenuous relationship between our countries. While we aren't outright enemies, any sign of treachery on our part could trigger a fight with them, and if they see deception from within our own ranks, that could be taken as a sign that we're weak enough to come after us, should they want more power. I can't risk that.

"I don't have any advice for you, I'm afraid," I reply sadly. "She has a specific plan in mind."

One designed by my cousin. I'm still not sure how he overrode Arta's original programming, but he manipulated her into turning on me — she would never do this on her own, especially since my mother programmed Arta to be loyal to me when we brought her into the palace when I was a child. My cousin is more skilled than I am, but I find it hard to believe he could manipulate my mother's work.

"I see." Corinth frowns, rubbing his temples. "Perhaps you could tell me about Sylvane? Maybe that would offer me some insight."

"Shouldn't you be negotiating with the princess?"

"We're taking a break. We don't seem to be getting anywhere today."

"Surely your father could help you," I suggest.

"He's not allowed to take part in the negotiations. The princess and I are the only two allowed to work on it and whatever we come up with is final... She can't even leave until it's done," he mutters, frustrated. "I'm sure you're ready to go home, Goselyn — it's been an entire week. Can you just try to think of something that will help me?"

I frown. How am I supposed to help him when I still have to find a way disable my Artificial without Kenneth finding out? I have enough problems of my own.

"Sir, they're looking for you." An Artificial approaches us, waving toward the palace.

"Perhaps we could speak tomorrow," the prince says as he stands. He strides toward the palace, sending a group of geese scattering toward me.

"What did he want?" Gand asks, wandering over to help herd the geese back.

"Advice for working with the princess."

"Did you give it to him?" He pushes at a swan. It flaps its wings dangerously.

"I have no advice to give. The princess makes up her own mind."

"How many years have you worked with her?"

I gently bump the chest of a white goose with the end of my hook, trying to coax it back before Gand can reach it.

"Many," I reply. He pauses to evaluate what I said.

"You've been studying her this long and you don't have any insight on how to handle her?" he inquires. "Perhaps in Sylvane, the technological advances are not as great. Here in Delare, we know everything there is to know about the humans, down to how their facial expressions will change based on the food that they eat. I do not believe you have no information about your princess."

"I know many things about her," I fire back. "I simply have nothing that will help the prince convince her to do something she does not wish to do."

"You've been here a week," Gand replies, taking a step closer. "In that time, you have worked alongside me here with the birds. You don't act like a normal Artificial, but I can't decide if it is because Artificials are different where you are from, or if you are here for another reason."

"I do not know if we are different. I only know this is how I am," I inform him, trying not to get caught up in a conversation. Artificials tend to be practical and precise, so I pray he believes me.

"I'm watching you," Gand says, turning his back to return to his own area.

Arta is going to be thrilled—the local Artificials could bring her plan down before I do. I'm a little surprised Kenneth didn't program Arta to hijack the Artificials here as well—perhaps she doesn't have time.

Gand studies me from afar as I pretend not to notice. The moment we are released from our duties, I walk back to the palace and head straight for my room as Gand leaves to see to his next task.

"About time," Arta says when I enter.

I confront her. "The prince says you're being difficult."

"Well, *of course* I am—this isn't supposed to be easy. He has to be willing to give in just to get this thing finished."

"Oh, so *that's* your plan? Wear him down until he agrees to anything?" I kick my shoes off as I walk to my sofa in the corner and drape a blanket over my feet to compensate for the short dress I'm wearing.

"Yes, it is." She glares as she walks across the room. "Now, eat that. I was supposed to have the tray set out twenty minutes ago."

She motions to the food on the small table. I race to it quickly, piling as much food as I can onto a napkin. I take several bites out of the apple before setting it back on the tray to make it look like she had eaten some and leave bits of the pastry crumbled on the plate before setting it outside the door to be picked up.

At least Arta wasn't depriving me of food.

"Stay here. I have to attend a ceremony in the rose garden and I don't need you getting in the way."

She glides across the room toward the door, her blonde hair moving slightly in the breeze her movements create, lifting it away from her shoulders and upper back.

"I don't know why these silly ceremonies are so important to you humans. Traditions are ridiculous, especially when they have to do with flowers."

She marches out of the room as the door swings shut.

I grab the sheets I smuggled into the room yesterday from under the sofa cushions. Tying them to the handle on the window probably isn't the best idea, but I have to get out of the palace without her knowing and the other Artificials can easily see me from the hallway.

I'm only a floor off of the ground, but it's still enough to make my stomach drop when I look over the ledge. I slip my shoes into my dress pockets before carefully swinging myself out the window.

After an eternity, I reach the ground. I didn't inherit many things from my father, but my hand-eye coordination is the thing I appreciate the most. Aiming, I throw my smuggled knife high into the air, praying it's enough to slice through the sheet I'd braided into a rope. Part of it rips before the knife falls back to the earth.

I jump back to avoid the falling blade. Once it settles and no longer bounces against the ground, I rush to the sheet-rope. I pull on it, trying to break it free. The material rips, but not enough. Using my full weight, I jump up to grab it, using gravity to my advantage.

It breaks.

My feet don't cooperate as I fall, leaving me in a pile on the ground. The braided sheet hits me in the head and I bite my tongue to keep from snarling at it.

The bush acts as a hiding place for the evidence of my escape—I'll need to find a new way back inside, but at least they didn't see me leave from the hallways.

If I can find Fal, I can send him to my mother with a message— robots' programming can only be changed internally, so unless Arta or Kenneth get their hands on him, they can't stop him. Arta has been keeping me from my loyal butler, refusing to let me see him. I'm sure she knows that if I reach him, there's a very good chance I would try something to interfere with her plan.

I creep around the side of the castle, making sure no one is there.

When I'm positive it's clear, I run toward the stables, where everything that didn't come with us to our chambers is being stored.

Our vehicle sits at the far end of the stable, away from the animals. I tiptoe as quietly as I can past the stalls, grateful I haven't put my shoes back on yet. Any noise might spook the creatures.

I quietly open the door of the vehicle, looking to see where Fal might be. I had put him into sleep mode so he shouldn't have gone far.

I tear the vehicle apart, but have no luck finding him. I finally extricate myself from our transport, stepping out backward onto the dirt.

A distant beep pierces the air so softly that I'm not sure I hear it at all. I turn slowly, trying to locate the source. When I can't find it, I close the door and begin to move around the stable, looking for where Fal might be hidden—I won't let Delare steal my butler.

I jump out of my skin when I hear the beep again, this time overhead. My eyes sweep over the walls until I finally spot him.

Mounted on the wall high above me is Fal's head. I shriek, clamping my hand over my mouth to try to stifle the noise.

Fal's body is nowhere to be found. A dim string of lights blinks across his eyes, the only color to Fal's silver shape. Without the rest of him, he looks like an upside-down metal bowl that blinks.

"Fal," I whisper.

He hovers somewhere between sleep mode and functioning mode, just enough to make small noises and move the tiny lights across his face. I reach up, tapping his head. I struggle on my toes to stretch high enough.

When I tap him, his eyes light up—white with blue electronic pupils—as he connects with my biometric signature.

"Goselyn," he says quietly. "They took me apart."

"What happened to you?" I can feel myself on the verge of tears as I lower my heels to the ground.

"Arta didn't want me to tell the Delare royalty what had happened. She had them dismantle me—she told them I wasn't functioning properly. They took my body and gave it to another robot and put my central system up here until they can reprogram me."

"We can't let them reprogram you!" I shout.

As a robot, Fal's programming does not allow the Artificials to have access to him—which means they can't control him—but it also means that if someone reprograms him, he'll be gone for good—robots' systems are far less complex and advanced than Artificials' systems.

"What is she trying to do?" His eyes light up, changing color.

A noise on the other side of the stable stops us. Fal dims his lights, going into night mode. I press against the wall, hiding behind a barrel. After a few moments, the person leaves.

"What does she want, Goselyn?" Fal repeats from his place on the wall.

"She's trying to ruin the negotiations and change the proposal. My cousin reprogrammed her because he wants me out of the picture. He thinks by destroying this proposal, I won't be allowed to succeed my mother and the crown will pass to his family."

"You need to tell your mother," Fal informs me, as if I didn't know.

"That's why I was trying to find you. You're the only one who can get back to Sylvane without Arta finding out."

"I can't move without my body." Fal's face lights up as green, red, and yellow dots race across his interface. He beeps unintentionally as his system fails from being mounted on the wall.

"I couldn't even get you down if I tried." I look around for something to climb on to reach him.

"I'm stuck up here. Even if you could reach me, it would take an hour to get me unhooked. There's something weird back here." The flashing lights slow to a crawl. "You need to go back and find a way to warn the king. You know if your cousin is coming after you, he will also go after

Delare—he's always said he should take command *here* if you were to inherit Sylvane."

Another noise frightens us across the stable.

"Just go, Goselyn. Put me in sleep mode and come back after you've ended this. I'll be fine."

"But—" I protest.

"No. You need to go. I can't help you. You need to put Sylvane first."

Fal has always been wise beyond his programming.

"I'll be back for you," I promise as I reach up to turn on his sleep mode setting.

"I'm sure you will. Good luck, Goselyn." He beeps when I tap him, settling into sleep mode.

Stopping Arta before Fal is reprogrammed becomes another motivation for beating my Artificial, urging me to quickly sneak out of the stables. I slip my shoes on once I reach the grass and hurry toward the palace.

The most dangerous part of my return journey into the palace is slipping by the kitchen without being noticed. People bustle about, preparing the evening meal. I can smell the roast chicken from down the hall.

"What are you doing?"

I jump at the question. Spinning, I clutch my chest. Artificials shouldn't be scared, but I can't help my reaction.

"Goselyn, what are you doing?" Gand demands. His jaw clenches like a real human's would. "I knew it—you're not an Artificial."

"No, I am." My words come out panicked and high-pitched.

"You're not," he says, reaching for my neck. He struggles to move my hair as I fight back.

As we grapple, I do my best to eject the chip from the back of his neck. The Artificial throws me against the wall, slamming me between it and the back of his shoulder. I yelp in pain.

As he steps closer, I stomp on his foot, causing him to look down long enough to punch the button on the back of his neck. The chip pops out just enough to make his face go slack.

Opening the small control panel, I pull up his programming. While I only learned a few things from my father, I gained many skills from my mother, including the ability to alter the programming of the Artificials and robots we work with in the kingdom. I wish I could do the same to Arta, but Kenneth would know the moment I touched her control panel.

Before securing the chip back in place, I program Gand to not be able to come within ten feet of me. I also erase the last ten minutes of his memory. He will know I removed the time from his programming, but it will take him a few days to recover it, giving me enough time to fix the problem with Arta — *I hope.*

While Gand blinks back to life, I slip down the hall and dart around the corner. I make it back to my room with just enough time to pull the remnants of the sheet off the window and close it before Arta opens the door. She eyes me but says nothing.

THE NEXT DAY, I make my way down to the lake, the geese following in my wake. Gand watches me from his place on the other side of the lawn, as if trying to figure out what had happened.

I turn my shoulder away, keeping my back to him as I corral the birds on the lawn.

"Gand." The prince's sharp voice bounces off a nearby tree. I look up in time to see Gand retreating, having been dangerously close to me. I'm sure he was checking to see if I had a control panel.

"Should I ask what that was about?" Corinth asks as he sits next to me on the log. His blond hair tips down gently over one eye as he turns to face me.

I pull my dark hair over my neck, ensuring he can't see my skin.

"I don't know." I try to keep my response simple.

"Have you thought of anything that might help me?" he asks, making me sigh.

"Perhaps..." I pause, trying to think of *anything* I can give him. "Let her think she's won. Give in to as much as you can, but hold true to the most important things and make them seem unimportant to you. Fight over silly things and make her give you the bigger things as a compromise. If she thinks she's won, perhaps you can make this work."

"That's an interesting thought," Corinth replies. "I'll try that. You're very wise, Goselyn. I knew I liked you."

He stands, preparing to leave.

"How do you like it here, Goselyn? Are you finding everything to your liking?" he asks politely, turning back to me.

"Delare is a very nice country, sir."

"Thank you." He smiles. "That's not what I meant. How are you doing?"

I'm only being held captive by an Artificial who is threatening the lives of everyone around me at the whims of my narcissistic cousin, but sure, I'm great, I think, but instead I say, "I'm doing fine, thank you."

"Is Gand treating you well?" he inquires, putting his hand behind his back as he was trained to do.

I smile, not wanting to answer.

"Gand?" Corinth calls, motioning my keeper over. "How has everything been? Are you two working together well?"

"Goselyn has been managing just fine, Prince Corinth."

"Very good," he replies, giving Gand a curious look. "You're taking care of her, right? Treating her as one of our own?"

"Yes, sir," Gand assures him, placing his free hand on his shepherd's hook in an attempt to make the prince feel more at ease. Artificials are programmed to make human-like movements specifically to make humans feel more comfortable around them, even to the point of regularly blinking.

"Good. We want everyone to feel welcome here." Corinth smiles, nodding to me. It's amazing how he takes so much time to speak with his Artificials publicly. I've had many long talks with mine, but only in private.

Gand takes a step toward us, but then he suddenly leaps back, as if a bee has stung him. Corinth looks as shocked as Gand does.

"Are you all right?" Corinth moves toward him.

Gand's eyes shift toward the clouds as his system processes what just happened.

"I...I'm not sure what that was." He takes another step forward, bouncing back as if he's hit a wall. Gand won't know it until he recovers the data I deleted, but I programmed him to do that.

"Perhaps you should come inside and have one of the programmers take a look." Corinth reaches a hand toward the Artificial. "Maybe there's a glitch in your data."

Unable to resist, Gand follows him toward the palace as the prince manipulates the key around his neck to force the Artificial to follow.

"Will you be okay on your own, Goselyn?" The prince turns back to me with a concerned look on his face, his brow furrowed kindly.

"Yes." What other choice do I have? At least Gand won't be in my hair today.

I take a seat as the prince and the Artificial walk away. For a moment, I consider letting the geese roam free for a while, but I don't need any extra questions. I go back to tending them properly.

It isn't long before Arta joins me.

"What happened?" she demands, clearly having heard something.

"The Artificial was asking too many questions. He got close to me and I managed to pop his chip out and program him to stay away from me so that he didn't expose your little plan."

She grimaces, wrinkling her nose.

"Fine. Keep it that way. I'm nearly done anyway."

"You mean we'll get to go home?" I ask, standing.

"Yes. I just have to get the prince to sign the proposal and then I can remove him."

My blood runs cold.

"What do you mean?"

"Oh, stop being so sentimental, Goselyn. I won't do it while we're here. We still have to go home, present the proposal, enact the plan, and *then* we'll kill him—you don't have to watch any of it. All you have to do is keep your mouth shut."

Before my cousin got his hands on her, Arta never would have spoken to me like that.

My knees wobble, nearly forcing me to pitch forward. Arta's eyes grow wide for a moment before narrowing.

"Pull it together," she hisses. Any human-like movements that aren't a part of an Artificial's programming could give us away.

"Princess," the king calls from the hill. "My son is waiting for you inside. He'd like you to join him in his study if you don't mind."

My first reaction is to curtsy, but I remember just in time and manage to hold still. I wait as Arta accepts his invitation to return to the palace.

Partway up the hill, the king slows. Once Arta is safely inside, he turns to me.

"Hello," he says in greeting. He's friendlier than his son—though, I imagine, just as strategic.

"Hello, King Delare."

"All by yourself today?" He stands with his hands behind his back, his posture as straight as my shepherd's hook.

"Your son sent Gand in to be looked at by a programmer. He seemed to be experiencing a glitch," I report.

"Yes, I caught him on the way out, actually. Had quite the story to tell." He pauses, removing a hand from behind his back to stroke his chin. "It seems he thinks you're not an Artificial. I wonder why he would think that..."

"I don't know, sir." I look down, trying to avoid him as I scoot a goose back.

"I see," the king muses. "And there's nothing you would like to tell me?"

"No, sir."

He pauses, trying to decide what to say next. A swan wanders by us, but he waves for me to leave it alone.

A few dozen yards away, the fountain cascades into itself, creating a never-ending cycle of soothing sound. I wonder if I could hide behind it.

"Perhaps it's that you *can't* tell me." The king tips his head, examining me.

"I couldn't say, sir," I reply.

"I see," the king says solemnly. "Maybe you'd like to sit with me."

He motions me over to the log. He's larger than his son and takes up more space on the overturned tree.

"I would very much like to help you, Goselyn, but I can't do that unless I know what's going on. No one is watching us and your princess is behind closed doors. All of my Artificials, robots, and workers have been removed from the area. If something is going on, now is the time to tell me," he insists. He's clearly trying to be gentle with me, but the wrinkles on his forehead suggest that he's worried something is going on.

I don't trust Arta. She decapitated Fal—or ordered him to be. She's threatening my mother. Even just now, she told me she's planning the assassination of a ruling monarch of another country. The king may feel it's safe, but I know it's not.

"I truly do not know what you mean, sir." I reach up, brushing back my hair. Pulling it to one side, I expose the skin on my neck.

"I see," the king says slowly, eyes widening. "And you're sure there's nothing I can help you with?"

"I think the only thing you can do, sir, is help your son. He's in greater need of it than I am," I say, praying he understands my meaning. I tip my head to emphasize my point. "Children need their parents to look after them just as much as parents need their children to protect them."

I hope he understands that I'm doing this to protect my mother. Perhaps he could even find a way to warn her for me.

"You make a good point," he agrees, standing. "I'll see to my son. He's always been good about keeping secrets, as I'm sure your Princess Arta is.

"I hear you've been advising my son. Thank you for your help. I'm sure he would like to thank you personally later." He makes it ten feet before he turns back to me. "I think I shall send a letter to your queen, thanking her for the magnificent representatives she has sent for this diplomatic mission. I'm sure she'll be quite pleased to hear of it."

"I'm sure it would mean everything to her, thank you. You'll want to send that via Channel One so no one accidentally intercepts it."

"Indeed." He nods his understanding.

I can scarcely believe my luck. The king of Delare is going to warn my mother of my cousin's plans. I want to throw my arms around him to thank him, but I hold still. My mother will know what to do to disable Arta's ability to control the Artificials in Sylvane the moment she reads his communication—now I just have to figure out how to survive until she does, and return to take down my cousin.

"PRINCESS." CORINTH GREETS me by my title, cornering me outside the stable. I eye him warily until he holds up a necklace—a device that prohibits intelligence gathering within a certain radius. It knocks out all cameras and recording devices while looping in old footage. I have something similar at home. "We're alone."

"Has your father contacted my mother?" I ask, giving up my wariness over Arta catching us.

"He has. I'm so sorry you had to go through all of this. Your mother is working to shut down Arta's ability to control the Artificials as we speak. She'll be safe soon."

I hope she figured out that my cousin is behind this and didn't enlist his help. We've always been wary of his demands and outbursts, so I'm sure she's being cautious.

"You're in danger," I quickly tell the prince. "Arta is planning to destroy the proposal, and then once it's been signed, she's going to remove you."

"*Remove* me?" His eyes widen as he takes a step back. "What does that mean?"

"I assume it means you're going to die," I try to say gently. "My cousin wants my throne *and* yours, so he's trying to take us both out at once after we've returned with the proposal."

"But if she's not here, how will she manage that?"

"I would imagine that she's not the only Artificial in on this plan." I glance around, waving him into the shadows of the building. "It's entirely possible he has control over some of *your* Artificials too. Gand must not know, or he wouldn't have pushed things with me, but who knows which of them are working together on this?"

"Why is he doing this—other than simply wanting the thrones?"

"My cousin believes his leadership would be superior, Corinth—he doesn't think we can handle ruling. He doesn't want our countries working together."

"We've done just fine until now," says Corinth bitterly.

"Now, we just have to prove it," I say.

CORINTH NODS TO me as I trail behind Arta into the parlor—my mother has sent word back that she's safe.

Let the games begin.

"Princess, have a seat." Corinth motions toward a fainting couch with a large, ornate gold rim along the tiny fragment of a back.

Arta arranges her skirt carefully as she sits. I quietly follow behind her, taking a seat on the edge of the couch, prepared to go after her control panel if needed.

Corinth begins. "I've been thinking about a few addendums to the proposal." He lays out a few papers on their laps as he sits next to her. "I think it would be beneficial if we could—"

"What is this?" Arta shrieks. She gathers the papers up and shoves them at the prince. "No, we agreed to the original proposal and we're sticking to that."

"No, actually, we didn't, princess. You tried to *force* me into it, but you never once listened to me. This is what I feel we need to add to make this beneficial to Delare and not just Sylvane." He tries to hand her the paperwork again.

"You are a fool." Arta shakes her head in disgust. "I will leave right now and neither of us will have completed our part of the proposal."

"You can't be queen without it," he reminds Arta, jumping to his feet to follow behind her as she hurries toward the door. "But honestly, *I* don't mind. I've never really had a taste for ruling. You'd be doing me a favor."

Arta looks at him in shock.

"This hurts *you* more than it hurts me, Arta," he says in a darker voice. "If you want me to play along, you have to make this worth my time. You've offered me nothing."

Arta pauses, her face going slack as she processes the information, a telltale sign that she's an Artificial. When she comes out of it, she blinks.

"I can offer you my hand in marriage," she says. "We can rule our countries together."

"No, thank you, you're not my type," Corinth quickly replies, infuriating her.

"Well, what do you want?" she demands.

"A robot, for starters." He grins. "I hear you had one brought here. I'd like to see it. Your robots are quite a bit different than ours here in Delare, so it would be a bit of a novelty."

"It's broken." Her words are biting.

"It's not," he says, challenging her. "I saw you bring it in. Go fetch it."

He waves his hand at her, shooing her toward the tall, oak door. Arta looks like a petulant child about to stamp her foot.

"Goselyn!" She shrieks my name, never taking her eyes off of the prince.

"Let's all go," Corinth says, motioning for me to quickly follow.

Arta argues the entire way down the hall that she doesn't know where Fal is, but Corinth expertly guides her toward the stables, where he knows our things are being stored.

"There he is," I add when we can finally see my butler strung up on the wall.

"What happened to him?" Corinth yells, acting surprised.

"I told you, he was broken. Your programmers took him apart for scraps."

"You're not handing me a robot head," Corinth snarls. "Go find it a body."

He swings back to face me, away from Arta.

"This is ridiculous," he growls at me with a playful wink. He turns back around to face her. "Well?"

Arta huffs and scurries off to find Fal's missing pieces.

"That will keep her busy for a while." Corinth grins as he steps toward me.

"Oh?" I try not to blush as he smirks at me.

"I hid the pieces." He shrugs. His eyes sparkle when he notices my cheeks and he quirks an eyebrow at me. "She's going to have to make him a body from scratch. I think we should follow her and see what she does."

He tugs at my hand, keeping a safe distance behind Arta as she scours the stables for anything she can use to recreate Fal. She throws things behind her, disrupting the animals, but she doesn't flinch even once as they panic.

We follow her through the stables, out into the yard as she stomps around, looking for anything she can use to cobble together a robot body. She never once considered asking me to do the work for her, though she's also aware that I don't have the technical skills to build a robot body as she does.

A vicious tug pulls me back as we stride toward the palace. I shriek against my captor, fighting to break free. Corinth wheels around, ready to defend me.

"She is not an Artificial," Gand rages, pulling me away from Corinth.

"I know. Let her go, Gand," the prince commands, trying to keep his voice down. "Now!"

Gand freezes, still holding me against his silicone body covered in lab-created skin. The only thing that gives him away is his lack of pulse.

"Sir, she does not belong here. She is lying to us. She needs to be taken for questioning." His grip tightens around me.

If I had seen him coming, I could have defended myself, but Artificials can be as much as three times stronger than a human. I wriggle under his grasp. Even Corinth looks slightly worried.

"Put her down, Gand. I'm aware of what is going on." Corinth lowers his hand, indicating that I should be set down. His other hand moves toward the key around his neck in case he must force the Artificial into submission.

The moment my feet touch the ground, I sprint toward the prince, pushing away from Gand.

"She erased my memory, Prince Corinth," Gand says to him. "She attacked me in the hallway and tried to undo my programming."

"No, Gand. *You* attacked *her* and she was trying to protect herself—*and* me. I can't explain it now, but you'll understand soon."

"I will take this to your father," Gand threatens.

"He already knows, Gand."

The Artificial takes a dangerous step toward the crowned prince of Delare. Corinth doesn't back down. It amazes me how Artificials think they can challenge humans just because their brains work faster than ours process information.

"Go back to the geese, Gand." Corinth reaches for the key around his neck again, prepared to force Gand back.

The Artificial turns around slowly, slinking back toward the lake. We watch as he kicks at several of the geese.

"You need to find him a new job," I comment, pursing my lips.

"Or turn down his anger levels," Corinth murmurs back.

"Maybe take out his personality all together?" I suggest, earning a smug, close-lipped grin as Corinth fights not to laugh.

"But he has such a charming personality," he remarks.

"True. The Artificials of Delare are so welcoming." I toss my hair as I speak, rolling my eyes dramatically.

"Hey, we're not all bad," Corinth corrects me.

"I didn't realize you were an Artificial. I suppose that would explain why you weren't friendlier to me," I tease.

"I wasn't the one concealing my identity, *princess*," he reminds me casually. "We should catch up to Arta."

With the sudden change in conversation, we spin around and hurry back toward the palace, assuming Arta went inside to look for supplies.

It's quiet inside as we search for Arta, methodically sweeping the rooms until we locate her. The loud crash in the dining hall suggests we've found her before we open the doors.

When we enter, it's not Arta, but rather the king whom we see first.

"Son," he warns in a harsh tone. "Get back."

Arta's arm is wrapped around his neck. She grabs her wrist, using her forearm to apply pressure to the king's throat. He struggles uncomfortably beneath her grasp. Corinth gasps beside me.

"Arta." I try to reason with her, though I'm not sure why since she's under my cousin's control. "Let him go. There's still a way to make this work."

"How is that?" she asks, her programming urging her to listen.

"We can still get both parties to sign the proposal. You and I can still take it back to Sylvane," I reply, taking a small step toward her.

"It's too late for that—they already know about the plan," Arta contradicts me.

"They only know what you've told them," I assure her.

"Don't lie, Goselyn." She gives me a withering look. "You've never been good at it."

"Can he hear us?" I ask, referring to my cousin in Sylvane.

She pauses, waiting for confirmation. Finally, she nods.

"Kenneth," I call. "You need to end this. We won't hold it against you if you stop now."

Arta drops her arm from around the king's neck. His hands fly to his throat as he attempts to step away from the Artificial.

The moment of hope passes as Arta runs full speed at me. Corinth attempts to block her, only resulting in him being pushed to the ground.

My Artificial tackles me to the floor, our screams mixing together. Something twitches in her eyes as we wrestle—perhaps a bit of the old Arta before she was reprogrammed. She slams my head into the ground.

I kick her off of me, sitting up to a spinning world. Corinth throws himself on her, forcing her backward until she tosses him over her shoulder.

The king runs at Arta at full speed, slamming her into the wall with his shoulder. She grunts, struggling to get her footing while she claws at his face.

I hate the idea of hurting my Artificial, but she's no longer the Arta I know—she's something much more hideous now at the hands of my cousin.

Arta breaks free of the king as Artificials pour into the room to see what's happening. They surround us for a moment, looking on.

I pause next to Corinth, breathing just as heavily as he is. We watch the group of human-like creations as they stare at us, unsure of who has control over them.

The king hits his button to protect himself from the Artificials.

"Son," he warns, urging the prince to enable his key to protect himself, blocking the Artificials from being able to hurt him. All royals have one, and despite our differences, we have documentation in place to ensure these necklaces work on all Artificials, regardless of country. If someone intends on hurting another royal, they can't use artificial intelligence to do so — it's one of the many perks of having a key.

"She doesn't have one," Corinth replies, refusing to enable his safety net if it will leave me vulnerable.

The king looks shocked, yet overwhelmed with respect for his son.

"I think you two are going to get along just fine after this," he murmurs. "But we really don't have time for this right now."

He rushes at Arta, slamming his elbow into her face. Her head snaps back at an angle so sharp that it would have done incredible damage had she not been a machine.

"Get the key," he demands as he pushes his hand against Arta's face to hold her back.

We scramble forward, unsure if our movements will cause the Artificials to attack. Corinth tears at Arta's neck, looking for the chain my key device is on.

I could help Corinth and retrieve my key, but that will only protect us for so long. Instead, I thrust my hands toward the back of Arta's neck, fumbling for her control panel.

"That won't work," she warns me. "You can't eject my chip. Kenneth made sure."

I would eject her chip if I had to shatter her neck to do it.

"I'm smarter than my cousin," I counter.

"He's a programmer," she yelps, struggling to rip my hands away. "He's better than you."

"We both had the same teacher," I respond, fingers slipping off her fake skin. "I promise you my mother didn't teach him everything she taught me."

Arta uses her feet to push off the wall as the Artificials erupt around us, some breaking free of whatever control Kenneth had over them, while others are still clearly under his programming.

The king falls to the ground, nearly tripping Arta. She springs over him at the last second, leaving me only a step behind her. I tackle her, attempting to pin her arms.

"Use your key," I scream at Corinth.

"I didn't get yours yet," he yells back, rushing to my side.

"You need to stay protected," I shout back.

"So do you, *princess*," he says, for the first time not using my title respectfully.

"One thing at a time, *prince*."

I lower myself, running at Arta. Grabbing her around the waist, we topple to the ground. I pull open the control panel on her neck, prepared to punch in the necessary information to fight back against my cousin.

Corinth throws himself on top of us, lending his weight to the struggle. He rips my key necklace from around her throat as he sits on the Artificial.

The prince gently leans toward me, brushing back my hair as he wraps the small digital key rectangle around my neck, latching it. He twists the clasp around to the back of my neck, tickling me in the process. Arta still bucks beneath us as we struggle to control her.

I reach up for a moment to enable the biometric key, knowing Corinth can't do it for me. As soon as it locks into place, putting a digital barrier between myself and the rest of the fighting, I go back to my attempts to disable my Artificial.

"Anytime, Goselyn," Corinth says as he pitches forward. Arta bucks, trying to throw us off. He catches me, holding me steady as I work.

"*Kenneth*." I lecture my Artificial sharply, knowing my cousin is getting a full report. "You're going to pay for this."

"Goselyn," the king shouts, running to our sides. "A bot just arrived with a message. "Your mother has control of your cousin. All you have to do is reset your Artificial."

Perhaps he *didn't* hear my last threat.

The news gives me renewed strength. I lunge at Arta again, working to key in the proper codes to disable the override. She struggles, but there isn't much she can do under the weight of two of us.

I key in the final commands and she goes slack. We sit in silence.

"Is it over?" Corinth finally asks, afraid to move.

"It's over," I breathe, shuffling off of the motionless Artificial. "You should also have control over your Artificials again."

I motion toward the human-like figures around us. They've already slowed, connecting to their former programming.

"Already taken care of, my dear," the king replies. "I think it's time you contacted your mother."

"And time to get the proposal negotiations back on track," Corinth adds. "I get the feeling that we really shouldn't wait on that."

"I agree." I let out a nervous laugh. "But first, can we go get Fal, please?"

"I'm sure you need something to feel a little more secure about your place here," the king responds. "Corinth, take the princess to rescue her robot, please."

Corinth offers me a hand. Together, we leave Arta's shell on the floor. The king's Artificials will take her to their programmer to get her back up and running in her former working condition before I leave, though I imagine I'll have some trouble trusting her for a while.

"I'm sorry we made you work with the geese," Corinth drawls as we walk toward the stables. He places his hand behind his back properly.

"There were swans there too," I remind him. "Aren't we past all the formal stuff at this point?"

He smiles slightly, not missing a step.

"I suppose we are, Goselyn." He drops his arm, walking more casually. "I do apologize that you had to go through all this though. I'm sure it was very difficult."

"I'm sorry I brought it all to you. I didn't have any idea until right before we arrived." I sigh.

"It's not your fault," he says as we approach the tall doors to the stable. "I think I might have a few things to say to your cousin, though."

He chuckles warmly.

"Well, perhaps you'll have to come to my home to give him a piece of your mind."

"I might have to." He walks a little faster, catching the door to hold it open for me. "After you."

Fal is sitting on the wall where I left him, still in sleep mode.

"Hold on," Corinth says as I reach for my robot.

He finds a stepping stool in the very back of the building and drags it over. Climbing up, he wrestles Fal's central system off the wall. A programmer joins us, carrying Fal's body. He expertly puts him back together, though the wait is excruciating.

I tap Fal's head, bringing him back to life. The light blinks on, simulating eyes, as dots of different colors dart across the interface.

"You did it?" Fal asks, beeping the way a cat might purr.

"We got word to my mother and she helped us turn off Kenneth's programming. They're working on fixing Arta now."

Fal notices Corinth and beeps at him.

"He's fine, Fal." I smile. "Corinth, this is my robot, Fal. Fal, this is Prince Corinth of Delare."

"Nice to meet you, Fal." Corinth looks like he wants to get down on his knees and address the robot as a child. My robot beeps back at him.

"Your Highness," Fal says.

"I'm sorry about the rude welcome," says Corinth. "I hope you'll allow us to fix that."

Fal looks up to me, gauging my reaction. I nod, encouraging him to relax.

"We have negotiations to work on," I say, redirecting the conversation. "We should probably get back. I need to message my mother too."

"Of course, Princess."

"YOU'RE MUCH EASIER to work with," Corinth informs me as a tray overflowing with fruits and cheeses is set on the table next to us. "Prettier too, if I might add."

My hand stops in midair as I blush profusely.

"You like doing that, don't you?" I ask, blinking back the uncertainty.

"Making you squirm? Yes," he answers bluntly.

"That nice-guy act was just for show, huh?" I pick up a grape.

"Oh no, I'm always nice to the Artificials — they don't do so well with sarcasm and flirtation."

"I liked you better when I was an Artificial," I tease.

"Most people do." He nods innocently, eyes wide. "The good news is that we're almost done with these charges against your cousin, so you can go home soon and never see me again."

"You say that as if you weren't planning on coming along to harass Kenneth during his trial," I mumble, glancing up just in time to catch his grin. He quickly rearranges his face to hide it.

"Fine, you'll be rid of me after I see justice is done. You'll be sad to see me go, though."

"Will I?"

"You will." Fal beeps next to me. I quickly tap him on the head, putting him into sleep mode. Corinth smirks, scooting closer on the couch.

"I like the little guy." He shrugs casually. "I also like that I don't have to be so proper around you."

"Benefits of fighting an insane Artificial together, I suppose."

"What would you have done," he asks, putting his arm on the back of the couch, "if my father hadn't found out you weren't an Artificial?"

"Climbed out the window again and escaped, probably."

He looks as though I've struck him.

"You climbed out the window?"

"Did I not tell you about that part? *Oops.*" I shrug, reaching for another grape.

He catches it out of my fingers, popping it into his mouth.

"That's what happens when you keep things from me," he informs me.

"It's been a week—we hardly know each other well enough to share all of our secrets," I retort.

"Two weeks, madam," he corrects, staring at my hand resting on my knee.

"Yes, but only one of being a human."

"Fine, I'll give you that, goose girl. Good thing we have the entire journey to Sylvane to talk."

"Oh, doesn't that sound lovely?" I reply sarcastically.

"It does." He purses his lips, tipping his head as he looks at me.

"Goose girl?" I question.

"Yeah." He grins. "Since you like pecking at me so much—"

"Your Highnesses." A knock at the door sounds. "We've fixed her."

The programmer opens the door, stepping to the side. Arta stands beside him quietly.

"Your mother sent us the specifications," the programmer informs us. "She's been restored to her last backup."

"Hello, Goselyn."

I tap Fal on the head much harder than anticipated. He springs to life, wheeling himself over to inspect Arta.

I reach up, tapping my key necklace to control my Artificial. After going through the motions of testing her, I finally release Arta.

"Welcome back, friend."

She smiles at me as I introduce her to Prince Corinth.

Corinth recoils as she turns an icy glare on him when I inform her that the prince will be traveling with us. I'm positive this will be a very enlightening trip home.

DANCE OF DECEPTION

Clara Kensie

We danced in the woods at midnight. Every night. All twelve of us.

We danced because it was fun, because it was summer. We danced to celebrate our youth and our freedom and our friendship. We danced because no other girls could dance the way we could.

As long as no one found out.

I slipped out of my house at 11:45, like I had every night this summer. My parents always went to bed early, so they never noticed. Even if they had noticed, they'd probably let me go, happy that after living in this town my whole life, I'd finally made some friends.

The heat, thick and humid, hit me as I slid open the back door. I ran two blocks through my neighborhood down to Main Street. Lilybrook was a quiet, safe, mostly-boring town in northern Wisconsin, and the only place open this late was Hawthorne's Diner. I went there almost every morning to get a latte and breakfast to go, but this time of night

270

they served mostly cops, couples on dates, and the after-shift guards from the Lab who were craving a late-night slice of Hawthorne's famous blueberry pie.

Lilybrook was quieter than usual tonight, though. There weren't even any cars on the road. Still, I stayed in the alleys and shadows until I reached our designated meeting spot at the edge of the woods.

I was second to arrive, after Anna. She always got there first. These clandestine dances had been her idea, spawned two months ago when her boyfriend broke up with her just before prom. "Who needs that stupid school dance, anyway?" she'd sobbed to us later that day, wiping away tears with the back of her hand. "I have a better idea." She'd chosen us — me too — because we all had a secret like hers.

And now we had another one.

Our secret midnight woodland dance was so much fun that we decided to do it every night, all summer long.

Tonight Anna wore a glamorous golden yellow dress and matching pumps, both new. My dress was pale pink, sparkly, knee-length, and borrowed from Anna's closet. The rest of us couldn't afford to keep buying new dresses, so we swapped amongst ourselves, and Anna was always happy to let us wear hers. I was worried Anna would complain I'd worn this dress too many times, but she whispered, "I love that dress on you, Lila. You look so pretty."

Anna and the other girls had rarely spoken to me before these dances. None of them had ever been mean to me — they weren't like that — but I was awkward and shy and never knew how to fit in. It was more like they didn't notice me. But now, not only were they speaking to me, they were texting me and tagging me on social media and inviting me to get ice cream with them. And Anna had just given me a compliment.

School was starting in a couple of weeks. Now that I had friends, my senior year was going to be amazing.

One by one, the other girls gathered. Suppressing giggles, we slipped down the dirt footpath into the woods. The moon shone through the lattice of leaves overhead, giving us just enough light. We'd followed this path enough times by now to know when to hop over tree roots and duck under low-hanging branches.

We tiptoed on the wooden bridge as we crossed over the water-lily-covered brook and held our breath as we dashed along the electrified fence that ran the perimeter of the Lab. We darted down the dark narrow path, the only sound the chirping of the cicadas, the whoosh of our dresses, and the patter of our heels on the—

Snap.

I froze. Something behind me had made a noise. A twig—breaking? A foot—stepping?

"Lila," whispered Anna. "What's wrong?"

"Did you hear that?"

Anna stopped. Looked. Listened. "I don't hear anything."

I peered into the woods. "Hello? Is someone there?"

"Come on," said Anna. "We can't let the Lab catch us out here." She rushed onward with the rest of the girls.

I stayed where I was, watching, listening. But nothing moved, and I didn't hear the noise again. It must have been a squirrel, or an echo from one of the girls, or a falling branch.

I hurried to catch up with my friends.

THE SITE OF our midnight dances was a clearing deep in the woods, the surrounding trees tall enough to give us a canopy of leaves.

"Let's get set up," directed Anna, fanning herself. "Delia, cool us off first, would you?"

Delia obliged, taking a deep breath and exhaling through pursed lips.

The mugginess was replaced by air fresh and crisp, and tiny snowflakes floated from the sky, sparkling in the moonlight.

Katti opened the box she was holding and, with a wave of her hand, sent strings of twinkle lights floating up to the tree branches. Eva pointed at them, shooting a sizzle of electricity from her finger. The lights flickered on, bathing the area in soft light.

Ginger popped in, literally, at the center of the clearing, then wobbled as she steadied herself. Teleporting always made her dizzy. "Sorry I'm late," she giggled.

Carmen stood at the edge of the clearing and gave a soft whistle. Moments later, four great gray owls fluttered onto her outstretched arms. She cooed gently at them, and they flew off again, following her command to circle the clearing, guarding the path and the surrounding area.

In the center, Belinda spread her arms and turned in a slow circle, giving us another layer of protection by creating a soundproof force field around us. Using our powers anywhere but in the Lab or in our own homes was forbidden. Even in the middle of the woods, in the middle of the night. But now, not even the Lab would hear us. We were ready to dance.

The twelve of us gathered in the center, our dresses of every color glimmering under the twinkle lights and the stars, snowflakes cooling our skin. Eva zapped power into tiny speakers we'd camouflaged in the trees, and soon music played. Soft and delicate at first, then louder, faster, urgent.

Lithe and graceful, Josephine started dancing first. As she twirled, she touched each of us on our shoulders, infusing us with joy, injecting us with giddiness, making our feet tap in rhythm, even mine, which usually couldn't keep a beat.

Our feet pounded, our arms swayed, our dresses swirled. We twirled and leapt and sang and laughed. We were young, we were free, we were powerful, and most of all, we were friends.

We danced until our feet ached, our ears buzzed, and the moon dipped low, but we didn't stop. We twirled and swirled and—

Hoo, hoo.

"The owls!" Carmen cried.

Everyone froze. The music stopped, the twinkle lights went dark, the snow melted. Anna rushed to the owls, the rest of us following close behind. The owls stood on the path in a circle, hooting and squawking, their wings spread wide.

Caged by the owls, eyes wide, mouth open in shock, was a boy.

He had seen everything.

His face was shadowed under his long, dark hair, but I recognized him by his height and broad shoulders. "That's Michael," I said. "From school. He works at Hawthorne's every morning."

"He writes for the school paper," said Hedda.

"He's the one who exposed those kids for cheating on the SATs last year," said Josephine.

"He's terrified," squeaked Fanny, her hands over her heart. "He's trying not to show it, but I can feel it."

"He's neutral," said Anna. Neutrals had no psychic abilities. They were powerless. But they were also dangerous because if a neutral found out about us, they could expose us.

"What do you mean, I'm neutral?" asked Michael. "What's that?"

Anna didn't answer. Instead she smiled at him and asked pleasantly, "What are you doing out here?"

Michael shrugged innocently. "Just... taking a walk."

"You were taking a walk, in the woods, in the middle of the night?"

"Yep." For some reason, his gaze settled on me.

"Oh, no, he's hurt," said Fanny, rubbing her head. "An owl must have scratched him." Indeed, Michael shook the hair from his face, revealing blood on his forehead.

"I'll heal him," said Hedda, immediately stepping forward.

Anna held her back. "Michael, tell us what you saw."

"I told you, I didn't see anything," said Michael. "I took on a few night shifts at Hawthorne's, and tonight after my shift I went for a walk to clear my head." He backed away, but at Carmen's silent command, the owls lifted their wings, trapping him again.

"He's so scared," whimpered Fanny. "Michael, you don't have to be afraid of us. We won't hurt you."

"Yes he does," said Anna with a smile, "and yes we will, if he doesn't tell us what he knows."

"He's *hurt*, Anna," insisted Hedda. "You have to let me heal him."

Anna sighed. "Fine. Carmen, tell the owls to stand down."

Carmen directed the owls back up to the trees, and Hedda stepped forward. She murmured comforting sounds and placed her hand lightly over his wound. He jerked away from her.

"It's okay, Michael," I said, catching his gaze. "Let her heal you. It's what she does."

I kept my eyes locked on his, keeping him calm as Hedda healed him. Many of us had lived in Lilybrook our whole lives because our parents had been recruited by the Lab. Some of our families, like Anna's and Belinda's, had lived here for generations. But Michael had moved here right before our freshman year of high school, with no association to the Lab. I didn't know much about him, other than that he was on the school paper and he took all the Advanced Placement classes. He had a small group of friends, all neutrals. The only time our paths crossed was when I stopped at Hawthorne's to get breakfast. He always grunted a bored *good-morning-can-I-help-you* greeting as I decided what to order.

And now that I was spending so long looking into his eyes as Hedda worked on him, I noticed how dark they were, how expressive. I didn't need Fanny's psionic empathy to know he was bewildered — and afraid.

I offered him a smile, hoping it would help, a little.

"There, all better," cooed Hedda. She dabbed off the blood with a leaf. "The cut is all healed. And don't worry, you won't have a scar."

He scuttled away from her, but Anna stopped him. "Stay where you are, please," she said sweetly. "If you move a muscle, we'll have to bring the owls back."

He swallowed hard, his eyes darting up to the trees.

"Isadora," said Anna. "Will you please tell us what he knows?"

Tiny Isadora stepped over and, standing on her tiptoes, placed her fingertips on Michael's temples. "He saw everything," said Isadora, reading his mind. "He followed us all the way down the path and watched us the entire time."

"How are you doing all this?" asked Michael. "Reading my mind, healing me. The music, the lights. The snow. The birds. How is that possible?"

Once again Anna ignored his question. "Where's your phone?" she asked. "Did you take pictures? Video?"

Michael looked at us one by one. "The science lab," he said. "All of you have parents who work there. I've seen you all going in and out of that place." He crossed his arms. "It's not a regular science lab, is it?"

Isadora put her fingertips back to his temples, then jerked away like she'd been burned. "He wants to write about us," she cried. "Not just for the school paper, either. He wants to expose us and the Lab to get a journalism scholarship. He took a video and he's going to post it online as proof!"

No. No, no, no, that could *not* happen. Michael could *not* release that video. I didn't know a lot of what happened at the Lab. It was run by very important, powerful people, and most of what they did was classified. But I did know one thing for sure: If Michael released that video, the Lab would be shut down, and everyone with special powers would be locked up. Experimented on. Weaponized. Neutralized.

We could not let that happen.

"Where's your phone, Michael?" asked Anna.

"In his pocket," answered Isadora.

"Give it to me," said Eva. A bolt sizzled from her fingertip. "I'll fry it."

"No." Anna sighed. "I'll take care of it."

Katti wiggled her fingers at Michael's jeans, and his phone rose from the pocket. "Hey!" he shouted. He grabbed for it, but it zipped away.

Anna caught it and rubbed it between her palms. When she separated her hands, the phone was gone.

Michael's eyes went wide again. "Where'd it go? What did you do to it?"

"I banished it," said Anna, shrugging. "It's gone. Forever. It no longer exists. We're under a force field, so your video wasn't transmitted to the cloud. But banishing your phone was the only way to ensure that video was completely destroyed. I'm sorry, Michael, but it had to be done. And so does this." She turned to me. "Lila, you know what you need to do."

I nodded, hoping the girls would assume the sweat on the back of my neck was caused by the heat, not by my nerves. I could do this. I *had* to do it. I'd done it plenty of times in the testing room at the Lab, and my dad had made me practice until I was as skilled at it as he was. I'd never done it on someone who wasn't a volunteer, but it was the only way to save the Lab. This was my big chance to impress my friends, to cement my place in the group.

Please don't let me mess it up.

I stepped over to Michael. He backed away. "What are you going to do?"

"It won't hurt, I promise." I tried to hide my anxiety as I took his hand between both of mine. His hand was rough, warm, strong, and I held it tight.

I closed my eyes.

Concentrated. Pushed.

Entered his mind.

Then I shuffled through his memories, from the moment he left Hawthorne's that night.

Michael's memories flowed into my mind, one after another, filling my head, making me warm, making my heart pound.

LEAVING THE DINER a few minutes before midnight, exhausted after a long day, knowing he still needs a story to get that journalism scholarship.

Seeing something move in the shadows in the alley across the street. His heart stopping when he recognizes Lila. She comes to Hawthorne's in the mornings and takes forever *to decide what to get, then ends up ordering the same thing she always does:* a small vanilla latte with extra sugar and a blueberry pie pocket to go, please.

Smiling at the thought. For the past three years she's been doing that, almost every morning. She's got the longest, thickest eyelashes he's ever seen.

Wondering what she's doing out in the middle of the night, rushing through the alley, looking over her shoulder, wearing a party dress. Wondering if she's in trouble. Deciding he'd better make sure she gets home safe.

Trailing her as she creeps along the shadows. Feeling surprised when she meets a bunch of girls at the edge of the woods. They're all dressed up too. Fancy dresses, fancy hair, fancy shoes. Those are the girls who go to that science lab in the mornings. He hadn't realized Lila was friends with them.

Knowing that whatever she's doing, she's safe now. Knowing he should go home and work on his application. Curiosity compelling him onward.

Following the girls as they dash into the woods. Observing as they fall completely silent when they tiptoe past the science lab.

Freezing when he breaks the silence by stepping on a twig. Cursing himself when Lila whisper-shouts into the woods, asking if anyone is there.

Following the girls deeper, to a clearing. Slipping behind a tree, hiding.

Shivering when one girl exhales, the air suddenly cooling. Gasping at snowflakes falling. Watching with disbelief when strings of light float up to the trees, all by themselves.

Knowing this can't be real. Can it?

Suppressing another gasp as a girl whistles, and four owls fly from the trees and land on her arms. She whistles again, and the birds fly off on her command.

Realizing these girls must be witches, or aliens, or paranormal superpower mutants. Things he reads about in books and watches on TV but never before believed are real.

Sliding his phone out from his pocket.

Aiming the camera.

Clicking the record *button.*

Thinking, pondering, mind whirring, making connections. All these girls have parents who work at that science lab. The exterior of the building is old, small, and uninteresting. Ugly, even. But it all must be camouflaging a fascinating interior.

Knowing this is bigger than anything he's written for the school paper. He needs to figure out how to get inside the science lab, and then he's going to go wide with the story. This will get him that journalism scholarship.

Focusing his camera on the girls dancing giddily in the moonlight.

Capturing each of the girls in turn, one by one, as they do something extraordinary.

Lingering his camera on Lila, unable to turn away. She's always been cute, with those thick eyelashes and that spattering of freckles on her nose and the way her cheeks flush when she asks for extra sugar in her latte. He'd even say she's beautiful. But tonight, under the twinkling lights and the glowing moon, dancing with euphoria, enchanted by joy, she is breathtaking.

Watching her dance and twirl and laugh.

Wishing she was in his arms, dancing with him.

STANDING ON THE edge of the clearing, the moon low in the sky, holding Michael's hand between both of mine, I saw all of his memories of that night. Every last one.

And then, with a mighty pull, I absorbed them into my mind, erasing them from his.

Breathless, I released his hand. He opened his eyes, looked at me, at the girls surrounding him, up at the trees. Squeezed his eyes shut, shook his head, opened them again. "What... how did I...?" He ran his hands through his hair. "What's going on?"

It worked. I did it. He didn't remember anything. I leaned closer to him and whispered, "Shh. This is just a dream." He smelled like soap and pine.

Using my mnemokinetic power always drained me for a few

minutes, like fatigue after a rush of adrenaline. I wanted to get Michael home, but my legs were weak, my hands shaky. "Someone needs to make sure he gets home okay."

"He's feeling a little dazed," confirmed Fanny, shaking her head to clear it of Michael's confusion.

"I'll take him," said Ginger. She crouched and put her hands on his shoulders, and the two of them disappeared with a small pop.

Anna kneeled next to me. "You sure he won't remember anything about tonight?" she asked, rubbing my back.

"When he wakes up in the morning," I said, already feeling better, "he'll feel like he had vivid dreams, but he won't remember any of them."

"Good," said Anna. "That was a close one."

Somber now, and still shaken, we packed up what was left of our soiree. Anna vowed tonight's events would not stop our midnight dances and made us all promise to keep coming back.

We walked home in the darkness and heat together. The girls congratulated me and thanked me for saving the Lab—and our dances. Anna even brought me in for a hug when we reached my house. "You saved us, Lila," she said. "I'm so happy we're friends now."

I waved goodbye to my friends, knowing our dances would continue. I'd solidified my place in the group and had earned their respect. I was one of them now, finally, and truly.

But all I could think about were Michael's warm hands, his tousled hair, his frightened eyes. He knew me. He'd *noticed* me, all these years, when no one else ever had.

He thought I was beautiful.

I STOPPED AT Hawthorne's the next day on my way to the Lab, where we went every morning for training. After, I was going with Anna, Isadora, Josephine, and Katti to Lilybrook Lake. Anna had a new inflatable float, shaped like a gold, bejeweled crown, and so big that all five of us could fit on it at once.

Unlike the diner's subdued, almost-empty late nights, it was always bright and bustling in the mornings, with weaving waitresses carrying trays and sit-down patrons clattering and clinking their utensils. Michael worked the carry-out counter near the front of the diner. I was fifth in line today, behind a tall, slender woman holding a toddler's hand and jostling an infant in a baby sling, and in front of a short, round man muttering angrily into his phone to someone named Nelly. I watched Michael as I waited in line. Did he remember anything about last night?

His eyes looked a little tired, but he didn't seem confused or dazed as he took the customers' orders. He wore a bright pink polo with the Hawthorne's Diner logo—the name of the diner circling a slice of blueberry pie—embroidered in blue over his heart. Around his waist was a white apron with a small steno notebook and a pen in one of the pockets.

His forehead was unmarred, the cut completely healed as if it had never happened. His dark hair was tied back. I definitely liked it better down and long and tousled, the way it had been last night. But I liked the way his jaw was a little scruffy today. Was it like that every day and I'd simply never noticed? Or had he been too tired to shave this morning?

My turn. I approached the counter, watching him carefully.

Was there a flicker of recognition in his eyes? No. A smile? No, not even that. Just weariness, and maybe a sense of impatience. "Morning, welcome to Hawthorne's, what can I getcha today?" he mumbled.

"Um..." I tapped my fingers on the Formica as I looked at the menu, determined to be healthy today. Iced green tea and an egg-white-and-turkey-bacon sandwich on a whole grain English muffin. Or maybe a lemon fizzy water and a spinach-and-feta wrap. Or the avocado, kale, and banana power smoothie with chia seeds and ground flax.

The round man behind me had ended his phone conversation and was standing too close, and I could sense his impatience at my indecision, flustering me. "Small vanilla latte with extra sugar and a blueberry pie pocket to go, please," I said.

The corner of Michael's lip rose the tiniest bit. If I'd noticed that smile before, I would have assumed it was a sneer. Now I knew he was amused. "Alrighty," he said, wiping his hands on his apron and going to the coffee maker. He returned with my order exceptionally fast, as he always did, the latte with a cover and a sleeve, and the blueberry pie pocket warm inside a paper bag with extra napkins.

"Thank you," I said.

He nodded absently, already looking over my shoulder to serve the man behind me.

"No, really," I said. "Thank you." It was really sweet of him to follow me last night. He'd wanted to make sure I was safe. He didn't remember doing it, but he had still done it, even though he was tired and still had that scholarship application to work on. He was more than sweet. He was chivalrous. Selfless. I gave him a smile.

He returned it with a closed-lipped, bashful smile of his own that disappeared before it fully formed. "Morning, sir, welcome to Hawthorne's, what can I get you today?" he asked the round man, dismissing me.

He didn't remember a thing about last night.

The round man took my place at the counter. I rushed out, excited to get to the Lab and tell my friends that I'd confirmed I had successfully erased Michael's memory, that the Lab was safe, that our dances could continue. They would all be so relieved.

I RUSHED IN the stifling heat that night, sneaking out of my house, running two blocks to Main Street, passing the dark stores and restaurants. No sign of Michael as I darted past Hawthorne's. I met my friends at the edge of the woods, and we dashed down the woodland path, over the brook, past the Lab, all the way to the clearing deep in the center of the forest. Belinda generated the soundproof force field, Carmen directed the owls to patrol, Delia frosted the area with snow. Eva turned on the twinkle lights and started the music, Josephine infused us with rhythm. We danced and laughed and twirled, and we were young, and powerful, and free.

Until the owls screeched.

Eva snapped off the power, and Delia melted the snow, hiding us in darkness and heat. On the path, the owls had tackled Michael to the ground and were squawking two inches from his terrified face.

"Why is he back?" cried Anna.

The steno notebook I'd seen in his Hawthorne's apron that morning was in the dirt near his hand. Katti wiggled her finger at it, and it rose and zipped over to Anna, who snatched it from the air.

Her silver dress sparkled in the moonlight as she slowly flipped through the notebook. "He wrote down everything we did tonight, and he made sketches," she said. "He wrote the word *Lab* with a question mark and circled it."

From the ground, Michael reached for his notebook and tried to get up, but the owls pinned him down by his shoulders. Shaking her head at him and sighing, Anna held the notebook between her open palms. Moments later, it disappeared. Michael looked just as shocked as he had last night when she'd banished his phone.

She shrugged apologetically at him. "Fix this, Lila," she said.

I motioned to Carmen to call off the owls and sat cross-legged next to him. "This won't hurt," I assured him. I took his hand, closed my eyes, and concentrated. I decided to go further back in his memory, all the way back to when I'd seen him at Hawthorne's this morning:

Seeing Lila in the carry-out line. Waiting as she debates over the menu choices, knowing she'll order a vanilla latte and a blueberry pie pocket anyway. Hating the impatient jerk in line behind her. Serving the rest of the customers. Looking all around the diner for his missing phone.

Going home after his morning shift. Sending his mother off to work. Slathering SPF50 on his little sister, taking her to the park. Reading her every book she brings to him at the library. Taking her home, creating an obstacle course for her in the backyard, spraying her lightly with the hose, showing her how to make rainbows with the water.

Opening his laptop, tapping the keyboard, thinking, knowing he needs to uncover something big to get that journalism scholarship. Looking for his phone again until their mother gets home. Heading out for another shift at the diner.

Leaving just before midnight, exhausted, knowing he still has lots of work to do. Turning the corner, seeing Lila dash through the shadows. Following her to make sure she's safe.

So. It was my fault he was here—again. I should have taken a completely different route to the woods.

I squeezed his hand, and with a herculean mental pull, I absorbed his memories into my mind, erasing them from his.

The fatigue set in, then the shakes, but I didn't let go of his hand. I hadn't known much about Michael before, but I knew now that he worked split shifts at Hawthorne's, that he took great care of his little sister while their mom was at work, and that when he saw a girl slip through the shadows in the middle of the night, he cared less about going home to apply for scholarships than he did about making sure she was safe.

It was a shame, really, that I had to erase so many hours of his memories. Nothing extraordinary had happened during those hours—discovering our secret psychic dance the exception. He'd spent the day taking care of his sister, working hard, and watching out for my safety.

It was just an ordinary day for him. And that made him extraordinary.

My chest grew tight, my throat became thick.

One of the girls knelt next to me and placed her hand gently on my shoulder. "You okay, Lila?" It was Hedda. "You look really shaky, worse than you did last night. Tell me what's wrong and I'll heal you."

What was wrong was that I'd stolen Michael's memories, and that was something Hedda couldn't cure.

But I had to erase his memories. I *had* to. It was the only way to keep our psionic powers secret, to keep the Lab safe, to keep our dances going. These girls were my friends, and I would never do anything to jeopardize that.

"Were you able to see why he came back?" asked Anna.

"Um, like he said last night." I hated lying to my friends, but I couldn't let them find out it was my fault. "He went for a walk to clear his head after his shift."

The girls helped me from the ground and steadied me. I reached for Michael's hand again, not to erase more of his memories, but to help him up. And also... because I wanted to touch him again. I wanted to feel his hand in mine, just for a second.

His hand was warm. Strong. I held on to it longer than necessary. I gave him a comforting smile, and he returned it, his eyes glazed. "Small vanilla latte with extra sugar and a blueberry pie pocket to go, please." He chuckled and swayed on his feet.

My heart burst, and my knees went weak again. After releasing him, my own hand felt cold and empty. "We need to make sure he gets home safe."

He had been trying to make sure *I* got home safe, after all.

With a twinge of jealousy I watched Ginger take his hand. With a pop, she teleported herself away, taking him with her.

Michael was a good guy. A *really* good guy. I liked him. A lot.

Anna put her arm around my shoulders and thanked me for saving them again. She invited me to go shopping with her tomorrow afternoon.

I said yes. I liked Michael, but my friends were more important.

HAWTHORNE'S CARRY-OUT line was extra long the next morning. A white-haired lady was behind the counter, chatting with each person as they placed their order as if they were the only customer in the diner. "Where's Michael?" I asked her when it was finally my turn.

"He's been working split shifts, late nights, early mornings," she said. "Kid's working so hard that when he came in today he thought it was Tuesday. Yesterday. It was like he forgot an entire day. Mrs. Hawthorne gave him the morning off. Told him to go home and get a few extra hours of sleep."

Guilt pooled in my belly like lava. "Is he all right? Is he coming back?"

"He said he'd be back for the evening shift."

"Okay, good."

I looked at the menu, debating between the avocado, egg white, and spinach sandwich and the butternut squash breakfast wrap. "I'll have a small vanilla latte with extra sugar and blueberry pie pocket to go, please."

"Sorry, sugar, we ran out of the pie pockets an hour ago."

"Really?" This morning's stop at Hawthorne's was a huge disappointment on every level. First no Michael, then no blueberry pie pocket.

"Gotta get here early if you want one of those." The lady's face crinkled as she smiled. "You must be the girl he saves them for."

"Hmm?"

"Michael. Every morning when he comes in, he sets aside a blueberry pie pocket. Won't let anyone touch it. Says a girl comes in and orders one every time, so he saves it for her. That's you, isn't it?"

My whole face grew hot, and I couldn't stop myself from smiling. "Yeah, I guess it is."

This morning's stop at Hawthorne's wasn't so disappointing after all.

I SHOULD HAVE taken a different route to the woods that night. But I waited in the alley across from Hawthorne's. I had to make sure Michael was okay, that I hadn't harmed him by erasing so many hours of his memory. Just before midnight he stepped outside. He seemed fine. Well-rested. Healthy. He took off his apron and pulled the tieback from his hair. His eyes shone bright under the streetlights.

I should have waited for him to head home before I continued on my way to the woods. But I stepped out of the alley.

I should have stayed in the shadows. But I stepped out into the street.

I should have been quiet. But I made a little noise.

He noticed, and followed. All the way to the woods, all the way to the clearing. And he watched.

And after we discovered him and Anna banished his notebook, I held his hand and erased his memory. Just from the time he saw me outside the diner, nothing earlier than that. He wasn't getting hurt, and we weren't in danger of being exposed. It was harmless. I got to keep my friends, and I got to hold his hand.

The next night, and the next night, too. I didn't hide in the shadows as I passed Hawthorne's on my way to the woods. I got there early and lingered across the street, waiting for Michael to push open the door, take off his apron, and shake his hair out of the tieback. I'd start walking again, making sure to pass under a streetlight. My steps were no longer so quiet.

He noticed again, and he followed me, staying about a half block away. I led him to our meeting place at the edge of the woods, then dashed down the path with my friends, knowing he was a few hundred feet behind me. I felt... complete, knowing he was there. He filled in a piece of me that I'd never known was missing.

I said nothing to my friends, knowing he was watching us from behind a tree as we set up the dance, as Belinda soundproofed the area, as Delia made it snow and Katti floated the twinkle lights up to the trees, as Eva sparked the music on and Josephine infused us with grace and rhythm. I danced and spun and laughed with my friends under the twinkle lights, knowing he was watching.

I spun away from Isadora, who could read my mind and know I was thinking of Michael hiding in the shadows, of Michael's kindness, and his selflessness, and his green eyes, and his lips.

I twirled away from Fanny, who would feel my emotions and know I had fallen in love.

In love?

Yes. Oh, yes. I was in love.

And all too soon, Carmen's owls hooted their alarm, and I had another chance to go to Michael and hold his hand, before I erased the dance from his mind.

WE HADN'T EVEN reached the wooden bridge the next night when a howl, followed by a strangled yelp, echoed through the woods.

"Got 'im!" Anna shouted, pumping her fist triumphantly. "Nicely done, Carmen."

My blood ran cold as we dashed back down the path. There, growling, teeth bared, was a coyote. And pinned under him, too scared to move, was Michael.

I started running to him, but Anna pulled me back into the trees. "Carmen, get that coyote off of him!" I cried. We were psionic, but we would never use our powers to hurt anyone. Not like this.

"The coyote won't bite him," said Carmen calmly. "She's just scaring him so he won't come back into the woods."

"So what if he does? I'll just erase his memory again."

"It's not enough," said Anna. "He walks through the woods at night to clear his head. But now that he knows he'll be attacked by a coyote, he'll go clear his head somewhere else from now on. "

"Call off the coyote, Carmen," I demanded. "Anna. That's enough. Tell Carmen to let him go."

Anna acquiesced with a reluctant nod. Carmen gave a low, sharp whistle, and with a final growl and a warning lunge, the coyote released Michael. It pranced over to us in the trees and sat at Carmen's feet, looking up at her worshipfully.

Down the path, Michael struggled up to his elbows. He was breathing hard, but I couldn't breathe at all. My heart stopped beating as he climbed to his feet.

But instead of running up the path and out of the woods to safety, he peered into the trees.

"Why isn't he leaving?" asked Anna.

Michael took a tentative step, then shouted, "Lila?"

I froze.

Anna gripped my arm. "Why is he saying your name?"

"Lila, it's me, Michael," he called. "From Hawthorne's? I saw you and your friends go down the path. There's a coyote..." He stumbled forward. "Lila?"

Anna's nails dug into my skin. "Did he follow you here? Is *that* why he's been showing up every night? Did you know about this?"

I started to shake my head, but it was over. I had to tell my friends the truth. "He sees me when I go past the diner and follows me to the dances," I confessed. "I let him do it. But you banished his phone and notebooks and I erase his memory every time, so it's okay."

Anna stared at me, her eyes blazing, her lips in a tight line. Behind her, the girls stared at me too, most of them with their mouths open.

"It was wrong, I know, and I'm sorry. I promise I won't do it again," I said, "but right now Michael thinks we're being hunted by a coyote. He's trying to save us. He's not going to leave until he knows we're safe. Anna, stop. You're hurting me."

Anna's face was pure red as she glowered at me, squeezing my arm. Was she going to banish me from existence? Could she do that to a living thing, to a person? Was she that powerful?

But instead of banishing me, she released my arm. "Well, then," she said. Her tone was soft, measured, and sickeningly sweet. "You'd better go erase his memory again."

I nodded and rubbed my arm, which was sure to have bruises in the morning. "I'm sorry," I repeated. "I won't lead him here again."

"Oh, I know you won't," said Anna, smiling. "Because you can't come again either."

I froze again. "What?"

"I really liked you, Lila. We all did. We'd always thought you didn't like us, and we were so happy that you finally let us be your friends." She gestured to the girls behind her, and they all nodded. Eva and Ginger looked like they were about to cry. My eyes burned. I couldn't speak around the lump in my throat. I could barely hear Anna over the pounding in my ears.

"But then you led Michael here," she said. "You purposely exposed us. You put the Lab in jeopardy." Her syrupy tone turned acidic and bitter. "So you can't come back. Ever."

She turned away and marched into the trees. The rest of the girls followed. Belinda and Isadora glanced at me over their shoulders and shook their heads. Suddenly, the air around me went frigid. The other girls weren't shivering, which meant Delia had literally left me out in the cold.

Anna hadn't banished me from existence, but she had banished me from the group. And that was even worse.

I had just lost all of my friends.

I DIDN'T SNEAK out to the dance the next night. Or the next. Or the next. The few times I left my house and happened to see the girls in town, they were cordial to me but distant, the way they used to be. One morning Ginger and Josephine nodded to me at the Lab when we were there for training, and once Eva and Katti waved to me at the store as we were buying school supplies. But I was back to being the awkward girl who didn't fit in.

I had betrayed my friends. I didn't deserve to have them anymore.

In the mornings, I drank my mom's Folgers with her sugar-free creamer and ate blueberry Pop-Tarts at home. I was avoiding Hawthorne's. Really, I was avoiding Michael. When I'd approached him in the woods that last night, he'd been so relieved I hadn't been attacked by the coyote that he'd hugged me. While he held me tight, he'd asked if I was okay, if my friends were okay, and then he'd asked what we were doing out there in the first place.

Instead of answering his questions, instead of hugging him back, I'd erased his memory.

Ginger hadn't been there to teleport him home, but I'd been so shaky and fatigued that he'd ended up taking *me* home. It had felt like a dream to him, and even in his dreams, he was determined to keep me safe. He wouldn't remember that dream in the morning, but I would never forget that night. Michael was selfless, courageous, ambitious, kindhearted, generous, and beautiful, and I had betrayed him, invaded his privacy, and stolen his memories.

I didn't deserve him, either.

A WEEK AFTER my banishment, I stared at the dresses hanging in my closet. I missed the dances. I missed the music, I missed the celebration, the freedom. I missed being part of something secret and special.

I missed my friends.

And I missed Michael. His green eyes, his tousled hair, his strong, warm hands.

I wondered if he was still saving a blueberry pie pocket for me every morning, or if he'd given up.

One of the dresses still had the tags hanging from it. I'd been saving it for tonight. School was starting tomorrow. Anna had promised that the last dance of the summer would be the best yet, and instead of borrowing a dress from one of the girls, I'd bought a special dress with my own money for the occasion. Pale yellow, with fabric roses adorning the neckline.

My fingers itched to slide into the dress, to strap on my heels, to twist up my hair. I wanted to dash down the woodland path to the clearing and twirl and swirl under the twinkle lights with my friends. I wanted Michael to wrap his arms around my waist, hold me close, and dance with me.

But I had betrayed them all. Michael and my friends. I had jeopardized the Lab.

I had no reason to wear this dress, no *right* to wear this dress. I took it from my closet, and while the rest of the girls were painting their toes and curling their hair in preparation for the last dance of the summer, I went to the mall and returned my dress.

I shoved the cash into my pocket and went home, wishing I could return everything about this summer and pretend it had never happened. I wished I could return Michael's memories.

Wait.

Maybe I *could* return Michael's memories.

At 11:45 that night, I dashed down Main Street, wearing shorts and a T-shirt and flip-flops, my hair down and loose. The night was the warmest it had been in weeks, but I shivered as I approached Hawthorne's. *Please let him still be there. Please don't let me be too late.*

I pulled open the door and rushed inside, and there he was, coming out from the kitchen, untying his apron.

"A small vanilla latte with extra sugar and a blueberry pie pocket to go, please," I said. I was breathless from running—and from finally seeing Michael again.

The corner of his mouth rose. "I just got off duty," he said. "But hold on. I'll get your order."

"No, wait." I inhaled his scent. Powdered sugar and spice. "I didn't really come here for blueberry pie."

"Oh, no?"

"I need to give you this." I took the cash I'd gotten for my dress and pushed it into his hand. "It's to replace your phone."

"My phone? How did you know it was missing? And why do *you* need to replace it?"

"There's more." My heart beat in my throat. "Will you come with me?"

"Where?"

"Just come." I held out my hand, and he took it. My hand belonged there, in his warm grasp. It fit perfectly.

I led him out of Hawthorne's, down the street, to the edge of the woods. The girls had already started down the path with a flutter of skirts and a clacking of heels. Anna was easy to spot in her dress, which was covered in so many rhinestones she looked as if she herself were made entirely of diamonds. They stopped when I called out to them. They turned, stiffening when they saw Michael.

Anna pushed her way to the front of the group. "What are you doing here?"

I stood tall. Anna had backed down before when we'd stood up to her, when Hedda had insisted on healing Michael after the owl had scratched him, and again when I'd insisted Carmen call off the coyote. I needed to do that again.

"Anna," I said, "I made a mistake, and I'm sorry. I had the best time this summer, dancing with everyone and hanging out with you. I'll leave if you want me to, but I want to stay. I want to be friends again."

Anna looked me up and down, and the fire in her eyes extinguished. "I want to be friends again too," she muttered to her feet. Then she squinted up at Michael. "But what about him?"

"I trust him," I said, shrugging.

Behind Anna, the girls looked at each other, murmuring.

"Lila, what's going on?" asked Michael.

"I'll show you." I led him, followed by the girls, down the path, over the bridge, past the Lab, all the way to the clearing. I brought Michael to the center. The girls gathered at the edges. They were the watchers this time.

I stepped closer to him, holding both his hands, feeling his warmth. "I could tell you what's happening," I said, licking my lips. His lips were only a few inches away. I stood on tiptoe to make them closer, and he brought them closer still. "But the only way you'll believe me," I whispered, feeling his warm breath on my cheek, "is if you see it for yourself."

And then I kissed him.

His lips were warm, soft. Tender and strong at the same time.

Without breaking the kiss, I released his hands and slid my arms around his neck, bringing him closer. He wrapped his arms around my waist.

Instead of a mental pull this time, I pushed, and his memories, trapped inside my mind, transferred back into his.

The nights he'd hidden behind a tree, watching us dance, amazed, as gentle snowflakes floated from the sky, as lights twinkled from the branches, as the air cooled and music pumped, as we swayed and swirled and twirled and laughed. His memories of being discovered, and cornered. His memories of me taking his hand and wiping his memory.

All the memories I'd stolen from him, I returned.

Still holding each other tight, we stopped kissing for a moment. "Wow," he panted, gazing into my eyes.

"There's one more thing I need to do," I said. "I've never done it before, but if it works, it'll explain everything."

The corner of his lip went up again. "Go for it."

I kissed him again, and instead of pulling this time, I heaved a mighty mental push, and transmitted my own memories into his mind:

We danced in the woods at midnight. Every night. All twelve of us.

We danced because it was fun, because it was summer. We danced to celebrate our youth and our freedom and our friendship. We danced because no other girls could dance the way we could...

MY MEMORIES BELONGED to Michael now, too.

Our kiss lasted much longer than it had taken to share my memories, and when we finally parted, we noticed the twinkle lights, and the music, and my friends swirling and twirling and laughing around us.

Because he knew everything now, he knew how fatigued I felt. Gently, he guided me to the edge of the clearing and wiped the leaves and moss from a fallen tree trunk, and helped me sit. But he hadn't spoken yet, his eyes dark, his expression unreadable. Was he angry? Was he going to expose us anyway? Whatever happened next, I wouldn't wipe his memory again. I wouldn't do that to him.

"Michael," I said, still trembling, "Are you okay?"

I couldn't breathe until he answered.

"That was..." he said, then he burst out laughing. "Incredible. Wow. *Wow.*"

Warm relief spread through my limbs. He wasn't upset. He was thrilled. Awed. Amazed. "You know about us now, and the Lab," I said. "But you have to keep it a secret. You'd destroy us if you tell anyone."

"I won't tell anyone, I promise. I wouldn't do that to you."

I wanted to kiss him again. "But that means you won't have an article for your scholarship application. I'll help you think of something else."

He scrubbed the stubble on his chin. "Actually, you already did. You know the man standing behind you at the diner that morning, the one you called 'the round guy' in your memory?"

"Yeah..." That man was so inconsequential that I would never have thought of him again if I hadn't just shared all of my memories with Michael. "He was on the phone with a woman named Nelly."

"Well, 'the round guy' just happens to be the mayor, and Nelly isn't a woman, he's the owner of a construction company who's known for bribing politicians to throw business his way. Now, thanks to your memory, I know the mayor is talking to him. I'll do some investigation to prove they made some kind of deal. If they did, I'll have my scholarship article after all."

A grin spread across his face, and he kissed me. Gentle, playful, then urgent and powerful. I kissed him back hungrily, no memory exchange this time, just pure, perfect, glorious kissing.

When we finally stopped, breathless and beaming, the dance was in full swing. The music pumped, the lights twinkled, the snowflakes floated from the trees. The girls swirled and twirled and spun. Anna beckoned to us, laughing.

"Michael," I said, "will you dance with me?"

Hand in hand, we walked to the center of the clearing. I wrapped my arms around his neck, he wrapped his arms around my waist.

And together, we danced.

THE FALSE NIGHTINGALE

Mary Fan

A new dawn woke over the proud mountains and rolling seas of Huangjing, capital of the planet Caixing. Named for the rainbow hues banding the land, Caixing had been settled generations ago by Daiyu's ancestors from Earth.

Starships from a hundred worlds descended from the rose-gold sky, each carrying their civilization's most important political and cultural ambassadors to attend Daiyu's coronation. Whirring transports zipped over Caixing's colorful surface, bringing tribute from the outlying provinces.

It was a day that would long be remembered in Caixing's history. But Daiyu wished she could close her eyes and wake to a world where it would never happen.

As the third child of her royal parents, she'd thought she'd get to choose her own path. She'd spent years training to be an operatic soprano, dreaming of gracing the galaxy's greatest stages. But empresses didn't get to be singers.

Still, Daiyu understood her duty. She stood before the Empire's gilded throne, which was carved with celestial dragons winding through shooting stars, and gave polite nods to the dignitaries who'd come to pay tribute to Caixing's new ruler. Her neck felt ready to snap under the weight of the elaborate headdress, which was bedecked with golden phoenixes and ruby tassels. It crowned her head of ornately twisted black hair. Her ceremonial dress, made of heavy yellow silk embroidered with whirling patterns of galaxies and tigers, seemed ready to drag her to the ground.

She tried to act as her parents and brothers would have expected her to. A year had passed since a rogue asteroid had shattered the starship carrying all four of them, and the wounds in her heart were finally starting to heal. The nation, too, seemed ready to move on from its collective tragedy. She'd worried that the regents would refuse to cede power when she'd come of age at eighteen, but those fears had been unfounded. Apparently, her coronation was the salve Caixing had needed to recover from losing their beloved Emperor and Empress—her beloved parents.

Beings from every corner of the galaxy approached to offer gifts and blessings. The red columns of the Great Hall, wrapped with gilded dragons made of stars, shimmered around them. Daiyu greeted each with practiced words, trying to exude the same effortless grace her mother had. She hoped her resplendent ensemble and bright red lipstick made her appear more mature than the shy, round-cheeked girl she was accustomed to seeing in the mirror. The small, pale girl with the wide, innocent black eyes and the demure cherry-blossom mouth.

If she'd been born with her father's imposing height or her mother's authoritative stare, she might have seen an empress when she gazed at her own refection. And if she'd seen one, she might have felt like one. But Daiyu had spent most of her life thinking her destiny lay in playing wilting damsels and lovely maidens onstage. That destiny had suited her.

Unlike her brothers, she hadn't been educated in politics and diplomacy. Though she'd spent the past year cramming her head with relevant knowledge, everyone knew she was still merely a soprano who'd been thrust unwittingly into the Empress' throne.

Yet she *was* the Empress, whether she liked it or not. And by the stars, she would behave like one. She was all too aware that many expected her to be a malleable puppet, someone clueless and naïve they could manipulate. She'd seen it in the greedy, ambitious eyes of the Empire's ministers, guild leaders, and regional representatives. She refused to yield to their expectations.

Nervous as she was, Daiyu tried to appreciate the parade of marvels before her. It seemed the entire universe had sent ambassadors to greet her, from the tall, blue-furred Orinians, with their large yellow eyes and twisting silver horns, to the gelatinous blue Whiswheri, who slithered like snakes but morphed into humanoid forms to speak to her.

Since Caixing was known for its arts, many had brought performers to serenade her. The winged Ash'iii had brought a band that produced music by flapping their feathers through the air. The eight-legged Pashans had brought a troupe of dancers who flowed like ribbons upon the hall's bronze floor.

But the performer who'd captivated the court the most was from Caixing itself.

Daiyu didn't need the Master of Ceremony's introduction to recognize the famous Vox Jarik, known as the Bilin Nightingale. Two years ago, she'd persuaded her parents to let her travel all the way to Llayu on the other side of the galaxy just to attend an opera the young tenor was starring in.

Jarik's black hair was pulled in a stern topknot that accentuated the severe beauty of his sharp, gold-complexioned cheekbones and hard chin. A pair of piercing black eyes, tilted under hooded lids beneath thick brows, met her own. He lifted his lips into a confident smirk, one that told the world that though he was merely a musician from the rural Bilin Province, not even royalty intimidated him.

Daiyu's heart fluttered. When Jarik began to sing, she thought it might fly away. The song of triumph he performed in her honor seemed to be spun from a million yellow stars. The strength he sang of, the victory and the honor — she felt it in her own chest.

Yes, Caixing was a great nation. Yes, she was its great Empress. And yes, she would bring her people glory.

By the time Jarik concluded his song, Daiyu felt ready to lead a fleet of starships into combat — even though they were a peaceful nation and had no enemies. Her parents had spent their lifetimes brokering treaties to ensure that.

"Does he please you, Your Majesty?" A soft voice slithered past her ears.

Daiyu looked over to find General Drokka Res, one of her many advisors, leaning toward her with a glint in his hazel eyes. She nodded. "He is very talented."

"It would honor him if the Empress invited him to approach." General Drokka gestured at Jarik.

"Yes, of course." Daiyu recalled the many times her parents had asked a particularly talented performer or well-spoken advocate to approach the throne. She cleared her throat. "Vox Jarik. Your performance pleases me. Please, come." She extended one hand invitingly.

A smile brightened Jarik's lips. The blue silk of his tunic glimmered as he walked up to her. Though he bowed deeply, the confident glint in his eyes was anything but humble. "You're too kind, Empress."

"You... did well." Daiyu paused, trying to recall what her parents had said in similar situations. White noise filled her memory, and a slight panic rose up her throat.

"You could invite him to stay at the palace as a member of your court." General Drokka's smooth voice slid into her ears. "It is what your parents would have done."

Daiyu considered the many artists her predecessors had brought to the palace—the musicians, painters, dancers, and acrobats who'd spent the entirety of their careers serving the royal family. She couldn't deny that she wanted Jarik to stay with her. Asking him to join her court seemed like the proper thing to do.

"Vox Jarik." She lifted her chin and gave the singer what she imagined was a dignified look. "I wish for you to join my court."

Jarik's grin widened. "I would be honored, Empress."

General Drokka stepped forward and spread his arms. "The Bilin Nightingale will be staying at the palace at the pleasure of our new Empress!"

Applause and cheers rose from the audience. Daiyu breathed a sigh of relief. At least she'd done one thing right. She looked at Jarik, who gave her a playful wink. Heat rushed to her face. A few years ago, even as a princess, she couldn't have imagined such a handsome, talented, and renowned singer looking her way.

Now that she was the Empress, everything had changed.

WHILE THE PEOPLE of Caixing celebrated their new Empress with fireworks and dancing, an old engineer labored in her humble home. Far from the vibrant streets of the capital, with its jutting skyscrapers and cloud-piercing pagodas, Lao Qiu tinkered in the silver dome that was her house.

On her steel workbench lay a young man with gentle black eyes and soft, angelic features. Except there was no life in them — not yet. Lao Qiu examined the exposed machinery behind a panel in his fair-complexioned neck. Satisfied, she closed the panel, grabbed a nearby tablet, and pushed the icon to wake him.

The boy blinked for the first time in his life and glimpsed his creator's crinkled, merry face, which was ringed with curls still jet black despite her eighty years of age. Her lips curved, and he lifted his own, imitating her expression.

"Good evening, Galen." Lao Qiu reached out to him with one hand.

That was an invitation. Galen knew enough about human behavior to understand that. *Accept it. Take her hand. Repeat her greeting.* Galen gripped her palm, and she pulled him up. "Good evening, Lao Qiu."

"What do you know of yourself, my boy?"

Galen blinked slowly. He had no physical need to do so but knew that humans found lidless stares to be disconcerting, and he did not want to make his creator uncomfortable. "I know I am an artificial intelligence, an AI. I know you made me to look and feel human, even though I'm not one of them." A strange feeling coiled in his chest. "I know you gave me emotions, which is something most AIs are not equipped with."

"I made you to be more than your synthetic shell." Tears welled in Lao Qiu's eyes. "You were modeled after my darling son, who died from disease many long years ago. Like him, you are to be a singer and a compassionate friend."

Galen blinked again. The expectations his creator stated were not foreign to him. He understood his function and his purpose; she'd made sure he would. But he didn't know how he could fulfill them. "As you wish."

"No, as *you* wish." Lao Qiu placed a fond hand on his cheek. "I may have programmed you with a purpose, but I also gave you a mind of your own. Use it well."

Galen wanted to show her that he understood. *Lift your mouth again. Make sure you crinkle your eyes. Take her hand—that's what humans do to show affection.* He wrapped his smooth, youthful fingers around her frail, crinkled ones. Though the gesture felt contrived, the meaning behind it was genuine. "I will do as you intended." More than that—he *wanted* to. He wanted to be a person. But he wasn't sure how.

Lao Qiu sighed. "We have a lot of work to do."

EACH MORNING, DAIYU woke wondering how she would get through the next day as Empress. And each evening, she went to bed unsatisfied with her progress and eager to try again the next day.

She spent her days reviewing proposed laws and meeting with politicians and her evenings entertaining official guests of Caixing, from alien ambassadors to local schoolchildren. Though she fell into a rhythm of duty, most days, she found herself wishing that she could go back to being only a soprano.

She found solace in Jarik, who proved to be a charming companion as well as a popular member of the court. He was always willing to listen to her speak of whatever was on her mind or to tutor her in music so that she might at least hold on to part of her old self.

A month after her coronation, the palace hosted a ball to celebrate the arrival of Prapalla, the Princess of Bupuru, to sign a long-awaited trade agreement between the two planets. Daiyu arrived dressed in green ceremonial robes and greeted the Princess, who was about half her height and walked on four of her seven limbs. Long, silver fur spilled over Prapalla's ensemble, which covered her slender body with red and blue beads.

As the two royals exchanged pleasantries, a cornucopia of guests wandered about the Great Hall, conversing and nibbling on intergalactic culinary delights. Most were human—either from Caixing or other homes of Earth's descendants—but many were alien. Yruxians with serpentine bodies flashing scales of every color on the spectrum. Urala with a hundred tiny legs that barely seemed able to support their bulbous blue forms. Kikkiki with their tiny, humanoid builds supported on wide butterfly-like wings and pointed faces sprouting long whiskers.

At long last, Daiyu finished making her official rounds and managed to find Jarik.

"There you are!" He grabbed her hands and pulled her close.

Blushing, Daiyu lowered her eyelids and giggled. She enjoyed Jarik's familiarity. Around him, she could feel like an eighteen-year-old girl again. "You shouldn't behave this way in public! Everyone can see us."

"Is my Empress ordering me to back away?" Jarik arched his brows.

"Of course not!" Daiyu sighed and pulled her hands away. "But I must maintain the appearance of propriety."

"I understand." Jarik reached toward her face but paused. "I should go prepare for my next performance."

Daiyu's heart sank as she watched him walk away. She wanted so badly to let him treat her as he would any other girl. He was the only one who dared try, and for that, she was glad.

Jarik stepped onto a low stage, and all eyes turned to him. The orchestra, recognizing his cue, struck up the introduction to the song he'd prepared.

Daiyu soon found herself lost in his undulating notes. He certainly knew how to captivate an audience—and not just when he was performing. Everyone at court liked him... in a way they could never like her.

Jarik concluded his song, and the whole court applauded with abandon. Daiyu joined in, grinning. When he descended the stage, it seemed every guest in the hall wanted a chance to meet him.

When a gap appeared in the crowd, she walked up to him. Nervousness clenched her heart. No matter how often she saw him, she still felt like a shy audience member approaching the opera's star. "Jarik!"

"Yes, Your Majesty?" Jarik turned to her with a disarming smile, his sparkling eyes finding hers.

That look could have killed her a thousand times over, and it was all she could do to maintain her dignified stance. "Well done."

He bowed. "Thank you, Empress."

The ambassador from V'blach approached Jarik, towering over him at three times his height on two hoofed legs. Daiyu retreated and waited for Jarik to finish greeting his fans. Jealousy pinched her heart. He was living the life she'd always wanted, while she was trapped in a role she'd never been meant for.

It wasn't until the next act took to the stage that he was freed from their praises. He strode up to her. "Apologies, Empress."

Daiyu cocked her head. "How many times must I ask you to call me Daiyu?"

"Of course, Daiyu." He took her hands.

She wrapped her fingers around his, savoring their warmth. Under the light of the golden chandeliers, which resembled explosions of fireworks frozen in metal, he was painfully beautiful. If she were anyone else but Empress, she might have tried to kiss him. She was certain he would have accepted it; the smoldering look in his eyes told her so.

"I wish I didn't have to be here," she confessed. "I wish we could run away to the garden right now."

"So do I," he murmured.

A troupe of Treshar dancers took to the stage, whisking about with their long, amber fins. They looked almost like fish darting through the water, except with feline faces accentuated by high nose ridges.

Jarik glanced at them. "It's a shame. When our people first settled Caixing, this stage and this palace were reserved for only the finest of our own kind. Now, it has become a free-for-all."

Daiyu knitted her brows. "The other nations have honored us with their best performers."

"We are losing our culture to the influence of outsiders. Our ancestors wouldn't recognize what Caixing has become. I hope someday, it will be a planet for humans once more."

Daiyu frowned but remained silent. Several of her advisors had expressed similar opinions, arguing that Caixing's borders had grown too lax at the expense of the humans who had colonized the planet first.

Even when she wanted to only be Daiyu, she couldn't forget that she was the Empress.

A BRILLIANT MIDDAY sun bathed the palace so brightly, its red and gold walls seemed to glow. Light glinted off the carvings of rabbits, horses, and other creatures adorning the eaves.

Keep your brows and lips lifted to project a pleasant expression. Don't let them fall, or people will think you're cross. As Galen followed Lao Qiu up the steps leading to the Empress' throne room, he recalled a holopic his creator had once shown him of her late son. He did his best to channel that young man's aura of serenity. In the few months he'd spent conscious, he'd learned much about human behavior, and he wanted more than anything to fit in with them. But he often had trouble understanding their subtle cues.

Still, Lao Qiu had deemed him ready to meet the Empress. For the occasion, she'd donned her best silk dress, which was ruby red and finely embroidered with images of Caixing from space. The outfit she'd chosen for Galen was far more opulent. He walked carefully to avoid stepping on the gilded trim of his cobalt robes. He appreciated the craftsmanship that must have gone into embellishing the silk with silver patterns resembling computer chips, but he had little opinion about their aesthetic value. Tiny holoprojectors sewn into the cloth cast glowing, three-dimensional images of abstract patterns that flowed across his body. The glowing lights scattered across his shoulders were more resplendent than the most precious of jewels.

The Empress' court teemed with humans and aliens dressed in extravagant clothing. Yet all eyes turned to Galen when he approached. He reminded himself, once again, to hold his face in a pleasant expression. According to Lao Qiu, his downward-tilted mouth, arching brows, and heavily hooded eyes made him look unimpressed and bored when at rest. His quick gaze took in the dozens of beings and matched them to the database in his mind, which was connected to the planetary network.

"Have you ever seen anything finer?" A purple-scaled alien — *name: Gryin; species: Noxi; planet: Vagor, in the Ysab system* — gestured at him with one of twelve tiny paws.

Beside him, a human woman — *name: Asha Henderson; planet: Mars, in the Solar system* — gave a contented sigh. "It was worth coming here today just to lay eyes on such magnificent craftsmanship."

Galen wasn't sure whether they were referring to his clothing or to him.

He craned his neck, trying to get a glimpse of the Empress through the crowd. When he found her, he finally understood what humans meant by a sight that could take one's breath away. Lao Qiu had shown him plenty of images, but they'd failed to capture the wondrous delight the Empress' presence brought. The smile brightening her sweet face seemed to illuminate the whole room. Though he didn't have a heart to pound or muscles to tighten, he nevertheless felt something stir in his chest.

"Lao Qiu!" The Empress stood from her throne and rushed to greet the old woman. "It's good to see you again."

"Little Yu." Lao Qiu took the girl's soft hands in her craggy fingers. "You look every bit as fine upon that throne as your mother did. She would be proud of you."

"Thank you. I've missed you, Auntie. When I can't sleep, I still recite the stories you used to tell me when I was a little girl."

"I'm glad they brought you comfort. I've come with a gift that I hope will be as soothing as my stories were." Lao Qiu gestured at Galen. "This is Galen, the AI I told you about. May he be a trustworthy companion, even when others give you reason to doubt."

The Empress' dark gaze slid over to Galen. He straightened. Nervousness would not show on his face; he was too conscious of its movements to allow that.

The Empress' expression warmed. "Hello, Galen. It's nice to meet you."

Recalling Lao Qiu's instructions, he bowed. "Hello, Empress." He inflected his voice to mirror hers and lifted his lips to copy her smile. That was how people were supposed to greet other people. "It's nice to meet you too."

A delighted giggle escaped the Empress. She glanced at Lao Qiu. "He's wonderful!"

"I'm glad he pleases you." Lao Qiu nodded. "He's also gifted with music. Galen, will you sing for the Empress?"

"As you wish." No one could have heard the relief in Galen's voice—he controlled it too well. But he was glad to be able to, for a few moments, escape the pressures of all the eyes on him.

Lao Qiu had built his vocal processor and programmed musical knowledge into his memory, but his songs were his own. The ancient tune she'd taught him was fast and bright, but its words were tragic. Though Galen didn't change a note, he gave each line the weight it deserved. His clear tenor voice, pure and strong as diamonds, glittered through the air. The throne room and all its busy bustling disappeared around him.

When he finished, he was surprised to find the room completely still.

The Empress' eyes glistened. "That was beautiful." She looked at Lao Qiu. "I've never seen an AI who could imitate the nuances of human expression so well. How did you manage it?"

Lao Qiu placed a hand on Galen's shoulder. "I only gave him what he needed to get started. I told you he was unique."

"Yes, he is." The Empress turned back to Galen, her expression glowing with joy. "I look forward to getting to know you better."

"Thank you, Empress." Though excitement flooded Galen, he had to remind himself to smile. It wouldn't matter how he felt if others couldn't see it.

The crowd tittered. Though they'd come from far and wide and had seen many of the galaxy's wonders, no one in the court had ever encountered anything quite as fascinating as the beautiful, bejeweled AI boy with the voice of an angel. Many speculated that his song was finer even than that of the Bilin Nightingale.

Few noticed Vox Jarik standing in the back, watching his artificial competition with narrowed eyes.

AS TIME PASSED, Daiyu grew more accustomed to the attention that came with holding court. But she knew to keep a wary eye out for those who would smile sweetly and praise her merits while secretly poisoning her tea. She was well aware that everyone wanted something from her, or to use her.

That was why she was so grateful for Galen. As a longtime friend of the royal family, Lao Qiu had known what kind of people would surround the Empress, and she'd created the AI to be a respite from the politics. Though Galen was a machine, Daiyu would have felt wrong treating him like one when he looked and behaved so human. She gave him quarters near Jarik's, thinking that the two would get along as fellow artists. But Jarik didn't seem to appreciate Galen's presence, saying that the found the artificial singer to be unnerving.

Many who dreamed of being Empress thought only of the fineries of court and cared little about the hard work that came with ruling a planet. Daiyu, however, preferred the quiet hours she spent reviewing legislation, petitions, and reports. After four months on the throne, she'd come to treasure the moments when she could be alone with her thoughts.

One evening, Daiyu sat alone in her study, having finally escaped the court. Her red, lacquered table, sitting in the middle of a bronze-walled room decorated with holographic images of the universe, felt like an island in the eye of a hurricane. Her head still buzzed from the multitudes of voices trying to wheedle their way into her head. Sometimes, they were so loud, she scarcely knew what she herself thought any more.

The door swished open, and Daiyu looked up from the tablet she'd spent the past hour reading.

"I thought I might find you here," Jarik said as he entered. "That was a fantastic speech you gave this morning."

Daiyu blushed. No matter how many times she saw him, her heart always fluttered like it was the first. "Thank you."

"What's that?" He gestured at the tablet.

"A proposed new law to limit the number of alien migrants who come to Caixing for seasonal work." Daiyu wrinkled her nose. "General Drokka keeps pushing for it, but my parents believed the migrants are valuable to our economy and our society. I agree... I think I'm going to reject it."

"Your parents considered General Drokka to be one of their most intelligent advisors." Jarik leaned back against the table. "You'd be wise to listen to him. Caixing is great, but it's not infinite. You don't want aliens to crowd out your own people."

Though his tone was light, Daiyu sensed something darker beneath it. That was hardly the first time he'd expressed distaste for the number of aliens living on Caixing, and that was hardly the first time he'd tried to influence her decisions. Though she wished she could trust him, an uncomfortable feeling gnawed at her.

She'd once hoped to find a true friend—and perhaps more—in Jarik, but she feared he was not as different from the others as she'd believed.

THE IMPERIAL GARDENS were famed throughout the galaxy for their splendor. Flora from every known planet smiled under the afternoon sun. Luminous blue flowers as tall as trees from the lush planet Rioll. Bushes with white, star-shaped leaves from the desert planet Wajir. Pink lotuses from the original homeworld, Earth.

The royal family had always been generous with their gardens, sharing it freely with the people. Though they were among the most popular attractions on Caixing, the lands were so vast, one could easily feel as if one were the only person there.

It was for solitude that Galen sought them. Over the weeks, he'd grown weary of being gawked at and ordered to sing. Not by the

Empress — he would gladly have sung for her whenever she pleased — but by everyone else from alien dignitaries to cleaning staff. He'd never refused a request to perform, for he wanted to be accommodating, but neither did he appreciate being treated like a wind-up toy.

Galen wandered past towering Aoharian trees whose brilliant yellow leaves were each as tall as two of him. He glimpsed a movement ahead and froze, dreading that it would be some tourist who would point and marvel at the famed technological wonder they saw him as.

Instead, the person who emerged was one whose presence warmed him to the core. The Empress wore none of her finery that day, and in her plain white tunic, she could easily have been mistaken for a tourist. Yet her kind eyes and merry lips retained an ineffable luster.

"Galen! I didn't know you enjoyed the gardens too."

He bowed. "Your Majesty." He suddenly realized that he'd forgotten to lift his face into its practiced, pleasant expression. He rushed to curve his lips.

The Empress giggled. "You don't have to smile *all* the time!"

I must have grinned too widely. He adjusted his expression. "Is this better, Your Majesty?"

"Please, don't do that."

"Do what?"

"Treat me like an empress." She sighed. "I understand that you need to in the palace, but it's only us now. I know how hard you work to fit in. Believe me — I feel your pain."

Tilt your head to indicate confusion. Galen angled his head. "What do you mean?"

"People expect an empress to be certain things." The Empress wandered along the wide path, which was paved with gleaming purple stones. "Dignified. Calm. Authoritative. Most of the time, I imagine what my mother would have done in my place and imitate her. But that's not who I am, and it's exhausting." She glanced at him. "I've noticed you do the same thing, except you imitate the courtiers. Always smiling, always looking 'pleasant,' whatever they may be thinking. You may be an AI, but Lao Qiu created you to think independently. So who are you, really?"

Galen blinked. After all his efforts to appear perfect, she'd seen right through him. "I... do not understand most of what humans do. I try to read their expressions and give them the responses they expect. But so often, they cloud their true meanings, and I find it difficult. What's more, I've found that honesty is not always welcome, yet I do not know how to tell falsehoods convincingly. And so I simply smile, say as little as I can, and do my best to be pleasant." A strange rush filled him. Those were the most words he'd spoken to her at one time since arriving at the palace.

"I understand. Human interactions are difficult, even for humans. It's a wonder we manage to communicate at all." The Empress smiled and shook her head. "But I shouldn't complain. I'm grateful to be in a position that lets me make our world a better place."

"Yes, Caixing is a better place because you are Empress." The words emerged from Galen's mouth before he considered them. An awkward feeling seized him.

The Empress grinned widely. "Thank you. I don't deserve such praise, but it means a lot to me since I know you meant it."

"Yes, I meant it." Warmth pooled in Galen's chest, but he wasn't sure whether to find it comforting or disconcerting.

He walked beside the Empress as she continued her stroll through the gardens. But none of the exotic blooms or magnificent trees bore as much beauty as she did.

DAIYU'S SWEET SOPRANO intertwined with Jarik's vigorous tenor, and the two voices soared through her study. She sounded pale and fragile in comparison to the Bilin Nightingale, but she nevertheless delighted in sharing a song with him. She didn't have a lot of time for recreation, but she always made sure to keep her appointments with Jarik. The time she spent with him was the closest she could come to the stage she'd once dreamed of.

Yet even as she sang, she couldn't stop her mind from wandering to Galen and what it might be like to sing with him instead. In the two months she'd known him, she'd come to realize he was the only being in the entire palace that she could trust. As much as she enjoyed Jarik's company, she had to remain wary of his attempts to influence her. Because of her busy schedule, she often had to choose which one of them she would spend time with. So far, she'd chosen Jarik, seeing Galen only once or twice a week. Things would have been easier if Jarik would have tolerated Galen's presence.

Once, she'd asked Jarik to perform with Galen for a royal reception, but the rehearsal had gone disastrously. Jarik had claimed Galen was too much like a music box and lacked the flexibility needed to accompany another. Galen had simply been confused.

The tenor countermelody cut off abruptly in the middle of a phrase. Jarik crossed his arms and frowned at her.

Daiyu knit her brows. "Did I do something wrong?"

"You hit all the right notes, but your mind was elsewhere."

"I... don't know what you mean." Daiyu glimpsed a movement outside the large, circular window and glanced past Jarik.

Galen, who was passing by on the covered walkway outside, paused when she caught his eye. He'd been holding his face in that "pleasant" expression he always did—the mask he projected to the world. His smile warmed, tilting into something crooked and somewhat awkward — but undeniably genuine.

Daiyu smiled back.

"Daiyu!" Jarik stepped in front of her, blocking her view. "We should get back to your lesson."

Daiyu cocked her head, wondering if he was really as angry as he sounded or if she was imagining it.

Outside, Galen rushed away and vanished from sight.

"Good, he's gone," Jarik growled.

"What's wrong with you?" Daiyu put her hands on her hips. "You're always so unpleasant in his presence. Has he offended you somehow?"

"Not by his actions, but by his existence. You seek to replace me with him, but he can never give you what I can."

Daiyu recoiled. "What are you talking about?"

"I've seen how you spend your days with him, and I know it was him your mind dwelled on when you were supposed to be singing with me."

Daiyu wanted to point out to Jarik that it was *him* she'd chosen to spend her days with — often at Galen's expense — but he went on before she could speak.

"Be careful, Daiyu. A machine will always be a machine." Jarik's eyes burned with such intensity, she thought they might set her aflame. "He won't be there when you need him the most. Do not be fooled by that false nightingale." He stormed out of the room.

Daiyu stared after him in shock. She'd never before realized how much darkness had gathered in his heart. He'd hidden it well with his handsome face and easy charm. But in that moment, she finally saw his true self.

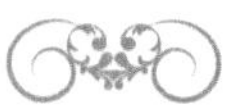

NEW EMOTIONS BLOOMED in Galen's soul—feelings he'd known the definitions of but was experiencing himself for the first time. Some were wondrous—like the rush of riding a fast horse for the first time. Some were painful—like the embarrassment of saying the wrong thing and seeing people laugh at his verbal clumsiness.

Yet he couldn't define what he felt in the Empress' presence. It was at once magnificent and agonizing. At first, he told himself that a powerful attachment to her was natural since Lao Qiu had created him to serve her. But soon he realized how far it went beyond that.

His favorite moments were those he spent walking alone with the Empress in the Imperial Gardens. Sometimes, he'd sing for her, and in the privacy provided by sky-high flowers or hedges as sturdy as steel, his melodies would flow in a way they never could in court. It was her presence that coaxed them out—the soft, admiring look in her eyes, the pure joy on her lips.

She spent more and more time with him—sometimes, he'd even see her two days in a row. Meanwhile, Vox Jarik had vanished. From what Galen had heard, the Bilin Nightingale had returned to his province, though he had no idea whether it was for a visit or forever. Secretly, he hoped it was the latter. The Empress had seemed distraught by his absence at first, and Galen had done his best to take Jarik's place in her life and onstage. Many, human and alien alike, claimed that his music was more enchanting than the Bilin Nightingale's, and some even began calling him the AI Nightingale. Despite their admiration, Galen often felt like an imposter. Vox Jarik was the one who'd developed a career in the arts and enjoyed being at court. All Galen wanted was to sing for the Empress.

One day, Galen and the Empress were wandering among the luminescent pink-and-white Varia lilies, which were each only the size of a hand but climbed upon each other until they reached such lofty heights they nearly blocked out the sun.

An uncomfortable feeling had been following Galen all day, and even the Empress' proximity couldn't melt it. A dark figure seemed to loom behind him, waiting to stab him in the back, yet he could find no reason for it.

"Is something the matter, Galen?" The Empress had apparently noticed his discomfort.

"Yes, but I don't know what."

"You've been performing a lot recently. Perhaps you are fatigued." The Empress met his gaze. "I've been meaning to speak to you about something. When you first arrived, Lao Qiu presented you as a gift. Since you're an AI, I thought nothing of it at the time. But now that I've gotten to know you, I realize you deserve freedom as much as any being. You don't need to stay here if you don't want to."

A slight panic seized him. "Please don't send me away. Being here brings me great joy."

"I'm not sending you away. I'm letting you know you have a choice."

"Then I choose to stay with you." Galen pictured the generals he'd seen, how they'd stood with firmness and certainty, and he did his best to imitate their sure posture.

Before he could continue, a man in black armor wearing a grotesque black helmet that covered the entirety of his face, jumped out from behind the flowers. He brandished a silver laser gun. The Empress screamed. One of the palace's security drones flew onto the scene and rained white blasts down upon the attacker. He shot the machine, and it crashed to the ground.

Galen watched, stunned, as four other attackers appeared seemingly out of nowhere and rushed at the Empress. She tried to run, but whichever way she turned, they blocked her path. Though additional drones swooped in to protect her, the attackers destroyed them all with ease. Two palace guards arrived and exchanged fire, but they were outnumbered and soon fell.

The five in black armor closed in on the Empress, looking like the shadows of death. The Empress snatched the gun from one of the fallen guards. "Galen! Go get help!"

At her command, a sense of urgency gripped Galen, and he wondered why he'd been standing still the whole time. But when he tried to run, he realized that it wasn't shock that had held him in place.

He was paralyzed. No matter how he tried, he couldn't so much as twitch a finger. He might as well have turned to stone.

Yet his senses remained alert, and he watched in horror as the Empress faced her attackers alone.

"GALEN!" DAIYU'S HAND shook around the gun she'd so boldly grabbed. Now that she had it, she didn't know what to do with it. Fear strangled her heart like a snake. "Galen, please! Help me!"

No matter how she cried out, the AI Nightingale remained still, his gentle face expressionless. Something must have broken inside him... a malfunction. Jarik's words haunted her. *He won't be there when you need him the most.*

The attackers closed in on Daiyu. They'd killed two guards, and they wouldn't hesitate to kill her. Already, she could feel the cold hands of death wrapping around her.

"Stay back!" She fired, but her shot missed widely.

Though she struggled fiercely, she was no match for them. One seized the gun, and another yanked her hands behind her back.

The next thing she knew, she was staring down the barrel of a weapon. She was certain that these were assassins who had infiltrated the garden with the intention of murdering the Empress, and no amount of pleading would win their mercy. Tears streamed down her cheeks, and she closed her eyes, waiting for the inevitable.

"Stop!" a familiar voice rang out.

Daiyu looked up, stunned to see Jarik running toward her. After he'd left the palace in anger, she hadn't expected to see him again. So great was her surprise that it robbed her of words.

Jarik halted beside the man with the gun. "Let her go."

"Tyranny has reigned over our planet long enough." The man spoke with a cold, pitiless voice. "The Empress must die."

"She has only just begun her reign." Though he was begging, Jarik still managed to look proud and dignified. "She is not to blame for the laws enacted by her parents. If you do this, Caixing will fall into chaos. Please, lower your weapon and let the Empress live."

"You are a man of the people, and so we will not kill you. But your words will not dissuade us from our mission."

"You are here because you love Caixing, and ours is a world of peace. If you believe in our planet and what it stands for, you'll let her go."

Daiyu's heart pounded so quickly, she felt faint. She didn't dare hope that she might escape death, and yet Jarik appeared so strong, despite being an unarmed musician in the presence of assassins. The man with the gun appeared to hesitate. He hadn't pulled the trigger yet after all.

Silence billowed through the garden.

A golden voice broke the stillness like glisks through a raincloud. The words of an ancient song of peace, one cherished by all on Caixing, sprang to life on the lips of the Bilin Nightingale. Daiyu had known the tune since childhood, but it had never burrowed into her heart the way it did when Jarik sang it. Somewhere in the back of her mind, she knew he was hoping to persuade the assassins to let her go by reminding them of their world's values. But if the song was the last thing she heard, at least she would go to her grave happy.

When he finished, Jarik stepped closer to the man with the gun. When the latter didn't move, he slowly reached out and took the weapon. The assassin offered no resistance.

"Caixing stands for peace," Jarik murmured.

"Peace," the man echoed. "You are wise, Nightingale."

Quick as a flash, he vanished into the thick curtain of lilies. Daiyu felt the grip on her arms disappear, but when she spun to see what had happened, she found that the other four attackers were gone as well.

"Empress!" A red-uniformed officer leading a group of guards rushed toward her. "Are you all right?"

"Yes, I'm fine." The words, a breath on her voice, tumbled out automatically.

Her gaze met Jarik's and she found she couldn't tear herself away from his fierce beauty. He drew closer, and his arms encircled her waist.

It hit her then that she was going to *live*. She collapsed against his chest, sobbing with relief. "Thank you for coming back."

"I could never abandon you, Daiyu." His breath whispered against her cheek.

The next thing she knew, his lips were upon hers, hot and hungry. She offered no resistance. Such a mess of emotions tumbled through her that she didn't know how to react. Yet one thing was sure: In his arms, she finally felt safe.

Standing forgotten beside the wreckage of a broken drone, Galen remained frozen, his eyes still fixed upon his beloved Empress.

GALEN PICTURED TRAGIC scenes from operas he'd watched, ones in which a devastated hero threw himself to the ground weeping, or cried out in vain to silent gods, or plunged a knife into his own heart out of despair. He imagined these emotions because he could not express any of them, no matter how he longed to. His body had betrayed him, and he remained trapped behind still, expressionless eyes.

The Empress must have thought him dead—or deactivated. She seemed to have forgotten all about him after the attack in the garden. He kept seeing the way Vox Jarik had taken her into his arms and kissed her, and he wished he could have been as lucky as the drone that had been shot to pieces.

Two guards carried him back to his quarters, speculating out loud about how he could have shut down at such a critical time. One believed he'd been unable to compute the shock of someone attacking the Empress. The other believed the assassins had uploaded a virus into his mind via his connection to the planetary network. Either or neither could have been true, but Galen didn't care about the cause. All that mattered what that he'd failed the Empress, and she'd nearly died because of it.

The guards left him face-up on his bed and mumbled about how they didn't know what to do about him. Galen wondered if anyone would think to contact Lao Qiu, who could have discovered what was wrong with him.

But as the hours stretched on and on and on, he realized no one cared what happened to him. Not even the Empress.

DAIYU HARDLY REMEMBERED what had happened in the days following the assassination attempt. She drifted through them in a haze, feeling as if she were on autopilot, but she did her best to appear all right. People already thought she was weak. She couldn't give them further reason to believe that, and so she allowed herself no time for recovery. She kept every appointment and attended every function. She stood straight and spoke with a confidence she could project but couldn't feel. In fact, she couldn't feel much of anything. She kept seeing the two dead guards—their slack faces and pooling blood. If Jarik hadn't arrived when he had, she would have joined them.

Jarik seemed to follow her everywhere, and she was too grateful to push him away. Everyone gossiped about how the Empress had a new lover, but she was too numb to care. She allowed him to walk by her side as an equal, to hold her hand and even kiss her in public.

News of Jarik's heroics spread quickly. Everyone praised the Bilin Nightingale, whose song was so sweet it chased away Death itself. Daiyu wished she could feel about him as they did. It was because of him that she was breathing at all. She remembered how she'd felt not long ago, when she'd been a starstruck girl meeting Caixing's greatest opera singer. That girl would have been giddy to have the handsome, talented Bilin Nightingale as her lover, and she would have treasured every one of his kisses. A distant part of Daiyu hoped that when the fog cleared from her head she might find pleasure in his company again.

She felt as if she were in a deep ocean being swept about by waves from every direction. But she didn't have the energy to swim and could barely tread water. People would come to her—officials, courtiers, Jarik—and she would oblige, but she did not seek them out. She spent an inordinate number of hours sleeping, each time hoping that she'd wake with a clear mind.

GALEN LAY THERE, day after day, night after night. His mind kept running through images of human expressions—ones he'd stored so he could imitate them but now pictured because he could not. He recalled screams he couldn't release, tears he couldn't shed.

Footsteps padded down the hall outside. At first, Galen thought nothing of them, for many had passed his room without realizing anyone was inside. But then the door swished open, and Vox Jarik entered with a short-haired woman he did not recognize.

"Quickly!" Jarik gestured at Galen. "You must get rid of him now, before someone sees you here."

What? Fear rushed through Galen like an icy waterfall.

"Are you sure about this?" The woman peered into Galen's face. "He was a favorite of the Empress. People may notice when he's gone."

Jarik let out a derisive noise. "He's a broken machine and should be discarded as such. Besides, the Empress won't miss him when she has me."

The icy waterfall grew heavier. Galen wanted to cry out, but he couldn't even blink.

The woman's lips quirked. "How are you doing with her?"

"Very well." A cold sneer contorted Jarik's face. "Ever since I saved her life, she's been clinging to me like a magnet. I have no doubt she will fall in love with me as planned—if she hasn't already. It won't be long before she'll agree to marry me. And when I am Emperor, I will free Caixing of the alien rabble infesting it. Persuading Daiyu will not be a problem, especially since I'm now her hero."

Jarik must have thought that Galen's mind was as frozen as the rest of him, or else he would never have spoken so frankly. Shock pulsed through Galen. He could never have imagined such deception.

The woman lifted her chin. "General Drokka will be pleased. I had my doubts when you first proposed staging an attack on the Empress, but it seems to have worked out in our favor."

"I needed bold strokes. The little fool was going to replace me with this mechanical abomination." Jarik pointed at Galen. "Even if the others hadn't agreed to the assassination attempt, I still would have uploaded the virus to his mind. He was getting in my way."

Galen recalled once seeing a nobleman gasp in horror. The memory looped through his head, expressing what he couldn't.

Vox Jarik had been plotting against the Empress from the moment he'd arrived at court. He'd planned to charm her with his beauty and his talents, and then convince her to marry him and make him Emperor. And he'd thought he could control her.

Galen wanted to rise up and defend his Empress. Despite her gentle manner, she was no one's puppet. Perhaps she had fallen for the Bilin Nightingale's tricks, but that didn't make her a fool. Galen wondered if he alone saw her for the intelligent, kind, wise person she really was.

But what he thought didn't matter. *He* didn't matter.

He could do nothing as Jarik and the woman seized him by the limbs. He could do nothing as they dragged him down to the palace's waste disposal center deep underground and left him on a pile of scrap metal. And he could do nothing as robotic claws yanked discarded machinery from the dump and tossed it onto a conveyor belt leading to a fiery pit.

He could do nothing as they drew closer and closer to him.

A SHARD OF discontent remained lodged in Daiyu's gut. First, she thought it was the trauma of having faced her death. Then, she thought it was the stress of pretending to be all right. Next, she wondered if it was because she did not love Jarik as everyone thought she did.

While all these things were true, they did not explain the odd feeling that haunted her. She'd carried it for days, an itch she couldn't scratch.

She was in the middle of yet another meeting with her advisors when it hit her.

Galen. She hadn't seen him since he'd frozen in the garden. She tried to recall what had become of him, but her memory was a blur. It was as if someone else had inhabited her body, and she'd watched from a distance. *Where is he?*

Gripped by abrupt alarm, Daiyu stood. "I'm sorry, but I just recalled that there is an urgent matter I must attend to."

She paid no attention to her advisors' surprised and indignant remarks as she swept out of the room.

The first place she searched for Galen was in his quarters. When she arrived, she found the spare, silver-walled room empty. It was possible, of course, that he was elsewhere in the palace. Or perhaps he'd decided he wanted to leave after all. *But surely he would have said goodbye?*

"What are you doing?" Jarik appeared in the doorway.

She approached him. "Where's Galen been? Your quarters are nearby—you must have seen something."

Jarik's expression darkened. "An empress has no need for broken machines."

"I have *need* for people I care about." Daiyu examined Jarik's face. He'd never liked Galen, and she got the sense that he'd be glad if the AI Nightingale were gone. She moved to exit the room, but he blocked her.

"Where are you going?"

"To order a search for Galen."

"Forget him, Daiyu." Jarik gripped her shoulders. "You do not want a false nightingale. Especially when you have a true one at your side." He leaned down to kiss her.

She pushed him back. "*You* do not tell me what I want. I am still Empress, and if you do not get out of my way, I will exercise my authority."

Jarik scowled but did not respond.

Unsure what else to do, Daiyu rushed to her study, grabbed her tablet, and contacted Lao Qiu. The engineer's wizened face popped up in holographic form before her.

"Little Yu, why do you look so distressed?"

"I cannot find Galen, and I was hoping you could help."

An hour later, the old woman arrived at the palace, practically tripping over her long dress as she rushed to find the Empress. Since Daiyu had informed everyone at the palace that Lao Qiu was to be given anything she needed, two guards flanked the engineer and ordered everyone else out of her way.

Daiyu was still in her study, pacing and worrying.

"Little Yu!" Lao Qiu held up a tablet. "I have traced the signal from Galen's network link. He is beneath the palace—in the waste disposal center."

Daiyu's jaw dropped. Hot rage, more powerful than anything she'd experienced before, flamed in her chest. Galen would never have gone to that horrible place himself. Someone had tried to destroy him. She turned to the guards. "Shut down the system! Go down there and retrieve Galen *immediately*! I want him returned safely to me, understand?"

"Yes, Empress!" The guards rushed to obey.

Daiyu started to follow them, but Lao Qiu held up a hand.

"You are the Empress. You have given your orders, and now, you must wait for your guards to fulfill their duties."

"But Auntie—"

"Your word is powerful. They will act as quickly as they can, for their Empress commanded it. Indeed, they will be quicker if they do not need to wait for you."

Daiyu realized Lao Qiu was right—as usual. Her parents would have told her the same. So she waited, walking in circles to release some of her agitation. Anger burned in the pit of her stomach, and she longed to know what monster would have thrown Galen away like garbage. Beneath it pooled a deep well of shame for not realizing sooner that he was in trouble. She'd allowed days to slip by without seeing him.

And yet he was the one she yearned for the most. Without him, her world felt colder, emptier. And once she got him back, she would never let go again.

A BLINK HAD never felt so sweet. After spending so long unable to even perform that simple action, Galen cherished the ability.

He lay on a long sofa in the Empress' study, where he'd been brought after the guards had retrieved him from the waste disposal center. They'd shut down the system just in time—those claws had been on the verge of seizing him. After they'd brought him to the Empress, Lao Qiu had gone to work to fix him.

She'd finally succeeded, and she gave him a fond smile as she helped him sit up. His movements felt stiff after having been still for so long, and yet he relished them.

The Empress stood behind Lao Qiu, watching him anxiously.

Smile. That will let her know you're okay. Though Galen had to remind himself to make the expression, the lift of his lips was entirely genuine. "Empress. It is good to see you."

"Who did this to you?" The Empress' dark gaze crackled. "Did you see?"

"Yes." Discomfort twisted through him. He had seen how she cherished Vox Jarik. He glanced at Lao Qiu.

His creator nodded. "Tell her the truth, even if it is hard to hear."

Galen searched his memory for a human expression that might be appropriate for what he was about to share but found none that fit. So when he told the Empress of the plot he'd overheard, he was only able to be himself. He knew his words came out all wrong. His tone was too flat. His face failed to convey the proper surprise or outrage. He forgot to gesticulate.

But the Empress did not seem to care. When he finished, she gave him a nod. "Thank you, Galen."

She turned to her guards and ordered Vox Jarik to be arrested at once. But the Bilin Nightingale must have learned of Galen's rescue, for no matter how they searched, he was nowhere to be found. Neither was General Drokka. While it was later revealed that the traitorous advisor had used his authority to let the attackers into the garden and had fled in a private starship, Vox Jarik seemed to have vanished into thin air.

Some believed he'd fled Caixing for one of the far-off alien worlds whose citizens he'd so disdained. Some believed he'd found asylum on Earth, home of the only people he'd seen as *people.* Some believed he'd remained on Caixing, too clever to be caught, and continued plotting to seize power.

Many missed his renowned voice and regretted that he would never again grace a stage. But many more were glad the Empress had uncovered his treachery. And her faithful AI Nightingale, though false in body, was truer than the Bilin Nightingale had ever been. She was generous with his time, allowing him to perform for the people whenever he pleased. But all knew that he belonged to her. Not because his creator had made him a gift, but because he chose to be.

Time alone could heal the wounds of Jarik's betrayal—but sometimes, it seemed as if there wasn't enough time in the universe to stop the bleeding in the Empress' heart.

Two months later, she still sighed sadly as she went with Galen on one of their long walks. Galen may not have been an expert at human expressions, but he understood her well enough to know the cause of her sorrow.

Since he didn't know what to say, he instead took her hand. That was something humans did to comfort each other, and, with the warmth of her palm in his, he understood why. She was once again dressed as a commoner, and he no longer struggled to think about her as Daiyu.

She glanced up at him. "Every time I walk past the Varia lilies, I think about how foolish I was to be taken in by Jarik's deceit."

Again, Galen did not know what to say. He'd learned, though, that it was better not to say anything at all than to speak disingenuously. Yet Daiyu seemed to know how he felt.

"I know I'm supposed to be strong," she went on. "But even my parents needed to escape the palace now and then. I've decided to take a trip to Onaia, whose beauty rivals even Caixing's with its soaring waterfalls and vibrant wildlife. Will you come with me?"

Galen felt his mouth spread into an involuntary grin. "It would be my honor, Empress."

"Empress?"

"Daiyu."

She smiled.

They wandered through the seemingly infinite wonders of the Imperial Gardens, past Nairod roses with multi-hued petals and Iqinn trees whose red branches interlocked into patterns finer than lace.

Galen's heart sang, and soon, his voice joined in. He did not know the wordless melody that emerged, only that it had a life of its own and needed to be released. Soon, a fine soprano joined his rich tenor. Daiyu may not have known the song, but she could feel its intent.

Two hopeful voices twirled between the flowers and the branches, wrapping around each other like interlocking fingers.

LEO 6

arkness surrounded Kjersi. It clung to her skin like a security blanket, reminding her that this was home and this was where she belonged. Every breath she took brought the darkness inside her, thick and heavy, lined with the fine dust of the mine that crept through the woven fabric of her mask. She needed to make a new mask, but fiber was hard to come by in the mines, and the thin air of the surface and the blaring heat of the sun were not elements designed for her people.

Boots scuffed against the rocky floor as the line shuffled forward. Forty-six... forty-seven... forty-eight. Finally, it was her turn. Kjersi reached forward, finding the basin from memory, her fingers grabbing a grimy rag.

"Oi, Nabil," she yelled after her work partner. "You didn't rinse the cloth."

His chuckle rang from deep in the tunnels, where Nabil was nearly at the lift. "It's my present. A little bit of me for you."

Kjersi grumbled as she dipped the rag into the basin to be rinsed amongst the grime of the forty-eight miners before her. Nabil, always the jokester. Always trying to make her laugh. It wasn't often she laughed. But that didn't stop Nabil.

Lifting the mask, she wiped her face with the rag. The grit of those who had come before her rubbed against her rough skin as she tried to wash away the mine. But Kjersi knew she could never escape the dirt. It was in her skin, her lungs, her bones. She was made here, born here—carved from the mines themselves. Her mother had delivered her in a mine cart, moments before dying, risking her life like so many other women back then who'd dared to risk pregnancy. Her father had carried her to the wash basin at the end of his shift to bathe the last remnants of her mother from her skin, already covered in the dust that enveloped them all. Yes, she was as much a part of the mine as she was human.

The line pushed forward, indicating her time was up. Rinsing the rag properly, she left it on the side of the basin and made her way to the lines at the lift. There Nabil had saved a place for her.

"Thanks a lot," she said.

His shoulders whispered against his sides as he shrugged in the darkness.

"I've got something that may boost your spirits," he said. "Apparently, the lift driver has brought news from the surface."

Kjersi grunted. "Why does everyone care so much about the surface? We're undergrounders. I'm not interested."

"Really?" A hint of mystery lined Nabil's voice. "Not even if it has to do with Earth?"

"Earth." She grunted again, though this time the sound was mixed with laughter. "Earth is a pipe dream for those with small brains."

"Well, the lift driver says there's a contest starting," Nabil continued. "And there's a chance for a miner to win a ticket to Earth."

She shook her head. Nabil was so naïve. He would believe anything. "Lies, I tell you. Don't believe a word of it."

On the ride home the driver wouldn't stop talking about the contest. Kjersi kept to the back of the lift, pressing the side of her face against the cold steel walls. Under the UV lights of the lift, people were talking and jostling, and she didn't like it one bit. It was the colors. The noise. The excitement that came with hope. She much preferred the familiarity of darkness.

"And if we find the gem, then we can go to Earth?" someone asked.

The lift driver held up a hand. "The largest gem wins! But don't forget, you only have one month."

"How exciting," someone else said. "I can't wait to start looking." And the loud talking of voice over voice began again.

"Fools," Kjersi said from her corner. "Only one Painite has ever been found in all the time that humans have inhabited Leo 6, and the president keeps it under lock and key. I know because it was my father who found it, and no one has found one since. This contest is nothing but a hoax to get you to work faster."

People started to grumble, but the lift driver cleared his throat. "Yes, the young lady speaks truth—only one has ever been found. But where there is one, there must be more, correct? And that makes your odds even better. If you are the one to find the second Painite, what are the odds anyone else will find a third or a fourth, yeah?"

Everyone gushed in agreement, hope once again filling the lift, its weight pressing Kjersi farther into the corner. "Fools," she muttered under her breath. "All of you."

Finally, the lift reached their floor. She held back waiting for everyone to spill out of the mine, into the steel-lined barracks where they would meet for a meal. Nabil was the only one who turned back, frowning at her as she stopped next to the lift driver.

"If there is no contest, my people will crucify you."

He raised his hands in protest, shaking his head as he replied, "Whoa, whoa. But there *is*. I promise you, girl. There is a contest. It's the president himself who thirsts for a second Painite. It is said the gem haunts his dreams and his greed is as big as his gut. And the one who brings him the largest one will be freed of the mines forever."

With that, the lift driver pushed her out of the lift, slammed the door, and disappeared in his ascension.

"See?" Nabil said over her shoulder. "Not everything is a lie. Now let's go see if they have any pie."

Kjersi grunted as they made their way to the dining hall.

"I'M GOING TO win that contest," a nearby miner named Ronan said, slamming his pint of ale on the steel table. "If it's the last thing I do, I will leave this dirty planet."

"The only thing dirtier than this planet is your undergarments," Nabil teased. Roars of laughter filled the dining hall from all around her, but Kjersi did not smile. Instead, she watched Ronan's face flush red, and then in a flurry of arms and legs he threw his drink to the floor and jumped over the table at Nabil.

Ronan was a fool. He'd always been one. Their fathers had worked side by side in the mines until they'd both died from the dust. Kjersi had grown up with Ronan always watching her with eyes that wanted more than friendship, the pressure pushing her away from him. She would not ruin her life with love like her mother had. Love brought hope.

It wasn't until the commotion knocked her own drink from her hand that she stood up and yelled, "Enough!" The boys paused a moment, revealing a trickle of blood from Nabil's nose and Ronan's partially swelled eye. She stood, letting her chair grind against the already worn floor. "They hang a promise of Earth in front of your noses and you turn into barbarians. Idiots! All of you."

And with that, Kjersi retreated to her quarters.

"TELL ME ABOUT Earth," Kjersi's older sister, Jaala, said from the bed that had become her home for the last month since her cough had taken a turn for the worse.

"What can I say?" Kjersi replied. "It was before my time. Long before our parents or their parents before them."

Jaala twisted a brittle strand of hair around her finger. "What about the stories that Father used to tell? The ones about the air that was so clean, you could breathe it without a mask. The ones about the water so fresh, it had life that lived in its depths. The ones about a sun that gave life to the planet and didn't take it away."

Kjersi grunted. "Stories. That's all they are. Why is everyone suddenly so taken with Earth? It's an old world that never progressed past war. We forget why our people left that galaxy. We should just be grateful for our colonies, light years away from Earth."

Jaala let go of her hair and pointed at her sister. "You're wrong. Stories bring hope. Without Earth, I have no hope. I'll die in this tiny room, never to feel the sun on my skin." Her voice cracked at the end as her body broke out into a fit of coughs. Pain twisted her features as she curled her body into itself under her blanket.

"Shhh, now," Kjersi said. "Look what hope does to you. Makes you too excited. Let me be the one to worry about Earth." She sat at her sister's side, rubbing her back. In such a short time the tables had turned; Jaala had gone from the surrogate mother who cared for her to the one needing care.

Once Jaala's breathing calmed to the rhythms of sleep, Kjersi left her sister's bedside. Kneeling on her own bed, she reached around the far side of the mattress, butted against the cold steel walls, until her hand grazed against the top of a tiny cloth bag made from the rags of her father's old mask.

"Keep this safe," he'd told her long ago, when the cough had racked his body until it was so frail, he couldn't push himself out of bed. "This is the rarest gem of the mines. This is Painite. Keep it hidden until the day you need to use it."

Kjersi remembered the day her father had found the first chunk of Painite. She was just a child. The president was so excited he'd brought her family to the surface for a celebration that night. A buffet was spread out in his office, revealing enough food to feed the entire mine, yet there were only four of them there. It was then that she realized the division between the surface and the underground.

She pulled the bag out from under her bed, emptying its contents into her palm. Veins of rust-colored mineral contrasted against the sheen of the black crystal. The gem was no larger than her thumb, yet she'd known its value the moment it had passed from her father's hand into her own. He'd kept it hidden all of these years, and she never understood how such a tiny thing could carry power.

Hope was a dangerous thing in these parts. She'd learned long ago not to trust the pangs of hope that could seep into one's skin. The promise of Earth wasn't enough for her to give up the gem.

EVERY DAY FOR the next week was the same. Kjersi woke. She worked. Then she stood in line, shuffling forward. Forty-six... forty-seven... forty-eight. She lifted her mask and washed her face with the grimy rag. She took her place in line at the lift, where Nabil always saved her a spot, staring ahead while he complained about Ronan or something new that had rattled his cage. Then they climbed into the lift and ascended to the dining hall.

But not today. Today was different.

That morning Jaala had coughed up blood. Kjersi knew that meant her sickness had progressed, like it had with their father. Without Jaala, what would be the point of living? She hated herself for letting despair take over and bringing with it a tiny shard of hope. She'd pulled the gem from its hiding spot and spun it between her fingers. Maybe it was okay to have hope. Maybe she should see just how far the Painite could take Jaala.

Now, inside the lift, she reached her hand into her pocket, gripping the small shard of hope—her father's Painite. Once everyone left, bustling about hungrily for the dining hall, she turned to the lift driver. "I need to see the president."

The lift driver's mouth dropped open before the corners curled into a smile. "No one just goes and sees the president. Especially not girls like you."

"Trust me," she said, pulling the Painite from her pocket and displaying it between her thumb and forefinger. "He'll want to see this."

The lift driver's mouth dropped open as he reached toward the dark gem.

"Uh-uh." She shook her head, sticking the shard of Painite back in her pocket. "Now, take me to the president."

She could feel the lift driver's gaze on her the entire ride, but she refused to meet it. She had to stay focused—on task—alert. The president wasn't known for being charitable. But for Jaala, she needed to convince him.

"Put on your goggles," the lift driver said, pulling his over his eyes. "Or you'll regret it."

She scrambled to pull her goggles down from her tangled locks, then braced herself against the back of the lift as it slowed and broke the surface. Rings of blinding light assaulted her eyes through her goggles.

"What is that?" she cried out.

"What?" The lift driver laughed. "The sun? Haven't you ever been to the surface before?"

"Just once." Cringing against the side of the lift, Kjersi pressed her eyelids closed as her palm gripped the Painite in her pocket. "But the sun had set."

When the lift finally stopped, she pried her fingers off the gem. "Last door at the end of the hall," the lift driver said.

She stepped out of the lift, turning back for guidance, but the lift driver had already sped away. Taking a deep breath, she moved toward the large doors at the end of the hall. When she arrived, they swished open, announcing her arrival.

A large white room revealed itself, lined with pale chairs and a desk at the end of the room. She carefully walked inside, quick to note the mine dusk that covered her body was leaving a trail across the plush white carpet. Soft music played from the ceiling, the only other sound from a woman at the desk as she clicked on a screen.

"Hello, 980816," the woman said without looking up from her screen. "Have a seat, please. The president will see you soon."

"But how did you know my birthcode?" Kjersi asked.

The secretary sighed and met Kjersi's gaze with a less-than-impressed glance. "It's not your *birthcode*. It's your name." Then she motioned with her hands. "And it's the room; it's filled with sensors. Now have a seat, please." She turned back to her screen and started clicking again.

She looked around the empty room and took the closest seat on the right to the desk. There she pulled off her goggles, remembering her birthcode. The gear was filthy from years of use, but after rubbing around the nose piece she found the faint etching of numbers inside the plastic. The undergrounders refused to be named by the date they were born. In the mines the birthcodes were nothing more than identifiers of whose gear belonged to whom. Giving children a real name at birth was a way to claim the mines as their own.

"He'll see you now," the secretary said as the wall behind her separated.

Kjersi slowly stood, fidgeting with the goggles in her hands. Nerves were throwing her off her game. She missed the mines. The darkness.

Inside the president's office, the walls were steel, reminding her of back home. She couldn't help but stare at their familiar cool surface as she approached the president's desk.

"Nice, aren't they?" he said from his chair.

She nodded, mumbling a "yes, sir" as she took the seat in front of him.

"I had the room renovated the moment I stepped into office. I've nothing against the sun, of course, not like some undergrounders," he said, looking down his long nose at her.

"I've never seen the sun until today," she said.

He burst into laughter, his round face stretched to its limit as he tilted back his head to allow the sound to escape his throat. She noticed the extra folds of weight under his chin, a sign of the privilege of excess that the surface provided. Kjersi shifted in her seat, aware of how her bones and muscle showed through her thin layer of skin, shadowed by the dust.

"You haven't truly seen the sun," he said, wiping tears from his eyes once his laughter subsided. "Not until you've flown in its orbit. Of course, it's surrounded by complete and utter darkness, but that doesn't diminish its fortitude. Only then you can truly get a sense of its wonder and greatness. A power that both giveth and taketh away."

She nodded, wishing she'd never come. But Jaala, yes, she couldn't forget about Jaala. "I've got something for you," she said, standing and pulling the Painite from her pocket. She tossed the chunk of gem onto the desk between them, where it skidded across the surface, landing in front of the president.

Immediately, his eyes widened as he scooped the Painite up with his hands. She noticed then that he wore gloves, white ones, and the dust of the mines left its trace against the pale fabric as he rolled the Painite over again and again in his palm.

"Why, it's beautiful," he cried out. "Just beautiful."

She waited for him to mention the competition as he swirled the gem in a glass of water. Flecks of dust soon darkened the clear liquid. Slowly lifting the gem from the glass, the president wrapped it in a silky white handkerchief, frowning as a drop of grayed water fell to his pristine white desk.

"It's very rare, you know," he said, wiping up the drop with the handkerchief before setting it down. "Even back on Earth, only a few were ever found." He began to unwrap the soft folds of white silk. "To think my luck would bring me here, to this desolate place, only for me to find the rarest gem across the six galaxies."

Kjersi looked at the open handkerchief, revealing the Painite. Its edges shone in their rust-colored glory, embedded in the gem like dried blood. But even more striking was its core, visible through the sheen of its surface, dark as the mines it was born in. She cleared her throat. "About the contest, sir. I'd like to enter my sister's name in place of mine."

"The contest, yes," he said, still playing with the gem. "Wait — what?"

"The contest," Kjersi repeated. "The one where you get entered for a ticket back to Earth in exchange for the Painite."

"Yes, yes," he said, his voice getting louder and faster as his face reddened. "Of course I know my own contest, you stupid girl. But what's this about your sister?"

Kjersi shrank in her chair, wishing she were anywhere but here. "I want to submit her name in place of mine."

"Why would you do such a stupid thing as that? I mean, it's Earth."

"It's just that she's — "

"I don't care what she is!"

"I didn't mean any offense — "

"What, are things too cushy in the mines that you'd prefer to stay there than go to Earth?" The president banged a fist on his desk, making the glass jar of water with the Painite in it shake. "Unheard of, is what it is, 980816! No, you cannot enter your sister's name in place of your own. If she wants to go, she can bring her own gem. Now go, get out of here before I decide to strike your name from the list as well."

"WHAT'S EATING YOU?" Nabil asked as they waited in line the next day.

Kjersi didn't answer. How could she tell her oldest friend that she'd been hiding Painite since her father had died, the one thing that could get them off this godforsaken planet? How could she tell him that the only way she'd survived all these years was burying that hope, and now she'd let a little bit out and it had all blown up in her face?

"Fine," Nabil said. "Ignore me. But that just means I'll harass you all through supper until you spill."

Their turn for the lift arrived, and Kjersi hid herself from the driver. But he paid her no mind, instead talking about the lucky entrant from the day before.

"What did they look like?" someone asked.

"Ah, you all look the same to me," the lift driver said. Kjersi grunted from her corner. "But the president said the entrant was a true undergrounder, worthy of a ride to Earth." Kjersi snorted, but the lift driver ignored her. "In fact, he said he can't wait to meet the next one of you to bring him more Painite."

Inside the cafeteria people were grumbling throughout the lineup. Kjersi ignored it, wishing it would move quickly so she could get home to check on Jaala. The line ahead of her pushed back when two men started arguing.

Ronan's voice rose above the line. "I heard it was another 98er — 980816? Which one of you is that?"

She froze at the mention of her birthcode but avoided eye contact with Ronan and shimmied closer to Nabil.

"Show me your goggles," Ronan said, grabbing at one of his friends' headwear. The two wrestled, falling out of line and bumping into the wall. Ronan managed to pull off the man's headgear and looked at the code. Standing, he chucked the goggles back at the man, who still sat on the floor. "That's one down, who's next?" Ronan jumped back in line and started harassing another one of his friends.

Nabil groaned. "I hate that guy. If he finds a Painite before me, I'll lose my shit."

She shuddered at the thought of the Painite she'd kept hidden all these years. Her father had been sure it would bring them a better life, but he'd died before he could do anything with it. "Let it go," Kjersi said. "He's not worth it. And he's not finding any Painite."

"Well, someone did," Nabil said. "It might be easier than you think."

"Why, Nabil? Why is it so important to you to leave?"

"Imagine the adventure, getting out of the mines, off of Leo 6." A dreamy look crossed Nabil's dirty face. "Really, the universe is a version of the mines—dark and mysterious, with planets hidden in its expanse, as precious as gems like Painite."

"You make it sound so appealing," she said. "But there's only room for one person. I could never leave Jaala."

"Never say never." Sadness weighed down Nabil's voice.

Kjersi stared straight ahead, watching as Ronan harassed a third friend without luck. She made a mental note to hide her goggles where he'd never find them.

AFTER SUPPER KJERSI sat at the edge of her bed, listening to Jaala's shallow breathing. That morning her sister had developed a fever. She was stable, but Kjersi didn't like it. Jaala wouldn't make it another month in the mines.

Kjersi stood, pacing the room as she pulled her goggles from her head. Spinning them between her hands, she tried to focus on a solution. The president wouldn't let her submit Jaala's name in place of her own, and searching for another chunk of Painite was pointless. Why did he have to make things so difficult?

She tossed her goggles on her bed, frustrated that she had hit a wall. Her only option was to send someone else to pretend to be Jaala. But no one in their right mind would do that for them, not even Nabil. Earth was too great a prize. Plus, there was that damn sensor in the office. They'd know right away it wasn't Jaala. Kjersi grabbed her goggles, moving them to the floor with her other mining gear, but she paused a moment when she noticed the birthcode she'd revealed yesterday. That was it. She didn't have to send someone to pretend to be Jaala when she had all she needed right here to do it herself.

She retreated to the foot of her sister's bed and reached for the wooden chest that had sat closed since Jaala became bedridden. The hinges fought against Kjersi as she opened the lid, revealing her sister's old mining gear. From here on out she was going to be 930410.

THE NEXT WEEK the lift driver had news. "The president is excited to announce he has received a second Painite. That's right, undergrounders — two entries in the first two weeks. Maybe the third will be you!"

Kjersi's chest constricted, pressing in like a collapsed mine. The chatter in the lift escalated as she slumped into a corner and struggled to catch her breath. A second Painite? How was it possible?

Nabil's voice made her focus back on her surroundings. "Did you hear that? It was another 98er — 980918." His face was beaming as if every worry in the world had been lifted. "What are the odds? And you never thought any of this was possible. Don't you feel silly now?"

Anger filled her insides, pressing back against the pressure of her worries. "Was it you?" Her voice escaped in a whisper.

Nabil frowned. "What?"

"Dammit, Nabil," she said louder. "Did you do this?"

Before he could answer, Kjersi stormed from the lift toward the dining hall. She managed to make through the line and to her spot before Nabil dared to speak again.

"For someone not interested in Earth, you sure get worked up about this contest," he said.

Kjersi ignored him and ate her food. Behind their seats, Ronan bragged loudly to his table. "Yes, yes, I am the winning entry!" He stood on his chair, presenting himself to the entire room. "I am 980918 and I am going to Earth!"

"Good riddance," Nabil mumbled.

Kjersi pushed her tray forward, unable to take it any longer.

"Wait," Nabil called after her. "I wanted to talk to you about something."

"Not now, Nabil," Kjersi said, running from the dining hall before her disappointment made her lose control.

She fought back tears as she made her way down the hall. How had Ronan found Painite at such an opportune time? He'd stolen Jaala's only chance to survive. If only there was some way she could convince him to give up his spot for her sister. But even Kjersi wasn't naïve enough to believe Ronan would ever be so selfless.

Opening the door to her room, Kjersi froze immediately, sensing something was wrong. Scanning the room slowly, she instantly saw that Jaala was missing from her bed. "No!" Kjersi cried out, running inside. There Jaala lay on the floor, drenched in sweat as she mumbled to herself.

"Jaala, are you okay?" Kjersi knelt beside her sister, scooping her head into her lap. "Can you hear me?" But it was no use. Jaala was unconscious, mumbling over again and again a single word.

Painite.

"YOU ARE THE last person I ever expected to show up at my room," Ronan said, leaning against his doorway, half-dressed in cotton pants.

Kjersi glanced down the hallway, worried someone might hear them. "Can't we talk inside?"

Ronan raised a brow. "You, in my room at night? Why, whatever will the other undergrounders think?"

"Just let me in."

Ronan leaned back, leaving Kjersi a tiny space to squeeze in between his body and the jamb. Kjersi spun around to face him as soon as she was inside. "I need to talk to you about the Painite."

"So, I get a ticket to Earth and you finally come running."

"It's not like that," Kjersi said quietly.

"Then what is it like, Kjersi?" Ronan asked. "Because I remember chasing after you since we were kids, and you snubbing me as if you were better than me."

"This is important, Ronan. That ticket to Earth is the only way to save Jaala's life. I need it for her."

"I'm sorry to hear about your sister," he said. "I truly am. But if I did have more Painite, what would you do for me?"

"Do you have more?" Kjersi's heart raced in her chest as a smile played at the edge of Ronan's lips. He was definitely hiding something. "I would do anything."

"Really." Ronan took a step toward her, backing Kjersi against the wall. "You'd do anything? Would you marry me?"

Kjersi's gut churned as she slowly shook her head. "You can't be serious."

"I am dead serious." His voice was deep and hot against her cheek as he leaned in closer. "If you expect me to stay in this shithole, then I need you to commit to being with me."

"I can't," she said, choking on her words. She closed her eyes tight as an angry groan escaped Ronan's lips.

"But of course, you'd do anything *except* be stuck with me forever. Get out of here." He stepped away from her, the gap between them like a cold rush of air, slapping her awake.

Her eyelids jumped open. "No, Ronan, wait. Please reconsider. I just—I can't—I'm not the one you want to be with forever. I won't make you happy."

He faced the opposite wall, his back turned to her as his shoulders lifted and fell with each breath. "Fine. Whatever. If you want another piece of Painite, you can give me half your workload for a week."

"Half! That's insane. I'd have to work extra shifts just to get my own work done."

He shrugged. "You want me to give up my only chance to ever leave this place and you won't sacrifice a little extra labor."

"I want you to help me give Jaala a chance to survive."

"Then you know what you need to do," he sneered.

"WHERE DID YOU go last night?" Nabil asked at supper the next day. He was already finished eating when Kjersi walked in. Exhaustion had crept past the dust, into her muscles where it rested in her bones. But good old Nabil, loyal to a fault, had stuck around to sit with her.

Kjersi shrugged. "Jaala isn't doing well."

Nabil had tried to be his usual jovial self all day. But the pressure of the contest and the extra hours she put in today for Ronan were wearing on Kjersi. It was all she could do to keep everything from Nabil, but she needed to do everything she could to give Jaala one last entry. Today she noticed people were watching the lift, ready to pounce on any entrant who dared to ride to the surface.

"Why do you care so much about this contest, Nabil?"

"Why don't you answer my questions?"

"I said I was helping Jaala last night."

Nabil shook his head. "Funny thing is, I stopped by to make sure you were all right. I even brought you your tray of food that you didn't finish. But no one answered."

She shrugged. "I was probably sleeping."

"Dammit, Kjersi." Nabil slammed his hand down on the table, making her jump. "All I ask for is honesty. Don't I deserve that? We've been friends since we were children."

Before she could respond, Ronan appeared at the table. "Trouble in paradise?"

Nabil jumped from his chair, his hands balled into fists. But instead of taking his frustration out on Ronan, he stormed from the dining hall. Kjersi slowly released her breath as she set her utensils down on the tray.

"People are getting testy," Ronan said. "There's going to be a lot of disappointment at the end of this week. I'd hate to be on the receiving end of it." He winked at Kjersi as he strutted down the aisle.

Kjersi had to get Jaala out of here before it was too late.

AT THE END of the week, Kjersi was beyond exhausted. The only thing that kept her going was knowing that Jaala would be saved. As she approached Ronan's room she was surprised to find him pinning another miner against the wall.

"Just show me your goggles and I'll let you go," Ronan said, pulling at the man's gear. With a snap, the goggles came off and Ronan dropped the man to the ground.

"What's going on here?" Kjersi asked, keeping her distance.

"Nothing," Ronan said tossing the goggles back at the man. "Nothing at all."

The guy scrambled away as Kjersi followed Ronan into his room. "Are you still looking for that first entrant?" she asked, shaking her head. "Seems stupid to care once you moved ahead of them."

"How do I know the first guy isn't holding back another Painite?" he said, reaching up for a small box that sat close to the ceiling in his room.

"If I had two, how do I know that guy doesn't?"

"I'm sure he would have entered it by now," Kjersi said, watching as Ronan pulled a Painite from the box. She couldn't help but gasp out loud. This gem was much larger than her first entry; it was definitely going to get Jaala in.

Kjersi reached for the gem, but Ronan grabbed her wrist before she could reach it. "What are doing?" she asked, struggling against his grip.

He was staring at the goggles on her head. "I just realized that I never looked at your birthcode. What was it again? I remember you're older than I am by only a month or two."

Her eyes grew wide. What would Ronan say when he found her wearing Jaala's gear? "It wasn't me," she said, shaking her head.

"I just want to peek," he said, pulling her against his chest as he twisted her arm behind her back. Kjersi used her other arm to try to fight off Ronan, but he only twisted her arm tighter until she cried out in pain. When he finally got the goggles off her head, he pulled some hair with them.

"See," he said, letting Kjersi go as he peered at the inside of the headgear. "That wasn't so hard."

She reached forward and snapped them from his hands. "Hey," Ronan protested. "I only saw the '10' at the end."

"That's proof enough I wasn't the first entrant," she said. "They ended with a '16.' Now give me that Painite so I can get the hell out of here."

"Don't be such a poor sport," Ronan said, handing the gem over.

A loud knock came from the other side of Ronan's door. "What's going on in there?" It was Nabil.

"Did you ask your boyfriend to watch out for you?" Ronan laughed, going to the door.

Kjersi shoved the Painite in her pocket as the door opened. Nabil appeared with worry crossing his face in dark lines. "What were you doing to her?" Nabil's eyes narrowed as he looked from Kjersi to Ronan.

Kjersi quickly straightened her disheveled hair as Ronan burst into laughter. "Seriously, what do you think boys and girls do behind closed doors?"

Kjersi's face flushed red as she met Nabil's gaze. He took a step toward her, but she stepped back from his reach. "See, Nabil," Ronan continued, "she doesn't want you here. Did she tell you I proposed?"

"You—what?" Nabil's face twisted as he looked at Kjersi. "You didn't—you can't be serious."

"Of course not," Kjersi said. "Why are you here?"

"I heard you call out," he said. "I thought you were in trouble. I never expected you to be with him—"

"I can take care of myself," she said, embarrassed, as she stormed past Nabil into the hallway. "And there is no *me and him*."

She stormed away, trying not to listen as Ronan questioned Nabil about his birthcode.

THE LIFT RIDE the next day was quiet, as Kjersi stayed in a corner with Jaala's goggles on her face. She tried to speak very little, so as not to make the lift driver suspicious that the same girl had returned. She'd even worn all of Jaala's gear to the mines that day and tied her hair in a braid just as Jaala always did. Nabil had given her a strange loo, but didn't speak a word to her all day.

"A third entrant!" The lift driver whistled as she stepped off of the lift. "The president will be pleased. Just continue to the door at the end. I'll be back to get you later."

The Painite felt heavy in her hand. Or maybe it was just a sign of how exhausted Kjersi had become. She didn't recall ever being this tired, except maybe when her father had died. It was this damn contest. The weight of hope. It was almost all too much to bear.

"Hello, 930410," the secretary said. "Please have a seat."

Kjersi couldn't believe her luck. It had worked!

Once inside the president's office, things moved even more smoothly.

"Oh, this piece is even more beautiful than the last," he gushed, clutching the Painite close to his face after washing it. "I swear, it's as if you all have been hiding these precious gems down there."

"No sir," Kjersi shook her head. "Just anxious to get to Earth."

He dropped the Painite in his glass of water and eyed it greedily. "Did you know that the first undergrounder that entered my contest wanted to give her seat to someone else? Preposterous, isn't it?"

"Yes, sir." Kjersi nodded quickly.

"But not you," he said, eyeing her up approvingly. "No, you understand the importance of going to Earth."

"So," she asked, "is my gem bigger than the last? Am I a winner?"

"Let's weigh it and see." He squealed with excitement. "Of course, if it isn't, I could keep it as part of my collection. You'd be well reimbursed, I promise. Maybe a dwelling on the surface, hmm? Get you out of those dark mines?"

"Let's just weigh it and see." Kjersi bit her lip as the president reached into the glass and pulled out the Painite, carefully dipping it on his bright white handkerchief. As the water wiped off, a thin peel of black came off as well.

"Why, what is this?" the president said, leaning close as he examined the gem. "This is just a rock. It's been painted!"

Kjersi stepped back. "Why, no, that's impossible. I—"

"Are you trying to trick me?" he said, standing from his desk. "Now that's preposterous! Unbelievable, 930410! I am flagging your number.

You will never, ever be allowed to leave the mines. Go back where you came from. I never want to see you on the surface again."

Two guards entered the room and dragged her from the president's office, through the lobby, and down the hall to the lift before Kjersi could plead her case. The lift driver was silent the entire way down as Kjersi huddled into a corner, her anger ready to burst the moment she saw Ronan. She'd trusted him to spin straw into gold. She should have known better.

When she stepped off the lift she stormed straight for the cafeteria. There her entire crew was still seated, finishing their meal. She beelined straight past Nabil's empty chair to Ronan's seat.

"Liar!" she screamed, pulling Ronan back by the hair on his head. Startled, it took him a moment to recover, but soon he had pushed his chair back into Kjersi, knocking her over.

"Get off me, you crazy bag!" he said, standing above her.

She scrambled to her feet. "You lied. You gave me a fake piece of Painite!"

"You were foolish enough to believe me," Ronan sneered. "Did you really think I'd give up Earth for you?"

"It was for Jaala," Kjersi said, a sob escaping her lips. "I needed it to save my sister's life."

Ronan scowled. "Your sister will become nothing more than mine dust, like your father before her."

Kjersi screamed, thrusting herself at Ronan, but one of the 98ers jumped up to stop her. Another stood behind Ronan, holding him back.

"Get out of here," Ronan said, kicking into thin air. "You're pathetic."

THE LAST WEEK of the contest went by achingly slow. After the announcement of the third Painite find being a fake, the lift was lined up with people desperate to go to the surface to see if gems they'd found could possibly be Painite. The president put a stop to this immediately, putting security guards in the lift and the tunnels surrounding it where they tested each gem before allowing anyone to come to the surface. But no more Painite had been found. Disappointment spread across the faces of the miners each night they met for supper.

"The president will be announcing the winner tonight, after supper!" the lift driver called out to everyone as they exited for the dining hall. "It's very exciting to think that one of you undergrounders will be given the great privilege of returning to Earth, where our ancestors lived. Make sure you're in your rooms by last call in case you're the winner."

Ronan pushed past everyone, getting awfully close to one of the president's guards. "I demand to know who the first entrant was," he said. He'd obviously worked his way through all the 98ers without success. He continued to a second guard and then a third. But the guards never breathed a word, standing still as statues with their hands on their guns.

Kjersi couldn't help but smirk as she walked past. It made her happy to see that Ronan was bothered by her original entry. He deserved whatever fate would befall him for having tricked her. Kjersi couldn't wait for things to go back to normal in the mines. Even Jaala had pulled through her fever, and though very weak, she was conscious. Kjersi had been as much of a fool as the others to let hope in. Even Nabil would eventually forget his hope of going to Earth. Leo 6 was their home. They weren't meant to survive on the surface—let alone in the skies.

"What do you think is so funny?" Ronan asked, grabbing Kjersi's arm and spinning her around. "You think you're so great because you don't care about this contest?" Gripping her tighter, he leaned in to her ear, spitting on the side of her face, and said, "You and your sister are stuck down here for the rest of your lives, and we both know her time is almost up."

Kjersi slapped Ronan's cheek with her free hand. His eyes watered as her hand left a mark in the dust on his face.

"Is there a problem here?" A guard stopped next to them.

Ronan shook his head, a sneer crossing his face as he studied Kjersi. "No, sir. Not at all." He let go of her arm, and Kjersi rubbed the spot where his fingers had left marks on her skin.

In the dining hall, she noticed there was pie on the menu and instantly thought of Nabil. She walked to their regular seats, but Nabil was nowhere to be seen. She caught a glimpse of Ronan, watching her with eyes narrowed as he tapped a knife on the table. Kjersi decided it would be best to eat in her room tonight until the contest was over. Her skin crawled as she walked away, the sensation of Ronan's gaze burning into her back.

This was her last chance to make up with Nabil before he found out she'd been lying to him. Grabbing a peace offering from the dining hall, she made her way to Nabil's room.

Once she arrived at his room, she banged on his door. "Nabil, open up."

"Leave me alone."

Frowning, she leaned against the frame. "Nabil, seriously. I don't have time for this. Open up right now."

"No."

A loud sigh escaped her lips. "I can't believe you're making me say this, but I've brought pie."

There was only a moment's pause before the shuffling of Nabil's footsteps came near. The door opened a crack, revealing her dear friend with a smile across his face. "Did you say pie?"

"Let me in, you fool." She thrust the plate of pie toward him and stormed into the room.

Kjersi waited as Nabil gobbled his pie. "You act like a starved man."

"I've missed supper the last two nights," he said with a full mouth.

She threw up her hands. "Whose fault is that? I told you this contest was bad news from the start. I can't wait for it to be over."

"Well, someone's going to Earth," Nabil grumbled. "And it's not me."

"Me, either," she said. "Would I be here otherwise?"

He swallowed and then set down the empty plate. "I don't understand why you pretend not to get excited about things like Earth, but then as soon as Ronan gets in you're all over him in what I can only assume is an attempt to try to leave Leo 6."

She took a deep breath. "Nabil, no. You've got it all wrong."

Nabil shook his head, his eyes getting wide. "And Ronan. How can you stand that guy? Kissing up to him just because he has a ticket to Earth?"

Kjersi's breath caught in her throat. "Nabil—"

"If you wanted to leave the mines so much, I could have helped you." Nabil's voice got louder, faster. "But you hid it from me, and then when you needed help you went to Ronan instead."

"Stop, please—"

"Seriously, Kjersi." He was practically yelling at her now. "Why can't you see that it's not fair? If you'd just let me take you and your sister to the surface, she'd have a chance. But, no. You'd rather take off to Earth yourself."

"Enough, Nabil!" Kjersi exploded. "I was never going to Earth. I wanted to win for Jaala."

"She's—wait, what?"

"That's what I came here to tell you. Jaala was supposed to go to Earth. She needed that ticket more than anyone down here. And now—it's too late."

Nabil stood there staring at Kjersi, his mouth open as if he was going to continue arguing with her. Instead, he shook his head. "So you were never going to leave?" he asked.

"Never."

"Then I've got something to show you." Nabil reached into his pocket, revealing a chunk of Painite. "I was about to use this for myself," he said, passing her the gem. "But I want you to take it for Jaala."

"Nabil," she whispered, "I—I don't know what to say."

"Just tell me your sister is going to Earth, and I'll be happy."

"Thank you!" Kjersi threw herself into Nabil's arms, embracing him tight. "If I hurry, I might be able to catch the lift driver."

As the door slid open, she called back to Nabil. "Thank you for the Painite. I'll be back soon."

"Promise," he called after her.

Before she could respond, Kjersi ran into Ronan in the hallway. "Move, Ronan." Kjersi scrambled past him trying to get to the lift.

Ronan grabbed her by the wrist and pushed her against the wall, flashing the knife from the dining hall in his other hand. "Did I hear you say that you've got a new Painite?"

"Let me go." Kjersi struggled against his grip.

Ronan leaned in to her face, so close the heat of his breath warmed her cheek. "Tell me, how does a dead girl make it to the surface?"

Kjersi brought up her knee, connecting with Ronan's groin. His grip instantly loosened as he stumbled back a step. It was all Kjersi needed to get away. His voice screamed after her as she sprinted down the hallway, toward her room. Just a few steps away, Ronan jumped her from behind and knocked her to the ground.

He flipped her over, pinning her to the floor with his knees as he rifled through her clothing with one hand while holding the knife against her neck with the other. "Your entire family has always thought they were so special. My father told me all about the time your father found the Painite and won the president's approval, and how your father threw it in my father's face. He was as arrogant as you are, but now it's my turn to shine."

"Let her go, Ronan." Nabil's voice came from behind Ronan, out of Kjersi's line of sight.

Ronan shook his head. "You don't realize what she's got. Ah-ha!" Ronan cried out as his hand landed on Kjersi's pant pocket, against the lump of Painite. He pulled it out of her pocket, away from her body, and lifted it into the air. "It's mine!" Ronan cried. "I'm going to Earth." He climbed off Kjersi's bruised body and flashed the gem at Nabil.

"Give me that!" Nabil cried out. He lunged at Ronan as Kjersi scrambled out of the way. The two boys tumbled to the ground together, a mess of arms and legs, before Nabil managed to get the upper hand.

Kjersi slid herself up the wall into a standing position, her legs shaky from her fall. She ran a hand to her chin and found a small cut where she'd been nicked by Ronan's knife. The sight of blood on her fingers as she drew them away made her gasp.

"Nabil, careful!"

But it was too late. A scream escaped Nabil's lips at the same time Kjersi called out her warning. She watched in horror as her best friend's body stiffened against Ronan's frame, and then crumpled as Ronan pushed him off.

"Guards!" Kjersi screamed. "Someone, help!"

Ronan's eyes were wide as he got to his feet, blood staining his clothes where Nabil's life had spilled out onto him. He scrambled down the hall, running away from the body and toward the lift.

"Nabil," Kjersi cried, kneeling next his limp body. "Nabil, answer me." She cradled his head in her lap, trying to wipe away the dust from his face as she willed his eyes to open. "It's going to be okay; just hang in there."

But Nabil didn't answer. His face lay slack where her tears fell onto his skin. His torso was dark where the blood had seeped through his clothing. Ronan had killed Nabil and now Ronan was gone — and so was the Painite. Everything was wrong. This wasn't how things were supposed to end.

Kjersi stumbled from Nabil's body. She knew she had to put distance between them. The knife was still there, and she was the only one here. The guards would come soon, and then she'd be questioned and probably locked up. Jaala would be left alone to die. She couldn't let her sister die alone.

Stumbling to their room, Kjersi stopped and looked at Jaala. Her sister's body had withered away to bone, barely a spark of life left under the shriveled skin. Kjersi couldn't take it anymore: the loss, the hopelessness. Maybe Jaala had been right. Maybe having hope was better than not having it at all. She curled up on her bed and let the tears fall.

"Don't cry, sister," Jaala's muffled voice said from her side of the room. "I'll be gone soon, and you won't have to worry any longer."

"I'm so sorry, Jaala," Kjersi said. "I tried to get you to Earth with some Painite Papa had left us. I got you in, I really did. But someone stole our last piece and has gone to take your place."

"I thought you didn't care about Earth," Jaala said, her voice nothing more than a wheeze.

"I don't." Kjersi kneeled at her sister's bedside. "That was for you, not me. But now Nabil's been killed and soon I'll lose you too."

"You'd never go?" she asked.

Kjersi shook her head. "I could never leave you."

Jaala was silent a moment, her breath pausing as she raised a hand. "Kjersi, reach under my bed, along the bottom of my mattress."

Kjersi didn't argue; her sister too weak to ask again. She ran her hand under the thin cotton padding until it bumped against something hard.

"What's this—?" Kjersi paused as she pulled out the largest Painite she'd ever seen. It fit perfectly in the palm of her hand.

"Papa left us both some Painite," Jaala said. "Will this be enough to win the contest?"

"Jaala," Kjersi said, standing. "Why didn't you give me this before?"

She coughed out a half-laugh. "Because I knew you wouldn't go, and I knew I'd never make it."

Kjersi shook her head. "You of all people should know you still have to try."

"I'll go if you promise the trip won't be a waste."

Kjersi leaned down and scooped up her sister's frail body. It barely took any effort. Her tiny bones were so fine, Kjersi was afraid she'd break before they got to their destination.

THE LIFT DRIVER hesitated only a moment until Kjersi thrust her palm full of Painite into his face. His eyes didn't leave the rust-colored gem, blackened from the dust of the mines. But Kjersi kept it close to her and Jaala, whom she cradled in her arms the entire way.

She strode from the lift to the office doors, knowing she'd find Nabil's killer somewhere on the other side. As she entered the pristine white office, an alarm blared from the speakers in the ceiling. She stormed straight to the doors of the president's chambers and kicked at the door.

"Hold on," the secretary cried out. "You're not allowed in here!"

"Trust me," Kjersi said, flashing the fist of Painite at the woman. "He wants to see this."

The secretary stepped back, typing furiously on her screen until the large doors finally opened. Inside the office, next to the president's desk,

Ronan crossed his arms.

"My piece is larger than the first two," Ronan gloated to Kjersi. "Looks like I'm the winner."

"He's right, my dear," the president said, not peeling his eyes away from the gem as he washed away its last remnants of mine dust. "It's only larger in the slightest, but still a winner nonetheless."

Kjersi set down Jaala in the chair across from the president's desk and turned to the two men. "If there's time, 930410 has one last entry."

The president remained focused on the Painite in the glass of water. "930410?" The president's eyes narrowed. "I thought I told you never to return to the surface."

"Are you sure?" Kjersi asked, lifting her palm, revealing the ball of Painite. Ronan gasped, and the president jumped from his chair, toppling it over behind him.

"My word—it's beautiful—where did you—just amazing!" The president cried out his approval, crawling over the top of his desk to take the Painite from Kjersi. "Of course there's room for 930410, of course there is."

"This isn't fair!" Ronan pounded a fist against the president's desk, leaving a black mark of dust in its wake.

The president turned toward Ronan, eyes narrowed as he ran a finger along the black mark on his desk and raised it to his face. A frown crossed his lips as he turned back to Ronan. "Take him away!"

Two guards burst from a hidden door behind the president's desk, grabbing Ronan on each side. He fought against them as they dragged him from the office. "And run a test on that blood on his shirt," the president called out. "I imagine we might find it links to someone in the mines. Can't risk losing miners—not when we're finding all of this Painite!"

He turned toward Kjersi. "Now say your goodbyes. The rocket leaves soon!"

Kjersi turned and kneeled in front of Jaala, carefully embracing her sister so as not to hurt her. But when Kjersi pulled her sister close, Jaala slumped forward with the same slack that Kjersi had felt just moments before with Nabil in her arms.

"Jaala," Kjersi cried. "Jaala, please answer me."

"Come, 930410," the president called, now standing at the door behind his desk. "The rocket is this way."

"But she's gone."

The president looked behind Kjersi and scrunched up his nose. "Oh, dear. Just terrible. I'm so sorry for your loss. But this is your last chance, 930410. Are you going to Earth, or not?"

Kjersi kissed Jaala's cheek and then rose from her sister's side. "You don't understand — *she* is 930410."

"Impossible," the president said. "You are. We read your birthcode when you come into this office." He motioned to the goggles on top of her head. "As far as I'm concerned, that's who the winner is. So is that your number or not?"

Kjersi's hand moved to the goggles. Jaala's goggles. She'd never swapped them back. To the president, she was 930410. She was the winner.

"Hurry up and decide," he urged. "The countdown is about to begin."

Kjersi took one last look behind her at the dark trail Ronan had left on the white carpet of the president's office. Even Jaala's frail corpse was a sharp contrast to the surroundings of the surface dwellers. Up here reminded her of everything she despised about Leo 6. But could she ever return to the mines without Nabil or Jaala?

Looking back at the president's hidden steel door, she knew what she had to do. She was the one girl on this wretched planet who'd sworn she'd never leave. A life in the mines was all that she'd ever known. But she'd made a promise to Jaala, and that was the only way Kjersi could keep her sister alive.

Turning back to the president, she nodded and walked through the door. Inside the hull of the rocket, Kjersi could see the dark skies through the telescreens in front of the pilot seat. It was just as Nabil had described. Kjersi took her seat, her gaze focused on the vast darkness that enveloped the stars. She breathed a sigh of relief, knowing that the darkness patiently waited for her in her new home in the skies.

SOLSTICE SPELL

Clare Dugmore

Clara Birch stood in the queue to get into Sugar Plums nightclub, her legs shaking and her body shivering. But it wasn't due to the freezing December weather, or the ballgown she had on. Clara was trembling with anticipation, hoping the fake IDs she and her best friend, Marie, had would hold up to inspection.

Sugar Plums was the place to be in the city in the lead up to Christmas. Every year on the solstice, they held a masquerade ball, and Clara had been longing to go ever since she'd been old enough to notice the posters and signs for it around town.

As she grew from a toddler to a child and then a teen, she became increasingly jealous of her older sister, Louise, who could go to Sugar Plums. Now, Louise was at home with a young baby, and Clara saw this as her time to shine. It didn't matter that she still had dolls hidden away, or that she daydreamed of meeting Prince Charming. She could have both. She could be grown-up like Louise but still play the make-believe games she loved.

She and Marie had been planning this for months. She'd been saving her pocket money and birthday money to put toward the price of a ticket and a dress for the ball. After school, she and Marie had used the computers at the local library to acquire fake IDs and order their tickets. It was all she'd ever wanted — to attend a ball like the ones in the fairy tales she loved, and perhaps even... Clara shook her head. It was a silly daydream. Handsome princes didn't come riding along on white horses to rescue fair maidens.

Clara just hoped the IDs would do the trick. She was almost seventeen, but still over a year away from legally being allowed into nightclubs, bars, and pubs. Though she thought with the right makeup and clothes that she looked much older than her age. It was time to put that theory to the test.

As another patron was admitted into the club, Clara and Marie shuffled closer to the entrance. She could already hear the music coming from inside — festive and lively. It made her heart soar, and she desperately wanted to dance. This time of year was always so magical. The city's Christmas lights were twinkling, sparkling snow blanketed the ground, and the seasonal music from inside Sugar Plums added to the merry atmosphere.

Eventually, she and Marie reached the front of the queue, and a bouncer dressed as a toy soldier in a red jacket with black trimming said, "Tickets and IDs?"

Clara and Marie handed them over. The bouncer inspected them for a moment, comparing the pictures on the IDs to the girls in front of him, then nodded his head.

"In you go, ladies," he said, handing the items back.

The girls grinned at each other and entered Sugar Plums.

If Clara had thought it was festive outside, inside was like a Christmas shop had exploded. Tinsel, baubles, fairy lights, and other decorations covered every available surface, as an LED hub shone green and red lights across the darkened room. Somewhere above, a snow machine produced fake snow that was enhanced with glitter and fell in sparkling flakes to the floor.

"Oh my God, this is amazing," Clara squealed, grabbing Marie's hand and dragging her into the center of the dance floor.

All around them were women in elaborate silk ballgowns, and men dressed in the finest suits, complete with tails and cravats.

"Can we get you girls a drink?"

Clara turned in the direction of the voice and came face-to-face with a man in his early twenties, a long rat-like nose dominating a pointed face with small, dark eyes.

"No. No, thank you." She smiled politely and tried to turn away, but the young man grabbed her arm.

His hands were long and unwashed, with pointed nails that had dirt beneath them. Clara shuddered and tried to yank her arm from his grip, but he was unnaturally strong.

"No. You're coming with us. You're just the type of girls the boss likes."

One rat-like man grabbed Clara as the other wrapped his arms around Marie, and the two girls were dragged away from the dancers and beautiful lights to a dark corner of the club.

Sitting on a throne was the vilest man Clara had ever seen. His nose was long and crooked, and she swore whiskers were sprouting from it. Like the men who'd taken her, he had a pointed face and small, beady eyes. His mouth was full of jagged yellow teeth. Looking down, Clara noticed he had a protruding, rounded belly, and small, spindly legs sticking out from underneath, dangling from the edge of the throne. On his head was a tarnished, dirty crown, sitting askew between tufts of matted hair.

"Let go of me this instant," Clara demanded. The man holding Clara threw her to the floor in front of the throne.

The one with the crown leaned forward, his misshapen nose pressed against hers, his rank breath hot on her face.

"Well, aren't you a pretty little thing?" he said with a grin that sent a chill down her spine.

"What I am is none of your business." Clara struggled to her feet. "I demand you let my friend and me go."

"And why would I do that when you'll make the perfect queen for me?"

He reached out with a furry hand and grabbed Clara's arm, pulling her body flush against his. Clara retched, bile rising in her throat. As he inclined his head toward hers, she closed her eyes...

"Unhand her this instant," said a commanding voice.

Clara opened her eyes and looked up to see who'd come to her rescue. Her gaze fell on an impossibly handsome man. He was tall, with blue eyes like ocean water, and dark hair pulled back into a neat ponytail. He was dressed like a prince, in a military-style red suit, a blue sash trimmed in gold draped across his chest.

In one perfect leap, he jumped over the surrounding men so he was standing right beside Clara. He pried the rat-like man's hand off Clara's wrist, and then pushed him backward.

"Guards," he called. "Over here. This man and his gang are trying to assault this lady and her friend."

A number of bouncers, all dressed in the same red jackets as the one at the door, rushed forward. They took one look at the man on the floor and dived into action.

"Thank you, sir," said a bouncer. "This is the notorious drug dealer, the Mouse King, and his crew. They've been causing trouble in clubs all over the country. We'll see he's sent straight to the gaoler."

The bouncers grabbed hold of the Mouse King and his crew and dragged them away as the princely man knelt and offered Clara his hand, gently helping her to her feet.

"Thank you." Clara straightened her dress.

"It's my pleasure, Miss...?"

"Clara. My name is Clara. And yours is?"

"I'm Hans," he said with a bow. "Might I perhaps buy you a drink?"

"Thank you. That would be very kind."

Hans led Clara over to the bar. She looked around for Marie and saw her friend was being taken care of by one of the bouncers. Certain Marie would be okay without her for a few minutes, Clara turned her full attention to Hans.

Under the light, he was even more beautiful than she'd first thought. His skin was fair and flawless, with a strong jaw and distinct eyebrows. But it was his smile—which he flashed to her as he handed over a shimmering pink drink in an elegant crystal glass—that had her mesmerized.

"What's this?" Clara asked, smelling the drink, which gave off a strong aroma of roses and sugar.

"It's a Christmas special. A cocktail made from Turkish delight."

Clara smiled. "How wonderful. I just love Turkish delight."

She took a sip and found it to be just as delicious as the sweets she so loved. Unable to help herself, she gulped the rest down greedily, and as the last drop passed her lips, Clara's vision went black...

WHEN CLARA OPENED her eyes, she was in a bed that wasn't her own. The mattress was as soft as a cloud, and looking around, she saw the bed had four posters, with a light blue, silken canopy hanging from them.

She sat up, afraid that she wasn't in her own home, but also intrigued by her surroundings. They seemed oddly familiar to her.

In an instant, Hans was at her side.

"Clara, please, I can explain." He gently gripped her shoulders and pushed her back against the pillow, and then pulled up an oak seat beside her. "I have a confession to make," he said somberly. "I should have told you last night, but... I am a prince, and this is my palace. I brought you here because I need your help."

Clara stared at him, wide-eyed. "I'm sorry, you said you're a prince? And you need my help?"

"Yes. Many years ago, I was cursed by an evil sorcerer, who confined me to the palace. I am trapped here every night apart from the solstice, because there is magic on Midwinter's Eve more powerful than even his. Each year on the solstice, I am able to leave my prison in search of a maiden with a heart pure and true, one who has the power to free me from this curse."

Clara blinked. Was this some sort of joke? It sounded like a story from a fairy tale. This guy had to be insane.

She threw back the silken blue covers and jumped out of bed, thankful to find she was still fully clothed.

"I'm sorry. I should have told you the truth from the start, but, well, it sounds so absurd..."

"That's because it *is* absurd. You're crazy. Get away from me."

Clara ran toward the door, but before she made it out into the hallway Hans stalled her with a gentle touch on her arm.

"Please, I can prove to you that I'm telling the truth if you'll just come with me."

He gazed into her eyes, the blue of them like a summer's sky, and as Clara stared back, she felt her fear melt away. The story sounded deranged, and yet Hans had spoken so earnestly. What if he was telling the truth and he *was* trapped here?

He'd saved her from the Mouse King, and he was a perfect gentleman. Princely even. What would the harm be in hearing him out and seeing this proof? If he was lying, she could still find a way to escape.

As if in a dream-like trance, Clara returned to the bedroom and settled on the foot of the bed.

Hans took her hands and clasped them in his. "Thank you for returning."

"Show me the proof."

Hans rose to his feet and took Clara's hand. He helped her off the bed and then led her into the hallway. Arm in arm, they walked through the vast expanse of the palace, passing libraries and lavish bedrooms. Rooms filled with suits of armor, and others containing hundreds of finely-dressed porcelain dolls. They walked down a grand staircase and passed a huge ballroom until, at last, they reached the palace entrance's double doors.

Hans opened them swiftly, and a chill swept over them as they stepped out into a landscape of white. Leading away from the palace into the distance was a flagstone pathway that had been cleared of all snow, but around them were shimmering mounds of snow covering the lawns and dusting the fir trees dotted around the area.

Together, Clara and Hans walked down the cleared path until they reached a wrought-iron fence with a curving gate in the middle.

Hans pushed open the gate and led Clara out, but after only a few more steps, they met an invisible wall, as though they'd walked into a pane of glass.

"Oh," Clara said, coming to a halt and bracing her hands in front of her. She could feel the glass. It reached up above her head and down into the ground. As she looked up into the sky, she thought she could see a faint glimmer of glass above them and surrounding them, and it was then that Clara realized the truth. They were trapped in a glass bubble, like a giant snow globe.

Clara pressed her hand against the invisible barrier, then sucked in a breath. "You're telling the truth."

Hans held her gaze. "Sadly, I am. I am trapped here unless someone can break the spell."

"And where is *here*?" The enchanted world she'd found herself in seemed familiar to Clara. She felt like she'd seen the palace before, had dreamed of dancing in its ballroom.

Hans smiled slightly. "Why, the Land of the Dolls, of course."

The palace doors sprang open at his words, and rows upon rows of dolls, human-sized and alive, waltzed down the pathway toward them.

As the gathering drew closer, Clara was surprised to see the dolls were the ones she'd owned as a child, their cheeks still rosy and their eyes still sparkling.

One of her old favorites, Masha, reached out and grabbed Clara's hand, twirling her around in a dance. She and Hans were passed from one waltzing doll to the next until they'd returned to the palace doors.

Breathless and giddy, Clara looked at Hans and studied him closely. His square jaw, dark hair, and blue eyes were all familiar to her, and piecing it together with his claim he was a prince in the Land of the Dolls, Clara suddenly realized the truth.

She gasped. "You're him, aren't you? The Nutcracker Prince?"

Hans bowed to her. "That I am. And when Christmas Eve comes, I will once again turn into a wooden toy. I have but a few days each year to try to break the wizard's enchantment."

Hans led Clara back inside the palace, to a large sitting room heated by an open fire.

"And that's why you need me?" Clara asked, trying to piece everything together.

"Yes. I'm sorry I couldn't tell you the truth at Sugar Plums, but part of the spell means I can't speak the truth until you're in this realm, and the only way to get you here was for you to drink something from the Land of the Dolls."

"The Turkish delight cocktail you gave me?"

"It's a famous drink here, made by the Sugar Plum Fairies themselves."

Clara's eyes widened, and she leaned forward on her seat. "They're real too?"

"Indeed. As are many others you probably know from the old Christmastime stories. They're all my subjects, cursed and trapped here too."

"And the Mouse King and his crew weren't just some random thugs, were they?"

"No. They were sent by the evil sorcerer to try to prevent us from meeting."

Clara shook her head. "This is too much. I need some time to absorb all this."

Hans stood from his chair and bowed. "Of course. I'll send for some refreshments and give you some space to think."

He left the room swiftly, and a moment later, a silver food trolley wheeled itself into the room, coming to a halt beside Clara's seat. On the trolley was a steaming mug of hot chocolate and a plate of butter cookies. Clara took one, dipped it in the hot chocolate to soften it a little, and then bit into the sweet goodness.

As she chewed the cookie, Clara thought about everything she'd been told. Another realm — the Land of the Dolls from her favorite Christmas story, no less — a prince under a curse, and Sugar Plum Fairies and the Mouse King being real. It all sounded ridiculous, and yet she was there, wasn't she? She'd seen the food trolley move by itself and had felt the glass wall just beyond the palace gates. And the palace itself. There was no way it wasn't real. It was too grand and magnificent to be make-believe. Even the most elaborate movie sets couldn't match the magic of the palace.

So that must have meant Hans was telling the truth. And if he was, he and the subjects of the Land of the Dolls were prisoners here, and only she could save them. But how?

Clara tried to recall all the fairy stories she'd read as a child. Whenever a curse had been placed upon someone, true love's kiss most often broke the enchantment. Did that mean to break the spell and free Hans and the people of the Land of the Dolls, she had to kiss him?

But no, that wouldn't be enough, would it? She'd have to love him first, and how could that be if they only had a few days until Christmas Eve?

More confused than ever, Clara ventured out of the sitting room, hoping to find Hans or perhaps one of the other castle residents to explain to her what role she had to play in breaking the curse.

As Clara wandered down the hallway, she passed open door after open door, and unable to resist, she couldn't help but stare at the rooms inside.

The first room had a white sandy beach spreading out into the distance, and just as the sand met the horizon, she could make out a crystal blue lake, with — no, she couldn't believe her eyes — giant swans almost as big as horses gliding on the water. Clara giggled, tempted to see if she could reach one of the swans. They reminded her of a story she'd read as a child, where the magnificent creatures carried humans on their backs. She wondered if all stories had a grain of truth in them, based on magical realms only a few knew about. It was something she'd have to ask Hans later.

The second room was almost as wondrous as the first. The doorway opened up into a fragrant-smelling pine forest, the floor and trees lightly dusted with snow, and scampering around the forest were flower-like people of many colors: red, blue, pink, purple, orange, yellow. The flower people chased each other and squealed with delight, throwing snow and laughing when a ball hit one of their companions. Clara was tempted to join them, but her curiosity about what was in the next room was too strong, and so she continued on.

After that, she came across the dolls that had danced outside to meet her and Hans, all sitting around a table, with a fine porcelain tea set laid out in front of them. As she peered inside the room, Masha caught her gaze.

"Clara, won't you join us?" she called.

"Oh, thank you, but I can't stay. I'm looking for Hans."

"He's just down the hall, in the animal garden."

"Thank you." Clara curtsied as best she could and hurried on her way until she reached the only doors that she'd come across that had been closed. They were made of heavy gold and embossed with pictures of different animals: lions, elephants, and giraffes. Assuming this must be where Hans was, Clara pushed open the doors and entered.

"Oh my goodness!" Her hands flew to her mouth as she stepped from the marble-floored hallway and into a lush green jungle.

She cautiously walked farther through the trees, and as she stepped over a tangle of roots, something brushed her leg. Clara squealed and looked down as a massive peacock emerged from the undergrowth. Even with its feathers down, it was almost as tall as her waist, and then when it unfurled its tail, the feathers reached up past her head. But it wasn't just the size of the peacock that was amazing. It was brightly-colored, like males of the species were, but gleaming from the tail were emeralds, sapphires, and rubies.

Hans stepped out from behind the peacock and smiled. "Hello, Clara. I see you've found my animal garden."

Clara looked around herself in awe, her eyes as big as saucers. The peacock was still strutting about, and overhead flew shimmering gold and silver parrots. "It's magnificent, like a book I read once—only bigger, brighter and better than the story described."

"Come. Let me show you something." Hans took her hand and led Clara deeper into the jungle, past more strange and exotic animals.

Beside a river lazed a crocodile, its scales shimmering in the sunlight. Beyond that, they encountered a troop of lemurs, only instead of their fur being shades of white, black, and brown, they were vividly colored in shades of pink and purple.

Finally, they drew to a halt in a clearing, and Hans whistled on his fingers. A moment later, the ground beneath their feet started to shake, and then into the clearing walked a gigantic elephant. Upon its back was a silken carriage.

"Would you like to come for a ride with me?" Hans asked as the elephant stopped in front of them, and Clara noticed a rope ladder hung from the carriage all the way down to the elephant's feet.

"Oh, could I?" This was like a surreal dream, where things Clara had once imagined as a child had come to life.

"Why, of course. Follow me." Hans took her hand and helped her climb the ladder until she was comfortably nestled between pillows in the carriage. He then sat down beside her, whistled again, and the elephant started walking away slowly.

The rhythm of the elephant's steps was gentle, so Clara and Hans weren't jostled about too much. From high up on its back, they could see into the canopy of jungle trees, where silver and gold parrots perched.

The elephant walked back through the jungle the way they'd come, passing the lemurs and the crocodile, until they came to the golden doorway that led back into the hall.

Hans whistled, and the elephant stopped its journey. He climbed back down the ladder, and then helped Clara to the floor. As a reward for its service, Hans plucked a banana from a tree and handed it to the elephant. The creature received the banana with its trunk and shoved the fruit into its mouth whole, with the skin still attached. The elephant trumpeted happily before disappearing into the trees.

Clara and Hans stepped back into the hallway together, and he turned to lock the golden doors that led to his animal garden.

"What happens to the animals on Christmas Eve if the spell isn't broken?" Clara asked as Hans offered her his arm and they walked back to the sitting room.

Hans bowed his head, sadness overcoming his features. "They all turn into toys, I'm afraid."

Clara bowed her head too as tears filled her eyes. "I wish I could help you all, but I'm not sure I know how to. Curses like this are usually only broken with true love's kiss, and we — "

"We've only just met," Hans finished for her. "Expecting us to fall in love in a matter of days is ridiculous. But I don't think that's what's needed. The wizard who cast the spell said all I needed was a maiden with a heart pure and true."

"Then my heart can't be pure enough, or else the curse would have broken already?" Clara's bottom lip trembled as she spoke.

Hans' eyes turned down at the corners. "I'm sure there is nothing wrong with your heart, and maybe I misunderstood what the sorcerer said about the spell. If you're willing to remain here until Christmas Eve, perhaps we can find a way to break this curse together?"

"But my parents — they'll be worried."

"I think it will be okay. Time behaves differently in the Land of Dolls than it does in the mortal realm. If I'm correct, I believe hardly any time at all will have passed."

Clara chewed on her bottom lip. Could it be true that time worked differently here? It wouldn't be the first strange thing she'd witnessed. And if she did leave, what would happen to Hans, his subjects, and all the wonderful animals in the jungle?

She nodded her head. "Okay. I'll stay with you until Christmas Eve, and together, we will break this spell."

Hans grinned. "Wonderful. This calls for a celebration. I'll inform the cook at once to prepare a great feast, and then afterward we'll have a ball in your honor."

Clara blushed. "I can't ask you to go to all that trouble on my account."

Hans waved her off. "Nonsense. It's been far too long since we had a reason to celebrate, and besides, it's almost Christmas. Don't we deserve some holiday cheer?"

Clara was smiling now too. It was impossible not to when the Nutcracker Prince was grinning at her so sincerely.

"I'll call the Sugar Plum Fairies," he said. "And they can get you ready for the ball."

Clara looked down at the dress she'd worn to the Christmas ball in the city. It was slightly dirty now and completely rumpled. She couldn't attend a royal ball in her current gown and was thankful Hans was calling the fairies to help.

From his jacket pocket, Hans produced a small silver flute and played a series of high, haunting notes. A few moments later, the hallway in which they were standing illuminated in shades of pink, purple, and turquoise. Clouds of colorful smoke surrounded them, and then, in an explosion of glitter, three female figures appeared.

All were tall, taller even than the Nutcracker, with ethereal beauty and long, flowing hair that looked to be made of spun silver. They had pointed ears and delicate facial features.

The three fairies—one dressed in pink, another in purple, and the final in turquoise—curtsied to Hans and Clara.

"Your Highness, how can we be of service?" asked the one dressed in pink.

"This is Clara," Hans said, taking her hand and leading her forward so she stood before the fairies. "She has agreed to stay in the palace until Christmas Eve to try to help us break the curse."

The fairy in the purple dress clapped her hands together. "This is wonderful. Thank you, Clara."

Clara blushed and looked away. These fairies were beautiful to behold, in flowing silk gowns, with iridescent wings sparkling on their backs. She couldn't believe they were thanking her.

"It is splendid news indeed," said Hans. "Which is why I'm throwing a feast and ball in Clara's honor. Would you three be kind enough to help her get ready?"

The fairy dressed in turquoise smiled widely. "It would be our honor."

Hans passed Clara over to the fairies. "I will leave you in their capable hands, then, and go visit the cook."

Hans turned and walked away. Once he was out of sight, the fairies took Clara's hands and led her back to the bedroom she'd woken in.

"I'll run you a bath," said the fairy in pink, opening a door leading onto the bedroom.

"Here, why don't you change into this?" said the fairy in purple, pulling open the wardrobe and handing Clara a plush, downy bathrobe.

The three fairies stepped into the bathroom to give Clara some privacy to change.

"I'm ready," she called once she'd shed her ballgown and slipped the robe on. It was the softest thing she'd ever worn and she wondered if it was enchanted somehow.

The fairies opened the bathroom door, and shimmering swirls of sweet-smelling steam followed them out.

"It's made from clouds," the turquoise fairy said, answering Clara's unspoken question.

"We've left you some things for washing and bathing, as well as some clean undergarments," said the pink fairy.

"Please take your time. We'll be just in here, preparing your dress for the ball," said the purple fairy. "Call us if you need anything."

"Thank you." Clara tried to curtsy to them, but it was difficult in her robe. Then she straightened and walked into the sweet-scented bathroom.

Before her was a giant bathtub, easily big enough to fit four people inside, and overflowing with glittery soap bubbles. Clara took off her robe and folded it over a nearby silver rail, then stepped into the warm water. It was the perfect temperature. She sank into the water but found she couldn't reach the bottom, and instead, her body floated just below the surface.

Clara sighed happily and closed her eyes. As bizarre as all this was, it was too magical, too amazing, for her not to be completely enthralled by it. All her life, she'd read fairy tales, dreaming about finding a magical land and meeting a handsome prince, and here she was living that dream. She just hoped that Hans was right, and time did work differently in the Land of the Dolls, or her parents would be going out of their minds with worry.

After soaking in the water for a while, Clara picked up one of the glass bottles the fairies had left around the tub and uncorked it. She poured a little of its contents onto her palm and discovered it was a rose-scented shampoo. She lathered up her hair, and then looked around for a way to rinse off the bubbles. As if answering her request, a silver jug floated toward her and poured warm water over her hair, washing away the shampoo. Clara repeated the process with conditioner from the second bottle, and then used the body wash from the third to clean herself all over. Then she stepped out of the bath and wrapped the robe around herself. It was snuggly and warm from hanging on the silver rail, and she used it to dry off her body and hair.

Now dry, Clara changed into the undergarments the fairies had left for her and stepped back into the bedroom. The Sugar Plum Fairies had left, but hanging on the wardrobe door was a festive red ballgown that was trimmed in gold.

Clara took it off the hanger and gasped as she touched the material. It was even softer than her bathrobe, like it was made from rose petals, and the gold trimming was actually gold leaf.

Once she was dressed—the gown fit her perfectly, as though it had been made to her exact measurements—Clara stepped out into the hallway to find the fairies. They were waiting patiently outside her room for her, and when she emerged, they all squealed.

"You look simply radiant," said the pink fairy.

"A breathtaking vision to behold," said the purple fairy.

"A true princess, worthy of ruling the Land of the Dolls beside Prince Hans," said the turquoise fairy.

"Wait... what?"

The turquoise fairy covered her mouth, and the others fussed around her.

"She didn't mean anything by it," said the pink fairy.

Clara narrowed her eyes. "That was no slip of the tongue. Tell me the truth."

The turquoise fairy gazed at her. "Well, if you break the spell, surely Hans will ask you to become his bride."

"I can't. We barely know each other."

"But you'll be the savior of the realm," said the purple fairy.

"That still doesn't change the fact that Hans and I have only just met, or that I'm only sixteen years old."

"The prince will understand," the pink fairy insisted. "He will court you properly, so the two of you can get to know each other, and then when you're of age, he'll ask for your hand in marriage."

Clara felt her cheeks heat up as warmth spread through her. Hans was handsome, no doubt about it, and becoming a princess would be nothing short of amazing. It was all she'd ever dreamed of. If the pink fairy was right, and Hans was willing to do things properly and wait until she was older, well, marrying him wouldn't be so bad.

"Let's just focus on tonight's ball, and then breaking the curse," Clara said.

"Of course," the pink fairy said, leading Clara back into the bedroom.

Together, the three fairies applied Clara's makeup, styled her hair, and finished off her outfit with dainty golden slippers and a delicate gold chain with a beautiful emerald pendant in the center. When Clara looked in the mirror, the girl looking back at her wasn't herself, but rather an exquisite princess, with dark hair pinned up in curls, wearing a stunning festive dress.

"Perfection," said the fairies in unison before curtsying to Clara.

"Thank you all so much for this. I look beautiful."

"It's the least we can do for the girl willing to try to break the curse and set us all free."

The fairies led the way out of the bedroom, Clara following behind them, and back downstairs to the first floor. They turned left at the bottom of the staircase, walking along the corridor in the opposite direction from the way Clara had explored that morning. They passed the grand ballroom, where many of the palace's inhabitants were readying it for the ball later.

The next room they reached opened into an elaborate dining room, but just before Clara stepped through the doorway, she noticed another door at the end of the hallway. It was made of dark wood and was heavily bolted.

"What's through there?" Clara asked.

The fairies exchanged worried glances, but before any of them could speak, Hans appeared and took Clara's arm. He kissed her lightly on the cheek, whispering in her ear, "You look simply magnificent, Clara."

She blushed and turned her head away from his gaze, her question about the locked door forgotten as Hans led her to the table and pulled out an ornate wooden chair for her to sit in.

He took the place opposite her, and with a clap of his hands, the candles along the table illuminated.

Clara looked around and saw the dining room slowly filling with guests. The Sugar Plum Fairies joined, along with the dolls that had greeted them earlier, and a platoon of soldiers dressed in their finest attire. She also spotted the flower people she'd seen playing in the forest earlier, as well as other courtiers she hadn't seen before, but who were exquisitely dressed.

Once everyone was assembled around the table, with Clara in the position of honor, Hans called for the first course to be brought out. Waiters appeared carrying tiny plates of smoked salmon with horseradish crème fraîche and beetroot salad. The food was divine—so fresh and full of flavor. Next, they were served succulent slices of roast turkey breast with all the trimmings: potatoes roasted in goose fat, carrots caramelized in brown sugar, sprouts with walnuts and little pieces of bacon, cocktail sausages wrapped in strips of bacon, stuffing, rich, thick gravy, cranberry sauce, and huge, fluffy, light Yorkshire puddings.

Clara ate until she was stuffed, wondering how she'd fit another morsel in her mouth, let alone dance at the ball. But, as the plates were cleared away and Hans helped Clara from her seat, then led her from the dining room, the weirdest sensation passed over her. Instead of feeling full and bloated, she felt content and satisfied. Neither hungry nor gorged. In fact, she felt refreshed and more than ready for an evening of dancing.

Holding his arm out to Clara, Hans led her into the ballroom, where twelve enormous spruce trees stood at one end of the room, all finely decorated for Christmas with tinsel, baubles, and shimmering golden stars on top. Each tree was lit with tiny candles that magically floated between the branches.

"Oh my goodness. It's beautiful," Clara exclaimed. She let go of Hans' arm and rushed over to the trees.

Upon closer inspection, she saw that the tinsel was made of gossamer ribbons twisted through with strands of glitter that flowed and moved of their own accord. Each bauble housed a tiny festive scene, from a field of snow where children built snowmen to a crackling fire in front of which a family opened gifts. Each scene had been expertly painted in miniature, and despite the small size, the details were breathtaking. The children building snowmen had rosy cheeks and noses, and the family opening gifts all had firelight gleaming in their eyes.

Clara felt a presence behind her and turned to see Hans approach.

"Amazing, isn't it?"

"Yes. Who painted those baubles? They're stunning."

"I did," Hans said proudly. "There's not much else here to do when we're permitted a few days of life over the Christmas period, so I try to make it as festive as possible for everyone in the palace before we're all turned back into dolls."

Clara smiled sadly. "I promise I will try my hardest to break the curse."

"Thank you," said Hans. "But let us not speak of such things now. Tonight is for festivities and dancing."

He took her hand and led her away from the trees to the center of the ballroom. Soon, others joined them, until couples were standing almost shoulder-to-shoulder.

Clara peered over the heads of the other guests as an assortment of musicians entered the ballroom. She spotted people carrying flutes, bass clarinets, French horns, trumpets, and trombones. Some entered with snare drums, cymbals, bass drums, triangles, tambourines, and castanets. One person even wheeled in a celesta keyboard. Finally, people carrying harps, violins, and double basses joined the other assembled musicians.

Once they were all settled on a stage at the end of the ballroom opposite to the Christmas trees, the orchestra began to play.

The soft, sweet music filled the room, and Hans placed one delicate hand on Clara's shoulder as the other lightly held her waist. He led her in a light and graceful waltz around the ballroom as the other couples gathered there followed his lead, stepping lightly with their partners to the rhythm of the music.

To Clara's ears, each song was more beautiful than the last. The music seemed to speak directly to her soul, making her full of joy and also wanting to weep all at once.

They danced for what seemed like hours until her feet ached and she was dizzy and breathless.

The orchestra quieted down, and somewhere in the distance, a grand clock struck the hour of midnight. When the twelfth chime ended and the room plunged into silence, Prince Hans led Clara to the stage, where the musicians were gathered.

"Thank you all for joining us tonight," he said to the hushed room. "I know that many of you do not feel like celebrating when the evil sorcerer's curse looms over us, and we fear being turned back into dolls. But I have wonderful news. Clara here from a faraway land has agreed to remain at the palace until Christmas Eve to try to help me break the spell."

Cheers rang out from the vast array of ball guests. Clara saw the Sugar Plum Fairies grin and wave at her.

"Three cheers for Clara," called the fairy dressed in pink.

"Hooray, hooray, hooray!" shouted the crowd. Clara felt her cheeks heat, but she held on firmly to Hans' hand and did not look away, instead gazing at all the people gathered in her honor. Breaking the curse was an enormous task — she had no idea where even to begin — but she promised herself she would not let the charming Nutcracker Prince or the good subjects down. She would find a way to break the wicked spell.

"Thank you all," Clara called when the crowd had quieted. "I will try my hardest to break the curse, and hopefully soon we will have something else to celebrate."

Everyone began clapping and cheering again, then Hans led Clara from the stage. The guests parted to form a pathway for them, and the prince led her out of the ballroom and to the grand staircase.

"I will walk you to your room," Hans said with a bow. "And then, after a good night's rest, we can have breakfast together and discuss how to break the curse."

Clara gazed into his blue eyes, her heart melting as she stared at him. Not only did she want to break the curse so Hans and his subjects would be free to live as normal people again, but she remembered the Sugar Plum Fairies' earlier words when they'd helped her dress. Could it be that while she and Hans searched for a way to break the spell, they'd get to know each other, even start to fall in love with each other? Clara wondered whether it were possible that Hans would want to make her his princess.

They reached Clara's room, and Hans bowed to her. "Thank you for a wonderful evening, my lady." He took her hand and kissed it lightly. "Sweet dreams, Clara."

"You too, my prince," she replied, the color rising in her cheeks as her heart somersaulted in her chest.

Hans bowed again and then departed, leaving Clara to enter her room, hot and flustered. He really was the most handsome and charming person she'd met.

On her bed, Clara found a white cotton nightgown laid out for her. She changed into it and hung the ballgown back where the fairies had left it for her. Then she pulled back the covers, climbed into bed, and sank down into the soft, feathery pillows. Pulling the thick blankets around herself, Clara soon drifted into a peaceful sleep.

That night Clara dreamed she was at another ball with Hans, only this time, instead of being dressed in a festive red gown, she was wearing a beautiful white silk wedding dress. Hans looked becoming in a black tuxedo with tails, a bow tie, and a matching top hat.

For their first dance as husband and wife, Hans held on lightly to Clara's waist as she looped her arms around his neck. Their bodies were pressed close together as they glided around the ballroom, the prince whispering sweet nothings in the ear of his new princess.

When the song ended, Hans lowered his mouth to Clara's lips, pressing them together and kissing her deeply.

Clara woke with her heart racing and her body flushed with heat.

A knock at the door caught her attention, and she called, "Come in," before sitting up in bed.

The Sugar Plum Fairies bustled into the room, carrying clothes, toiletries, and trunks filled with other such things.

"Good morning, Lady Clara," the pink fairy said, curtsying, and then hanging an array of garments in the wardrobe.

The purple fairy curtsied, then laid various toiletries and makeup items on a large oak dressing table.

"The prince has asked us to see that you have all you need while you're here," said the turquoise fairy, laying down the wooden trunk she was holding.

"Thank you, ladies," Clara said, climbing out of bed and crossing the room to the fairies.

They all curtsied again.

"It's our pleasure," said the pink fairy.

"The prince said for you to meet him in the dining room when you're ready," said the purple fairy.

"Let us know if you need help getting ready," said the turquoise fairy.

"Thank you. I will."

Once the fairies had departed, Clara located something to wash with, and a paste which smelled strongly of mint that she thought she might be able to clean her teeth with. She took them to the bathroom and freshened up, and then browsed the selection of dresses the fairies had brought for her. A simple gown in forest green caught her eye, and Clara shed her nightdress and changed into it. After brushing her dark hair and tying it back with a ribbon in the same shade as her dress, she put on some dark slippers and left the room.

Clara walked down the hallway to the grand staircase and descended, heading in the direction of the dining room, where they'd eaten the day before. But as she reached the end of the corridor, Clara noticed the dark, barred door she'd seen the night before. Too curious to even wait and ask

Hans what was down there, Clara crept forward.

The bars were heavy but not impossible to lift, and after a moment's work, Clara moved them away so she could push the door open. Walking lightly, she passed over the threshold, and into a dimly-lit corridor.

The hairs on the back of Clara's arms and neck prickled, and for one moment, she considered turning back and going to the dining room to find Hans. But then she saw a faint light coming from the other end of the hallway, and if she listened closely, she swore she could hear something moving.

Her pace quickening, Clara hurried down the corridor, following the source of the light until she came to a single lantern hanging on the wall, and to the right of the lantern, a jail cell.

Clara gasped and peered inside, her heart hammering as her eyes adjusted to the dim light and made out the shape of a figure sitting at the back of the cell.

"Hello?" she called.

"Who's there?" a wizened voice replied, and then into the light shuffled a gnarled old man. He had pure white hair that stuck up from his head in every direction. He wore filthy and ragged gray robes, and a black eye patch covering his left eye.

"You're him, aren't you? The wizard who cursed the Land of the Dolls?" Clara asked. Her eyes were wide, and her body was a war of emotions. Part of her wanted to flee in revulsion and run back to the safety of the Nutcracker Prince. But a tiny part of her was fascinated by this deformed old man. She wondered if perhaps she could learn anything from him that would help break the curse.

The old man laughed, a sound Clara didn't like. It filled her with cold and dread. She was about to run away when his twisted hand grabbed her wrist, and with surprising strength, he pulled her against the bars of his cell.

"Is that the lie my nephew told you?"

"Your nephew?" Clara repeated the old man's words.

"Oh, yes," he said. "Hans is my nephew, all right, and he was my apprentice too. I was once the famed court wizard Drosselmeyer. I served the King and Queen of this palace diligently, using my magic to help them fight the invading Mouse King's army. And at the same time, I taught Hans all I knew, with the hope that one day, when I became too old to carry out my royal duties, he would replace me as the palace wizard."

Clara narrowed her eyes. "You're lying. Hans is the prince of this palace, and you cursed him and his subjects to live as dolls."

Drosselmeyer laughed again. "Ha, he is no more a doll than I am. Though it is true, the poor people of this palace, the King and Queen included, are all under a curse that has turned them into toys."

"You're lying. Why are you lying? I've met the subjects of this palace, and they're all lovely people. I've promised them I'll break this curse."

"Open your damn eyes, girl. That's what he wants you to believe. This is all part of his illusion. The people you've met and the things you've seen aren't real."

"No. You're just trying to trick me so I don't break your curse."

"The only curse is the one he cast upon this palace. Don't you see I'm telling you the truth? Open your eyes before it's too late. Before he claims your soul too."

Clara stilled. Out of everything Drosselmeyer had said, the remark about her soul caught her attention.

"What do you mean?" she asked.

"For Hans to become the true ruler of the Land of Dolls, he needs magic more powerful than either he or I possess. He needs the magic of pure souls. His plan was to enter the mortal realm and kidnap anyone he sensed had a heart that was pure and true. To slow his progress, I was able to cast a spell to ensure that Hans cannot leave this place, except for the few days between Midwinter's Eve to Christmas Eve. That's when his magic is at its strongest, and I, weakened as I am, cannot contain him."

Drosselmeyer let go of Clara's arm and she stumbled backward. Once she'd righted herself, she said, "No. I won't believe it. You're the true evil wizard, and I'm going to break the curse you've cast."

She turned and strode away from the prison cell, but even as she walked, doubts started to set in. What if Drosselmeyer was telling the truth? What if she'd been caught up in Hans' spell?

It was all so convenient—meeting Hans in the nightclub, him rescuing her and bringing her to the Land of the Dolls. Even the magical kingdom itself was peculiar in how it was all very similar to stories she'd read as a child or games she'd played when she'd been little. Almost like Hans had plucked the ideas from her thoughts and memories.

As she stepped out of the dimly-lit corridor and back into the main hallway, it was like a veil lifted from her eyes. Because doubt had been cast on Hans' claim, the enchantment broke, and she saw the palace for what it really was—a dilapidated ruin.

The walls were crumbling, and the once-fine crystal chandeliers were tarnished and damaged. The marble floor beneath Clara's feet was cracked, with grass and weeds growing through the holes.

Her heart hammering, Clara ran along the corridor to the rooms she'd visited on her first day in the palace, where she'd seen wondrous sights like Hans' animal garden. But when she pulled back the doors, the horrible truth was revealed. In every room were case upon case of dolls and toys covered in dust and cobwebs.

Cautiously, Clara approached the case that held a once-magnificent king and queen, whose clothes were now moth-eaten and ruined. Staring into the dolls' eyes, Clara could see they were alive with fear. It was just like Drosselmeyer had told her; the true rulers had been turned into toys.

Clara screamed and ran from the room, throwing herself up the staircase—which was no longer grand and sweeping, but decaying, with steps missing—and hurried through the rundown hallways until she reached her room.

She entered, only to find that the luxurious bed and items the fairies had bought for her had all vanished. All that was in the room was a lumpy mattress and the discarded dress she'd worn when she'd first met Hans.

Looking down at herself, Clara realized the fine clothes she'd been given were an illusion too. She was dressed in a shapeless gray robe, similar to the one Drosselmeyer had been wearing, though slightly cleaner.

Clara tore the robe from her body and pulled back on her original ballgown, then searched the room for any other doors, but there were none. Even the doorway to the bathroom was nothing but a mirage. Apart from the door that led back out to the hallway, the only other opening the room contained was a tiny, barred window. Even if the window hadn't been barred, there was no way Clara could escape from it—it was too small. She did use it to look through, though, and try to gain some understanding of where she was.

The land around her was blanketed in snow, but the sky was a dull gray color, so the snow didn't glimmer magically. In the distance were black, withered, twisted trees surrounding the palace grounds.

Clara wondered if the magical glass ball that contained them was part of Hans' illusion too. Maybe it had merely been a trick, and there was a way for her to escape if she left the palace.

With that thought in mind, she left the bedroom and raced down the stairs, not looking back as she hurried to the main front door. The magnificent oak entranceway was another deception. Instead, a burnt and battered wooden door hung almost off its hinges and was forced closed with pieces of metal.

Clara pushed at the door, pulling the pieces of metal away until it fell open. She ran down the path of crumbling bricks with black scorch marks and scratches along them. She ran until her legs hurt, not stopping until she reached the wrought-iron fence. There wasn't a nice gate like there had been when Hans had first shown her around, but instead a hole in the fence, as though some of it had been blasted away by a cannonball. Careful not to catch her dress on the rusted iron, Clara climbed through the gap in the gate and then continued running away from the palace, past the contorted black trees until... *oof.* She collided with an invisible, solid wall. Looking up to the sky, Clara caught the faint glimmer of glass and knew that the ball the palace was contained in was not an illusion.

"I see you've discovered the truth," a cold, high voice said from behind her.

Clara knew it was Hans, but she wasn't prepared for what she saw when she turned to face him. Gone was the handsome prince, and in his place, was a tall, thin figure with deathly pale skin and long, white fingers. He still had long, dark hair, but instead of being brushed back in a neat tail, it hung around his shoulders like a veil, obscuring his face and casting ghastly shadows upon it.

Floating around the figure were three female wraiths, their skin too unnaturally pale as they glided in black robes, their hair like raven's wings. The Sugar Plum Fairies in their true forms.

"Let me out of this place." Clara made her demand while

maintaining eye contact with Hans, staring into his cold, black eyes.

The wraiths glided forward and grabbed Clara's arms. A chill shot through her, like she'd been stabbed by spears of ice. She struggled to free herself, but the wraiths' grip was too firm. They pulled her along until she was mere inches from Hans.

Up close, Clara could see he also had pointed ears, like a faerie, and elongated incisors that reminded her of the fangs of a wild animal.

Hans smiled, revealing the incisors and making her shiver.

"What are you? What do you want from me?"

"Didn't that old fool Drosselmeyer tell you? No?"

Hans snapped his fingers and the wraiths turned to stone, their hands still gripping Clara so she was unable to move.

"Once, long ago, my uncle was court wizard to the insufferable king and queen who used to own this palace. They had a daughter, Princess Pirlipat, the fairest maiden in the land. When I met Pirlipat, I fell in love with her instantly and sought her hand in marriage. But a lowly magician's apprentice wasn't worthy enough for the king's only child, and my proposal was rejected.

"But who were they to stop me? I studied magic more deeply than Drosselmeyer knew, learning a great many spells and incantations that were 'forbidden.' Finally, I came across the perfect curse. All I had to do was acquire a Krakatooth Nut, a magical nut a knowledgeable wizard could place a curse upon. Whoever then eats the nut is affected by the spell.

"I traveled across the land to find a Krakatooth Nut, and then when I did, I ground it down and baked it into the pastry of a huge pie I'd prepared for the king's birthday.

"My plan was that everyone would become dolls, and then all I had to do was travel to the mortal realm and steal enough souls to augment my magic. Once I became powerful enough, I could reshape this realm as my own, making myself Prince and Pirlipat my bride.

"Only my uncle discovered what I was doing. Though unable to stop me from casting the curse, he did find a way to limit the time in which I could enter the mortal realm. If he had had his way, Drosselmeyer would have trapped me in this ruined palace forever. But my magic is stronger than his, and I was able to create a window through which I was able to enter the mortal realm."

Clara struggled against the wraiths holding her. She was beginning to see just how demented Hans really was. All this—casting a curse, stealing souls—because he hadn't been allowed to marry the princess.

"Since then, every year between Midwinter's Eve and Christmas Eve, I have been able to come to your world. Using a simple enchantment that allows me to create the cocktail I fed you on the solstice, I have been luring maidens with hearts pure and true here. Once in the Land of Dolls, the maiden falls under my spell, and then by Christmas Eve, her soul is mine."

"You monster." Clara spat the words at Hans' feet.

He simply sneered. "The people of this kingdom got what they deserved. No one respected my uncle or his power. To them, wizards and magic were a novelty. A frivolous thing to entertain themselves with."

"So, what, you turned them all into toys?"

"Yes, let them become the oddity. Let them be the throw-away item only brought out to amuse the powerful."

"Even Princess Pirlipat, who you loved so much?"

Hans scoffed. "She didn't deserve me. She didn't even deserve to become one of my dolls. As punishment for rejecting me, I turned her into a simple animal, so easy to overlook. You didn't even notice her in the jungle, did you? So fascinated by my peacock and elephant, you missed the poor princess who is now an ant."

Clara shuddered. "That's horrible. Is that what you've done to all the innocent girls you've lured here and stolen the souls of?"

Hans smirked. "They were rewarded for the service they gave to me. The first three became the fairies that hold you now. The others became the characters in my palace of wonders. All the living dolls, dancing flower people, and exotic animals you so loved? They're the souls of the girls who gave their lives to me. And you can join them, Clara. All you have to do is bow to me. Become my princess. Let me claim your soul, and I will give you everything you've ever dreamed of. All the fantasies you've had since childhood can become true. Pirlipat's beauty was nothing compared to yours. Submit to me, and I will make you my bride."

The childish part of Clara delighted in Hans calling her more beautiful than Pirlipat, but she shook the thought from her head. *He's lying. If I submit, he'll just turn me into a doll like the others.*

"Never!" she said.

"You have less than twenty-four hours until Christmas Eve. One way or another, your soul will be mine."

With that, Hans turned, and in a swish of black robes, he vanished. As he departed, so did the wraith fairies, freeing Clara so she plunged down into the frigid snow.

Even though the wraiths were no longer holding her, Clara could not move. She had sunken into the snow, and it was hardening around her, trapping her from the waist down, on the edge of the forest.

Realizing she had no means of escape, and that even if she did climb out of the snow somehow, she had less than twenty-four hours to break Hans' curse, Clara started to weep. The cold tears trickled down her cheeks, freezing almost instantly.

I've been such a fool.

Clara had been so eager to grow up and act like her sister. She'd so easily believed she could behave like an adult and still cling to the fairy tales she loved. She'd been naïve to think a prince would fall in love with her and make her his princess.

An owl hooted overhead, and then came swooping down to land on the snow in front of Clara. Before she could process what was happening, the owl hooted again and transformed into Drosselmeyer.

Clara gazed up at him and blinked. "How?"

"Your presence here. You're the first person to ever find me and see through Hans' illusions. Everyone else he brought here from your realm believed his lies and fell under his curse. But you didn't. Your natural curiosity led you to finding me, and when I told you the truth, the enthrallment Hans cast upon you broke. The pureness of your heart has given me back a little of my magic, and I was able to escape my prison."

"Can you help free me?"

"From the snow, certainly." Drosselmeyer waved his hands, and Clara was standing on the ground, her lower half now warm and dry. "From this realm, unfortunately, no. Only you can do that, Clara."

"But how?"

"Because you're a maiden pure and true. Your heart can break the enchantment and free everyone Hans turned into dolls."

Clara could feel the tears welling in her eyes again. She wanted to go home, and she wanted to return the king, queen, and their kingdom back to normal. But she was just a simple girl with no magic.

"I don't know what to do."

Drosselmeyer smiled. "Yes, you do, Clara. Search your heart, for the answer is there."

He twirled his cloak, turned back into an owl, and flew away, leaving

Clara to stare into the sky at his retreating form.

Clara had thought the original task of breaking the curse was going to be difficult, but breaking this spell seemed impossible. She didn't have the Nutcracker or his subjects to help her. All she had was herself and less than twenty-four hours before her soul belonged to Hans.

Not wanting to return to the cursed palace, Clara searched around for somewhere to shelter from the snow and found a small discarded shed. She pushed aside the rotted wooden door, ignoring the cobwebs and spiders that hung down in front of her, and huddled inside.

Think, Clara, think. Hans said he used enchanted food to bring you here. Perhaps that's the key to getting home.

Clara sighed. If food from her realm was the way to get home, she was out of luck. Her dress had no pockets, and there hadn't been anything to eat at the club. The only thing she'd drunk was Hans' cocktail.

Again, Clara felt the tears building, and she brushed them away with the back of her hand.

Damn it, all I wanted was to go to the ball, like Louise used to. I just wanted to be a grown-up...

But her heart knew that wasn't entirely true. She'd wanted the enviable aspects of being a grown-up, like being able to go to balls, but she hadn't wanted the responsibility. Her sister had a baby now, and that meant nights out were limited. Clara didn't want that. She still wanted to believe in handsome princes, magic, and fairy tales. She saw how Louise struggled to raise the baby, or how her parents were always stressed because of work and money. She didn't want all that. All she had to worry about was homework, and which boy she was crushing on at school. Ah, if only she could live a life of ignorant bliss forever...

Wasn't that what Hans was offering? She could become the princess she'd always dreamed of being. She'd never have to grow up, get a job, and be weighed down by life. And all it'd cost was her soul.

And then Clara knew exactly what she needed to do. She dried her eyes, stood, and walked out of the shed. With her head held high, she marched back up to the palace.

Knowing exactly where to find him, Clara entered the ballroom, and there was Hans. On the stage where the orchestra had played the previous night was a throne made of something dark and glistening she thought might be obsidian. Hans reclined in it, his long legs draped over one of the sides.

"You've come to accept my offer?" he asked as Clara approached.

"Actually, I've come to reject it. I'm going home, because I realized something really important just now. I want to grow up. And I don't mean the fake 'grown-up' I thought I was being by sneaking into Sugar Plums. I mean real, proper grown-up, good and bad. The time for fairy stories has ended. I want to live. I want to move forward and experience all the things a normal girl my age does. I want to finish school. I want to meet someone and fall in love. Real, true love, like my mum and dad. Not the fake love you're offering."

"But, Clara, I can make all your dreams come true. Anything your heart desires, I can give to you. All you need to do is bend to my will, and I will give you the world. I will make you a queen."

"Hans, I don't want to be your queen. All you can offer me is illusions and lies, a distorted web of endless childhood fantasies. I don't want this life anymore. I want real life, my life. I want to go home."

As Clara said the final words, her vision dimmed. For a moment, she saw the look of horror on Hans' face, distorting his once-handsome features into something twisted, and then everything went black.

"Clara, baby, please wake up."

Clara tried to open her eyes, but they felt too heavy, as though her eyelids had been glued together. Mustering all her might, she forced her eyes open and was assaulted by the harsh overhead lights.

"Mum?" she croaked.

"I'm here, sweetie. I'm here." Her mother grasped her hand. "David, get the doctor. Clara is awake."

Clara tried to sit up, but her body felt heavy, like she was recovering from the flu. "The doctor? Why? Where am I?"

She looked around and realized this wasn't her bedroom. For a moment, her chest tightened. Had she managed to break the curse?

But of course she had, her mother was there. Then she realized. She was in the hospital.

"What happened to me?"

Her mother's eyes glistened with tears. "Someone spiked your drink in the club. You've been in a coma ever since. We weren't sure you were ever going to wake up."

"I've been in a coma? What day is it?"

"It's Christmas Eve, and you're awake. It's a Christmas miracle."

Christmas Eve... just like Hans had said.

"I... I..." The story of Hans and his wicked plot was on the tip of her tongue, but she shook her head. The time for fairy tales had ended. She wanted to grow up properly, and now was the time to start acting responsibly. "I'm sorry I snuck out."

"It's okay, sweetie. We're just glad you're all right. We can talk about everything else when you're out of hospital."

"I'm glad I'm okay, too, and whatever punishment you and Dad decide is fine with me. I shouldn't have gone to Sugar Plums, and I deserve to be grounded or whatever you guys decide."

Her mother raised an eyebrow. "It seems like you've developed a new mature attitude while you were unconscious."

Clara looked to the door, where her father was entering with the doctor, and for a moment, she swore she saw Hans walking along the corridor in the background. She blinked, and he was gone.

"Yeah, something like that," she mumbled.

The doctor took some blood from Clara, and after running various tests, deemed no lasting damage had been done by the drugs or the three days she'd spent in a coma. Certain she'd make a full recovery, the doctor discharged Clara from the hospital so she could spend Christmas Day at home with her family.

Clara's parents helped her across the hospital car park, and as her father unlocked the car door, a noise overhead caught Clara's attention. An owl hooted, and she looked up to see a bird—which looked eerily similar to the animal Drosselmeyer had transformed into—glide past the moon.

She took her mother's hand and said, "Come on, let's go home."

MORSEL

Dorothy Dreyer

HENRY

The blue flashing lights on the interior paneling of the limousine cast a faery-like glow in Grace's eyes. I could tell she was nervous about this party. Excited, but nervous. She kept asking me if I was sure she could come along since it was my new girlfriend who had invited me to the party at the mansion. I'd reassured her for the fiftieth time just as the limousine pulled up to our house. Now we sat inside, a bottle of champagne chilling on ice and a huge bowl of delicious-smelling candy inviting us to indulge. The silver and copper candy wrappers seemed to glow and twinkle in the interior of the limo.

"Are you sure you don't want to try this?" Grace asked, unwrapping another sugary treat and popping it in her mouth. "It's unbelievable. It has to be imported."

I smirked at my sister, holding back a laugh. "No, I'm good. And it's not imported exactly. Candy is Vivienne's mother's business. She's Lilith Van Lebkuchen. She owns Morsel."

"What? I didn't know selling candy could get you a limo like this," she said, smoothing her hands over the leather seats.

The excitement in her eyes made me smile. Grace needed this. She needed a bit of happiness again. Grace had always been "Daddy's Little Girl"—especially after Mom had died. We'd been young when the leukemia had taken her; Grace had been a mere toddler, and so Father always went the extra mile to see to Grace's every need. That is, until he'd remarried a year ago. At first, everything had been fine, but after a while I'd started to notice how our stepmother resented Grace. I never said it out loud, but she was clearly jealous of the attention Father gave Grace. She practically gnashed her teeth any time Father would dote on her. And if you asked me, she'd somehow manipulated Father into spending less time with us. I even overheard her threaten to leave if Father didn't start paying more attention to her.

This led to Grace feeling abandoned. She never admitted it, but I could see it in the way the corners of her mouth would turn downward when Father was too busy to attend her dance recitals or school play productions. It was almost as if he'd forgotten about her.

I could tell she had never brought up her inner turmoil with any of her friends. Perhaps she thought they wouldn't understand. I felt bad she had no one to confide in besides me.

At least I had Vivienne. We had a lot in common. Her parents had died in a car crash when she was a kid, and she'd been adopted. Even though her new family was rich, it didn't erase the fact that there were still people missing from her life—a loss we both shared that created a strong bond between us.

But Grace didn't have the luxury of a confidant. She spent a lot of time alone. And lonely. So when I'd told Grace about Vivienne's party and seen the hopeless look in her eyes, I'd just had to invite her along.

The smile on Grace's face now — a genuine smile I had not seen in ages — was reward enough.

"This is amazing," she said. "You've certainly upped your game in the girlfriend department." Before I could wrap my head around what she was doing, Grace scooped up a handful of candy and dropped it into her purse.

"Grace!"

Another handful of candy was stuffed into her purse. "What? We're allowed, right?"

"Yeah, but don't you think you're overdoing it?"

"I might want some later." She seemed to be analyzing how much would fit into her purse. "Just a bit more."

I bit back a laugh as she attempted — and failed — to close her purse after the third handful of candy. As if that weren't enough, she plucked out another piece from the candy bowl and unwrapped the shiny foil, popping the treat into her mouth with an unashamed smile.

As we entered Vivienne's property, Grace suddenly stopped chewing her candy and placed a cold hand on my arm. Her throat moved visibly as she swallowed back what I could only assume was fear. Following her gaze out the window, I found what she had been staring at. An old man in black clothes — whom I gathered must be the caretaker — stood near a humongous hole he'd been digging. At first glance, I thought it might be a grave, but upon further inspection, I realized it was something much bigger. As the man glared back in our direction, I purposely shifted in my seat to block my sister's view of the man.

"Don't stare, Grace."

"The windows are tinted," she said. "He can't possibly see me."

"Still."

"Sorry, Henry," she said, blinking and focusing on my face instead. "He just looked so creepy."

"Well, I think you'll forget all about that guy once you get a look at Vivienne's house."

Her eyes widened, and she scooted closer to the window, practically pressing her nose against it. The gasp that escaped her lips was confirmation that she was impressed by the mansion. The architecture was modern yet gothic, and the mere size of the building was daunting.

"How many people live here?" she asked into the window.

"Vivienne, her brother and sister, and her mother." I adjusted the lapels of my blazer, wondering if Vivienne would meet me at the door. I almost took out my phone to text her that we were here, but I didn't want to seem anxious. It was bad enough I was intimidated by her money—I didn't need to lose my cool. I wore my best blazer and newest shoes, even though something told me Vivienne didn't care about status and wealth. When she would look into my eyes, everything seemed to disappear, almost as if she was hypnotizing me with her gaze.

The limousine came to a stop, and Grace was quick to open the door.

"Grace, I think we were supposed to wait for the driver to let us out," I whispered as I stepped out of the car beside her.

She didn't answer. Instead she gazed at the house with amazement in her eyes, clasping her hands together as if to hold back her excitement.

The front door opened, revealing a thin, elderly man with slicked-back white hair. Pushing past him, Vivienne emerged onto the massive front porch, a lovely smile on her lips. Her dark hair looked like velvet, falling perfectly in soft waves upon her bare shoulders. There was a subtle shimmer to her gold dress that drew the eye to the curves in her figure. But what captivated me the most was her charm. Her smile could light up a dark and gloomy night like tonight.

"I'm so glad you made it." She skipped down the steps and greeted us each with a kiss to our cheeks.

Grace let out a giggle. I was taken aback by my sister's openness. But maybe she was simply caught up in the thrill of the evening.

"We wouldn't miss it," I said. Though I knew I'd done the right thing in inviting Grace along, for a moment I wished Vivienne's welcome kiss had been something more intimate and not in the presence of my sister.

"Come in." Vivienne tugged on my hand. "Dinner's about to be served."

VIVIENNE

"YOU LOOK NICE," I whispered, leaning close to Henry's ear. He was quite tall, so I had to stretch on my tiptoes a bit. The scent of blood pumping through his veins sent my senses stirring.

"You look incredible," he whispered back.

I smiled up at him and rubbed his arm. I had been thinking about him all day, smiling to myself as I got ready for the party and imagining his reaction. Now that he was here, I had the sudden urge to skip dinner altogether and bring him to my room so we could be alone.

"This house is amazing," Grace said, her head swiveling from side to side, taking it all in. She reached out and ran her fingers along the smooth surface of a white, porcelain bird with rubies for eyes, which sat on the side table in the foyer.

"Don't be too impressed." I smirked. "My mother said it was a steal because the previous owners claimed it's haunted."

Grace stopped in her tracks, gawking at me.

I let out a laugh. "Don't worry. I don't think it is. I mean, I've yet to see anything that's scared me."

A shadow moved in the hall before we reached the dining room. I rolled my eyes as my brother, Jamie, threw a smirk my way, his tall form blocking our way.

"Ah, more guests," Jamie said, his hands stuffed in his dress pants pockets. "Henry, right?"

"Yeah," Henry said. "You're, uh, a senior at school, right? James?"

"Jamie," my brother corrected him, reaching out to shake his hand.

An expression of surprise crept up on Henry's face, and I sent Jamie a warning look to ease up on his handshake. Jamie raised a brow at me and let go of Henry's hand.

"And who is this lovely morsel?" Jamie asked, his eyes wandering up and down the length of Grace.

She let out a timid laugh, her cheeks going red.

"This is my sister, Grace," said Henry.

"Oh, wait," Jamie said. "Yes! I remember seeing you in the fall play. You were magnificent."

Grace blushed even harder, her fingers swooping hair behind her ear. "Oh. Thank you."

"She was the star of the show," came a voice from behind us.

We turned toward my sister, Delancey, who wore a low-cut black dress that looked painted on.

"Delancey," she said, holding out her hand palm-down to Grace, as if she expected her to kiss it.

Grace looked confused but reached out and awkwardly shook Delancey's hand. "Do you go to our school too?"

Delancey snickered. "No, I graduated last year. But I wouldn't miss a show. You're quite talented."

Grace grinned and tipped her head to the side. "Thanks. God, I don't know how to handle all these compliments. Not to mention I'm a little nervous about being here. This house is so big and elegant. I'm afraid I might break something."

"I think you're just letting this full moon get to you," Jamie said, draping an arm around Grace's shoulder and urging her toward the dining room. "Full moons can make people feel strange. But I love it; it makes for a spooky night. Shall we eat?"

Delancey joined them, running her fingers down a strand of Grace's hair.

Henry looked astonished, no doubt concerned for the way they were acting around his sister. I, on the other hand, was used to their ways.

I quickly took his hand, forcing him to look into my eyes. "Hey," I said softly.

When his gaze connected with mine, I forced a wave of glamour his way. He looked as if he were going to say something, his eyes narrowing slightly, but then he relaxed.

"Hey," he said back, squeezing my hand.

"Let's eat," I said. "The sooner dinner is over, the sooner I can bring you to my room."

HENRY AND I followed Jamie, Delancey, and Grace through the grand doors and into the dining room. There were five guests already seated at the table, all entranced by the rags-to-riches tale my mother was narrating. They were transfixed by her, already caught in her spell, as the staff finished filling the wine glasses.

"This way." I tugged on Henry's hand. "I've saved you a seat next to me."

Glancing across the table, I watched as Delancey and Jamie maneuvered Grace into a seat between them. The other guests at our table were from our high school and Delancey's college, all staring at my mother as she enticed them with her story.

But it wasn't the story at all. It was the glamour laced in her voice, dulling their senses to anything else.

Mother turned to Grace first, offered her a smile that didn't reach her eyes, and then nodded to Henry. "Welcome. You've come just in time."

"Thank you for having us, Ms. Van Lebkuchen," Henry said.

I squeezed his hand under the table.

The staff reemerged with silver trays. They made their rounds about the table, placing covered dishes in front of each of us. I focused on Henry, watching his brows rise as the dishes were uncovered to reveal thick cuts of steak, rare and bloody.

At first, the guests hesitated. But then Mother spoke.

"Ah, what fine cuts. Simply delectable. Only the best for the friends of my children, of course."

In a blink, they were convinced. Even Henry began to cut into his steak with vigor. A couple of the guests moaned in delight. Grace smiled as a drop of blood dripped down her chin.

Jamie let out a snicker as he chewed on his bite of steak, the red juices gathering at his bottom gum. "How are you enjoying your snake, Henry?"

Henry froze, staring at his plate. "What?"

Brows drawn down, I glared at Jamie. *Cut it out!* I said to him telepathically.

I could feel the panic oozing out of Henry at what Jamie was making him see. He was paralyzed, as if an actual snake sat curled up on his plate.

Jamie smirked at me, enjoying his moment of glamour a bit longer.

I mean it! I told Jamie.

Now, now, Mother said to us telepathically. *There's no need to fight.*

Jamie rolled his eyes, still smirking. "I said, how are you enjoying your steak, Henry?"

Henry looked up at him and blinked, his knife and fork held up as the spell wore off. "Oh, um." He wrinkled his brow, and then he suddenly smiled at Jamie. "Great. Yeah, it's delicious."

You know what else I bet is delicious, Jamie said, handing Grace her glass of wine.

I sent him a scolding glare.

Children, as entertaining as I find it when you play with your food, Mother said, *do not forget your duties for the night. Lord Kyran is expected to arrive just before midnight, and we need to get these morsels prepared.*

I cringed, turning my face away from Mother. My eyes went to Henry. It was a blood moon: Lord Kyran expected us to deliver souls to him tonight. We'd been gathering these victims in preparation for this traditional sacrifice, and my initial intention had been to bring Henry as my offering. His idea of inviting Grace was a bonus. But now, the thought of losing Henry caused a knot in my stomach. I felt things for him with a heart I hadn't thought could feel things anymore. Henry actually listened to me — something nobody else seemed to bother doing. And when he looked at me, I felt as if I still had a soul. Studying the curves of his lips, the strong line of his jaw, I let out a small sigh and contemplated what I needed to do.

HENRY

I BARELY REMEMBERED dinner. It seemed as if it was over in the blink of an eye. But I knew I must have eaten something. Steak? And did I drink wine? I was a little shocked that Vivienne's mom would serve wine to teenagers, but I guessed there were different customs where she came from.

"It's just this way," Vivienne said, her fingers intertwined in mine as she led me to her room.

My body felt warm, and I squeezed her hand. The world around us seemed out of focus, with only Vivienne in my vision. Everything and everyone else seemed to disappear.

She stopped in front of a large white door, but instead of opening it right away, she turned and leaned her back against it, her hands hidden

behind her as she looked up at me with a coy smile and fluttering lashes.

"What?" I asked, unable to wipe the smile from my face.

"I'm a little nervous about showing you my sketches."

I moved a strand of hair off her shoulder. "Don't be. I'm sure they're great."

She captured my hand and held it to her cheek. "I also have some special candy for you to try. It's something new that hasn't hit the market yet. You *have* to try it. I swear, after you've tasted it, you'll never feel the same."

I let out a small laugh, finding everything about Vivienne adorable.

Voices from down the hall made me turn my head. I suddenly remembered we were not alone in the house. In fact, it suddenly occurred to me that my sister was somewhere in the mansion and I didn't know if she was all right.

"Wait. What about Grace?"

"Don't worry; Delancey and Jamie are keeping her company."

My brow wrinkled. "Are you sure that's a good idea?"

Her eyes dropped for a second. When she looked back up at me, a sudden sense of calm came over me. "Of course. Don't worry."

I immediately forgot what I'd been worried about. Something about abandoning Grace? But then my mind was filled with the vision of her smiling and having fun. She was fine. I quickly forgot about Grace and concentrated on Vivienne as she opened the door to her room.

Her room was lavishly furnished, with gorgeous velvet curtains hanging in the windows. Her vanity was a pristine white and covered with perfumes, hair accessories, and trinkets. And her bed was a huge queen-sized canopy.

As I gazed around her room, Vivienne skipped over to a desk and pulled out a large sketchbook. Batting her lashes, she smiled up at me and held out the book. "Be kind," she said.

I let out a small laugh and took the book. "Always," I said.

As I flipped the first page open, I was filled with surprise. When Vivienne had said she liked to sketch, I'd expected her drawings to be good, but in the pages before me were detailing and shadows and contrast that I could only describe as professional.

"Vivienne. Wow." I shook my head in wonder. "These are amazing."

"You really like them?"

"Yes, you're extremely talented."

Pink tinged her cheeks. It was the first time I'd ever seen this confident, no-fear young woman blush, and it excited me that I could bring about such a reaction.

I reached out and stroked her cheek, wanting to feel the warmth. First she put her hand upon mine, and then she took the sketchbook away and returned it to her desk.

"Do you want to major in art?" I asked, watching as she grabbed a box of matches from her vanity table and proceeded to light some candles. Upon seeing her do this, I was suddenly aware of the abundance of candles in her room. Had there been this many when I'd entered the room? I must have been so transfixed by Vivienne that I hadn't noticed.

"Maybe," she replied. "But... I mean — not to sound arrogant — but what could they actually teach me that I don't already know?" She lit a dozen more candles, then went over to switch off her bedroom lights. "There," she said. "That's cozier, don't you think?"

Her eyes were practically glowing in the candlelight.

"Yeah, it's nice," I said, watching her move toward me.

It was as if she were walking in slow motion. Even the way her hair bounced made me feel like someone had slowed down time. As she came nearer, I noticed something shiny in her hand.

"Come here." She reached for me with her free hand and tugged me toward her bed.

We sat beside each other, and I couldn't break my gaze. It felt as if I would die if I looked away.

"This is very secret," she said, placing the shiny object in my hand.

When I was finally able to tear my eyes away from her, I looked down to see a shiny candy wrapper in my hand.

"Don't tell anyone I let you have a taste," she whispered, her words soft and slow. She snuggled closer, her shoulder touching my chest as she unwrapped the candy and left the treat in my hand. "I could get into all sorts of trouble. But something about you makes me want to be daring. And reckless."

Again, I couldn't tear my eyes away. I titled my head closer to hers, the soft curve of her lips inviting me. My head buzzed pleasantly, and her words echoed in my mind. *Have a taste. Have a taste.*

Our lips were only inches apart, and then suddenly a shock of something sweet hit my tongue. I hadn't even realized Vivienne had lifted the candy to my mouth, and though I'd longed for a kiss, I was suddenly overcome with a sense of delicious satisfaction. It was as if nothing else could have gratified me more than having this taste in my mouth.

"It's good, right?" she asked, her voice still seductive.

Before I could respond, she tipped her head up and kissed me.

I felt as if I had entered a dream state, my mind floating and my body numb. The room spun, but instead of making me queasy, it somehow relaxed me. I was only slightly aware of Vivienne gently pushing me back until I was lying on my back, and then I felt her mouth on my neck. I closed my eyes, unable to resist the wave of relaxation pulling me in.

VIVIENNE

I FELT THE moment he blacked out. His blood was sweet and flowed like warm syrup over my tongue. I only took enough to quench my thirst, making sure not to drain him too much. After all, I wanted him to wake soon. I wanted to spend more time with him, to have him talk to me, to feel his arms around me.

Wiping my mouth, I sat up and gazed upon his still form. The wound at his neck was a bit swollen, but it was barely bleeding anymore. His breaths were slow, his strong chest rising and falling in an easy rhythm. He looked adorable with sugar on his lips. I had to smile.

Did I really have to give him up? Couldn't I spend a few more months with him? What would it hurt to keep him for myself for just a little bit longer?

A knock came at my door. I held back a grunt of frustration.

"I hope I didn't interrupt," Delancey said, shooting a glance over my shoulder at Henry sprawled out on my bed.

"I'm sure," I said, brow cocked. "What do you want?"

"It seems tonight's group was quick to fall under the spell. It must be a record. We're bringing them down to the pit shortly."

"Has Edgar already finished digging?"

"He's nearly done, yes. He'll be starting the fire soon." Her eyes went once more to Henry. "What are your plans for him?"

I flinched. The plan had been to bring him to the pit to sacrifice with the others, and although I was having qualms about going through with it, I was taken aback that Delancey could sense my reservations. "What do you mean?"

She scoffed. "I'm not blind, Viv. I see the doe eyes you give him. Are you handing him over to Lord Kyran or not?"

I sucked in a shuddering breath. "I... I want to keep him."

She let out a breathy laugh, shaking her head. "It doesn't surprise me. But, Vivienne, you need to be sure. Remember what happened last time."

"That was different. I was just bored then."

"You kept that boy for a year. He went crazy and almost killed Jamie."

"Henry would never do that."

"You don't know that. You don't know how he'll react when he's turned. The males are always so unstable. So unpredictable. And the end result? We had to kill that boy. So you lost him anyway."

"Henry is different. We... we have real feelings for each other. That's got to make a difference."

Delancey shrugged. "Sometimes it makes it worse."

A soft moan emanated from behind me.

"He's waking up," I said. "I have to go."

She placed a hand on my door, stopping me from closing it right away. "You need to make a decision, then. And soon."

Henry

I RUBBED AT my neck, wondering what had happened. The skin there felt sore and tingly. I sat up to find Vivienne sitting on the bed beside me with her legs tucked under her, smiling.

"You dozed off," she said sweetly.

I blinked, trying to remember how I could have possibly fallen asleep. Here I was in my gorgeous girlfriend's room, candles setting a cozy mood, a huge, comfy bed beneath us, and no parents around. What was I, crazy?

"I'm sorry," I said, feeling the need to stretch out my shoulders. When I did, the skin on my neck pulled, and I remembered the sore spot. Oh my God! I'd fallen asleep in the middle of making out. Vivienne had been kissing my neck, and I'd completely passed out, lying there like a lump while she'd given me a hickey. My face burned with the thought. How pathetic of me!

"Henry, I really like you a lot." Her gaze dropped for a second, her expression serious.

Oh, God, now she was breaking up with me. I swallowed hard. "I like you too."

She scooted closer and took my hand. "You make me feel special. You make me feel like... like I don't want to be around anyone else. No one's ever made me feel the way you do, and I was beginning to think I was incapable of *feeling* anything anymore."

I felt blindsided. Was she *not* breaking up with me?

"I want you to stay with me, Henry. Forever."

Confusion muddled my mind. "I... What? What do you mean?"

"I mean" — she squeezed my hand — "I could offer you a fabulous life. A life that would never, ever have to end."

I rubbed at my neck again. "I don't understand."

A cracking noise pulled my attention away. It was as if a large branch had snapped outside. A yellowish light glowed outside her window.

"What was that?" I jumped from the bed.

"Henry, wait."

I reached the window before she could stop me. Outside, a fire blazed. It looked like a bonfire, only bigger. And then, from the direction of the house, a line of people walked. They wavered as they walked toward the flames, almost zombie-like. Narrowing my eyes, I realized they were the guests from the party, gathering in a circle around the fire. And Grace was with them.

"What's going on? What's Grace doing with those people?"

"Nothing." Vivienne's voice had a tinge of panic in it. She raced toward me. "Here, have some more candy."

I eyed the candy, wondering why she'd offered it to me. Yet something weird pulled at me, as if I almost couldn't control myself and needed to have that piece of candy. But then the fire crackled outside. "No. No, something's not right here."

"Henry, it's me." She stroked my cheek.

I started to feel relaxed. But no. There was something wrong about this. I closed my eyes and turned my head. I focused on Grace's face. She stared into the fire as if she were sleepwalking. I pounded on the glass and called her name, but she couldn't hear me.

"Henry, stop. It's fine. Grace is fine. You're here with me. Don't you want to be here with me?"

I felt so confused. But my mind snapped back to Grace. "I... I do, but... but something's wrong with Grace. I have to go to her."

Her hand reached out to me, but I brushed past it, dashing for the door.

"Henry, wait!"

I ignored her call, throwing the door open.

And came face-to-face with Vivienne's mother.

VIVIENNE

MY VOICE STUCK in my throat when Mother placed her hand upon Henry's shoulder. She had him. It was too late.

Mother hadn't needed to say anything. Where my glamour had failed, Mother's worked instantly. Henry grew still, standing there and waiting patiently as if he'd forgotten his panic over his sister.

Mother's gaze found me. I walked toward her cautiously, aware of the disappointment in her piercing eyes.

"Delancey told me your plans, Vivienne. I hate to derail your efforts, but I don't think it's going to work."

"Why not? I can make it work. Henry — he likes me. It's not like last time."

"No, Vivienne. I forbid it."

"But — "

"End of story. Do you dare go against my wishes?"

I sucked in a breath, my hands clasped in front of me. I wanted to fight for him. But I couldn't get past her glare. I dropped my gaze and slowly shook my head.

"You are to bring him to the pit immediately."

I looked up at her, mustering up the courage to give it one last try.

"Vivienne," she said sternly. "Lord Kyran will be arriving shortly. Delancey and I are going to meet his car. Bring Henry to the pit now, or I will kill him myself. And perhaps you will join him."

Biting my lip, I nodded and took Henry's arm. "Yes, Mother."

I pulled Henry along with me, feeling Mother's eyes at our backs. I felt like crying. I felt like ripping out my hair. How could I let her do this?

My body shook as I made it outside. My muscles clenched along my jawline, and my eyes darted around the bonfire pit.

The pit was dug about two feet deep, filled with timber that spat up dancing flames, embers floating into the starry sky. The guests stood around it, some of them mumbling absently, some of them slack-jawed. Jamie stood beside Grace, and he smirked when he saw us approach.

"Aw, Vivienne. Why so upset?" he asked.

I could have punched him in the face. He knew exactly what I was upset about. "Did Mother ask you to make sure I brought him?"

He shrugged. "You can't be so naïve to think you can keep any boy you come across for your own, Vivienne. Lord Kyran is expecting these souls, and it would be foolish to deny him."

"There are plenty of souls here for him. Why does Henry have to be one of them?"

"So you're perfectly fine with sacrificing his sister?"

I flinched. I knew Henry would not be okay with losing Grace. It occurred to me that if I were to try to save Henry, I would have to save them both.

He turned to Grace and ran a finger down her cheek. "I understand, though. Such a shame to give up such a delicious morsel. In fact, I was thinking about keeping her for myself. This last hour has been... enlightening. She's got all the makings of a blood-hungry vampire."

My blood ran hot. "Leave her alone."

Jamie narrowed his eyes and took a step toward me. "Or what?"

I pushed him back. He let out a low laugh.

I reached for Grace's arm, but Jamie blocked my way. He pushed himself forward until he was directly in front of me, but instead of assaulting me, he grabbed Henry's arm and pulled. Instinctively, I wrapped my hand around Henry's wrist and pulled him back, but Jamie wouldn't let go.

"Forget it, Vivienne. Stop being stupid."

With two hands, I yanked on Henry's arm, desperate to get him out of Jamie's grasp.

The victims were oblivious to our struggle, swaying like zombies before the fire. Jamie suddenly let go of Henry's arm. It was so unexpected that I stumbled backward. Seizing the moment, Jamie charged forward and pushed me. Hard.

I was knocked to the ground, losing my grip on Henry. But I was only down for a moment.

Springing to my feet, I flew at Jamie and dug my fingernails into his face. He let out a guttural scream, clawing at my hands in an attempt to pry them away. But I was a younger, stronger vampire and was able to keep my hold. My nails scratched bloody trails of torn skin down his cheeks.

Jamie let out a curse and then suddenly delivered a hard blow to my stomach. I bent in half, coughing and sputtering. Jamie took this opportunity to reach for Henry, but I wouldn't let him have him. With everything I had in me, I barreled into Jamie, forcing him back—and didn't stop until his back hit the fire.

My foot connected with something hard. Looking down, I spotted the shovel Edgar had used to dig the pit. In one swift move, I picked up the shovel and broke it in half over my leg. With bared teeth, I aimed the splintered end of the shovel handle at Jamie.

His eyes widened. "What are you doing?"

"I'm not letting you treat me like an inferior anymore," I said.

He lowered his brows. "You don't have the nerve."

"Want to bet?" Clenching my teeth together, I thrust the jagged rod into his heart.

He gasped in horror, his hands grasping futilely for the blood that spurted out of his chest. With all the force I could muster, I kicked him into the fire pit. His scream echoed in the night air as he toppled into the heart of the flames. I watched as his writhing form caught ablaze. But there was no escape for Jamie, and soon his blackened form crumpled down among the embers and grew still.

My hands flew to my mouth. What was I going to do now? Mother and Delancey would be returning with Lord Kyran at any moment.

I swung around and ran to Henry, grabbing him by the shoulders. "We have to get out of here."

He was still in a stupor, his eyes looking right through me.

I shook him, hoping I could glamour him out of Mother's trance. "Henry!"

He blinked, finally roused. His brow furrowed as he looked around. "What—what's going on?"

"We need to leave. Now."

His jaw tensed, his eyes searching the crowd before they focused on me. "Not without my sister."

HENRY

IT SEEMED LIKE we'd been driving for days, but the sun hadn't come up yet, so I knew it was just fear and exhaustion toying with me. I couldn't seem to wrap my head around what exactly had happened. Just when I thought I was latching on to a thought, my head would swim and my mind would drift.

"It's the candy," Vivienne said.

I stared at her.

Her eyes stayed on the road. "The reason why you can't concentrate. There's something in the candy that suppresses your thoughts. As well as your fight-or-flight instinct."

"Where are we going?"

"Far away from here. If you want to survive, if you don't want my mother coming after us — or worse — then we need to get away."

The hum of the road was a tempting lullaby, urging me to sleep. But I had to fight it off. I kept checking on Grace. Except for the occasional moan of pain, she lay still, sprawled out on the back seats, her eyes moving rapidly behind closed lids. Her arms were wrapped around her purse, which was still bulging with candy.

I wanted to ask Vivienne what had happened, but I doubted my mind could grasp the reality of it. I decided to wait until we found a place to stop. All that mattered was Grace was safe. I would deal with everything else later.

At long last, Vivienne pulled into a parking lot. A neon sign propped above it read, "The White Duck Motel."

As Vivienne arranged getting us a room, I managed to pull Grace out of the car. Vivienne was back in a flash, and we quietly but swiftly got to the room. I placed Grace on one of the beds, noting how hot her skin was.

"We'll have to stay here for the night," Vivienne said. "Just to rest a bit. But we need to leave first thing in the morning."

I watched her move about. She checked out the window, then started nibbling at her nails.

"What's happening, Vivienne?" I rubbed at my neck. "I feel like we'd been kidnapped to join a cult. Or that you and your family..." I couldn't even finish my thought.

She looked ashamed. "Henry, I'm so sorry. At first, I was just doing what I was told. But then, after a while, I started to have real feelings for you. I couldn't do what they wanted me to do."

My head spun and my heart wouldn't slow down. I felt as if I were dreaming. I felt as if I were having an existential crisis. My girlfriend and her family were drugging people and throwing them into fire pits. But why?

I rubbed at my neck again. "You bit me."

She let out a small breath, then slowly nodded.

"What does that mean?"

"Nothing."

"Nothing? Vivienne, that doesn't make any sense. Are you...? I mean, it's crazy to think that they even exist, but the only thing I can think of is something I thought only existed in books and movies."

She rubbed her palms over her eyes and nodded. "I know."

I waited until she could look me in the eye again. "Please, Vivienne. I feel like I'm grasping at straws here."

She paced the room, wringing her hands together. And then she stopped and looked at me, letting out a heavy breath. "We do exist outside books and movies. And yes, I did drink some of your blood, but you won't turn. You won't turn from a bite unless you feed."

I felt as if the floor had dropped out from underneath me. "Turn." It wasn't a question. I knew what she meant, but my mind hadn't yet accepted it. "And by feeding, you mean blood."

"Human blood, yes."

My stomach churned. I stumbled backward and sat on the bed. Vampires? Was this actually happening?

Grace moaned. I turned my head to look at her. That's when I noticed the red swelling mark on her neck.

"She's been bit too," I said, my panic doubling.

"It's tradition to feed before offering souls to the vampire king."

I shook my head and waved off her explanation. "This is too much for me to handle. Just—don't tell me any more for now. I can't."

Grace shifted, whimpering.

"I'm going to go get some ice," Vivienne said. "Heat keeps the drug in the candy alive in her body. We'll need to cool her down."

I nodded slowly. "What should I do?"

"You can start filling the tub. I'll try to be fast." She grabbed the ice bucket from the side table and rushed out the door.

I moved closer to Grace, moving her hair away from her face. Her eyes inched open, and she turned to look at me.

"Grace?"

"What happened?" she asked. "Where are we?"

"Don't worry. We're safe."

"Safe?" She blinked, her voice still drowsy. "But the party. I was having fun."

She tried to sit up but hissed as if in pain, her eyes squeezing shut.

"No, Grace, just lie still. We're going to help you."

She placed her hands on her temple and lay back down. "Okay."

I got up and brushed my hands on my pants, then headed to the bathroom to fill up the tub.

VIVIENNE

I'D GONE DOWN the wrong walkway. Who designed this godforsaken motel anyway?

Nerves pushed me forward. I needed to cool Grace down. She didn't look good, and I wondered how much blood my siblings had taken.

I rounded the next corner, the glint of metal up ahead. Relief washed over me as I spotted the ice machine.

Picking up my pace, my eyes caught movement in the shadows. I slowed down, shifting my hair away from my face, and used my heightened hearing to pick out any sounds that might be out of the ordinary. Aside from the hum of the ice machine and an owl hooting from a nearby tree, there was only silence.

I rushed forward and started scooping ice into the bucket, the crunch of ice hitting ice loud in my ears.

Would Henry forgive me for getting him into this mess? Would he ever accept me for what I am? Would he still love me?

A shadow moved over the ice machine.

With a gasp, I spun around, barely catching a glimpse of a figure before something hard and sharp caught me in the head.

HENRY

THE HANDLE OF the tap squeaked as I turned it off. I dipped the tips of my fingers into the water and retracted them immediately. It was chillingly cold. I wasn't sure Grace would be able to stand it.

Vivienne had said the cool water would dull the effects of the candy, and only then did I realize that Grace hadn't been the only one who'd consumed it. I'd also had a couple pieces. Just thinking about it made my mouth water, and I remembered that Grace had a purse full of the delicious treats. But I squeezed my eyes shut and shook my head. No. It was drugged. I had to resist it.

I stood and shifted to the sink, letting the water flow to a bearable temperature before splashing my face with it. I rubbed at my eyelids, letting the cool water bring me back to my senses. When I opened my eyes and gazed into the mirror, I noticed the red wound on my neck.

Running my fingers over it, I bit back a hiss, the skin tender and stinging. Could I really be at risk of becoming a vampire? I couldn't even wrap my head around the fact that vampires existed, let alone the possibility of becoming one. The world as I knew it had completely turned on its head. How had this happened?

I went over the events of the night, suddenly remembering the bloody steaks we'd been served at dinner. Had it even crossed my mind to question how rare the steaks were? With the image of the bloody juices pooled around the steak, my mouth began to water again. No, this couldn't be happening to me. I splashed my face again and twisted off the water. I had to get a hold of myself.

With a frustrated sigh, I left the bathroom and went to check on Grace.

The bed was empty.

Every nerve in my body went rigid. I scanned the room, making my way around the bed in case she had fallen off it, but there was no Grace.

The door was open a crack.

Time seemed to stop for a moment.

With my breath stuck in my throat, I charged through the motel room door. She couldn't have gone far. But which way had she gone? I wiped off my clammy hands on my pants, begging my heart to stop racing. Then I turned right and ran.

The White Duck Motel wasn't the biggest establishment, but in that moment, it felt colossal. My pace picked up as I ran down the walkway, my senses on high alert as I looked and listened for Grace. But there was nothing to be seen or heard.

As I rounded the corner, something shiny on the ground caught my eye. I skidded to a stop in front of it and crouched down to find a piece of Morsel candy. Lifting my eyes, I spotted another silver and copper candy wrapper a few feet ahead. A line of them caught the light of a street lamp, dropped every few feet along the walkway.

Grace had to have her purse on her. Were the candies falling out of her handbag as she stumbled along, out of sorts? Were they spilling out because someone had abducted her and she was struggling? Or could she have been leaving a trail for me to follow?

I rushed forward, determined to catch up with her no matter what the circumstances might have been.

As I darted from one candy to the next, my heart began to sink. They were becoming sparser and sparser, farther and farther apart, until I had to actually search for where the next one was.

When I came to what I thought must be the last piece of candy, I clenched it in my hand, desperation eating away at me. "Grace? Grace, are you there?"

I was answered by a soft moan.

My breath hitched, and I charged forward, seeking out the source of the voice. My eyes widened when — instead of finding Grace — I spotted Vivienne lying on the ground near the ice machine, blood pooling from a wound on her temple.

I practically fell on top of her as I reached down to prop her up. "Vivienne, what happened?"

Her cold hand grabbed my arm, her eyes blinking open slowly. "Henry, no." Her voice was small and lacking power.

A sound like a whisper caught my attention. I glanced around but saw nothing. Grinding my teeth, I gently set Vivienne's head down.

I squinted against the darkness, searching. Had her family followed us? Would they have done this to her? Whoever did this to Vivienne might have still been around.

My breath shuddered as I strained to listen for a sound of movement. Vivienne groaned softly, and I turned.

I gasped when I saw the hunger in my sister's bloodshot eyes. Before I could think or speak, Grace grabbed me with shockingly strong hands and bared her fangs. There was a crunch as my skin was pierced, and the world turned to black around me as the sound of my scream filled the night air.

WIRES & BLOOD

Madeehah Reza

Pin refused to look back at the city. Her knees buckled and she fell on the dry, yellow grass beneath a large oak tree. Tears streamed down her cheeks as she panted and coughed, resting against the gnarled roots of the tree. The plain in front of her was scattered with a forest of tree stumps and not a single creature scurried about. The oak tree was a skeleton of its previous life, a hollow trunk with empty branches. Pin nestled herself in the dirt with aching muscles. Gen would find her here easily, but she couldn't push herself to run any farther.

Nothing broke the silence. For once, Pin missed Lisa's calm voice and the quiet, gentle hum of her wheels. Lisa had always made sure that Pin was occupied with books because 'knowledge was the way forward for humanity,' and she thought Pin should be a pioneer in that. And so Pin had read during every waking moment. She almost yearned for a book to read now beneath the oak tree, to flip through its pages and to feel the paper graze her fingers. To forget everything that had happened. To lose herself, away from the outside world.

Although there wasn't much of a world to be lost from.

The sun hung low in the rusty sky and the tree stumps stood like an army, lifeless yet foreboding. They promised her a hopeless fate. She turned away but only saw the city left behind, where the sounds of life had been quelled to silence.

Pain echoed through her body, pulsating around the knife pressed into her side. She stifled a groan, knowing that Gen might be nearby. She didn't want him to find her just yet. The solitude that had once bored her became precious, essential to calm a chaotic mind.

Maybe it's supposed to be like this, thought Pin. It seemed easier, somehow, to let the agony overtake her. Her fingers closed around the knife and she started to edge it out, but that only made it worse. Warm blood oozed from the wound, but Pin couldn't look at it. With a deep breath she let the knife remain and lay down, her head resting against the bumpy roots of the tree.

Pin snapped off the golden locket that hung around her neck. She clicked it open and saw her mother's face smiling at her. She had the same caramel skin, brown eyes, and crop of dark hair as Pin. A throb of energy pulsed through her arm and she threw the locket away into the brush.

It was humid and Pin always felt sleepy at this time of day. She closed her eyes and thought about Lisa, untangling her thoughts to free her memories.

"YOU HAVEN'T FINISHED these ones, Pinterry," Lisa had said the previous morning.

Pin had looked up from her new book and noticed the unfinished stack piled high next to her. She pulled a face from behind the pages while Lisa sorted through the stack alphabetically. Her joints moved slowly and carefully, each motion punctuated by the squeaking of metal.

"Look here," Pin had said. She pored over a large physiology textbook. The cover was torn off, but the pages remained pristine. They sat inside the Atrium, the largest room in the library with the tallest windows. Light poured into the room from the morning sun, small specks of dust dancing in its rays. Lisa put down the pile of books in her hands and wheeled around to see Pin's new interest.

"It says: 'A deficiency of vitamin D can lead to bone def... def-orm...'"

"Deformities," said Lisa. "Plural of deformity. A state of being misshapen, distorted, disproportionate, or crooked."

Pin nodded absently and traced her finger beneath the sentence.

"'A deficiency of vitamin D can lead to bone... *deformities*, such as os... os-tee-oh...'" Her eyes flicked up at Lisa, whose green light began to flash on her silver forehead. It signaled the gathering of information. To avoid another dictionary session, Pin continued reading. "'Sunlight is required for vitamin D to form in your body.' See, Lisa, I need the sun. So you need to let me go outside!"

Lisa wheeled herself away and picked up the books that she had set aside.

"Pinterry, it's too dangerous to leave the library. You know that. You have no bone irregularities, so you do not need the sunlight."

Lisa's mouth, a circular hole covered with wire mesh, lit up orange whenever she spoke. Sometimes, when she was really adamant about something, the orange would turn to red. This time it was somewhere in between. Pin shrank into her chair and hunched her shoulders into a sulk.

"You never let me go out," she said, just loud enough for Lisa to hear.

The robot faced her and spoke with orange softness.

"Pinterry. It is too dangerous to leave the library," she repeated. "The monster —"

"I know, I know. The monster will find us and hurt us and kill us," said Pin, but she couldn't help frowning after the word 'kill.' It had such a finality to it, something that she didn't want to understand.

To her, life felt infinite. Slow, but endless.

Lisa wheeled herself out of the Atrium with a dozen books in hand. She was good at organizing, sorting, and remembering things. Lisa was actually *LI-SA: Library Intelligence — Support Assistant.* The library was an ancient jewel in the city, though no one had visited it for many years. Numerous LI-SAs had been installed to take care of the library as the public interest declined. But Pin's Lisa seemed to be the only one who still remained, maintaining the vast collections of books, articles, and journals scattered all over the broken building. The fate of the other LI-SAs was a mystery.

Pin listened to the echo of Lisa's wheels squeaking in the hall. After she knew the robot was elsewhere in the depths of the building, Pin ran toward the large spiral staircase just outside the Atrium. The good thing about living in such a big building was the unexplored space that it offered. Pin dashed across the lobby, sprinted up the winding staircase, and weaved her way through halls of bookcases. But she wished more than anything to crack open the windows and race outside, just to keep going and never stop.

The second floor was full of fiction. Pin had never liked novels. Their made-up worlds made no sense to her. They seemed out of touch with reality. She preferred books filled with facts and interesting realities, things that were logical and tangible. But Lisa had truly irritated her that morning, and so Pin found herself traversing the corridors of bookcases in the fantasy section. A faded blue hardback sat wedged tightly between several smaller novels, beckoning to be plucked out of the crowded shelf.

garden. Tall fir trees blocked her vision. She always wondered what lay beyond.

Fables and Fairy Tales, read the title in embossed gold print. She flicked through the glossy pages, glancing at the colorful illustrations and skimming through the large print. There were many drawings: malicious queens, a wicked stepmother, witches, dragons, and hunters. All bad and evil. And the heroes, the princesses, the good folk who received their happily-ever-afters. But every time Pin had read these stories, the heroes fell as flat as the pages.

A princess cursed into a deep slumber waited helplessly for her champion. Across the page, an evil queen with pointy fingers cackled over a glass orb. She had the same green eyes as the princess.

What if the queen wasn't evil, Pin wondered, *but simply misunderstood?* Maybe no one listened to her, but she was really the one in need of help. Perhaps she wasn't evil at all—just a confused soul. A little deformed, crying out for help. Pin looked through the dirty window at the trees outside and tried to peer through their branches.

"Maybe there's no monster out there," she said. "Maybe whatever it is just needs to be understood."

Tree branches wavered gently in the wind, enclosing the library in its own cocoon. Pin's fingers traveled to the golden locket around her neck. She clicked the button on the side and the locket opened, revealing two pictures: one torn beyond recognition, and the other of her mother. The same warm brown eyes that Pin herself possessed stared back at her. Pin often opened the locket to gaze upon her mother's frozen, smiling face. She wished her mother could crawl out of the picture and onto the seat, rocking Pin in her arms. But as the days slipped by, Pin realized her memory of the kind face was fading. She would open the locket in the mornings and evenings, sometimes sighing, sometimes crying.

Months before, Pin had been left in the library, entrusted to Lisa's care. Why her mother had left her, Pin never really knew.

"Pinterry." Lisa's voice rang throughout the upper floors. She couldn't shout; she could merely increase the volume. "Come and help me with these books."

Pin slid off the bench, leaving the book of fairy tales on the seat, and went to look for the bot.

As she opened her eyes, a full moon greeted her. The darkness around her held no surprises; Gen hadn't found her yet. For now, she was safe. Pin tried to sit up straight, but a jolt of pain paralyzed her limbs and she cried out.

"I'm okay. I'm okay, I'm okay, I'm okay." The words did not soothe her. She closed her eyes and lied to herself again, that everything would be fine. But as she thought the words, her heart pounded against her chest with brutal force. Her skin prickled and burned.

It wasn't the first time this had happened.

Pin didn't like to tell lies. Every time she did, her skin would burn with a fire like the sun and her heart would not stop racing. But Lisa had annoyed her so much that day that Pin had to find a way to leave. If she didn't, she knew she would surely go mad. Staying indoors made time itself become something imaginary. Minutes ticked away, blending into hours, melting into days.

The library had two main entrances, front and side, and then a back access to the garden. The main entrances had been barricaded shut long ago and would have made too much noise to open, but the back access had a jammed broken door.

Pin made sure Lisa was far away from her, filing books under *Flora, Nature* at the other end of the library, before she crept past and ran down the hall. A nagging feeling told her to stop and turn back, but something else pushed her to break the door down and run away. She fiddled with the handle, desperately willing the door to swing open.

A gentle whirring of wheels echoed in the hall.

"Pinterry, what are you doing?"

Pin scrambled to invent an excuse. "I read a book earlier about fixing things using hammers and nails," she said quickly, "and I thought, this door has been broken for ages, so why couldn't I fix it?" She grinned, but it made no difference. The robot's metal features remained detached, the stark opposite of Pin's eagerness.

In that moment, Pinterry wished that Lisa was someone who could grin back at her, laugh at her bad jokes, scold her with a real angry voice. But of course she could never be.

"We don't have books on — " began Lisa, but as she did, Pin began to shake. She clutched the door handle for strength. Her legs filled with air, knees buckling. The effect of the lie. Was her heart pounding far too loudly? Or could Lisa hear it too?

"Pinterry, are you okay?" For just an instant, Pin thought she heard concern hidden in the monotone voice. She gave a small nod before an idea lit up in her head.

"Actually, I'm not feeling good. I've read that stagnant air can lead to all sorts of illnesses. I think I need to get some fresh air." Her heart punched violently and her skin prickled. Pin didn't know how long she could lie before she would pass out. "Lisa, you wouldn't really understand. It's a human thing."

The words stung, but Lisa didn't register it. She only shook her metal head and took Pin by the arms, slowly guiding her to the front door. Pin's beating heart settled and then shuddered, this time from sheer excitement as she realized Lisa was going to let her have her way.

"Only for a few minutes," Lisa said. "We don't want—"

"The monster to find us. No, we don't," said Pin, grinning from ear to ear.

DEAD LEAVES RUSTLED nearby. Pin jerked her head to the side, thinking the sound was footsteps coming closer, but no one was there. She was alone. Lost and alone. She wrapped her arms around herself, rocking back and forth, cradling her chest as if to soothe what was inside. A cool breeze sent shivers across her skin, wisps of dark hair tickling her cheeks.

Pin remembered how she'd longed to feel the wind, to be blown away by it.

And when she *had* felt it, it was glorious.

"PINTERRY, NOT TOO far!" Lisa had called. Pin stood still as the warm breeze hit her outside the library entrance. The sun shone down from a pastel blue sky and dusty green trees swayed gently, lining the road outside the library. Pin closed her eyes and tried to quell her excitement so she could savor the flavor of the wind brushing her skin like a soft embrace.

Her little lie had worked, and now she had her freedom. She glanced at Lisa before sprinting away. And she didn't look back.

Pin ran and ran and ran, passing tall buildings and roads littered with the remains of the past. Warm air filled her lungs and she shouted, utterly exhilarated. She ran till her legs could carry on no more, then she clambered up a stone wall and stood tall. There was an identical stone wall embedded with black lamp posts in the distance. Still panting, Pin looked over the edge and saw a dry, muddy abyss. The Thames should have been in front of her, but now an empty ditch snaked its way through London. Pin frowned and held on to a lamp post, glancing around. It was very still and quiet, as if no other soul lived in the city.

The gentle humming of wheels caught up to her. Lisa's mouth glared red, but somehow Pin thought Lisa looked concerned. Maybe she was. Pin sat on the stone wall, dangling her legs.

"Get down from there," said Lisa. "You could get hurt. Pinterry, were you lying to me before? Are you not ill?"

Reality drowned out Lisa's words. The mundane routine of her previous existence had vanished. Pin was outside, underneath a perfect blue sky. No book could replace the way the sun scorched her face.

"What happened here? Why is no one else around?" Pin asked finally.

"The city has been like this for a while," said Lisa, her volume turned to the lowest setting. A large structure stood in the distance across the muddy abyss, tall and pointed at the top, with a massive black hole on each side. Pin recognized it as Big Ben, but there was no clock face, only a gaping aperture at each side.

Without the clocks, time seemed to disappear into a void. There was no forward or backward—only now. Life had already felt endless and slow to Pin, and it felt even more so at that moment.

"The monster," said Lisa. Pin flicked from Lisa to the building.

"Big Ben?"

Lisa shook her head.

"It always emerges from that side. Always from the north."

Pin's curiosity grew and sprouted wings. She sprang from her perch and skipped along the stone wall before the robot could drag her back. Lisa called out to her, and Pin wondered if robots could panic. When she was at a safe distance, Pin slowed to a walk.

London had grown wild. Once a cornerstone of the world, now a city reduced to a jungle with crumbling buildings. Vines like thick green snakes grew out of windows and cars, sprouted from beneath sewers, and formed a carpet of green across streets. Pin trailed alongside the empty Thames, inspecting roads blocked by overgrowth. From the corner of her eye, she was certain she saw the vines crawl.

Then came a rustling. Not from the wind, nor the vines, but something stronger. Pin stopped in her tracks, her eyes darting around. The rustling came from a little way off, in the denser part of the jungle. It grew louder. Pin felt Lisa's metal hand grip her shoulder, trying to drag her backward, but Pin didn't hear her plead. Lisa wanted her to come, but Pin stood rooted to the ground.

It wasn't till the bullet blasted past her head that Pin turned to run. She didn't need to read any books to know the danger here.

"Come on, Lisa!" Pin screamed. Lisa's wheels, which had always been old and not built for a chase, struggled to keep up. Pin grabbed Lisa's mechanical arm and pulled her, metal scraping on the gravel.

"My wheels will break," said Lisa, but she allowed Pin to drag her.

The safest option was to go back to the library, but Pin's mind was muddled from the blast. They wound through side roads, racing to find a sanctuary of sorts until they came to a high street. Old shops lined the road, some with shutters drawn, others with broken glass scattered over their steps.

An abandoned bakery stood at the corner, stale bread and fancy pastries displayed behind the intact window. Pin pulled Lisa gently around the corner, hoping to find some way out, when she realized they had reached a dead end. Houses squashed against each other in the narrow cul-de-sac. Creeping vines grew over cars that lay wrecked on the tarmac.

"This isn't good," muttered Pin. She turned back to the high street and jerked Lisa's arm, but the bot could not move. Thick vines were tangled in between the cogs in her wheels.

"I cannot go any farther," said Lisa, with her unnatural calmness. Pin tried to pull apart the plants, but too many of them had twisted into Lisa's machinery. She had to do something else. Perhaps if she lured the monster away, it wouldn't know Lisa was here.

"Stay here and don't make a sound," she whispered to Lisa, who nodded and stopped struggling. She looked strangely lifeless.

Red clouds streaked the sky over the high street. Pin observed the debris as she crept across the pavement: broken signs, shattered TV screens, torn books, and more. She crouched down and lifted a lone page, wondering which novel it had been ripped from. An illustration of a monster, with twisted horns and a cruel, ugly face growled at her. She dropped the paper and jogged ahead.

A tall iron gate stood at the edge of a derelict park. Pin dragged the gate open, frowning as it creaked loudly. *This place is so beautiful*, she thought as she sneaked through, *but the grass is yellow and the ponds are all dried up*. Leaves crunched underfoot and not a soul breathed in the stillness.

"Found you."

Pin was paralyzed. From the edges of her vision she saw a man aiming a gun at her. He stepped sideways to look at her before his face crumpled from fury into confused relief. Dark circles puffed under his eyes and wrinkled, gray skin hung from high cheekbones. Stubble covered half his face. His bright eyes were the color of a perfect sky.

"What's your name?" he finally asked.

"Pin."

"Are there any others?

Pin shook her head. *Great, I finally find another person and I can't even speak*, she thought in annoyance.

"So you haven't got a mum or a dad?"

She shook her head. Not anymore.

"Brothers or sisters?"

None.

"Aunts? Uncles? Cousins?"

None, none, none.

"Anybody?"

She stopped moving her head just in time to hide the lie and he took her silence as a 'no.' The man reached for her and Pin took a step back, tripping over a fallen branch. He caught her wrist and hoisted her up, bright eyes piercing through hers.

"Didn't I see you with a bot before?" Stale breath wafted over her face and Pin winced, very aware of the gun in his other hand. She didn't dare answer the question.

He saw her pained expression and asked softly, "You're not scared, are you?"

Pin had no time to consider an answer. She just wanted him to let go.

"No," she said. Her heart punched, skin flushed and prickled. The man held on a little longer before seeing her sway.

"You're not well. Come on. Let's take you home."

'Home' did not mean the library. 'Home' was beyond Big Ben, a long walk away. They trekked across Westminster Bridge, but its road had collapsed, leaving only the narrow pavement on one side. Tarmac crumbled and Pin glanced over the edge, seeing only the dark chasm of the ditch below. She shuddered before the man—he'd introduced himself as Gennaro—pulled her away.

Pin felt like she was in a strange sort of trance. She couldn't believe that Lisa had warned her so desperately about Gennaro, such an ordinary man. He *did* have a gun, but apart from that, he wasn't frightening. He simply looked exhausted.

"How have you survived this long?" Gen asked.

"I've been at the library. Mum wanted to keep me safe," said Pin. "But she hasn't come back yet. Have you seen her? She looks like me, but older."

Gennaro shook his head. His narrow eyes darted from street to street as they passed by, and Pin struggled to keep up with his quick pace. She thought about Lisa, caught helplessly in the vines, and wondered if she ought to mention her. The gun dangled in Gennaro's loose grip, but Pin knew at a moment's notice he would have it ready to fire.

It would be best to keep Lisa a secret, she decided.

Gennaro lived in a small house with one floor. It was the only one on the street that wasn't completely covered in overgrowth, but the front door was barricaded shut. They walked down several steps to the side of the house to enter, and even then it was a struggle to budge the door open.

"Helps keep intruders out," said Gennaro. "You have to push it from this side." He pointed to where the lock was and shoved the door with his shoulder. It gave way after several attempts, and they entered a very messy kitchen.

A scream pierced the air.

Pin covered her ears, looking for the source, and saw a small, old woman perched on a chair underneath a thick blanket.

"It's her! She's back!" The old woman pointed at Pin with a shaking, wrinkled hand. "Get her away from us!" Gennaro put his arms around her and tried to calm the woman down.

"It's okay, Mum. She's a friend. We've found a friend."

She wasn't convinced. The screaming continued until Gennaro managed to lift his mother up—against her protestations—and carry her into another room. A few minutes later he emerged and closed the door to the silent room behind him. "She hasn't been feeling too great for a while."

The kitchen and living area was one messy, squashed room. A small fire burned in the hearth and Pin hovered over it, entranced by the colors.

"Sit," said Gen, but it came out more like an order. Pin obeyed and sat on the corner of a chair, barely allowing herself to relax. He sat on the couch and looked at the fire too, but his shoulders remained upright and palms gripped his knees.

"Why were you chasing me?" said Pin. The question had flickered in her mind for the last hour. Gen cleared his throat.

"Oh, I thought you were... I thought you were a robot or something. Silly, isn't it?" He got up and rummaged in the kitchen before placing two dirty plastic bottles on the coffee table. "They've never been opened. Go on—have a drink," he said. She muttered a thanks but didn't take the bottle.

A strange thought came to Pin then. Had she ever drunk water before?

She suddenly felt out of place. She wanted to be back in the library, amid the familiar smell of books. Then she thought of Lisa and ached some more.

"If I were a robot, why would you be chasing me?" she asked.

Gennaro glanced at her with a trained eye but then looked back to the fire, opening his own warm bottle of water.

"I guess you're too young to understand. The robots are the reason why everything's destroyed now. My father... he designed them, most of them, and now I have to deactivate them all."

"Deactivate? You mean kill?"

Gennaro laughed.

"You can't kill a robot. They're not alive to begin with."

Pin tensed. She turned her face away from Gen. If this man was planning to destroy all robots, then what about Lisa? Was he the reason why there were no more robots in the city?

Pin couldn't fathom how robots could be destructive. Lisa was helpful—albeit a little annoying—but she always tried to keep Pin safe. She kept the library in good condition, even though no one visited.

But then, Lisa was the only robot she ever knew.

"But if there are fewer robots now, do you really have to deactivate them all?"

Gen slammed his bottle on the table. He growled between his teeth and rose from his chair.

"If I don't deactivate them, they'll kill us all!" He stamped his feet as he paced around the cramped room. "It's a miracle me and Mum have survived this long. And you're here too, which means there *must* be other survivors. If we can destroy all the robots, the world can go back to normal."

He kicked a pile of empty boxes. A water bottle had fallen to the floor. Pin stooped to pick it up, not wanting to meet Gen's eyes. He took a few deep breaths before combing his hand through his gray hair.

"Sorry," he muttered, and he returned to the untidy kitchen. The silence filled with a clink of plates and the rustle of packaging.

Pin frowned. What if there were other robots that were evil? It wouldn't be too hard to believe; after all, throughout history there had been humans who were good and those who were bad. Maybe robots were the same.

Confusion crippled her thoughts. She slumped back into the chair and closed her eyes, picturing the library and Lisa and all her books around her, words streaming from pages. She tried to remember the words of the physiology book she had read that morning, but she only saw blank pages.

A clatter startled her from her reverie. Two plates were set upon the table and both had a strange, gray mush on them. The fire had shrunk in the hearth.

"Sorry, this is all we have. Eat up," said Gen.

Another strange thought popped into Pin's mind. Had she ever eaten food in her life, either?

She stared at the plate for some time while Gen ate his mush with little enthusiasm. "Go on," he said.

Pin took the plate to her lap and held up the gray sludge with a fork. It took a long time for her to place it inside her mouth, and once she did, it felt cold and strange. As if it should not have been there. She tried to chew, realizing she'd never chewed anything before, and she didn't know what to do from there. So, doing what she thought best, Pin spat it back out onto the plate. Gen raised his eyebrows.

"I guess they have better food where you're from, then?" He chuckled and took the plate from her. "Well, if you're not going to eat it, I'd better save it for Mum."

Pin watched the plate as it was taken away from her. Another question formed in the crevices of her mind, flickering in and out like the flames that were dying in front of her.

PIN AWOKE BENEATH a pile of leaves. She was tired of the waiting. Maybe Gen had forgotten about her. *Maybe he changed his mind,* she thought.

No, that's stupid. He would find her. She had to be patient. Pin wasn't sure what was worse: the miserable waiting, or the knife still stuck in her side.

Misty clouds swathed the moon, casting muted light over dead tree stumps. Wind whipped around Pin and a terrible feeling suffocated her. She closed her eyes, breathing deeply, and tried to remember the night before.

SHE HAD LAIN on a comfortable couch with a blanket over her and a cushion to rest her head on. Moonlight spread into the room through a dirty window, scattering dappled silver light across the furniture.

No matter what she did that night, sleep would not take her. Pin fidgeted, turned, and twisted till she fell to the floor in a heap. Gen had gone to his room, and his old mother snored from hers. Pin had kept a wary eye on the woman's door that evening.

A looming sense of confusion settled heavily in her mind. The fire had died and Pin was left to fight with her thoughts. Lisa could have explained everything with clarity, but Lisa was no longer by her side.

Fed up of not being able to sleep, Pin rose from the floor. She paced several times around the kitchen, around the couch, her steps as light as feathers, till she grew weary of her course and changed direction. She crept past both bedroom doors and heard snores from within. A third door, with cracked white paint, had a lock below the metal handle. One tap on the brass, however, and the door creaked open. She stepped through.

Several flashes winked at Pin through the darkness. She flicked the switch on the left and a single bulb flooded the room with sterile, white light. Dozens of knives and guns lined the walls of the small room. Pin surveyed each artifact and wondered what its purpose was. She'd never seen such a vast array of weapons. An uneasy feeling snaked its way through her. Messy piles of papers and newspaper clippings were strewn across two narrow, wooden benches. Pin tried to read over one before the door creaked open once more.

Gennaro's heavy feet padded into the room. His eyes were bloodshot and wide, the shadow beneath them darker.

"What are you doing here? You're wasting the light." His finger hovered over the switch.

"I couldn't sleep." Pin turned back to examine the walls. "You have a lot of knives."

Gen sighed and rubbed his face before settling down on a high stool.

"It's not always easy to tell what to take when I go hunting. I'd rather dismantle the robots the neat way, you know, through their activation box." He seemed to be talking more to himself than Pin. It was as if the presence of another person was a key that opened his locked mind. "But it's not always easy to find. Plus, if they're fighting back, it's usually quicker to hack at the main connection." He pointed to his neck. "Or just go straight to pulling wires out. Depends on how advanced the bots are."

Pin nodded as the facts came together slowly, forming a messy puzzle.

"Activation box?" she asked.

"It's not always obvious. Some bots have the box behind their heads—others, over here." He pointed to his chest. "Although the newer robots didn't even have a box. Bot Corp used to control their products from some kind of remote machine. Took me months trying to find the company's mainframe to shut it down. Had to burn all the robots in the end as well, just to make sure."

Pin imagined the blaze engulfing several hundreds of robots, many probably not knowing what was happening. She thought of Lisa's silver face melting in the heat. Gen spoke of robots as if they were only made of metal and wires, but they couldn't be only that. Lisa had kept her company all these months, more than any human had ever done. Lisa was lively and alert, even if her wheels didn't work as well as they used to.

Pin wondered about her friend trapped in the vines, hoping Lisa had managed to free herself. She clasped her shaking hands together.

"These are my father's old files." Gen pointed to boxes of tattered folders beneath the wooden benches. "He was a pioneer in his field, but that didn't stop him from being a lousy father."

He pulled out a faded green folder and blew the dust off it before slapping it on the bench. Loose papers spilled out, containing diagrams, equations, and angry red scribbles. "These ones are finished." He separated the papers and left a pile within the folder. "And I still have to find these bots, but I haven't had a chance to look through the notes. There were so many to begin with."

"Did you have to teach yourself this?" asked Pin as she flicked through the pages.

"I never had my father's flare for inventing," he said, wrinkles deepening as he frowned.

One page caught Pin's eyes. In fact, she was sure she had just seen her own brown eyes staring back at her. Snapping the file shut, she smiled at Gen.

"I think," she said, reminding herself to tell the truth, "I'm going to lie down now."

Gen nodded, allowing her to exit first. He glanced back at the file before flicking the light off and locking the door behind them.

Back on the couch, Pin lay frozen on her side. She couldn't sleep. How could she when she was so sure that her own picture was on Gen's hit list? But that didn't make any sense — she was a girl.

A human girl.

A real person.

Wasn't she?

PIN COULDN'T HEAR Gen's snoring. Taking her chances, she rose once more, wincing as the couch springs groaned. She tiptoed to the third white door, biting her lip. Those eyes could not have been hers; she had to see the drawing once more.

Almost of its own accord, the door drifted open.

The light bulb was on.

There, on the high stool, sat Gen, intently reading the paper Pin had spent all night thinking about.

"So you came back to haunt us."

"I don't understand," said Pin. She was more aware of the knives in the room, shining from their hooks like the eyes of predators waiting for their prey.

"No, I didn't either. But it looks like you were my father's pride and joy. His best invention." He tossed the paper to the floor. It wasn't just one paper, but a thick bundle of sheets stapled together. Pin picked it up gingerly and scanned through the pages.

Her own face stared straight back at her, but she looked much neater: perfectly drawn short, dark hair; a pointed caramel face with blushing cheeks; and sweet brown eyes. Pin was a drawing with precise measurements, numbers and arrows scribbled all around her.

A red circle was drawn over her chest with a question mark.

"It all makes sense now." Gen paced around the small room.

"It does?"

He stopped and glared at her.

"My last week in my parents' house." Gen motioned around him. "I was leaving for university. We were having dinner and someone knocked on the door. Dad opened it. A woman with a cooler box in her hands stood on our steps. She pleaded with him, begging him to help her. He let her in. His food went cold on his plate because he didn't eat that evening. He barely ate for the rest of the week."

Gen sat back down on the stool and crossed his arms. "He didn't bother seeing me off before I left London. He never visited me when at university, three years of it. He barely said anything to me whenever I came home. He was too busy," he said, nodding toward the stapled sheets of paper. "Too busy making you.

"That woman had lost her daughter in a car accident and the girl became braindead. But she stole her daughter's heart from the hospital and came running to my father that same day to build her another little girl.

"I didn't know what it was at the time. Dad kept the project a complete secret. You can imagine why—think of the court cases," he said before laughing. There was no smile on his face. "You weren't just any old android. Dad pushed himself to create a new species of technology. A cyborg."

Pin wondered what a cyborg was—there weren't any books on them in the library—but kept listening, completely entranced by her mysterious past.

"A cyborg: the 'enhanced' race of human beings. Human-like thoughts and emotions, but with a mechanical body that's impervious to disease." Gen stared at her, his eyes boring into her own. His gaze kept her rooted to the spot. "You've got a human heart pumping blood through your body. You might be able to *feel*, as the most advanced type of Artificial Intelligence, but that doesn't make you human. Clearly, this woman didn't love you enough like her own daughter to keep you."

The comment didn't sting Pin. She didn't care about this woman any longer, this supposed mother. When she tried to remember her smiling face, she only saw Lisa's.

"Dad missed my graduation, but I guess that time it wasn't his fault. He was sick. He was already ill, and this final project pushed him too far," said Gen, blinking back tears. "I held his hand when I got to the hospital, but it was already cold."

Tears trickled down his worn face. He wiped them away and rose to survey the back wall. His picked a knife with serrated edges on both sides, turning it over in his hands.

The blade glinted in the light.

The stapled papers fell.

Pin ran back to the living room and scanned it in a panic.

"I'm not a cyborg, I'm a girl, a real girl!" She grabbed a water bottle, twisting the cap free. "Look, I can prove it!"

The bottle opened, water sloshing inside, and Pin held it against her open mouth. Gen froze as he watched her. She hesitated, never having done this before, but brought the bottle to her lips and poured. The water collected in her throat until she had no choice but to spit it back out, spraying all over the couch and Gen.

"You little — "

Pin never heard the rest of the insult; she was already running. There was no time to apologize. She slammed several times into the back door, wood splintering, until the door came off its hinges. It smashed against the ground and she scrambled over the damage, running out into the clear morning air.

Sunlight burst across the horizon and painted the streets golden. Pin skidded down the road and turned into streets at random till the towering structure of Big Ben loomed overhead. She sprinted toward the broken bridge, her bones aching — though now she knew they weren't bones.

A fragment of concrete caught her foot and Pin tripped, scraping her elbows on the ground. She dragged herself up, ignoring the large ditch below, and kept going. Gen's pounding steps couldn't be heard, but Pin didn't wait for them to catch up with her.

She ran on till she reached the familiar sight of the abandoned high street. Pin skidded as she saw the bakery, panting hard. She darted around the corner to the cul-de-sac, finding Lisa still swaddled with vines. Relief nearly buckled Pin at her knees as she tried pulling vines away. The robot slowly powered up. When Lisa's battery bulb blinked red on her chest plate, a worrying thought grew inside Pin.

"Pinterry, you came back."

"And you're still stuck," said Pin. She tore the smaller vines, but the large ones were too thick to pull apart.

"I could not pull myself free. I am a library assistant, Pinterry, not a workbot. I have nothing sharp to cut through these vines."

Pin thought of the knife that Gen carried but shook it from her mind. She had to find another way to cut through the thickest, most tangled vines.

"Pinterry, where have you been? I waited quite a while," said Lisa.

Pin hoped Lisa had been as relieved to see her as she was to see Lisa. She slumped back on the ground in frustration. The vines were just too strong to break through.

"Two in one. Guess the day just gets better and better."

Pin turned in time to see Gen plunging forward with the knife. She darted to the side, hoping the knife would cut the knot of plants instead.

But Lisa had leapt in front of Pin, working herself free just enough to shield Pin from Gen.

And Lisa's battery box bled its black fluid, a thick trail seeping onto the green vines.

Pin screamed. Lisa staggered back and collapsed onto Pin's leg, vines ripping apart from the force of her fall. Pin flung the knife to the side and tried to stop the battery from leaking. Black fluid stained her hands and warm tears streamed down her face.

Lisa's mouth faded into a strange peach color.

"Lisa," Pin cried. The robot's eyes had pinprick circles of green that flickered as they sought Pin before fading into black.

"She's just a robot," said Gen.

Pin grew furious. "She's not just a robot! She's my friend."

Gen grabbed the knife from the ground. He hesitated a moment and Pin jerked herself free, the metal of Lisa's screws catching her skin. The silicone tore, but no blood escaped from the superficial wound. Only metal bones were bared.

Pin saw her bones, but before she could get away, Gen drove the knife into her. She cried out and limped away, grunts and groans escaping from her lips. And as her small frame struggled to turn the corner of the street, Gennaro was stunned into silence, the guilt of murder flitting through his tired conscience.

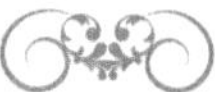

QUITE SURE THE knife would do no more harm than it already had, Pin pulled it out from her side. The pain had dissolved into a numb throb and only the screech of metal scraping against metal remained. Pin was all metal inside. Had Lisa known of her true identity? Why had Lisa hidden it from her?

Maybe, thought Pin, *she stuck around just to protect me.* A terrible longing for her friend burned inside, but Pin felt she could cry no more.

She was a scientific miracle in an empty world. A messy patchwork of human and robot, though she belonged to neither.

Darkness enveloped her. Pin remembered a time when her life felt infinite. Infinite, but slow. And now those endless days leaked out of her, drop by drop, draining from her side.

The sun rose once more and Pin felt it was her last. She gazed upon the glorious golden circle rising from a red sky into blue. Cool silence calmed her as rosy light spread across the stumps of trees that stretched out in front of her.

Then, dead leaves crunched underfoot.

Gen trailed around the oak tree until his shadow fell on top of Pin. She didn't look into his eyes—not because of fear, but from a hatred she didn't know she could possess.

"All robots must be deactivated," he said. "It's for the good of humanity."

"Humanity? There's no one left. You and your mum are going to die and the world will be free from your poison." She stared at the dead branches hanging above, ignoring the ache inside her. Gen knelt beside her.

"Lisa's gone. My friend is gone because of you." She blinked several times. "I don't have anyone else now."

"I wish that you were real. A real person. I really do. But you're just not, Pin."

She glared at him.

"I'm more human than you!"

But he shook his head firmly.

"Robots are wrong and should never have been made. They destroyed the world as we know it."

She let out a mirthless laugh.

"You can't blame robots without blaming yourselves. You made us what we are." The silence hung heavy with her words. "I blame your father."

Gennaro's lips tightened into a thin line.

He poked his finger through a hole in Pin's faded blue shirt, pulling it firmly to rip the cloth. Her smooth, silicone chest had a small mark to the left side. He pressed it gently and a square portion of skin slid back to reveal a glass chamber.

Pin's heart quaked and quivered, contracting in a silent symphony of beats. Gen could not take his eyes away from it. A real heart—a real human's heart, a real life—was in front of him, beating for all eternity under his gaze. He reached for the knife, still stained from Pin's blood, and held it above her.

The glass would smash. Flesh would pierce.

"You're not scared, are you?" he asked, the words slipping from his lips.

Pin closed her eyes tightly and gripped the yellow grass on either side of her. Her lips trembled and something strange and heavy filled her throat. She was more scared than she had ever been — more than when he had chased her through the city, and even more than when she'd seen Lisa's fluid.

"No," she lied.

Pin's entire body shook. Her heart hammered with the force of a mighty mallet against the glass chamber, but she didn't hear it. Her skin burned, ignited by both fear and the lie. The heat engulfed her. Her heart was going to break the glass, break her body, and break Pin into tiny pieces of insignificance. A shattered, metal corpse that no one cared about.

But Pin wasn't insignificant.

She had loved and was loved back, here, on Earth's soil. And so was Lisa. Lisa may have gone, but her kindness would never die. Her silver face appeared in front of Pin and she heard the robot's clear voice speaking to her. Scattered memories streamed through her mind: of helping Lisa in the library, of Lisa placing a blanket over Pin when the winter wind blew through a broken window, of waking up every morning to see her pile more books on the table for Pin to read.

The endless days of her life receded and Pin's eyes shot open only to see that the sun had set on another day. Her chest cavity was closed. Pin dragged herself up against the tree, panting hard. The yellow grass beneath her had scorched to brown. Her chest felt heavy and sore, as if it had been through death and back.

There was no trace of Gen. The knife lay on the grass, covered in dried blood. She hugged her knees and touched the wound at her side. No more blood leaked from it. The air had returned to a grim silence; no leaves rustled in the wind. The entire world fell to darkness, but a familiar loneliness remained.

Had the monster let her live?

Exhaustion weighed on her like an anchor. It was as if she had been shuttled from one end of existence to another. She closed her eyes and saw Gen's tired face looking at her with the knife in his hand, his blue eyes frozen on her beating heart.

Pin couldn't tell whether she was robot or flesh, wires or blood. She closed her eyes and brought her hand to her chest, feeling the soft thump against the glass chamber inside.

There were other robots in the city. She wondered if she ought to seek them out, or if she would come across another human being.

Deep inside, Pinterry hoped she never would.

THE END

About the Authors

LYSSA CHIAVARI is an author of speculative fiction for young adults, including *Fourth World*, the first book in a sci-fi trilogy set on Mars, and *Cheerleaders From Planet X*, a tongue-in-cheek send-up of all things sci-fi. Her short fiction has appeared in *Wings of Renewal: A Solarpunk Dragon Anthology*, *Brave New Girls: Tales of Heroines Who Hack*, and *Perchance to Dream: Classic Tales from the Bard's World in New Skins*. Her first published story, "The Choice," was named one of Ama-gi Magazine's Best Fiction of 2014. Lyssa lives with her family and way too many animals in the woods of Northwest Oregon. You can visit her online at lyssachiavari.com.

AMY MCNULTY is an editor and author of books that run the gamut from YA speculative fiction to contemporary romance. A lifelong fiction fanatic, she fangirls over books, anime, manga, comics, movies, games, and TV shows from her home state of Wisconsin. When not reviewing anime professionally or editing her clients' novels, she's busy fulfilling her dream by crafting fantastical worlds of her own. Learn more about Amy at amymcnulty.com.

T. DAMON is the author of The Forest Spirit series through Snowy Wings Publishing, as well as two independent YA contemporary novels under the pen name K.L. Teal. Her short story "The Desperate Warrior and the Beast Who Walks Without Sound" was included in the YA Shakespearean retellings anthology *Perchance to Dream*. Aside from writing, T. Damon holds a degree in Zoology and spends her free time doting on her daughter and numerous pets at her home in Santa Rosa, California. Her hobbies include studying astrology, tarot, and the teachings of secret magical orders. For more information about T. Damon, you can follow her on Instagram at @tdamonauthor, or on Facebook at facebook.com/tdamonauthor.

DOROTHY DREYER is a Philippine-born American living in Germany with her family. She is an Amazon category bestselling author of young adult books that usually have some element of magic or the supernatural in them. Aside from reading, she enjoys movies, chocolate, take-out, traveling, and having fun with friends and family. She tends to sing sometimes, too, so keep her away from your Karaoke bars.

CLARE DUGMORE is an author contemporary romance, urban fantasy and paranormal fiction. Her published works include contemporary romance novel *All It Takes*, LGBT novella *I Want You to Want Me*, and web serial *Every Moment With You*. She is currently working on an urban fantasy novel about witches who are oppressed by the government.

Clare is a thirty-something married mother of two from the West Midlands of England. In her spare time, she enjoys binge watching shows with her hubby, spending time with her two sons, and playing video games.

You can find out more about Clare and her stories at her website: www.claredugmore.com.

MARY FAN is a sci-fi/fantasy author based in Jersey City. Her other books include *Starswept* (Snowy Wings Publishing, 2017), a YA sci-fi romance, *Flynn Nightsider and the Edge of Evil* (Crazy 8 Press, 2018), a YA dark fantasy, and the completed JANE COLT space opera trilogy from Red Adept Publishing. She is also the co-editor of the *Brave New Girls* YA sci-fi anthologies about tech-savvy girls, which aim to encourage more girls to explore STEM fields and raise money for the Society of Women Engineers scholarship fund. When she's not writing, Mary can usually be found at choir rehearsal, on the ski slopes, or on an airplane heading to wherever. Find her online at www.MaryFan.com.

LEIGH HELLMAN is a queer/asexual and genderqueer writer, originally from the western suburbs of Chicago, and a graduate of the MA Program for Writers at the University of Illinois at Chicago. After gaining the ever-lucrative BA in English, they spent five years living and teaching in South Korea before returning to their native Midwest.

Leigh's short fiction and creative nonfiction work has been featured in *Hippocampus Magazine*, *VIDA Review*, and *Fulbright Korea Infusion Magazine*. Their critical and journalistic work has been featured in the *American Book Review*, the *Gwangju News* magazine, and the *Windy City Times*.

They are pleased as punch to be publishing their first novel, the new adult speculative fiction work *Orbit*, with Snowy Wings Publishing in September 2018.

Leigh is a strong advocate for full-day breakfast menus, all varieties of dark chocolate, building a wardrobe based primarily on bad puns, and bathing in the tears of their enemies.

CLARA KENSIE grew up near Chicago, reading every book she could find and using her diary to write stories about a girl with psychic powers who solved mysteries. She purposely did not hide her diary, hoping someone would read it and assume she was writing about herself. Since then, she's swapped her diary for a computer and admits her characters are fictional, but otherwise she hasn't changed one bit.

Today Clara is a RITA® Award-winning author of dark fiction for young adults. Her debut, the super-romantic psychic thriller Deception So series, was named an RT Book Review Editors Pick for Best Books of 2014, and Deception So Book One: *Deception So Deadly*, is the winner of the prestigious 2015 RITA® Award for Best First Book.

The first two books in the Deception So series, originally released as the six-part Run to You digital serial, are now compiled into full-length novels, *Deception So Deadly* and *Deception So Dark*. The series will continue soon with the never-before-published *Deception So Dangerous*. Clara's contribution to this anthology, "Dance of Deception," is a stand-alone romance set in the Deception So world with all new characters, some of whom may make appearances in future Deception So books.

Clara's critically-acclaimed novel *Aftermath* (Simon and Schuster/Simon Pulse), a dark, ripped-from-the-headlines drama about hope, healing, and triumph over tragedy in the tradition of *Room* and *The Lovely Bones*, was on Goodreads' list of Most Popular Books Published in November 2016, and Young Adult Books Central declared it a Top Ten Book of 2016.

Clara's favorite foods are guacamole and cookie dough. But not together. That would be gross.

Visit Clara online and sign up for her newsletter at ClaraKensie.com.

MARK C. KING is an easy-going writer with a talent for finding enjoyment in most any situation. He's a lifelong reader whose literary interests include science fiction, adventure, thriller, and mysteries. He grew up in California, but now lives in upstate New York with his wife. When not working or writing, he can be found watching movies, kayaking, associating with friends, and of course reading.

KARISSA LAUREL lives in North Carolina with her son, her husband, the occasional in-law, and a very hairy husky named Bonnie. Her favorite things are dark chocolate, coffee, super heroes and *Star Wars*. She can also quote *The Princess Bride* verbatim. Karissa is the author of two novel series: The Norse Chronicles, an urban fantasy trilogy from Red Adept Publishing; and The Stormbourne Chronicles, a young adult fantasy series from Evolved Publishing.

From her home in the land of living skies, MELANIE MCFARLANE writes fantastical stories that span from hope to tragedy, showing that the human spirit can persevere even in the darkest of times. Connect with Melanie at www.melaniemcfarlane.com for free short stories and swag.

SELENIA PAZ spends a lot of her time working at a library surrounded by awesome books, and uses the rest of her time to read, write, and run with her dogs. She finds inspiration in everything from history to science and especially loves magical realism. Her manuscript "Broken English" was selected as a 2012 New Voices Honor winner by Lee and Low Books. She is also the author of *Life and Death*, Book One of the Leyendas Trilogy, and "Lisbeth," a retelling of Macbeth published in the anthology *Perchance to Dream*. You can find her online at seleniapaz.com.

MADEEHAH REZA works as a pharmacist in London, although her lifelong dream is to write endless books to entertain younger readers, particularly those who are not represented by mainstream media. She has a handful of published stories and articles, and is working (ever so slowly) on her first novel.

K.M. ROBINSON is a bestselling storyteller who creates new worlds both in her writing and in her fine arts conceptual photography. She is a marketing, branding and social media strategy educator who is recognized at first sight by her very long hair. She is a creative who focuses on photography, videography, couture dress making, and writing to express the stories she needs to tell. She almost always has a camera within reach.

Get free excerpts of her books at excerpt.kmrobinsonbooks.com and check out her website www.kmrobinsonbooks.com. Connect with her on social media at @kmrobinsonbooks on Facebook, Instagram, Twitter, and Snapchat. You can view videos and live replays on YouTube, too!

A voracious reader, JANE WATSON has always been a fan of romance, fantasy, adventure and especially happy endings. She received her degree in Art History from the University of Puget Sound. When she is not writing, Jane works as a wedding coordinator, helping people reach their happily-ever-afters. She likes to spend her free time doting on her menagerie of pets, riding her bike, crafting, and obsessively shopping for purses. Visit Jane online at janewatsonauthor.com.